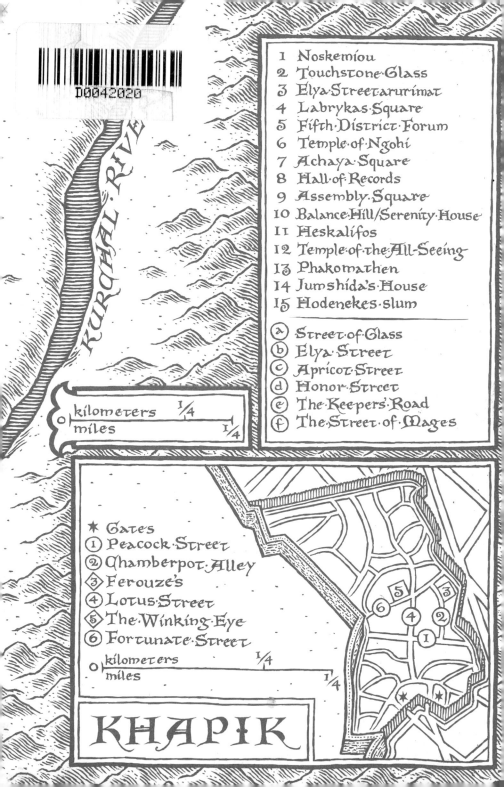

KURQAL·RIVER

1 Noskemiou
2 Touchstone·Glass
3 Elya·Streetarurimat
4 Labrykas·Square
5 Fifth·District·Forum
6 Temple·of·Ngohi
7 Achaya·Square
8 Hall·of·Records
9 Assembly·Square
10 Balance·Hill/Serenity·House
11 Heskalifos
12 Temple·of·the·All-Seeing
13 Phakomathen
14 Jumshida's·House
15 Hodenekes·slum

ⓐ Street·of·Glass
ⓑ Elya·Street
ⓒ Apricot·Street
ⓓ Honor·Street
ⓔ The·Keepers'·Road
ⓕ The·Street·of·Mages

0 kilometers   ¼
   miles   ¼

★ Gates
① Peacock·Street
② Chamberpot·Alley
③ Ferouze's
④ Lotus·Street
⑤ The·Winking·Eye
⑥ Fortunate·Street

0 kilometers   ¼
   miles   ¼

KHAPIK

SHATTERGLASS

BOOK FOUR OF
THE CIRCLE OPENS
QUARTET

• TAMORA PIERCE •

SCHOLASTIC PRESS

Library of Congress Cataloging-in-Publication Data

Pierce, Tamora.
Shatterglass / by Tamora Pierce.
p.   cm. — (Book four of The circle opens quartet)
Summary: Tris and her mage-student, a young man whose glassmaking
magic has been amplified and mixed with lightning, team up to track a
killer who may be nearer than they suspect.
ISBN 0-590-39683-8
[1. Magic — Fiction.   2. Fantasy.]   I. Title.
PZ7.P61464 Sh 2003
[Fic] — dc21
2002075862

10 9 8 7 6 5 4 3   03 04 05 06 07

Printed in the U.S.A.   37
First edition, March 2003

The text type was set in Adobe Caslon.
Book design by Elizabeth Parisi

To my father, Wayne Franklin Pierce

You taught me to soar with my stories.
Now, at last, the Old Eagle flies free.
May you find good winds, clean air,
and the universe under your wings.

Tharios, capital of the city-state of Tharios
On the Ithocot Sea

The short, plump redhead walked out of the house that belonged to her hostess and looked around, her air that of someone about to embark on a grand adventure. She shook out her pale blue cotton dress and petticoats, then wrapped a collection of breezes around her chubby person as someone else might drape the folds of a shawl before she went to market. The breezes came obediently to her call, having become so much a part of her in the girl's travels that they no longer rebelled. They spun around her black cotton stockings and sensible leather shoes, raced along the folds of skirt and petticoats, slid along the girl's arms and over her sunburned, long-nosed face. They swept over the spectacles that shielded intense gray eyes framed by long, gold lashes, and twined themselves over and along her head. They followed the paths of her double handful of copper braids, all pinned neatly to her scalp in a series of rings that left no end visible. Only two long, thin braids were allowed to hang free. They framed either side of her stubborn face.

With her breezes placed to her satisfaction, guardians against the intense southern heat, the girl whistled. The big, shaggy white dog that was busily marking the corners of the house whuffed at her.

"Come *on*, Little Bear," ordered Trisana Chandler, known to her friends as Tris. "It's not really your house anyway."

The dog fell in step beside the girl, tongue lolling in cheerful good humor. His white curls, recently washed, bounced with his trot; his long, plumed tail was a proud banner. He was a big animal, his head on a level with Tris's breastbone. Despite his size, he wore the air of an easy-to-please puppy as effortlessly as the girl wore her breezes.

Tris strode down the flagstone path and out through the university gates without so much as a backward glance at the glory of white stucco and marble that crowned the hill above the house. She thought that the university, called Heskalifos, was fine, in its own right, and its high point — the soaring tower known as Phakomathen — was pretty, but there were perfectly good universities in the north. She was on her way to see the true glory of Tharios, its glass-makers. Let her teacher, Niko, join their hostess, Jumshida, and many other learned mages and apprentices in their long-winded, long-lasting presentations on the nature of any and all vision magics. Tris, on the other hand, was interested in the kind of visual magic wrought by someone who held a blowpipe that bore molten glass on its end.

At one of the many side entrances to the grounds of Heskalifos, Tris halted and scowled. Had Jumshida said to turn left or go straight once she was outside the university enclosure?

A girl her own age stood nearby at a loading dock, emptying the contents of a trash barrel into the back of a cart. The muscles of her arms stood out like steel cables. Though she was clearly female, she wore her hair cut off at one length at ear level, and the knee-length tunic worn by Tharian men. She was also extremely dirty.

"Excuse me," Tris called to her. "Do you know the way to Achaya Square?"

The girl picked up the second barrel in a row of them and dumped its contents into her cart.

Tris cleared her throat and raised her voice. "I *said*, can you tell me the way to Achaya Square?"

The girl flicked her eyes toward Tris, then away. She dumped her empty barrel next to the others, and picked up a full one.

Well, thought Tris. She can hear me; she's just being rude. She stalked over to the cart. "Don't you people believe in courtesy to visitors?" she demanded crossly. "Or are all you Tharians so convinced that the world began here that you can't be bothered to be polite?"

Though the barrel she had taken to the cart was still half full, the girl set it down and fixed her gaze on Tris's toes. "You *shenosi*," she said quietly, using the Tharian word for foreigners. "Don't they have guidebooks where you come from?"

Tris's scowl deepened. She was not particularly a patient girl. "I asked a simple question. And you can look at me if you're going to be snippy."

"Oh, it's a simple enough question," replied the girl, still soft-voiced, her eyes fixed on Tris's no-nonsense shoes. "As simple as the way is if you just follow that long beak of yours. And I'll give you some information for nothing, since you're obviously too ignorant to live. You don't talk to *prathmuni*, and *prathmuni* don't talk to you. *Prathmuni* don't exist."

"What are *prathmuni*?" demanded Tris. She chose not to take offense at the remark about her nose. It was not her best feature and never had been.

"I am a *prathmun*," retorted the girl. "My mother, my sisters, and my brothers are *prathmuni*. We're untouchable, degraded, *invisible*. Am I getting through that thick northern skull yet?"

"Why?" asked Tris, curious now. This was far more interesting than a simple answer to her question. "Why should a *prathmun* be those things?"

The girl sighed, and rubbed her face with her hands, smearing more dirt into it. "We handle the bodies of the dead," she told Tris wearily. "We skin and tan animal hides.

We make shoes. We take out the night soil. But mostly, we handle the dead, which means we defile whatever we touch. If you don't move along and a *giladha* —"

"What?" asked Tris.

"One of the *visible* people," replied the girl. "If they see you talking to me, they'll demand you get yourself ritually cleansed before you go anywhere or do anything. Now will you go away?" demanded the *prathmun*, impatient. "You'll get cleansed, *shenos*, but I'll be whipped."

She said it so flatly that Tris believed her. She walked two steps away, then asked without turning around, "What's *shenos*? And how do you tell who's a *prathmun*?"

"A foreigner is *shenos*," retorted the *prathmun*, dumping the rest of her trash barrel into the cart. "And we all have the same haircut and the same kind of clothes, and straw sandals. Now *go*."

Tris followed the road that lay straight before her, the direction the *prathmun* had indicated with such flattery. "Niko said I'd find some of the customs here barbaric," she informed Little Bear when she was out of earshot of the *prathmun*. "I'll bet you a chop for supper this is one of the ones he meant. Whoever heard of people not being people just because they deal with the dead?"

Once she reached Achaya Square, Tris found the Street of Glass easily enough. Reading about Tharios on the way here, she had formulated a plan of exploration with her usual care to detail. She would start at the foot of the street where most of the city's glassmakers kept their shops, beginning with the smaller, humbler establishments near the Piraki Gate, and work her way back to Achaya Square until her feet hurt. She meant to spend a number of days at the shops that caught her interest, but first she wanted an overview. Tris was the kind of girl who appreciated a solid plan of action, perhaps because often her life, and her magic, was in too much of an uproar to be organized.

As she walked, she looked on the sights and people of Tharios with interest. Buildings here were of two kinds, stucco roofed with tile — like those in her home on the Pebbled Sea — or public buildings built of white marble, fronted with graceful colors and flat-roofed, with corners and column heads cut into graceful lines. The Street of Glass and Achaya Square fountains were marble or a pretty pink granite. Statues carved from marble and painted to look lifelike stood on either side of the paved stones of the road. It was all very lavish and expensive. Tris might not have approved, but her view of people who spent so much on decoration was leavened when closer inspection showed her soft edges on statues and public buildings, and fountain carvings worn almost unrecognizable by long years of weather. Tharios was an old city, and its treasures were built to last.

The Tharians themselves were a feast for her eyes. The natives ranged in skin color from pale brown to black, and while their hair was usually black or brown, many women used henna to redden it. Men cropped their hair very short or even shaved their heads altogether. Ladies bundled their hair into masses of curls that tilted their heads to the appropriate, sophisticated, Tharian angle. The *prathmuni,* male and female, sported the same rough, one-length cut Tris had seen on the girl she spoke to. All *prathmuni* wore a ragged, dirty version of the knee-length tunic worn by Tharian men. Tharian women dressed in an ankle-length, drape-sleeved version called a *kyten.* In summer these garments were cotton, linen, or silk, with sashes or ribbon belts twined around waists and hips. On top of the tunic or *kyten* upper-class Tharians also wore colored stoles, each of which indicated the wearer's profession. She knew that mages here wore blue stoles, shopkeepers green, and priests of the All-Seeing God red. Beyond that she was lost. No matter what color the stole, it was usually made of the lightest cotton, or even silk, money could buy. The Tharians looked cool and comfortable to Tris.

Since the *prathmun* girl had called her attention to shoes, Tris noted that better-dressed Tharian men and women generally wore leather sandals that laced up to the knee. Many of the poorer residents went barefoot. This wasn't as risky as it might be anywhere else: Tris saw *prathmuni* collecting trash and cleaning the streets on nearly every block.

Though Little Bear was content to stay with his mistress, Tris's breezes were not. They roamed freely around her, tugging at curls, tunics, *kytens,* and stoles, exploring people's faces, then returning to Tris like excited children gone for a walk with a favorite aunt. They brought scraps of conversations about trade rates, fashions, family quarrels, and political discussions from all around her, pouring those scraps into her ears. She half-listened, always interested in local gossip.

Some conversations mentioned her. A few of the Tharians she passed had discovered her way to stay cool. Perhaps her breezes wouldn't have been noticed if the air were not perfectly still. The only winds outside Tris's circle of influence were those made by handheld fans and those roused by pigeons in flight from uncaring feet.

Tris sighed, and drew the breezes closer to her. People continued to stare as her dress and petticoats stirred in different directions. She ignored them. It was too hot to give up her fresh air so a number of stuck-up southerners weren't made nervous. If they were as clever as they claimed, they'd find ways to hold breezes of their own, Tris told herself.

She had a number of breezes tied up in knots of thread back at the house. Perhaps she could peddle some at the market, and make a bit of extra money. There were two more moons of summer to go, and the problem with city walls was that they tended to keep out the wind. She ought to be able to sell a knot, or two, or three, for pocket money. She would ask Jumshida how to go about it.

On she walked, planning and observing. She passed between shops filled with wonders: vases, bowls, platters, glass animals in a multitude of colors and sizes. In the shops on the Achaya Square end of the Street of Glass, windows were made of small panes of glass, treasure troves in and of themselves that gave a watery, rippling shape to the beautiful objects behind them.

Mingled with the higher-priced glass was glass that had been spelled in some way. Magical charms and letters in the sides and rims of pieces, suncatchers magicked to catch more than just sun, rounds of glass imbued with magic to capture and hold an image in them, all glinted silver in Tris's vision, showing her the work of the glass mages of Tharios. It was for this reason that she chose to start among the poorer shops, those more likely to sell plain glass and few charms. Tris knew she would spend most of her time later among the glass mages, comparing notes and learning how they practiced their craft.

Closer to Labrykas Square the shops had ordinary, shuttered windows, with the wares arranged on shelves to tempt passersby. Tris lingered at one and another, admiring the curve of a bowl or the blue-green hue of a cosmetics bottle, but she always made herself walk on after a moment. She was determined to start at the very bottom of the glassmakers' pecking order.

As Tris approached Labrykas Square, the first public square beyond the Piraki Gate, her breezes carried a conversation to her. "— a disgrace!" someone cried. "One of the riffraff, murdered and left in the Labrykas Square fountain like, like so much trash!"

"It will take a powerful cleansing to purify the fountain again," a woman replied soberly. "Surely the All-Seeing God will take offense against the district for the defilement —"

"The district? I think not!" retorted the first speaker. "It's obviously the work of some *shenos* who respects nothing and no one. The All-Seeing knows that no Tharian would commit so foul an act."

"The Keepers of the Public Good will put a stop to it," the woman said with the firmness of complete belief. "They have —"

The breeze had not caught the rest of the discussion. Tris shook her head as she walked on. *Someone is murdered, and all these people care about is the purity of the square?* she thought, baffled. *That's pretty heartless.*

She also wasn't inclined to believe these Keepers would be able to do much about the killing. How effective could they be? They were each elected to serve a three-year term by the Assembly, a body of the oldest families and the wealthiest landholders. They would not have the experience or cunning of a proper ruler who'd been raised for the position, like Duke Vedris of Emelan, Capchen's king and queen, or Empress Berenene of Namorn. She was amazed that the Tharians got anything done, if their entire political system was run by a mob. She had seen at home how much a governing council could quibble, fuss, debate, argue, and fight, with nothing to show for it — and Winding Circle's governing council was only twenty people. She'd heard there were more than three hundred in the Assembly.

"It's different when one man or woman is responsible for a country," she told Little Bear as they passed through Labrykas Square. The fountain, which she had seen on her arrival in the city, was shrouded in a kind of white, roofless tent. "They have to jump on this kind of nonsense right away, or everyone knows they're to blame. Here, all the rulers have to do is point to the other Keeper, or someone from the Assembly, and say *they're* supposed to be in charge of that." Disgusted, Tris shook her head and thrust all such dissatisfactions from her mind. She was here to learn, not to let the strange ways in which other people governed themselves get on her nerves.

At last she reached the part of the Street of Glass that she meant to explore first, the part that stretched between Labrykas Square and the pleasure district known as Khapik. She took a moment to look around using her magical vision. One thing she would say in favor of the Tharians, they looked after the magic that was used in public places. She saw very few tag-ends of old charms and spells gleaming silver on walls or around windows and doors. Spells there were in plenty, the usual creations for protection, health, and prosperity that anyone who could afford it paid to have laid on their homes and businesses. The thing that Tris admired was that local mages either got rid of what remained of older spells, or wrote the same kind of spell afresh, so that the magic in them shone in bright silver layers, an indication that differences in the spells did not conflict and cause the magic to go astray.

Tris walked idly up the street, admiring the lacelike patterns of spells on the shop walls, tracing a curve here, a letter there, with her finger. She knew most by heart, but this Tharian way of copying them over and over seemed to extend their power, even if the mage who added the most recent layer wasn't particularly strong.

Suddenly she felt a twist in the air. Most of her breezes, all of the ones she had acquired in recent months, fled. Only those she had brought from Winding Circle stayed, though she felt them struggle against some powerful call. The escaping breezes whipped around the corner of a nearby workshop: TOUCHSTONE GLASS, according to the sign.

The breezes weren't the only things on the move. Power from every charm and spell within fifty feet of the shop streamed past Tris to round the corner in silvery ribbons: protection magic, fire-damping magic, health magic, wards for luck and prosperity, it didn't seem to matter. Something flexed in the air a second time. Without stopping to ask if she did the wisest thing, she pelted around the corner into the rear yard of Touchstone Glass.

She plunged into a stream of magic. All of it poured through the open doors of a workshop set apart from the main building. It swirled around a man who toiled in front of a furnace. He stood sidelong to the door, a glassmaker's blowpipe to his lips as he tried to give form to an orange blob of molten glass. Twirling the pipe with one hand, he shaped the base of his creation with a mold clasped in the other.

For a moment Tris thought all was well. Then she realized that despite the glassblower's twirling of the pipe and the steady stream of air he forced into it, the orange blob wriggled, bulged, and then sank like a burlap sack with a cat inside. She had never seen glass do that before. Magic flooded into the man, sliding under his leather apron, squirming into short blonde hair cropped close to his blocky head, tugging at his sleeves, then merging where his lips met the pipe. Down its length the magic streamed, disappearing into the molten glass.

The man thrust the glass back into the open furnace, waited a moment, then brought the pipe to his lips. He cupped the base of the glass with his mold and blew into the pipe. The material at its end bulged, twisted, and thrust about even harder, plainly fighting him. It grew longer and snakelike, with big lumps on top and underneath. Magic gleamed, as if the glass were shot through with silver threads as it stretched away from the pipe. As it pulled free, its connection to the blowpipe stretched thinner and thinner. Only a thread connected it to the rod.

Tris shook her head. The man had obviously lost control

of his magical working. "You'd better let it go," she informed him. "And what possessed you, that you didn't draw a protective circle?"

The man jerked and yanked the pipe from his lips. The glass wriggled, spiraled, and broke free, tumbling in the air as it flew madly around the room. Little Bear yelped and fled into the yard.

"Why didn't you undo it?" Tris demanded. She ducked as writhing glass zoomed over her head. "Didn't they teach you, the more power you throw into magic gone awry, the more it will fight your control? Forget reusing the glass. It's so full of magic now you'll have *real* trouble if you try to make it into anything else."

The glass thing — she couldn't tell what it was — landed on the man's skull. Smoke and the stench of burning hair rolled away from its feet. The man swore and slapped at it. Terrified, his creation fled. As it flew, its features became sharper, more identifiable. The big lumps became very large, batlike wings. Smaller lumps stretched out to become powerful hind legs and short forelegs. Lesser points shaped themselves as ears, an upright ribbed fin rose on its neck; another point fixed the end of the glass as a tail. When the thing lit on a worktable, Tris saw the form it had fought to gain. It was a glass dragon, silver-veined with magic, clear through and through. It was twelve inches long from nose to rump, with six more inches of tail.

The man had dumped a pail of water on his head as soon as the dragon left him. Now he flung his blowpipe across the room, shattering three vases.

"Tantrums don't do the least bit of good," Tris then informed him, hands on hips. "Old as you are, surely you know that much." She noted distantly that there was a circle of dead white hair atop the man's head, almost invisible against the bright, closely cropped blonde hair that surrounded it.

He wheezed, coughed, gasped, and glared at her with very blue eyes. "Who in Eilig's name are you? And what did you do to me?" He spoke slowly and carefully, which didn't match his scarlet face and trembling hands.

Tris scowled. "You did it to yourself, dolt. You threw good magic after bad, *including* power you drained from all around this neighborhood because you didn't protect the workshop. *Now* look. You'll have to feed it and care for it, you know. And what it eats is beyond me. Living metal feeds on metal ores in the ground, but living glass?" She tugged one of the thin braids that framed her face, picking the problem apart. "Sand, I'd suspect. And natron, and seashells, since that's what you make glass with in the first place. And antimony and magnesium to make it clear."

"Will you be *quiet*?" the man cried, his voice still low. "I have — no magic! Just — a seed, barely enough to, to make the glass easier."

Tris glared at him. "I may only be fourteen, but I'm not stupid, and you're a terrible liar."

The glassblower doubled his big hands into fists. "I — am — not — a — liar!" he cried, his slow words a sharp contrast to his enraged face. "How dare you address me like that? Get out!"

Little Bear didn't like the thing that zipped so dangerously around the workshop, but even less did he like the glassblower. He thrust himself between Tris and the man, hackles up, lips peeled away from his teeth, a low growl rumbling through his large chest.

"Now look," Tris said with a sigh. "You upset my dog."

The glassblower backed away. "I am a journeyman of the Glassmakers' Guild," he said, forcing the words past clumsy lips. "I have no magic. I am no liar. I want you and your dog gone. And that *thing* you made, too!"

"*I* made?" Tris demanded, aghast. "As if I didn't see the power flow from you into the glass! Look, Master Jumped-Up Journeyman, that dragon is *your* creation —"

The glassblower yelled and grabbed a long pair of metal tongs. The dragon had landed on a worktable and was trying to climb into a jar on top of it. "Get out of there!" he cried, smacking the tongs on the table a half-inch from the dragon's tail. "Coloring — agents cost — money!" His sluggish speech was in sharp contrast to his quick strike at the dragon.

The glass creature leaped clear before the glassblower

could shatter it with a second blow. It flew to a shelf on the wall, its front half covered with powder. Clinging to the shelf, it spat blue fire at its attacker. Once clear of its muzzle, the flames solidified and fell to shatter on the floor.

"Don't you dare hit that creature!" cried Tris. "It's alive — you might break it!"

"I'll smash it to bits," the man growled. He poked the dragon with his tongs as it scrabbled a new jar with its claws. For a moment it teetered, then righted itself. The man advanced on it, tongs raised in his hand.

"It's a *living thing*," Tris called. "You may have made it, but that doesn't give you the right to break it." She yanked one of her thin braids free of its tie and combed it out with her fingers. Sparks formed in the crimped red locks, sticking to her palms.

The glassblower ignored her. The dragon glided to another shelf, one that supported an uncorked jar. Curious, it stuck its head inside. "That's it," the man said grimly. "You're dead." With tongs raised high, he went after it like a man in urgent pursuit of a mouse.

"I'm warning you," Tris said clearly. She had to tell people when she was about to use particular magics: in her hands, magic was a deadly weapon and had to be treated as such. "You can't kill that."

"Watch me." The man struck at the dragon, missing by half an inch. When he raised his weapon again, a hair-thin lightning bolt slammed into the tongs. The man shrieked and dropped them, nursing a hand and arm that twitched in the aftermath of a moderate shock. He whirled to stare at Tris, white showing all the way around his irises.

She waited, her loosened braid hanging beside her face, sparks glinting along its strands. In her open right hand a circle of lightning played, leaping from finger to finger. "Try to break that poor creature again and what you just got will seem like a love tap," she said, crimson with fury. "You can't kill it — didn't your teachers make you learn *anything*? Once you make a working that lives, you have to treat it like you would a human child. You're not allowed to destroy a living creation."

The dragon knew a champion when it saw one. Voicing a cry like the sound of a knife striking glass, it flew to Tris and perched on her shoulder, wrapping itself around her neck.

"Yes, that's fine," she reassured it, stroking the creature where it crossed her neck. "Calm down." She kept her eyes on the glassblower, who now huddled in the corner farthest from her, clutching the hand she'd shocked. His face was ash gray; his hair stood on end. "Who's your teacher?" Tris demanded.

"I don't have one," he replied, his speech agonizingly slow.

"Nonsense. You may as well tell me. I'll find out," she said. "I'll have your master's name before the week's done."

The man shook his head.

"And if your teacher said you were fit to practice magic and turned you loose on the world, I'm reporting you both to the Mages' Guild," Tris snapped. Was something wrong with him? she wondered, puzzled. Was he slow of mind? He spoke as if he were, though his eyes were too intelligent, compared with the simpletons she had known. He had to be twenty if he were a day, yet he was huddled down like a child who expected a beating. She hadn't given him enough of a shock to hurt him permanently. Something here wasn't right, but clearly she would get nothing else from the fellow. "What about the dragon?" she wanted to know. "Do you claim it as yours? Will you be responsible for it?"

The glassblower shook his head vehemently.

Tris scowled at him. "Well, that's of a piece with everything else I've noticed about you," she said tartly. "If *you* won't take responsibility for it, then I — Trisana Chandler, educated at Winding Circle Temple, take charge of this magical creation. Be sure I'll mention *that* at the Mages' Guild, too!"

Outside Tris fed the lightning in her hand into her pinned-down braids. With fingers that still trembled with anger she tucked the braid she'd pulled apart behind one ear. She would visit more shops and calm down. She wanted to talk to Niko about the dragon before she tracked down the local Mages' Guild, and he wouldn't be back until his conference ended late that afternoon. She might as well use her time profitably.

"Come on, Bear," she ordered the dog. "Let's find someplace sane."

*   *   *

Kethlun Warder, journeyman glassblower, didn't know how much time passed before he found the courage to get to his feet. The hand and arm that held the tongs had gone from painful jerking to a pins-and-needles sensation. When he touched his good hand to his head, he found that his hair was nearly flat again, though it crackled still.

Slowly he closed the hand that had taken the lightning's power. It was stiff, but it worked. He moved each finger, then his wrist, forearm, and at last the entire arm. Everything worked. The motion was slow, but at least he wasn't paralyzed a second time.

What about the rest? he thought as he tried to stand. Last year it had taken weeks, even months, to get all of his body working again.

On his feet he wavered, then dropped to his knees. Fear swamped him: had she paralyzed him? After a moment's thought he tried again. Carefully he stretched first one leg, then the other, leaning on his hands. Only when his knees responded as they should did he try to stand a second time.

His mind was functioning, he thought as he leaned on a worktable. But what of his mouth? He was scared to try, in case he learned that she had turned him back into a gobbling freak, but he was also scared not to try. His ability to speak had taken the longest to return, and he was still unable to talk quickly.

He drew himself upright, took a long breath, and blew

out, thrusting all emotion away. He emptied his lungs completely before he filled them again. Once he was calmer, he said, "My n-name is Keth-lun W-warder. I am-m a journeyman." Heartened, he went on, "I come from — Dancruan in N-namorn. My family is in the glass tr-ade."

Relief doused over him like cold water. Yes, the stammer was back, but it wasn't as bad as it had been. He could manage it by speaking slowly. His hands were steady enough. He was all right, or as much so as he'd been in the past year.

He'd heard his mother say that he was damaged, not incapable. As usual, she had hit the nail on the head. He was damaged, but he was getting better. He would *be* better. He just needed time.

A year ago he had not needed time. Glassblowing had been natural to him. He had expected to succeed every time he thrust a blowpipe into the furnace. He'd pitied apprentices who inhaled by accident, burning their tongues or throat with drops of molten liquid. He'd smirked as they singed their eyebrows, burned their arms, or dropped half of the gather into the flames. The basic work had come easily, greased by his tiny drop of magic, but the artistry had been all his own. Whenever the subject of his lack of greater magic came up, he reminded his family that at least he had considerable talent.

Then he'd gone for a walk along the Syth one summer afternoon. The storm caught him in the dunes between the beach and the Imperial Highway, tearing at his clothes and hair, driving sand into his face. In a panic, he ran for shelter instead of dropping into a dip between the dunes and lying flat on the ground. The lightning bolt caught him as he scrambled over the last dune between him and shelter. The only warning he'd had was the eerie sensation of all of his body hair standing straight up, before his old life ended in a flash of white heat.

That he'd survived was a miracle. The discovery that he was half-paralyzed and unable to speak made his survival a mockery.

But his youthful conceit had a tough core to it. He fought the living tomb of his body. He forced a finger to move, then a toe, then two fingers, two toes. Hour after hour, day after day, he reclaimed his own flesh. When his family saw that his mind still functioned, they brought in the best healer-mages in Dancruan. The happiest hour of his life was in the morning when he returned to his uncle's factory, ready to work once more.

By noon that day his happiness was dust. His old ease was gone. Even as a first-year apprentice his hands were never clumsy with the tools, sands, salts, ashes, and woods that were the basis of glasswork. The first time he tried to blow glass, his breath had hitched, he'd jerked the rod up, and a fleck of red-hot glass rolled onto his tongue. When he tried to pour glass into a mold, it shifted, making one side of a bowl far thinner than the other. For weeks every piece he made ended in the cullet, or waste-glass barrel, to be remelted or used in other projects.

The other apprentices and journeymen smirked as his gathers dropped in the furnace or onto the floor. They grinned as the masters rejected piece after piece. Once Kethlun had never measured how much of a coloring agent to add to a crucible of molten glass: he just knew. When he measured now, the colors came out wrong.

He did not dare say that he thought the glass itself had turned on him. He had the notion that it was trying to tell him things. It wanted him to shape it in ways that differed from what *he* wanted. Keth feared that if he spoke such thoughts to any of his family, they would turn him over to the healers who specialize in madness, and never let him near a furnace again. Even the mages in his family never talked of glass as if it were alive.

One spring day he came home to find the guildmasters seated with his father and uncles. All of them, men and women, looked decidedly uncomfortable when they saw him. Keth's brain, so much quicker than his tongue or hands, told him what was in the wind. The guildmasters meant to strip him of his journeyman's rank, and send him back among the apprentices until he regained his old skill, if he ever did.

He could not bear it. "I've been th-thinking," he said, trying to keep from stammering. He leaned against the receiving-room wall, hoping to look casual, hoping they would not sense his fear. "A change of scene, th-that's what I need. Fresh in-spiration. I'm a j-journeyman. I'll journey. South, I th-think. Visit the cousins. Learn new techniques."

Guildmistress Hafgwyn looked at Kethlun's father. "It might be for the best," she said. "I am not comfortable with the matter we discussed." Her bright black eyes met Keth's. "It will do. You may go with the guild's protection. Bring fresh knowledge back to us, along with your old skill."

And so he had worked his way down the coast of the Endless Ocean, going around the Pebbled Sea and continuing south and east. At last he reached the shop of his fourth cousin once removed, Antonou Tinas, in Tharios. By then he'd recovered some of his ability with molds and pulled glass. Antonou was getting old. He preferred to do engraving and polishing in the main shop as he waited on customers. Keth could make the pieces Antonou needed, then practice his glassblowing in private, with no one to see how badly he did it.

Just when he felt safe, along came this girl, and her lightning.

Trembling, Keth forced himself outside, to the well, and drank some water. Then he returned to the workshop. It was a shambles. He'd broken finished glass, thrown his blowpipe, knocked over jars of coloring agents. He had to clean up before Antonou saw the mess. He reached for a broom.

The plump redhead had held lightning in her hand as casually as if it were a bracelet she had just taken off. It glinted in that free lock of hair by her face like the bits of mica the *yaskedasi*, or entertainers, used to make their hair glitter in the torchlight. The girl had *thrown* lightning as a soldier would a spear, shocking his hand and arm into numbness. She'd done it to save the abomination that had wriggled out of his breath and into a gather of molten glass.

Keth never wanted to see that girl again. Please, he prayed to any gods that might be listening, I don't even want to see her *shadow* again.

Dema

Earlier that day

Dema Nomasdina was asleep. In his dreams he saw the four dead women whose killer he had yet to find: Nioki the tumbler, Farray the dancer, Ophelika the musician, and Zudana the singer. All four women wore the yellow veil of the *yaskedasi*, licensed entertainers who worked for the most part in the garden district called Khapik. Instead of floating around their heads, pinned over curls or braids, their veils were wrapped tightly around their necks and knotted. Each woman had the swollen, dark face of the strangled.

"He left me dumped in an alley like trash," said Nioki. Despite the silk knotted around her throat, her voice was perfectly clear and damning in its grief.

"I was thrown down a cellar stair," whispered Farray.

"He sat me against a building at the intersection of Lotus and Peacock streets for the world to see," Ophelika reminded him.

"Me he laid in front of the Khapik Gate for some trades-man to find as he stumbled home," Zudana said bitterly. "That tradesman fell over me like I was a sack of onions."

"What are you doing?" asked Nioki. "Why does my ghost still drift in the great emptiness?"

"What are you doing?" moaned Ophelika through swollen lips. "My spirit is not cleansed."

"What are you doing?" the dead women asked, their voices sharp in Dema's ears. "Avenge us," they said as they faded from view. The last thing Dema saw was their out-stretched, straining hands, and the flutter of yellow silk.

"Nomasdina!" A rough hand shook his shoulder. "Wake up, *dhaskoi*. You're wanted."

Dema sat up, his eyes barely open, the taste of last night's greasy supper in his mouth. He'd gone to sleep at his worktable, on top of the pages of notes taken on the mur-ders of the four *yaskedasi*. No wonder he dreamed of them. A glance at the window showed him rays of sunlight that leaked through cracks in the shutters. The room was hot and stuffy. "I'm off duty," he mumbled.

"Good," the sergeant on duty told him with false good cheer. "Then you're free to ride to Labrykas Square. The district captain has sent for you." The sergeant upended a ladle of water on Dema's head. As Dema sputtered, the woman added with real kindness, "She knows you've been on duty all night. Don't try to fix yourself up, just *go*."

Dema went, though he couldn't imagine what the Fifth District commander of the *arurim,* Tharios's law enforcement agency and his employer, wanted with a very new mage like him. Dema had been an *arurim dhaskoi,* investigator mage, for only eight months. He'd done little to draw anyone's attention. True, he was working on the murders of four Khapik *yaskedasi,* but he also knew that he'd been given the task of investigating the first murder and the three that followed it because no one cared if he caught the killer or not. One of the first words of *arurim* slang he'd learned was *"okozou,"* which meant "no real people involved." It was a phrase used to describe crimes among *yaskedasi, prathmuni,* or the poor of the slum called Hodenekes. It meant no one really meant Dema to *work* at finding the killer. He'd expected to be summoned before his watch station captain to explain why he'd made no progress weeks ago, until he realized the captain simply did not care.

A mounted *arurim* waited in front of the Elya Street station with a horse for Dema. Groggily he mounted up, thinking that it was a good thing he wore his tightly curled black hair cut very short. It was probably the only thing about him that was presentable. He scrubbed at his teeth with a finger, which he wiped on the edge of the saddle blanket. "You're sure you want *me?*" he asked the messenger.

The woman looked as if she'd spent all night on duty and

should have been home herself. She glared at him. "You're *arurim dhaskoi* Demakos Nomasdina, in charge of the investigation of four murdered *yaskedasi,* are you not? This *is* the Elya Street *arurimat,* and not my house, where I should be fixing breakfast for my children right now."

"Sorry," Dema replied, feeling guilty, even though he hadn't been the one to assign the *arurim* to find him.

The sergeant emerged from the station with a flask in each hand, one for the *arurim* and one for Dema. It held smoking hot jailers' tea, guaranteed to take the finish off wood and to wake the dead. "You're a lifesaver," the woman told the sergeant. "I may live to go home after all."

"They owe you the time you've spent after your shift getting our greenie, here," replied the sergeant with a nod to Dema. "Make sure they give it to you."

"I will," the *arurim* replied.

"And try not to dent the *dhaskoi,*" added the sergeant. "He's a good enough sort, for all he belongs to the First Class."

Dema wasn't sure which would bother him more if he were awake, the slight to his class or the fact that even after eight months of service they still thought he couldn't take care of himself. It was too much to think about now. He thanked the sergeant for the tea instead and followed his *arurim* guide down the street.

Drinking hot tea at a trot was a thankless effort, but

Dema made it anyway, catching the spilled drops on an end of the blue stole that marked him as a mage. As he drank and dodged people in the streets, he reflected on how badly he'd been cheated. He had chosen the *arurim* as his area of advancement because it seemed far less regulated than the army or navy, and infinitely less boring than the treasury or law courts. Few people would be able to order him about among the *arurim,* while every person with one more stripe, dot, or sword on his sleeve would make military life into something very much like work. Even when his *arurim* superiors gave him night duty, Dema was pleased. The Elya Street station was just four blocks from Khapik. If things were dull at work, a short walk led him to the best food, drink, and entertainment in Tharios, all neatly tucked inside the walls of the pleasure district.

The nettle in the garden of his service, the first dead *yaskedasu,* sprouted five months after he'd finished his training and settled in at Elya Street. He hadn't realized that the easy service of an *arurim dhaskoi* was due to the fact that, more than nine times out of ten, the victim knew the criminal. It was a family member, or a friend, or a neighborhood roughneck. These were all offenders that regular *arurim* found easily by talking to the family, friends, and neighbors of the victim, then tracking down all who looked suspicious, questioning them until they confessed. The *arurim dhaskoi* were called in only when the criminal was a mage, or when no one with a motive or chance to get at the victim could be traced. When the investigation of *yaskedasu* Nioki's murder produced no possible killers, the case had come to Dema.

Now, three dead women later, Dema felt like those animals must feel who chewed off a limb to escape a trap. His service to the *arurim* was no longer fun. He wanted to destroy the one who ruined the harmony of Khapik, and he couldn't even get his fellow *arurim* to care about it as much as he did. One *yaskedasu* or three *yaskedasi,* the others told him, *okozou* still meant no one was supposed to work up a sweat over this.

So Dema did his best, and knew it wasn't good enough. He was too ignorant. Most of his spells for uncovering events could be used only when he had a suspect or when the crime had taken place elsewhere or had not led to death. Trying to find the killer was like sifting through a ton of barley in search of a pin. No one knew anything. No one saw anything. The priests who had ritually and magically cleansed the murder sites saw nothing irregular, and Dema found no traces of magic. He was at his wits' end, even dreaming about the case. What was he doing wrong?

"I see word's got out," grumbled his *arurim* guide. Dema's head jerked up. He'd done it again, forgotten what he was supposed to be doing as he worried over the case. He'd been so preoccupied that he hadn't even noticed they had reached the square. Despite the very early hour — the sun was just up — the outer edges of the square were packed with human beings. Unlike most Tharian crowds, this one was a hushed, silent, nervous gathering. The *arurim* had to poke and nudge people aside to clear the way for herself and Dema.

At last they emerged onto open ground, the Labrykas fountain. It stood in its full glory, each of its four lower basins six feet wide, fed from the mouths of three rearing horses. A long stone pillar topped by the double-headed axe called a *labrys* spouted water to bedew the heads of the beautifully carved white marble horses. It was the first official Tharian monument seen by new arrivals who came through the Piraki Gate, and Dema never got tired of looking at it. Many mornings he would sit on the rim of a lower basin to listen to the water and relax after his night's service, calming down until he could ride home, serene.

When Dema saw the blot that fouled the south basin, he gasped. Inside a ring of priests and *arurim* who stood around the fountain, a dead woman sprawled, her legs hanging out of the basin, her upper body in the water, her arms flung wide. Her makeup showed dead white against her swollen face. Her long black curls floated in the water, creating a chilly semblance of life. Her *kyten*, the longer, feminine version of the Tharian tunic, was streaked with filth. The long ends of her yellow veil had been carefully straightened to grip the basin's edge, like a yellow arrow that ended at her neck.

A short, stocky man in *arurim* red, wearing the silver-bordered white stole of the district commander, stalked up to Dema's horse. "Why haven't you caught this monster, *Dhaskoi* Nomasdina?" he growled. "Why didn't you stop him before he committed this, this atrocity!" He glared at the ring of priests and *arurim*. "A week, the priests of the All-Seeing tell us, a *week* before the fountain can be fully cleansed!" Already the priests were placing the anchor posts and white cloths that would shroud the entire fountain while they performed a major spiritual and magical cleansing. "A *week* before the people can begin to forget this offense against the order of the city!"

Dema tumbled from his horse's back and stood at attention as the commander raved. Finally, when the man fell silent, Dema said, "I've been doing my best, sir. This is a canny murderer, not the usual sort of criminal at all. He has found a way to hide his tracks from magical scrutiny, there are no witnesses when he kills them, and he transports them where he likes. I've only eight months in the *arurim,* and I *did* request extra people to patrol Khapik. He kills them there."

"You will do the proper work with those you have," snarled the commander. "With this abomination in a public place, the people will be more eager to come forward, to name this murderer and cleanse Tharios of him."

Dema's heart plummeted into his belly. According to the advice given him by the Elya Street *arurim* and the *arurim dhaski,* he *had* been doing all the proper things. "May I get a ban on the cleansing of this site, then?" he asked, his voice breaking. "Until I have a chance to go over it with spells of investigation?"

The commander leaned in close, his eyes fixed on Dema's. "Ban the cleansing?" he whispered in a voice more frightening than a yell. "Take one more moment than we must to erase this specter of disorder? It's not just the fountain that must be cleansed, you young idiot. It's the pipes and the source of the water itself. Apply yourself to proper investigation, and let us purify the square!"

Dema bowed his head. "I spoke rashly, without thought," he whispered. With the taint of death hanging over the square, the least he could expect was sin and riots in the Fifth District. The immediate cleansing of the city had stopped the violence and disease that followed the fall of the Kurchal Empire. Ridding Tharios of all taint of death in those days had purified her, had kept the city safe and standing while the rest of the world ran mad. Its purity had guarded the city from barbarian attacks and made her leaders strong enough to do all that was necessary to restore order. Asking the priests to delay their cleansing was to open the door to madness. He hadn't stopped to think of that when he'd made his request.

The problem was, in crimes of this sort, cleansing nearly crippled investigators. It was both physical and magical, erasing all trace not just of the death, but of the killer and how the killer had come and gone from the death site.

"You had best *start* thinking, Demakos Nomasdina," the commander whispered, gripping Dema's arm in a hold that would leave bruises under Dema's brown skin. "Remember the pride of your clan. Now go look at that mess, then let the priests do their job."

Dema swallowed. He walked between two priests who were setting up the tentlike veil that would hide the long process of cleansing from the people's eyes, so they would not carry the taint of death away from the square. He approached the south basin of the fountain, steeling himself to view another murdered woman. There were men and women at Elya Street, *arurim* and *dhaski,* who could look at someone who'd been robbed of life and eat a hearty meal after. Dema didn't know how they could do it. Even after eight months he still felt as if someone had offended him personally, had killed a member of Dema's own family — which was true enough. The other classes of Tharios were the responsibility of the First Class, Dema's class. Someone had taken the life of a young woman in *his* charge.

That she was young he guessed from her hands, unlined, with well-tended nails, and the fresh, tight skin of her belly, feet, and legs. She wore the halter top, semisheer skirt, and tight, calf-length leggings of a tumbler or dancer; her brown arms and legs were muscular. Dema glanced away from her eyes, so startled at the fate that had come upon her.

As he leaned over the edge of the basin, he noticed two priests closing in. "I'm not going to touch her," he snapped. "Stand away and leave me be."

They took a step back and waited, hands clasped at their waists, their eyes level as they watched Dema. The morning breeze tugged at their white head-veils and the ends of their complexly draped red stoles.

Dema glanced at the knot in the yellow veil — under the left ear, just like the knot on the other four victims. Bending, he squinted at the ends of the veil, laid so neatly on the basin's rim.

A gloved hand thrust its way into his vision, holding an ivory rod. "Use this," the priest of the All-Seeing told Dema, a kind note in his voice. "We will send you such tools, blessed for this work, *dhaskoi*."

"Do other *arurim dhaski* have them?" Dema wanted to know, meeting the priest's dark brown eyes.

"None of them want to get so close as you," replied the priest. "We have seen this in you before. Do not let curiosity take you too far. Yours is a noble house, free of the stain of corruption. We will protect you, as best we may."

Dema hesitated, then accepted the rod with a nod of thanks. He used it to straighten the curled ends of the veil. By law *yaskedasi* had to carry their home address stitched along the hem of their veils, one of the ways the city kept watch on their disreputable ranks. While most were fairly honest, everyone knew that their ethics in matters of theft were flexible.

Here was the dead woman's address: *Ferouze's Lodgings, Chamberpot Lane, Khapik.* Dema would start his questioning there. He straightened and returned the rod to the priest, fixing the woman in his mind. Then he turned to be cleansed before he went to find her name. The *arurim prathmuni* moved in to take charge of her body.

Tris put the rest of her time in the lower part of Tharios
to good use, visiting other glassmakers. Most of the people
with shops on the Street of Glass understood that they
were there to entertain as well as to create, and that some
one who saw a piece being made often bought it. They
were happy to welcome Tris into their workshops and to
answer her questions, though the sum of what she learned
was not comforting. None of them knew of any glass
mage at Touchstone, only that the owner, Antonou Tinas,
had a distant kinsman from the far north working there.
His name was Kethlun Warder, they told Tris, and they
described the man that Tris had met. They also had never
heard of anything like the glass dragon, though all of them
were fascinated by the creature and insisted on giving it
a thorough examination. From the way the glass dragon
preened, it enjoyed the attention.

Tris would have talked to the city's glass mages as well,
but found only their students in the workshops near Achaya

Square. The mages themselves were at the same conference as Niko, since glass magic was often used in order to see things or to make a problem clearer. Talking to the students did teach her one thing: while glass mages were as common as dirt in Tharios, a glassmaking capital, for the most part they were academic mages, people who worked with charms, spells, and signs worked onto the material. Tris knew, since she had seen the dragon shape itself, that in all likelihood this Kethlun was an ambient mage, one whose magic came from something in the world around him. Tris had always thought the balance between academic mages and ambient ones was equal, until Niko explained that it only looked that way to her, because she had been schooled at the single greatest center for ambient mages in their part of the world.

For every ambient mage there were four academic ones, not counting those with ambient magic who could also practice academic magic. Moreover, some types of ambient magic were more common than others: the magics for stones, carpentry, healing, cooking, thread and needlework, pottery, fire, and the movement of weather in the air. Ambient glass magic, one of the mages' journeymen told her, was "middling rare," though Tris had no idea what that meant.

With such a scant amount of information, Tris returned to Heskalifos and Jumshida's house. If memory served her, Jumshida's private library held a number of books on magic. Tris might learn more there.

Inside the house, she banished Little Bear to the inner

courtyard and carried the glass dragon to her room. Jumshida had granted Tris and Niko the whole second floor on the east wing of the house: rooms for each of them, as well as a workshop they could use during their stay. Tris put the dragon in her room, freshened up, then went downstairs.

Jumshida's cook welcomed her. Preparing supper for an unknown number of mages was always tricky business. Even with the help of a maid hired for the length of the conference, there was still plenty for Tris to do. She chopped, grated, washed, and peeled, soaking in kitchen scents and listening to the servants talk about their lives and the schedule for the week. Muscle by muscle, Tris relaxed. Kitchen life comforted her. It was a place where she knew the rules and knew how to act. Since the staff only knew her as Niko's student, they didn't watch themselves around her as they would around a fully accredited mage. Tris could be ignored as long as she made herself useful, and she could hear about the university and the people who lived on its grounds.

The bell that marked the closing of the city's gates had just rung when the front door of the house burst open, admitting a flood of chattering men and women. The maid picked up the waiting tray with its pitcher of wine and many cups; the housekeeper gathered the tray of fruit juice and cups. "Tell my husband I will greet him in the next world," the maid said drily as she walked out.

Tris snorted with amusement as the women braved the guests. "Is it that bad?" she asked the cook.

"Girl, there is nothing worse than a crowd of hungry mages who don't have to pay for the food," the cook informed her. "I'd as soon be hunted by wolves. Aren't you going out there?"

Tris shook her head. "I don't like parties," she confessed. "I never fit in." If older mages knew her as Niko's student, they treated her like an idiot, not fit to converse with adults. If they'd heard of her, they treated her with distrust and suspicion. Her own talents, so broadly distributed over forces in the air, ground, and water, intimidated those who actually believed she had them. Many chose instead to think Tris lied about the extent of her power to make herself look more important. Tris preferred to stay with her own circle: her foster sisters and brother, their teachers, a handful of mages and students from Winding Circle, and Duke Vedris of Emelan. They not only knew her; they treated her as one of them, someone they loved.

"Shall I have the girl bring a tray to your room?" the cook asked, checking a sauce.

"No, not when you'll all be so busy. I'll come here when I'm hungry, if that's all right," replied Tris. Assured that it was, she took the staircase from the courtyard to the second floor.

She had just set an armful of Jumshida's books on her bed when she heard Niko call from the workroom they shared, "Trisana, why is there a glass creature eating our antimony?"

Tris walked over to the open workroom door. There stood her teacher, hands on hips, surveying the glass dragon. Despite his long day at the conference, Niko looked fresh and crisp. His clothes, made by Tris's foster sister Sandry, a thread mage, showed not a single wrinkle. Niko wore a sleeveless gray linen overrobe and breeches, and a paler gray silk shirt, its full sleeves neatly buttoned at the cuffs. On his feet were black slippers. He refused to wear Tharian sandals, telling Tris that he would reserve the sight of his bare toes for himself alone.

At five feet ten inches Niko was half a foot taller than Tris was, and wiry, with silver-and-black hair worn in a horsetail most of the time. He possessed a full, natty, black-and-silver mustache of which he was vain, heavy black-and-silver brows, and deep-set black eyes. His face was craggy, the strong nose jutting from it like the prow of a ship.

Niko stared down that formidable nose at the dragon, who sat on its hindquarters, staring up at the mage. Its muzzle was coated with antimony; its belly was filled with the stuff.

"Is that even good for you?" Tris asked it.

As if in reply the dragon twitched, its belly roiling. A moment later it opened its jaws. Antimony surged from its gullet to form clear glass flames that dropped as soon as they broke away from its mouth. Niko quickly thrust a hand under the dragon's chin to catch the pieces. When the creature finished, Niko had a palmful of glass flames.

"I can't think of the last time I held dragon vomit in my hand," Niko remarked, his voice dry. "Why, never, in fact. There are no such things as dragons. Need I also point out there are no such things as living *glass* dragons?"

Tris picked the creature up and cradled it in her arms. "You shouldn't stuff yourself that way," she told it. "You couldn't absorb it. Surely you can't be hungry after all you ate at the shop."

"Perhaps eating is how she learns the nature and substance of things," remarked Niko, sidetracked by the thought. "After all, who can tell if she truly sees or not?"

"It's an it, not a she," protested Tris. She held up the dragon so Niko could see its belly was unmarked by male or female organs.

"Nonsense," he replied. "So elegant and dainty a creature, with such wonderful eyes, *has* to be female."

"You just say that because you like women better than men," Tris retorted. The dragon climbed up her arm and draped itself across her shoulders, rubbing its head on her braided hair.

"With good reason. Few women spend the first weeks of an acquaintance trying to prove how much more they know than you," Niko said as he gently poured the dragon flames onto the counter by the antimony jar. "You haven't explained how this creature came to be here, Tris."

"It's a long story. You're supposed to be down there,

aren't you?" she asked, nodding in the direction of the noisy first floor.

"For this lady, I will set aside the conference for the moment. I've never seen anything like her," Niko pointed out. "And you've been using your lightning. What for? You know I can see it on you and the dragon."

Tris shrugged. "It wasn't much." She set the dragon on a worktable and fitted the cork back into the antimony jar. "Some glass mage was having a tantrum. I don't think much of the teachers here, if they can't make a grown man learn self-control."

"Some students don't want to learn," Niko offered, rubbing the dragon's chin with a gentle finger. "Let's hear the whole of it."

Tris went around the room, making sure that every jar was tightly corked, as she told Niko how she had made the dragon's acquaintance. "I don't know which was sillier," she remarked as she finished, "him thinking I'd believe his story about not being a mage, or treating me as if I were a monster. I asked him if he would take the responsibility for the dragon and he refused, so I kept her."

Niko sighed. "Lightning scares people," he reminded her. "I thought you were going to keep a grip on it — and on your temper."

"I *did*," she retorted. "I just gave him enough of a shock to make him drop the tongs, *and* I warned him. He would have killed her," she said defensively, rubbing the dragon between its tiny ears. "I can't abide people who blame others for their mistakes, Niko, you know I can't. I'd like to give his teacher a piece of my mind."

"And if he's a new mage?" inquired Niko.

Tris snorted. "How could that be? He's a grown man!"

"Lark didn't know her gift with needlework was magic until she was nearly thirty." Lark was one of Tris's foster mothers, a powerful thread mage. "It isn't unusual for the person not to know, if his power, or hers, comes from things used every day," Niko added.

"Hmpf," replied Tris, unconvinced. "Well, he knows now. And it's not like there aren't fistfuls of glass mages in this city, so I won't be stuck with him." Any mage who was certified by Lightsbridge University in Karang or Winding Circle Temple in Emelan agreed to a pact to get a mage's credential: he, or she, had to teach any new mage if there was no teacher with that same magic on hand. Despite their age, Tris, her foster sisters and her foster brother all wore the medallion that marked them as accredited mage-graduates of Winding Circle. Sandry and Briar had written her about the mage-students they had taken on since Tris and Niko left Emelan. Tris preferred to avoid their fate. She was responsible for Little Bear and now, it seemed, for the dragon. That was more than enough for her.

"You should check on him in the morning. Make certain that he has a teacher," Niko said. "No fooling about, Tris. A student is a serious matter. Can that thing even *digest* charcoal?"

The glass dragon took her muzzle out of the box that held sticks of charcoal and belched. This time she produced semitransparent black glass globes that rolled over the worktable.

Niko stretched a hand out to the creature and twitched his fingers. "Come here, you," he ordered.

The dragon looked from Tris to Niko, plainly thinking it over. "It's all right," Tris assured her. "He's my teacher."

Niko smiled at her. "One of the strongest bonds between mages, isn't it?"

Tris nodded.

Gingerly the dragon walked over to Niko and, leaning back on her haunches, sat up. First the mage looked her over, inch by inch, examining the seamless joins of wings to body and claws to feet. Then he conducted an examination with his sensitive fingertips. He got nipped once for putting a finger into the dragon's gullet. "Don't do that," he said absently. "Now, stay."

He patted the dragon on the head as if she were a dog, then set his bony fingers on his closed eyelids. Tris raised a hand to shade her vision as white fire sprang from Niko's eyes. Startled, the dragon fell onto her back. Quickly she scrabbled to her feet and turned to see if her tail was still there.

When Niko opened his eyes, the glass dragon sneezed noiselessly.

"Very likely," Niko told her. He looked at Tris. "She's . . . strange," he said, frowning slightly.

Tris bridled in defense of her newest stray. "Of course she's strange," she retorted. "The one who made her tried to kill her." She didn't even notice that she had accepted Niko's decision that the dragon was female.

Niko sighed. "That's not what I mean. I don't know if I ever told you, but I hold a credential in glass magic —"

"In addition to your credentials in teaching magic, seer's magic, and star magic," the girl replied. "That's why they wanted you for *this* circus." With a wave of her hand she included the boisterous gathering of mages downstairs.

"Yes, Trisana," replied Niko patiently. "Now, I learned to make glass to expand my magical vision, and because I like glassmaking. I can tell you that this creature contains a surge of glass magic, but it's not focused in the way that a trained glass mage would do it. Her skeleton is made of glass magic. I'm also picking up traces of protective magics, wind magics, healing magics, prosperity magics, and love magics."

"Kethlun pulled all that in from the neighborhood," Tris explained. "Every loose bit of magic from a block all ended up in her. I told you he didn't raise any barriers."

"As I have now seen for myself," replied Niko. "Her blood though — her blood is lightning."

Tris sat on a stool, frowning, then turned her attention to the dragon. Carefully she removed her spectacles and set them on the table. Once they were off, everything in the everyday world went grainy: without her spectacles, she was nearly blind. On the other hand, if she wanted to look at highly detailed magic, her vision was sharper without the lenses. She rubbed her eyes for a moment, then surveyed her new charge.

The dragon blazed, the silver fire of the neighborhood magics rippling over her surface. Through the ripples shone a skeleton as bright as real silver, needle-thin bones that supported the dragon's elegant form. Twined around those bones was the hotter, blue-white fire of pure lightning, moving in streams like blood. Lightning shone in the small round bumps that served her for eyes, glinted along her thin teeth, and swirled down the length of her forked tongue.

Tris sighed as she hooked her spectacles back over her ears. "I wonder if he even could have killed you."

The dragon shrugged, her magical skin rolling with the movement.

"That isn't your lightning," pointed out Niko. As her teacher, he knew the many shapes of Tris's magic better than anyone.

"No. I didn't use mine till after the dragon broke away from the blowpipe," Tris admitted.

"Do you suppose it's his? Kethlun's?" asked Niko.

The dragon toddled over to Tris and stepped down into the girl's lap. There she curled herself, catlike, into a ball.

"I thought that lightning mages either learned to control themselves before they got to be my age or they died," Tris replied quietly. "That's what you told me." She smoothed a hand over the length of the dragon's spine. A pure musical note rose from the creature as Tris stroked her, a lingering tone like those drawn from the lips of glasses filled with water. The girl smiled. "Is that your purr?" she asked. The ringing tone rose each time she ran her fingers down the dragon's spine. The sound continued, first low, then higher, a melody that grew softer and softer, until it stopped. "I think she's asleep," Tris whispered to Niko. "I'm going to name her Chime."

Niko was still fixed on Chime's lightning blood. "It's true, if this Kethlun Warder were born with lightning magic, he wouldn't survive to adulthood without mastering it," he pointed out, smoothing his mustache with a bony finger. "There has to be an explanation of some kind."

"You're welcome to find it," Tris replied. She kept her voice soft, not wanting to wake the dragon. "Are you going to have time after the conference?"

Niko cleared his throat. "Actually, that was something I wanted to discuss with you."

Tris raised her eyebrows and waited.

"We, er, had a vote today," Niko explained, tugging the cuffs of his sleeves. "You know that from time to time mages get together to do some encompassing study of a particular sort of magic."

Tris knew that. She had handled the result of such research over the past four years, a substance which, after years of research on the part of a handful of mages, helped others to fashion cures for diseases. "The conference is something like that?" she asked.

"It is now," replied Niko. "In an outburst of magely fellowship and affection, it was resolved that all of us work together to create the single biggest compendium of visionary magics ever written, ambient and academic, truthsaying, past seeing, scrying in water, flame —"

"On the wind?" Tris asked eagerly. "You're going to write about scrying on the wind?" She knew that some mages were able to see images on the wind, glimpses of things the wind had touched. Being fond of winds herself, Tris thought that being able to see things on them would be well worth learning. The problem was that Niko, the finest seer she knew, couldn't do it, and thus couldn't teach it. "Who have you got for it? Can I meet her? Him?"

Niko sighed. "We don't have a wind seer. I hate to think of leaving this out. . . . I suppose we could dig up what's been written about it until now, though it would be wonderful if we had someone who could actually write about it as they do it."

Tris slumped on the stool. "Oh."

"Scrying the wind is very difficult, Tris," Niko said gently.

"It's like scrying the future. You're assailed with thousands of images — fragments, really. It drives many who try it insane."

"You learned to scry the future," Tris pointed out.

"And a number of people have informed me they think I am mad," Niko replied, his voice *very* dry.

"Niko!" someone yelled from downstairs. "Will you hide all night? We're *starving*. And Lieshield refuses to discuss anything else before we choose who will do the index!"

"And so it begins," Niko said wearily, straightening his clothes. "We could be here for decades." He stopped to give Chime a gentle caress. "You could always bring her down to distract my colleagues," he suggested, hope in his eyes. "You could meet some of your peers."

"I could always pull my ears from my head, too," replied Tris. "It would be just as much fun. You know I hate parties."

Niko sighed. "You've always been too sensible for me. Check on this Warder fellow tomorrow," he reminded her. "Make sure he has a teacher."

Antonou Tinas had agreed to give Kethlun shop room, but that didn't include sleeping quarters. The small building on the other side of the shop was just big enough to hold the old man, his wife, their youngest daughter, and her husband. From the sound of the quarrels, Kethlun wasn't even sure that there was room for the younger couple. There was certainly no room for Keth.

At the end of the day, Keth closed the workshop. After saying good night to Antonou, he walked down the Street of Glass to his home, located inside the entertainment district known as Khapik. It wasn't the best housing, as the district hosted quite a few people who regarded theft as an art form, but it was interesting and cheap. Students and young journeymen like Keth could afford Khapik's prices and also be entertained for free. Residents and guests spanned the full spectrum of performance, all lumped together under the name *yaskedasi:* poorer mages, actors, musicians, tumblers, dancers, illusionists, singers, gamblers, and fortune-tellers. Other residents and employees included outright criminals; servants and cooks at the many eating-houses, theaters, inns, coffee and tea houses; and clerks who served in the multitude of shops that offered everything under the sun: clothing, souvenirs, jewelry, art, flowers, and musical instruments.

Keth liked Khapik. There were things to see and do no matter how late the hour. Everyone came here sooner or later: foreigners, nobles, students, and merchants, male and female, going from attraction to attraction. Keth's slow speech, occasional stammer, and slight clumsiness went unnoticed in a district where the beggars were missing body parts and the poorer folk were missing teeth. No one cared that he didn't talk much. Here good listeners were in popular demand. Best of all, the occasional storms that swept through Tharios spent their lightning bolts on towers. There were no towers in Khapik.

After a few changes of address, Kethlun had settled at Ferouze's Lodgings on Chamberpot Alley. Ferouze let rooms cheaply, to *yaskedasi* and anyone else who could pay. Keth couldn't see what had brought fame as a *yaskedasu* to this old, fat, snaggle-haired woman, but her house and her linens were clean and she had enough healing skills to treat the small injuries that befell even the most careful performer. She also played chess. With her help Keth was regaining his old skill at the game.

When he entered the house, built like other Tharian homes around a central courtyard, Keth was surprised to find it so quiet. This was the hour when the place should be waking up, with six *yaskedasi* in residence. Ferouze's watchdogs came trotting down the corridor to sniff him, then returned to their normal pursuits, allowing Keth to pass into the courtyard. The rooms on all three floors opened onto this small square of green where Ferouze had a kitchen garden and the well.

Normally the *yaskedasi* would be talking back and forth from the upstairs galleries around the courtyard, trading gossip and insults as they prepared for work. Today Keth found three of the girls seated on one of the staircases, and no sign of their landlady or the other two men who lived there. The girls were still in day clothes, undyed wool *kytens*. None of them wore a speck of makeup; all had been crying. Yali sat with the absent Iralima's four-year-old daughter curled up in her lap. Little Glaki's black curls were tangled. Her face was red and swollen with weeping, and she slept with her thumb in her mouth. Xantha, the blonde northern dancer who lived there, still wept, her face puffy.

Keth looked at Yali, who raised wet brown eyes to his. "What's wrong?" he asked. All thought of the redheaded girl and her lightning fled his mind; goosebumps rippled over his skin. He didn't have to be a mage to know he was about to hear bad news. "Where is everyone?"

"Ferouze and the men are at Noskemiou Thanas," replied Poppy. Her green-and-brown eyes, normally filled with anger, were dull. Her brown skin was ashen.

Keth had to think for a moment to translate what she had said into his native Namornese. The city's great hospital for the poor was called Noskemiou; Thanas was the wing where the dead were brought. "Why?" he asked when his brain sorted it out. "Who died?"

"Iralima," Yali whispered, her full mouth quivering. "*Dhaskoi* Nomasdina, who's been investigating for the *arurim*, he came and described her." She covered her mouth with a hand that shook. Keth hesitated, then reached out and clasped her shoulder, trying to comfort her. He had liked Ira, and his heart went out to Glaki. Iralima was the child's only family. Ira's clan had kicked her out when she declared her intention to be a Khapik dancer.

"Where have you been all day, in a hole in the ground?" demanded Poppy. "The Ghost got her. He got her, and he strangled her, and he dumped her in the fountain on Labrykas Square like she was garbage."

"Hush!" scolded Yali in a whisper, covering Glaki's ear. "Not in front of the child, Poppy, for the All-Seeing's mercy!"

"I shouldn't have told Ira that she was a selfish old hen," wailed Xantha. "It's my fault."

Yali and Poppy exchanged disgusted glances. "We forgot the whole world spins around you, Xantha," said Poppy, her voice as tart as vinegar. "Just don't fight with us and we'll have long, happy lives."

"Girls." If Poppy and Xantha got started, Keth knew they'd be at it all night. "Did you tell this *dhaskoi* when you saw Ira last? Where she danced?"

"We told him," replied Yali, rubbing her arm over her eyes without disturbing the girl in her lap. "It's not like he broke his back finding out who killed those other *yaskedasi*, is it?"

"*Arurim* have a word for crimes against people like us, remember?" Poppy demanded.

Defeated, Kethlun repeated it: "*Okozou.*"

"*Okozou,*" Poppy repeated. "No one worth a *bik*" — Tharios's smallest copper coin — "got hurt."

"If they scurry on this one, it's because Ira fetched up in the Labrykas fountain," added Yali. "They've had the cleansing tent up all day. They can't have a dead *yaskedasu* defiling a public place, now, can they?"

"Tell us your own *arurim* back in the north would care about the likes of us," taunted Poppy. When Keth didn't reply, Poppy nodded. "I didn't think so." She struggled to her feet. "I have to get dressed."

"You're working *tonight*?" cried Xantha. "With Iralima at Noskemiou Thanas?"

Glaki whimpered. Yali bent over her, smoothing the child's rumpled curls with a tender hand.

Poppy glared at Xantha. "And you're not? Ira would be out there if it was you in Thanas. Didn't you say you don't have the rent money yet?"

"Deiina!" muttered Xantha, naming the patron goddess of Khapik. "I forgot!" In a flash she was on her feet, pushing by the other two on her way upstairs.

"It's not right," Kethlun told Yali. She was the cleverest of the three, the one he could talk with most comfortably. "*Yaskedasi* are Tharians, too."

"You're sweet, Keth," Yali said. "It won't last if you stay here." She got to her feet with a grunt, balancing Glaki's weight on her hip. The child was all cried out and didn't even stir. Yali said, "There will be a Farewell at the Thanion." It was the temple dedicated to the god of the dead. "Shall I tell you when they have it?"

"Please," Keth replied. Tharios's dead were burned outside the city, so there were no burials, only Farewell ceremonies. As Yali continued to climb upstairs, he called after her, "Yali, what about her?" He nodded to Glaki.

Yali kissed the little girl's hair. "She's mine, now. I'll take care of her."

"If you need help, just ask," Keth said. "I'll watch her, help pay for her food, whatever you need."

His reward was a slight lifting of the cloud in Yali's brown eyes, and a smile that made his heart turn over. "You're truly a good fellow, Keth," she told him. "I'll take you up on that."

"I want you to," he said as she finished the climb to her room.

The night was close and hot, bringing very little rest with it. Around midnight Keth took a sleeping mat up to the roof and placed it between Ferouze's potted herb garden and the wall. He placed a jug of water beside him — he'd been unable to drink wine since his encounter with a lightning bolt — and lay down, locking his hands behind his head. Heat lightning played in sheets under the clouds in the sky. It made him edgy, but not enough to go back inside. Heat lightning didn't strike, it only taunted those trapped in the baking city with the promise of rain.

As always, once he was in the open air, the tangled ball of thoughts that had kept him awake began to unravel. Here in the dark, alone, with the sounds of the crowds on the main street of Khapik muffled, he could think about the girl who threw lightning. His gut twisted over the memory, but he could think about it, and he could admit some truths to himself. The glass in the blowpipe *had* fought him. When, before his accident, had he ever felt that the stuff he'd worked with all his life had a mind of its own? That idea had grown since his travels began, along with the notion that glass had come to life while he wasn't looking. It never even occurred to him to call that feeling magic. Perhaps that was because none of the glass mages in his family had mentioned sensing the glass was alive. He was used to thinking of glass magic as his family described it: a matter of charms, signs, special twists in pulled glass, special shapes in molded glass, and blown glass shaped to hold and direct spells. They spoke of glass as Keth and his friends did: a substance to which they did things, not a living being.

As much as it pained him, Keth finally admitted the redhead was right. He should have been relieved to find an answer, but he wasn't. He'd had plans, important ones. His master's credential, marriage, a family, a rise in the guild until, one day, he led it. He would make glass for the imperial court and have the power and wealth to work on his own projects.

Now he was back at the foot of the ladder, a student, a beginner along with children. The study of magic would cut into his time with glass for years.

He had regrets; of course he did. He supposed he would always have them. But watching heat lightning ripple through the clouds, Kethlun Warder faced facts. Tomorrow he would find a glass mage to teach him.

3

Tris had used shawls to make a nest for Chime by the window, but when morning came, she turned over in bed and felt a glass corner poke her right eye. She opened the left: the cause of her discomfort was Chime's tail. The rest of the glass dragon was draped over an extra pillow, just as Little Bear sprawled over her feet. Tris grumbled and gently moved Chime's tail, then rose to begin her morning cleanup. At least she didn't have to worry about feeding her starling, Shriek. After four years of screaming at Tris the moment she woke up, Shriek had joined a flock of Hataran starlings when she and Niko passed through that country. Tris, secretly a romantic, told herself that a particularly comely lady starling must have caught her bird's eye. She never let on that she missed the speckled bird's chatter any more than she admitted to missing Sandry, Daja, or Briar.

Screams in the kitchen and Little Bear's deep-throated

barks interrupted Tris as she made her bed. She raced downstairs. The maid was in hysterics, having discovered what she called "a monster" — Chime — in the honey pot. Little Bear had already decided Chime was family. He stood between the maid and the glass dragon, barking a warning. The cook scolded the girl for being upset while Tris ordered Little Bear outside. Together Tris and the cook managed to get Chime clean. By the time she was free of honey, the glass dragon had begun to produced flames like bits of amber glass.

"May I keep some?" asked the cook. "They're so pretty."

Tris, glad to find a way to calm the servants, shared out the flames with the cook, the housekeeper, and even the trembling maid, then went to finish straightening her room. She hated to let others do housework, but looking after her own room and the workroom that Tris shared with Niko was all Jumshida's staff would permit her to do. After a light breakfast, she made a shawl into a sling, tucked Chime into it, then set off for Touchstone Glass with her dog at her heels. She would check on Kethlun as she had promised Niko, then explore more of the city's glass shops.

She had almost reached Touchstone when the flare of magic caught her eye. Three priests, two in white tunics, one in a *kyten*, all in white head-veils and complex red stoles that marked them as servants of Tharios's All-Seeing God, stood where an alley opened onto the Street of Glass. One priest wielded a censer of smoking incense: cypress,

Tris's nose told her, with myrtle, cedar, and clove — cypress for death, myrtle for peace, clove for protection, cedar for purification. A white candle burned on the ground between the priests. The female priest carried a basket full of candles. The third priest was the mage. Power flowed from his moving hands and lips to sink into the ground under the candle.

"What's going on?" Tris asked the stocky older man who leaned against the open door of Touchstone.

"A man dropped dead there last night," the Tharian replied. He was plump and gray-haired, light-skinned for a Tharian, with small, sharp brown eyes and a chunky nose. He wore a pale blue tunic. His shopkeeper's short, dark green stole lay over his shoulders, its ends hanging even with the hem of his tunic. "Once the *prathmuni* collect the remains and scrub the site, the priests must cleanse the area of all taint of, well, death. No one here may do business until then."

"Everything dies," Tris pointed out, watching as the air between the three priests turned magic-white. "Do you also cleanse for dead animals and insects?"

The shopkeeper shrugged. "You are a *shenos*. You're not used to our ways. The death of humans, the highest form of life, clings to all that it touches. It must be cleansed, or everyone who comes near will be polluted."

The priests turned their backs on the space they had just cleansed. As one they clapped their hands three times, then walked off. It was neatly and precisely done, with the deftness of long practice.

"Well, thank heavens the *prathmuni* were here first thing," remarked the shopkeeper. "Sometimes they don't come until late in the day. The place can't be cleansed until the remains are gone, and we can't open our doors until the cleansing is done. Lucky for us the district *prathmuni* are as reliable as their kind go."

Tris wiped her forehead on her sleeve to hide her scowl. Of all the peculiar foreign customs she had encountered since traveling north with Niko, she wasn't sure which she disliked more: the creation of the *prathmun* class, or the need to ritually cleanse anything touched by death. Tris thought the treatment of *prathmuni* was cruel and the pollution of death stupid. Thinking about it called on every speck of control over her temper that she had.

"Have a good day," the man said. He started to open the shutters on his shop. Tris, remembering why she had come, said, "Actually, *koris* . . ." She didn't know the man's name.

"Antonou Tinas," the shopkeeper informed her and bowed.

"*Koris* Tinas," Tris said, with a polite bow in reply. "I'm here to see a man who works for you, Kethlun Warder."

"Keth's not in just now," Antonou replied. "I'm not — Hakkoi's hammer," he whispered, calling on the Living Circle's god of smiths and glassmakers, "what is *that*?" He pointed to Tris's bosom.

Tris glanced down. A small, clear glass muzzle with hair-fine whiskers stuck out of the shawl as Chime peered up at her. The girl smiled and tickled the dragon's chin with a gentle finger. "*That* is why I need to talk to *Koris* Warder," she explained.

"May my fires never die," murmured the older man. "Come in, *koria* —?"

"Chandler," replied Tris, following Antonou into the shop. It was a relief to get out of the sun, even with her usual cocoon of breezes wrapped around her. "Trisana Chandler."

"Please sit down, *Koria* Chandler," Antonou urged, indicating a chair. This shop was meant for customers, unlike the workroom in back. The floors and countertops were covered with pale tiles in cream or beige to best display the glassware. Arranged on shelves throughout the room were plates, bowls, vases, figures, bottles of every imaginable size, even pendants, and ear and hair ornaments.

Tris sat and helped Chime out of her sling. "Don't start flying about and breaking things," she warned. "I can't afford to pay for them."

"May I?" asked Antonou, holding out his hands. "It's not *koria*, is it? It's *dhasku.*" He had properly identified her as a female mage.

"It's just Tris," she replied as she offered Chime to him. The glassblower gently wrapped his square, blunt-fingered hands around the willing dragon and sat on a stool, steadying Chime on his knees. Chime looked up into his face and nibbled one of his fingers.

"You should be careful," warned Tris. "She tries to eat anything she sees."

"I would be old and gamey to the taste," Antonou told Chime. He surveyed the creature with wonder, noting each detail of her eyes, muzzle, feet, and mouth. "You say Keth knows something about this creature?"

"He made her," Tris replied, watching the glassblower's face. Antonou was no mage; she had already looked inside him for that.

"Keth?" repeated the man, shocked. "Kethlun *made* this lovely being?"

A low, musical, steady note rose from Chime. "That's her purr, I think," explained Tris. "Be careful. You don't want her to be vain."

"A beauty like this has every right to be vain," Antonou replied. Chime gnawed one of his shirt buttons. "Well, if Keth did this, it explains this morning," Antonou commented. "He came here just after dawn, looking as if Hakkoi's Firewights were on his trail. When he told me he's got magic, like it's a disease to be caught, and he needed to find a teacher, I thought he'd been drinking."

Tris thrust her brass-rimmed spectacles up on her long nose. "I'm sure he thinks magic is a disease," she said drily. "That's how he acted yesterday. You say he's looking for a teacher now?"

"At Heskalifos," Antonou replied. "And magic explains more than it doesn't. He was struck by lightning, you know."

Tris stared at Antonou, mouth gaping, before she remembered her manners and closed it. When she had enough wit to speak again, she said, "He neglected to mention it."

"Oh, well, he usually does, poor lad. He lived, but it made a shambles of his life." Suddenly Antonou beamed at her. "Actually, this is wonderful news. A proper teacher can rid him of the *malipi* that's gnawed on him since he came. Anyone could see he was troubled. I kept saying, go to *Dhaskoi* Galipion over on Witches Row. Whatever *malipi* rides you, he'll be able to banish it.

"But young people, they don't understand how many troubles come from the unseen world," he continued, shaking his head. "They insist that all this reason and rationality that's so popular these days proves there is no supernatural, only what the mind can grasp and make plain. 'How about magic?' I ask them, but they tell me magic is also governed by reason. Pah." Antonou shook his head. "Law and reason are very well, but to say the gods are only tales told to comfort us . . . Hey, you!" Tris jumped. Antonou lunged over to a counter, where Chime was attempting to thrust her muzzle into a low, fat jar. "What is she looking for?" Antonou demanded.

"Food," Tris said, getting to her feet. "Actually, *Koris*

Antonou, what substances are used to color glass, and where might I buy them? At this rate Chime's going to eat all of my mage supplies."

Antonou was happy to assist her. Half an hour later, he sent her off with a list and explanations for every item on it, and directions to the Street of Glass's *skodi*, or marketplace. There Tharios's glassworkers bought raw ingredients and residents could buy whatever they fancied in the way of plain glasswork. Tris would find all she needed to feed a glass dragon there.

She went happily, just as curious to see the raw materials of glassmaking as she was to see the work itself. A small part of her mind was uneasy about the information she had gathered from Antonou regarding Keth's search for a teacher. That part of her demanded constantly: And what of the lightning? Lightning and glass don't go together in the day-to-day world. Lightning *melts* glass. How can a glass mage teach him to combine the two?

Tris ignored that part of her mind. Keth was no longer her problem. That was all that mattered.

Still, she might cut her day of exploration short, she thought. Go back to Heskalifos, to the Mages' Hall library, and see what books they had on the subject of glass magic. In the past she'd never thought about it much, but now that she had, she wanted to find out how it was worked, and what could be done with it. If she had a motto, it was "New learning never hurt anybody." She wouldn't know what insights she could or could not get from glass magic until she learned more.

Rather than wander the Street of Mages, Kethlun went straight to the source, Mages' Hall at Heskalifos. He presented himself to the clerks at the third hour of the morning, when he was informed that few mages were available. It seemed most of them were at some kind of conference in Philosophers' Hall, and would not return to their offices until midday. In the meantime, a clerk sat with him to ask a number of questions, writing Keth's answers down as he gave them. The clerk made it plain that he was not surprised to find a northerner who hadn't recognized his power until he was twenty. His attitude was that it was a wonder that northerners, unschooled in logic, reason, and discipline, discovered their magical skills at all. Keth tried to explain his near lack of power before his encounter with lightning, then gave up. Perhaps the mages would be more understanding.

After the questions, Keth was interviewed and tested by three student mages. One of them gave Keth a glass ball to hold as the student gazed into it. One used a glass wand to perform the same exercise. The third used a mirror made of glass and backed in silver. Each young mage reacted to his testing in the same way: they inspected their devices, then summoned the waiting clerk. After a few words from the student, the clerk made a note on the paper of information about Keth, then led Keth to the next student. After the third student, the clerk sent Keth off to eat his midday meal, with instructions to return in the afternoon.

Several hours passed after he came back. He spent them in the Mages' Museum, marveling at the many objects they had created, and briefly in their library, flipping through books. For a moment he thought he'd glimpsed braided red hair and the gleam of light along a long, curved glass edge passing by a stack of shelves on his right. Rather than see if it was the lightning girl or not, he went back to the museum.

At midafternoon his clerk-escort brought him to one of the university's mages, Vishaneh Amberglass. Keth felt better the moment he was ushered into her ground floor offices. Amberglass's office was a glassmaker's workshop, stifling hot from the fire in the furnace.

The mage herself was a tiny creature in her sixties, perched on a high stool. She had icy gray-green eyes, olive skin, and black hair worn in a coil ruthlessly pinned to her scalp. Instead of the Tharian *kyten* and stole, she dressed in the long tunic coat and leggings of a Trader or Bihanese. "I am told that you are a journeyman glassmaker," she said, eyeing him through round spectacles.

"Yes, *dhasku*," replied Kethlun.

"There is a crucible in the oven. Blowpipes over there."

Amberglass pointed them out. "Have you studied breath control through meditation?"

"Of course," he replied, startled by the question. "You don't get past your 'prenticeship without it."

"Do you know that meditation is a form that mages use to get at their power?" Her voice was crisp.

"Yes, *dhasku.* I learned from my uncles, who are glass mages."

"Then blow me a round glass ball, meditating as you do so," the mage instructed. "Don't take forever about it."

He didn't take forever. He did take his time, inspecting several blowpipes before he chose one that suited him, then eyed the crucible in the glory hole of the oven. "*Dhasku* Amberglass, you do understand that it's blowing glass where I get into trouble. It's why I'm here at all."

She inspected a thumbnail. "Either you are a journeyman, or you are not," she said tartly. "Which is it?"

Kethlun sighed. Closing his eyes, he fell into the breathing rhythms he had learned years ago. Meditation and breath control were as much a part of his family life as meals. Slowly he counted to seven as he inhaled, then held his breath to a count of seven, let it go for a count of seven, stopped for a count of seven, then began to inhale once more. Like magic his troubled mind instantly calmed. He could almost smell his mother's lavender sachet, his father's spicy hair pomade, the scent of baking bread in the kitchen. Gently he slid his pipe into the crucible, into the mass of molten glass, and collected a glob of it at the pipe's end. Bringing it out, he began to spin the pipe as he blew into it carefully.

"Let your mind drift," murmured that sharp voice, its edges blunted. "Close your eyes — I'll watch for you. Clouds go by, you smell spring rain —"

His mood shattered. He smelled hot metal and death. The hairs on his arms went stiff: lightning was here! He had enough sense to yank his mouth away from the pipe before he gasped in panic. The bubble at the end of the rod shimmered, then flashed with lightning. Miniature bolts rippled on its surface and through the center of the globe so thickly, it was impossible to see inside it.

Amberglass raised her hands and snapped her fingers. The bubble tore free of Kethlun's pipe and flew to her. She caught it in her palms. If the hot glass burned her, she gave no sign of it.

Trembling, Kethlun lowered the rod. "I did say —"

"Be quiet," she snapped, eyes fixed on the ball.

He knew the voice of a master; he shut up. Quietly he cleaned the excess glass from the pipe, cleared the inside of it, and put it away. When he finished, he glanced at the stool. Amberglass was gone. She soon returned, with his companion clerk, who carried the lightning ball, tucked into a silk-lined basket. Keth noticed that the lightning that covered the outside of the ball seemed to have no effect on the silk.

"This is beyond my skills," Amberglass told him. Her gaze gentled slightly. "I'm sending you to *Dhaskoi* Rainspinner. He works on weather."

With anyone else Kethlun might have complained, but not with this woman. She had gone to some trouble to see precisely what was wrong with him. He bowed to her, resigned, and followed the clerk to the upper floors of Mages' Hall.

By the end of the afternoon, Kethlun was more adrift than he had been that morning. He had seen two more mages after Rainspinner. Like Amberglass, they had sent him on to other glass or weather mages. Keth yearned to go home. If he spent much more time up here, Yali would have left Ferouze's and gone to perform by the time he got home.

When the clock struck the fourth hour, his guide led him back to the area where the mages' clerks sat, copying out schedules and lessons and reviewing correspondence. "You'll have to return tomorrow," the clerk said, wetting a reed pen in a pot of ink. He had placed the basket, with its sparking glass ball, at the farthest corner of his desk. The clerks at neighboring desks inched away from it. "Present yourself at —"

"Come *back?*" Keth asked, cursing his slow speech. What he *wanted* to do was scream, but he couldn't. If he didn't force himself to speak carefully, the stammer would return. Then no one would be able to understand him. He leaned on the counter between him and the clerks, his head and feet aching. "I have a debt to pay, work to do. I cannot spend my l-life h-here waiting like a pet dog. Aren't y-you p-people sup-posed to help?" There, he heard it: the stutter. He thrust the knuckle of his index finger into his mouth and bit down just hard enough to grab his attention, pulling it away from his fury. He did meditation breathing until he thought he could continue. None of the clerks had budged since he started talking. "Your charter says you are duty bound to instruct new mages," he said, letting each word finish its journey from his mouth before he tried the next sound. "Well, here I am. All new and shiny, fresh from the lightning strike. I need help *now*. Who knows what I will make next, when I do not know what I am doing?"

People were emerging from their offices. Most wore tunics and *kytens,* with the mage blue stole looped to waist-length in front and left to dangle to the knees behind. Kethlun looked around, counted, and gulped: twenty-three mages now stood in the room.

"How is it, my peers, that anyone can make such a complaint on this of all weeks?" The speaker was a tall chestnut brown woman with startling blue-gray eyes. Her nose was long and thin with broad nostrils, her wide mouth smoothly curved. She wore her graying dark hair in curls bound up with ribbons, covered by a sheer blue veil weighted with tiny glass drops at the hems. Like most Tharian women she wore the *kyten* and sandals that tied around her calves. Her ribbon belts were the same shade of blue as her mage's stole. Kethlun hadn't seen her or her companion, a white-skinned older man, emerge from an office behind him. The woman continued, "Here we have gathered a conclave of seers, glass mages, truthsayers, and masters of visionary magics from half the world, and we cannot name one man's power?"

"It is a mixture, *Dhasku* Dawnspeaker," explained the clerk who had shepherded Kethlun all day. "Something the mages and assistants who have seen *Koris* Warder have never encountered before."

"You give it a try, Jumshida Dawnspeaker," said the mage Amberglass with a sigh. "I've never gotten such a mangled reading of someone's power."

"Then perhaps we must stop wasting everyone's time, and go to the best vision mage present," replied *Dhasku* Dawnspeaker. She looked at her male companion. "*Dhaskoi* Goldeye?" she asked with a smile that Keth judged too warm for a woman who addressed a mere colleague.

Goldeye was a lean, wiry fellow, dressed in a sleeveless lilac overrobe, light gray silk shirt, and loose gray breeches. His long hair was black-streaked gray, held back from his craggy face with a tie. His eyes, dark and fathomless, set between heavy black lashes, caught Kethlun's gaze and held it well past the time Keth would gladly have looked away. At last he nodded, freeing Keth of the power in his eyes.

"I see why those who tested you were confused," he told Keth. "You have ambient glass magic, which means you draw power not from inside yourself, as academic glass mages do, but from glass and the things that go into making it, including earth, air, water, and fire. The thing that has transformed it, however, is lightning. That lightning gives your power strength *and* unpredictability. Your power flickers, jumping from element to element within you."

"Then we have a problem after all," Dawnspeaker admitted. "We have the finest glass mages in the world in Tharios, but lightning . . . changes matters. Does anyone here work in lightning at all?"

One of the other mages replied, "None. Lightning mages are rare, if any even exist."

"They exist," Goldeye said. "There are lightning mages among the Traders, and one of the academic mages at Lightsbridge has learned to handle it. For that matter, there is a lightning mage in Tharios. A very accomplished one, as it happens." He looked at Kethlun. "How advanced in the Glassmakers' Guild are you?"

"Journeyman, *Dhaskoi* Goldeye," Kethlun said politely. His brain was racing with new ideas. His problem had a name, and a solution, right here in Tharios. He could gain control over it, and return to his *real* life. And his family would be pleased. Keth's lack of magic had always disappointed them. In the world of the Namorn trade guilds, mages equalled power for their guild.

Goldeye smoothed his mustache with a bony finger. "Since you know your craft, it seems to me that any spells you might need could be learned from books, perhaps with advice from a glass mage once your power is controlled." There was a glint of mischief in the mage's eye, one Keth didn't understand. It vanished as the mage continued, "The lightning aspect is the thing that requires most of your attention."

"You mean you can help me?" Kethlun's voice cracked with desperation. He blushed hotly. He didn't want these people to know how scared he was. "What must I do?"

Goldeye put a comforting hand on Keth's shoulder and squeezed, then let go. Kethlun looked down a scant inch into the older man's face. "Come to supper with Dawnspeaker and me," Goldeye said. There was understanding in his gaze. "We'll sort you out."

After she had chased the glass dragon first from the alum, then the salt, then the myrrh jars in the workroom, Tris used a ribbon to make a leash for Chime and secured the dragon to a chair leg in the downstairs dining room. "I can't concentrate on these books with your rattling things," she scolded as she made sure Chime could retreat under the table. Little Bear enjoyed washing his new companion, and Tris wanted Chime to have a place where the dog couldn't reach her if the dragon decided she had endured enough.

Tris also left a small bowl of water, though she wasn't sure Chime drank water, and a dish with a tablespoon each of red and blue luster salts, as well as the powder that turned glass a deep emerald green. These she also tucked well under the table. Little Bear was as convinced as Chime that there was no harm in trying to eat everything at least once.

With dog and dragon settled, Tris returned to the upstairs workroom to read. At first glance all that she had found was academic magic, not ambient. This troubled her. While any ambient mage could and did use spells, signs, talismans, and potions to amplify her power, the source of ambient magic came from outside the mage. It had to be approached differently. Academic mages reached first for spell books, ambient mages for the things that gave them their power. Only another ambient mage held the truth of that difference in her very bones. What if Keth didn't find an ambient glass mage?

I just need to look harder for books on ambient glass magic, she told herself. I'm sure they have them.

Downstairs Little Bear was barking. Tris ignored him, fascinated by the instructions for making a bowl to scry with; the Bear tended to bark at anything and everything. Another sound did shatter her concentration, a bone-shivering screech like a shard of glass dragged over hard stone. She raced downstairs and into the dining room.

Chime had climbed a table leg to the top. She clung there, tucked into the corner of the table's frame as she made that awful sound. Tris scrabbled to undo the ribbon leash. The moment she freed the dragon, Chime threw herself at her, digging her claws into Tris's clothes and skin.

Tris crooned gently to the trembling creature, trying to calm her. Looking at the dragon's food, she saw a few glass flames beside the dish. Holding Chime with one hand, she set the flames in the dish with the coloring powders and put it on the table, where she couldn't break them by accident. Chime continued to screech. Over and over Tris stroked the dragon, trying to breathe meditation-style, hoping she would calm the frightened creature.

The front door opened as Little Bear continued to bark. Tris's breezes swirled into the front hall and returned to her with voices: Jumshida's, then Niko's.

"It's all right," she assured Chime. "They belong here. You remember Niko, don't you?" Now she was really puzzled. Chime had been admired by total strangers all day and had voiced nothing louder than her musical purr. What had upset her?

Red-faced with effort, several of her braids knocked free of their pins, she edged out from under the table. Once in the open air she sat back on her heels and straightened, holding Chime to her chest with one hand.

"Oh, no," said a man with a slightly husky, slow, familiar voice.

Tris whirled, forgetting that she still knelt, then fell on her side. Chime leaped free, taking flight. As the dragon zipped around the room, Tris glared up at Niko, furious to be caught unkempt and awkward before a stranger. Looking past him, she recognized the newcomer.

"You!" she cried at the same moment as Kethlun did.

"I take it you two have met?" asked Niko mildly. "Kethlun, Tris — Trisana Chandler — is the lightning mage I told you about."

Chime screeched, that same earsplitting sound of a nail on glass, and flew straight at Kethlun. A foot away from him the dragon spat a flurry of glass needles into her maker's face.

"Chime, no!" cried Tris. "Bad!" Quick as a flash — she had practiced the movements for weeks so she could do this bit of magic in a hurry — she stripped the tie from one thin braid and collected a handful of sparks. She threw them at the dragon, imagining each spark as a tiny ball of thread connected to her fingertips. The balls spun around Chime to form a lightning cage with the dragon suspended inside. Tris reeled in the cage. Only when she held it in her hands did she look at Keth.

He'd flinched when the dragon came at him, saving his right eye, but that side of his face and head was peppered with thin red, blue, and green needles. Niko tried to pull one out and cut himself.

"Serves you right," Tris informed Keth, scowling at him as she pinned up her loose braids. "You *did* try to kill her."

Keth looked from Tris to Niko. "Oh, no," he said, voice shaking. "Not her."

"I'm afraid so," replied Niko. "She *is* a lightning mage. You may have noticed," he added drily.

"I don't understand," said Tris, but she was afraid she did, all too well. She had tried to find other lightning mages, just as she had tried to find other mages who could master the forces of the earth or of the sea, with little success. It seemed that, of all the ambient magics, weather was the most dangerous. It drew its power from all over the world. Mages who tried to do more than call rainstorms or work the winds often misjudged their ability to handle the forces that supplied their power, and were crushed. It had been in the back of her mind since Niko had shown her the lightning in Chime, that Keth would have trouble finding a teacher who could help with that aspect of his power.

"Of course you understand," replied Niko.

Tris glared at him. Niko knew her too well.

"Moreover, you will do your duty," Niko added, looking down his nose at her. "You accepted that when you donned the medallion of your certification."

About to argue or even refuse, Tris made the mistake of looking at Keth. He was the picture of misery, blood dripping from the needles in his flesh, lines of exhaustion bracketing his mouth, dark circles under his eyes. Instead of speaking as she had meant to, she pulled out a chair with one hand. "Sit," she ordered Keth. "Let's get you cleaned up."

Dema

For once the Elya Street *arurimat* was quiet when Dema sat at his desk. The night patrols had gone out; the higher-ranking officers had left. With no one to hang over his shoulder, Dema took out the envelope of reports on the Ghost murders, from Nioki's, the first, to Iralima's, the most recent. He'd had two *arurimi* carry in a long work-table: now he used it to lay out the notes on each killing in order, so he could look for a pattern.

He was studying them when an *arurim* rapped on his door. "*Dhaskoi* Nomasdina, there is something you should see."

Dema turned, scowling. Standing beside the *arurim* was a little Tharian who wore the yellow stole of a clerk or scribe, hemmed with the white key pattern of Heskalifos. He clutched a covered basket with hands that shook. The silk of the cover shone to Dema's magical vision: spells for purification and containment were stitched into every inch of the cloth.

"I took it to the Heskalifos *arurimat*," the clerk explained, wheezing. "The captain there said to bring it to you. It was blown by a man who claimed to possess magic. He was at Heskalifos looking for a teacher. When he made this, it was just *covered* in lightning."

"And now it is not?" asked Dema, taking the basket. If this was a joke at his expense, he would seek revenge, he thought as he pulled the silk covering aside. He had too much to do without dealing with jokes.

Inside the basket was a globe of clear glass that sparkled. Curious, Dema touched a spark: it stung.

"Lightning, you say?" he asked. He went to his mages' kit and got his leather gloves.

"Miniature," replied the clerk, wheezing still.

Dema glanced at his two guests as he pulled on his gloves. "*Arurim*, perhaps a cup of water for the *koris*?"

The *arurim* bowed and hurried off. Dema lifted the globe from the basket. The globe was fully six inches wide and perfectly round, with something inside. When Dema held it before his eyes, he saw a room in its depths. It looked to be some public space. He saw a foot-high dais with seven backless chairs. Beyond it was a good-size room furnished with benches, and another, smaller dais with a podium set to face the chairs.

A dead woman lay on the big dais before the chairs. Dema knew she was dead: there was no mistaking the swollen, dark face of a strangler's victim, even under a *yaskedasu*'s makeup. She was dressed in a tumbler's leggings and short tunic, with brightly colored short ribbons stitched into the seams. The yellow noose itself was lost in the swelling of her neck, but the bright yellow ends of a *yaskedasu*'s veil once more lay straight from her side, almost as if they were placed to make the delegates seated in the chair look right at the body.

"What did the captain at the Heskalifos *arurimat* tell you?" Dema inquired.

"That this was a matter on which you are chief investigator," replied the clerk, "and that if I spoke to anyone else before you gave me leave, I could be arrested for promoting disorder."

"He was right," Dema said, continuing to examine the ball. He looked at the proscenium that framed the dais. There, in mosaics, was Noskemiou, the charity hospital, and the brightly painted walls that wrapped around Khapik, with the yellow pillars that marked the main entrance. There on the right side was the Elya Street *arurimat*. He knew this place. It was the Fifth District Forum, where the affairs of that part of the city were discussed and voted upon before the seven District Speakers. The place was closed during the day, when everyone worked. He glanced out the window of his office: the sun was reaching the horizon. They would open the Forum any minute.

Dema shoved the ball into the basket. "You're with me," he told the clerk, who was drinking the water the *arurim* had brought. To the *arurim* Dema said, "I want a full squad at the Fifth District Forum, soonest. We'll need barricades, *arurimi* to watch them, and *prathmuni* with a death cart. Scramble!" He grabbed his mage's kit in his free hand and strode out of his office.

"Can't I go home?" whined the clerk. "I've been all over the city. My wife will be worried —"

Dema turned and faced him. "Are you a citizen of Tharios?" he demanded coldly, glaring at the shorter man.

At the word "citizen" the clerk straightened, thrusting out his bony chest. "Of course I am," he snapped, indignant that anyone might question his status.

"Then I, Demakos Nomasdina, of the First Class, call upon you to do your duty as a citizen. Do you serve Tharios?" he asked.

The clerk hung his head. "Always and forever," he replied wearily. The formula was a part of his oath of citizenship. If a member of the First Class called on any resident of the city as Dema had done, that person was obligated by his oath to serve in whatever way he might be commanded.

Dema thrust the basket into the clerk's hands. "First we're going to see if this means anything."

They reached the Forum just as its custodians laid hands upon the wooden bars across the doors. Dema showed them what he'd been taught in school, the "face of the First Class," the expression, bearing, and crispness that anyone of his rank put on when necessary, to uphold the dignity of the First Class and of the city that was the final responsibility of the First Class. Even the weakest-willed children learned to act as if they knew what they were doing. Their duty was to assure the lower classes that Tharios was eternal, as long as order was kept. The duty of the lower classes was to obey those who bore ultimate service to Tharios in their very bones. Dema was grateful for that long, hard training now; it hid his fear of what he might be able to see.

The custodians opened the doors for him and the *arurimi* who had caught up with him, then closed the doors to keep the public outside. Only a few idlers were present, either for the night's Forum debates or because they had seen *arurimi* on the move, but Dema knew their numbers would soon grow.

Inside, he motioned for the clerk and the *arurimi* to keep back. He advanced on the dais, a ball of mage fire drifting beside him to light the way. When he reached the podium, he wrote a sign in the air. It gleamed, then faded. His mage fire grew until the front half of the room was mercilessly lit, without a shadow anywhere.

It had looked like a Ghost murder in the globe, and it looked like a Ghost murder now. Dema crouched beside the dead woman and opened his kit. A pinch of heartbeat powder sprinkled over the *yaskedasu* darkened to scarlet: she'd been dead almost an entire day.

Why did no one report that she was missing? he wondered. If they had, he would know. These days any word of missing *yaskedasi* came to him first.

Dema ground his teeth in vexation. The *yaskedasi* drove him crazy with their secrecy. Even when it was to their benefit they would not deal with the *arurimi* unless forced to it.

They made it that much harder to find who had seen these women in their last hours of their lives, just as they made it harder to identify the dead. The *yaskedasi* just didn't understand that cooperation was for their own good.

With a sigh, Dema opened a bottle of vision powder and sprinkled a pinch over each of the woman's open, staring eyes. The killer's essence began to fade fifteen hours or so after a slaying, but Dema wanted to try it anyway. If the victim had seen her attacker, the powder would reveal at least a smudge over her eyes, if not the killer's face. This time there was not even a smudge. Dema bit his lip: she must have been taken from behind. Her fingernails were broken, yellow silk threads caught in their shredded edges, from her fight to get free of the noose. The killer had to be strong, because the tumbler was solid muscle.

Dema selected one of the blessed ivory rods that had arrived at the *arurimat* the day after he'd spoken with the priests at Labrykas Square. He used it to pull the veil's ends out flat. "Melchang Lodgings, Willow Lane" was embroidered at the edge.

"Stand aside, Demakos Nomasdina, before you are in need of cleansing yourself," called a clear, female voice. "You are too close to the pollution."

Dema looked around. The *prathmuni* in charge of the dead had come and, with them, the priests of the All-Seeing, ready to cleanse the Forum. Like the fountain, it would need prolonged cleansing. It was a public place. The Fora were also the heart of Tharios, the reason the city had grown and succeeded without emperors and their follies.

"I haven't touched her," he replied sharply. "And your cleansings wipe away all traces I can use to track this *mirizask*." The clerk with the globe, standing behind the priests, squeaked at Dema's coarse language.

Turning his back on them, Dema selected the bottle of stepsfind from his kit, took a mouthful, stood, and sprayed it in the air over the dead woman. When it fell to the ground, it revealed blurred foot marks leading to the back of the dais. He followed those smudges off the dais, down two steps to the small meeting rooms behind the Forum, past the privy set aside for the use of any government officers, and through the hallway to the rear entrance. He tracked the smudges through the unlocked door and ran smack into a wall of silver fire. With a yelp Dema sprang back. He'd just tried to walk through a circle of enclosure. Not only was he unable to pass, but his face and hands felt as if he'd scrubbed them with nettles.

"How can we catch him if you erase any trace he leaves?" he cried, maddened, to the white-veiled priest outside the circle.

"What good will his capture do, if his infection spreads to the city? If you take on his pollution at the risk of your clan?" demanded the priest coldly. "Our souls are more important than these sacks of putrefaction and disease we call bodies, Demakos Nomasdina. Go and be cleansed yourself."

Dema shivered and walked back into the Forum, thoroughly ashamed of himself. For a moment he'd been so caught up in the need to catch the murderer that he had lost sight of his duty to his family and to Tharios itself, to keep the pollution that accompanied death from tainting the city. At the very least he risked his own soul and his status; at most, he risked dragging all of his kinsmen, everyone who'd had contact with him or his immediate family, into exile or, worse, into the ranks of the *prathmuni*. He had nearly ruined one of the great clans of Tharios.

There has to be another way to find the killer, he told himself as the priests inside the Forum cleansed him with prayer, ritual, and incense. Then he remembered the clerk. The man sat on a bench at the rear of the Forum, the basket at his side, a glum look on his face as he watched the priests go to work over the dead woman.

Dema took the globe from its basket. "Who made this device?" he asked.

Removing each needle from Kethlun's face was an exacting task. Tris sat on the table, Keth on a chair in front of her. As she worked, he told her, Niko, and Jumshida about his life before and after one summer day on the Syth.

When he finished, Niko regarded his fingernails. "The seed of magic you had all along probably saved your life when you were struck, Kethlun."

"I'm not thanking it for any favors," grumbled Keth. "I'd pass it to anybody else in a heartbeat."

"You don't have that choice," Niko retorted. "Moreover, until you master the lightning side of your power, you won't be able to make another satisfactory piece of glass — not blown, anyway. Not shaped by the breath that keeps you alive. That is why you need Tris, not a glass mage."

Tris scowled. "There isn't *anybody* else?" she demanded. "Oh, don't bother answering, I know there isn't." All the needles were out. She dipped some cotton into a jar of balm made by her foster brother and dabbed it on the bloody spots on Keth's face.

"Ow!" Keth snapped, flinching away.

"Don't be such a baby," Tris ordered. "You bore getting hit by lightning, you can bear a little sting."

Keth let her continue. "But she's a *student*," he protested to Niko. "Students don't teach!"

"It's unusual," Jumshida said, her voice comforting. "But lightning magic is so rare. . . ."

Jumshida and Keth had made an understandable mistake. Normal mage students got their credential in their twenties, and taught only after that. Tris, her two foster sisters, and her foster brother, were unique. They had mastered their power when they were all thirteen or so. Winding Circle gave them their mage's medallion, spelled so that, until they were eighteen, the four would forget they had them unless asked to prove they were mages. It was a useless exercise: Tris's ability to see magic and detect metal meant that she always knew what she wore.

Now she glanced at Niko; he nodded. Tris set aside the balm, reached under her collar, and drew out the ribbon from which her medallion hung. The metal circle had a silvery sheen to it, but it was a blend of silver and other metals. The spiral sign for Winding Circle was stamped on the back, to show where Tris had earned it. Tris's name and Niko's were inscribed on the edges of the front of the medallion: student and principal teacher. At the center, small but still clear to the eye, the smith-mage Frostpine had engraved a tiny volcano, a lightning bolt, a wave, and a cyclone, to show where Tris's weather magic worked. She hated bringing it out where people could see it. It felt too much like bragging.

"If she's a mage, why do I never see her with a mage kit?" demanded Keth. "You both carry yours, even though you're just attending a conference." He pointed through the door to the hall, where Jumshida's and Niko's mage kits, fitted into good-looking packs, lay on a table.

Tris let go of her medallion and picked up the balm again. She dabbed more on Keth's wounds. "I carry a mage kit all the time," she replied, squinting to get the bloody spots under his short-cropped gold hair. She pointed to her head with the hand that held the cotton. "Right there."

"Your skull is your mage kit?" asked Keth.

Tris scowled at him, though her touch remained gentle. "My *braids*, Kethlun," she replied. She sat back with a sigh; she thought she had gotten every puncture. The ones she had tended first were already healed. By morning he wouldn't know he'd been hurt. Briar, her foster brother, brewed good medicines with his plant magic. "I store power in my braids for when I need it. They hold it because I pin them in certain patterns." She set the balm aside and pointed to the thickest braid. It ran from the middle of her forehead to the nape of her neck. "Earth force here, bled out of a few earthquakes. Tidal force in these braids." She touched two on each side of her head. "If I'm tired, I can draw a little strength off of these, or a lot, depending on what I need."

"And then you collapse after you run out of it," Niko said. "Actually, you collapse once you use any of your braids but the little ones."

Tris shrugged and quoted a great-aunt's favorite saying: "All business requires some risk." She looked back at Kethlun and saw that he didn't believe her. "These" — she indicated four more braids, two on each side of her head — "are heavy lightning. The two by my face are just for quick things."

"Like shocking me," Keth said drily.

Chime voiced a shushing sound that Tris thought was probably a hiss of warning. "I *did* tell you to stop," she reminded Keth. "If I'd known you were afraid of lightning, I might have used something else, but you rushed me."

"Any other braids I ought to know about?" Keth wanted to know, smiling indulgently.

"Oh, there's a few wind ones in there, some heat ones. No rain, sadly. It makes me go all frizzy. Then power starts leaking out through the loose hairs. It's hard enough keeping everything smooth with lightning in my braids as is." Tris spoke in her most matter-of-fact voice. He probably thinks Niko won't ruin the joke about weather in my hair by telling the truth, she thought. That's all right. If I have to teach him — and I *do* know how few lightning mages there are — it won't go well if he's afraid of me.

She glanced at Jumshida and her heart sank. Their hostess was ashy under her bronze skin. "Well," Jumshida said. "One assumes the Initiate Council of Winding Circle knew what it was doing."

"There were unusual circumstances," Niko explained. He had not told Jumshida, or anyone, of the extent of Tris's skills. Tris had asked him not to unless it was necessary. She had seen shock like Jumshida's — or worse, jealousy, dislike, even hate — directed at her and her friends over their last year at Winding Circle, never mind that they had not chosen to be what they were.

"Events made Tris combine her power with that of her foster brother and sisters," Niko went on. "As a result, they expanded and structured their original abilities. Later events made them separate their magics again, but they kept certain abilities from one another. The result, and the work they put in afterward, brought their control over their magics to the level of an accredited, adult mage."

Jumshida shook her head. "I did not receive my credential until I was twenty-eight."

Tris knew what the woman thought, what other mages thought, when they knew what she had achieved. It was too much power, too much accomplishment, for a mere girl of thirteen or fourteen. They saw only the awe of it, the ability to move hurricanes and earthquakes, the ability to do complex workings alone and without sleep, because she could borrow strength from currents in the air, in the ground, and in the water. Others dreamed that with Tris's power and control they could live in grand palaces, dress in silks, and be given all they could wish for by the rulers they served.

They didn't understand that she meditated every day to control her emotions. Without a grip on her temper, Tris didn't just hurt someone's feelings or start a fight. When she lost control, she destroyed property; she sank ships.

They didn't understand that she had yet to find a way to earn a living. Rainmaking was chancy. She always had to be sure that if she moved one storm, she would not upset weather patterns for miles, creating floods or droughts. She was best suited for battle magic, but her dreams of the floating dead after her first battle still left her screaming in the night. She wanted to be a healer, but even now her control wasn't tight enough, unless people wanted her to do surgery with a mallet.

And she hated the palaces and courts she and Niko had visited on their way south to Tharios. They all seemed *wasteful.*

"We didn't *ask* to be singled out," Tris told her, silently begging the woman to think Tris's situation through. Jumshida had been friendly since she and Niko had arrived. Tris wanted that back. "We didn't ask the Initiate Council for the medallion." She stuffed it back into her dress and jumped down from the table. When she sat on a chair, Chime curled up in her lap.

Niko told Jumshida, "The Initiate Council felt Tris,

Briar, Sandry, and Daja should be sworn to a code of conduct, to the rules of the mage community, in case they were tempted to use their power unwisely. As the council saw it, the choice was to grant the four the medallion and its responsibilities, or bind their magics until the council felt they were old enough to know what they held." Niko smiled. "Fortunately, cooler heads prevailed. They were given the medallions."

At the thought that *anyone* might try to restrict her ability to get at her magic, Tris drew herself up, gray eyes flashing. "They could *try* to bind my power," she snapped. This was the first she had heard of *that* debate.

"Spoken very like Sandry," Niko teased gently.

Tris looked down. Her foster sister was a noble who forgot her rank until anyone questioned her right to hold it. "What do you expect after living with her four years?" she grumbled. She petted Chime. "And it's true all the same," she added stubbornly.

"The difficulty of actually binding you *was* a consideration," Niko admitted, smoothing his mustache. "It would look very bad if we tried, and failed. Not that any of you would have had the bad manners to resist," he added, raising his eyebrows at Tris.

She met his gaze defiantly, and saw a world of things in his dark brown eyes: the time they'd spent on the road, the many nights they'd discussed books, the way they looked out for each other. He'd been the first person she'd ever known who understood her.

She smiled ruefully. "Well, maybe not," she said. "Though I can't vouch for Briar's manners."

Kethlun, steeped in depression, said gloomily, "Splendid. She's a freak, and I'm a freak. We should be quite happy together."

Tris scowled. "Get used to freakishness, my buck," she informed him. "You have nowhere else to go, and lightning isn't exactly the most biddable force in nature."

Kethlun glared at her, red spots of fury burning on his cheeks. "I never asked for it! Never! I'd give it up if I could!"

"Well, you can't," retorted Tris. "Nobody can. Even the ones who *want* magic end up hating it sometimes. You have to work your life around *it*, not the other way around. Join the party and stop whining."

"That isn't kind," Niko said with gentle reproof.

Tris lifted her chin. "I'm not a kind person. Everyone says so."

"You mean you don't want people to think you're kind. You believe they'll see it as weakness," retorted Niko.

"Put yourself in this young man's shoes," added Jumshida.

"I don't want anyone in my shoes," Kethlun muttered, his voice slow. "*I* don't want to be in my shoes."

"Be silent," Jumshida told him. To Tris she said, "Here is

someone who has had this news dropped on him at an age when other mages are completing their studies. He —"

"I was going to be head of the guild," Keth interrupted, the slow words falling from his lips like stones. "Even without magic there was talk of me being named Glassmaker to the Imperial Court. You can always have a glass mage engrave signs or bless the sands for imperial work. I almost had enough to pay for a house. I had a good marriage arranged, with a pretty girl I like who doesn't bore me. Then I had to go for a walk by the Syth. For inspiration." A harsh noise that might have been a laugh came out of his mouth. "I got all the inspiration I can take."

Tris propped her chin on her hands and glared at Keth. Lately she'd begun to think that her greatest flaw was her imagination. Listening to him, imagining herself in his place, she could see how it *might* have been easier if the lightning had killed him. Instead he was newly born, forced to grow up in weeks, not years, with all his thoughts as a man still in his head. He'd already mentioned the long struggle to make his body and his tongue work. Would she have the patience and determination it must have taken to do that for long, weary months, not knowing if she would succeed?

"Then we're stuck with each other," she told him, not allowing her surge of pity to touch her face or voice. "The sooner we get started, the sooner you can wield your magic, instead of it wielding you."

"But first, I'll tell Cook it's two for supper, not one," Jumshida said, getting to her feet. "Niko, we're expected at Balance Hill at sundown. We must change our clothes."

"What's Balance Hill?" Tris asked.

"It's where the Keepers of the Public Good live during their three-year terms of office," Jumshida explained, walking toward the kitchen. "Our entire conclave has been honored with an invitation to Serenity House."

"Better you than me," said Tris as Niko ran upstairs and Jumshida entered the kitchen. She looked at Keth. "Well."

"Well," he said, looking back at her.

Tris inspected him. He was tall and broad-shouldered, with strong, wiry muscles. His nose was short, his teeth white and even. His head was blocky, his gaze level, as if he were a rock she was not about to move. She'd noticed his short blonde hair and the blueness of his eyes the day before, just as she had noticed his very large hands. Now she saw the burn marks that stippled his hands, and the way the last two fingers on his left hand stayed curled even when the other fingers and his thumb were straight — another legacy of the lightning strike, like the white spot in his hair, and his magic.

He dressed like a northerner in a plain white shirt, frayed a little at the shoulder seams, brown homespun trousers, and calf-high boots that had seen a lot of wear. His belt was nicked in spots, his belt purse made of cheap leather, his belt knife a fine one that had seen long use. All in all he looked as if he'd once been more prosperous than he was now. If determination were any indication, though, she would bet he would regain his place in society before much longer.

"So where do you come from?" he demanded as the cook came out with a tray of food. She set it out on the table, then returned for tableware and plates. "Not around here, anymore than your master Goldeye does."

"I was born in Capchen, in Ninver," Tris said, pouring water into their cups. "To a merchant family. They sent me to Stone Circle Temple when I was ten. That's where Niko found me and saw my magic." She wasn't about to tell this stranger that her family had passed her from relative to relative, each keeping her only until they grew so terrified of the strange things that happened around her that they couldn't wait to get rid of her. Stone Circle was her family's way of washing their hands of Tris. "Niko took me to Winding Circle temple in Emelan, where they specialize in ambient mages. Do you know what ambient mages are?"

"We *do* have mages in our family," Keth informed her drily as he cut up a baked chicken and served her. "Sometimes I listened when the big folks talked."

"There's only one person on this earth who's allowed to pull my tail, and you aren't him," Tris retorted.

"Let me guess. Your foster brother." He watched as Tris added spiced chickpeas to his plate, then hers.

"That's right. He and I and two others lived in this one

cottage. We trained with the mages who ran it and other mages around the temple."

"And you never went back to your family?" he asked, curious. "You don't think they'd be proud to have a mage? My parents' biggest disappointment was that I didn't have more power than just a seed."

"They'd be delighted, I suppose," Tris replied. "And that's the only reason they'd be happy to have me back."

"Oh." Keth looked at his plate. "It was that way for a friend of mine, back home. He said he'd never return." He glanced at her. "But you have family now, your foster family." Tris nodded. Keth went on, "And you look after each other, and study together."

"Lots of studying," Tris replied with a smile as she helped herself to the seasoned cantaloupe. "We were all in the same basket with our power, you see — none of us knew we had any, even though it was breaking out all over the place. It wasn't until we learned to meditate that we got any kind of control. That's where you have to start, too. Meditation, the whole thing. Breathing, clearing your mind, exercises to strengthen your grip on your magic." She held Chime away from her plate as the dragon tried to inspect it for anything edible.

"I know how," Keth told her, then took a bite of chicken.

Tris pursed her lips. It sounded as if he claimed he could, simply to shut her up. "You know how to meditate. And where, pray, did you learn?"

Now he looked up into her face. "We all learned it," he said impatiently. "In the Glassmakers' Guild. It helps you get control over your breath, so you can blow long and steady and not swallow molten glass. It was the first thing we learned as 'prentices. Well, that and how to tell what's good charcoal and what's bad."

Tris propped her chin on her hand. "Show me."

"Now?" Keth demanded. "I've been pounding around Heskalifos all the blessed day."

"If you're to be a mage, you must control your mind — your power — anywhere, at any time, tired or no," she retorted. "Now."

Keth put down his fork with a sigh. He shut his eyes and took a deep breath. Slowly he inhaled as Tris counted silently to seven. He held the breath for the same count, released it for seven, and held for seven. As he continued Tris closed her eyes briefly, concentrating on her vision. When she opened her eyes again, Kethlun's magic was as plain as day to her sight.

His breathing and stillness served to calm him, that was clear, but his power was unaffected. It jetted from his skin in erratic flares, fluid like molten glass one moment, crooked like lightning the next. Then the lightning shapes grew, racing over Kethlun like groping hands, splitting into more bolts, until he was nearly covered with light. He opened his eyes and the lightning vanished.

"Well?" he demanded irritably. "I said I know how."

For a moment Tris didn't reply, stunned by the fiery lacework that had covered him over. Then she remembered to breathe herself. How could Keth hold such beauty and not know it?

She remembered something Briar had once said while her friends cowered under a tree in the rain. Tris was dancing in a field as lightning flashed and thunder roared overhead. "Not everybody thinks it's a play-pretty like you do, Coppercurls! Send it on its way so we can go home!"

"So you can meditate," she said to Kethlun now. "That saves time. Let me see —"

She was interrupted by someone banging on the street door. "Open for the *arurim!*" a man cried. "Open in the name of the law!"

Little Bear dashed into the hall, barking furiously. Tris leaped after him and seized his collar. The housekeeper passed them both, opening the door only when she saw that Tris had the big dog under control. Tris hung onto her pet with both hands, dragging him back with all her strength as men and women in bright red tunics shouldered past the housekeeper, heavy batons in their hands.

"What is this?" the servant cried. "We are law-abiding people!"

"We seek Kethlun Warder," said a man who wore a sergeant's black sword border on his tunic sleeves. "We have information that he is present here."

"I'm Kethlun Warder," Keth said. He came to stand by

Tris and the nearly hysterical dog. "Why would the *arurim* look for me?"

A man stepped through the *arurimi's* ranks. He was young, with dark brown skin, kinked black hair cut in a short cap around his head, and sharp brown eyes. Like the men of the *arurim* he wore a scarlet tunic, but his was topped by a blue mage's stole bordered in scarlet braid. "Kethlun Warder, is this your work?" The mage held out a round glass ball. Sparks glinted faintly on its surface.

"It looks like my work," Kethlun answered slowly. He leaned in to better look inside the ball. "Or rather, it's like something I made this afternoon, but there was nothing in it then. It was all lightning."

"According to a clerk from Mages' Hall, the lightning cleared to reveal this scene just before he was to leave for the day. He brought it to us," replied the mage.

Tris squinted at the ball and frowned. "That woman looks dead."

To his sergeant the mage said, "Arrest him." The *arurimi* surged forward to grip Keth by the arms.

"Stop!" cried Tris, outraged. "You can't march into a private house — can they?" she asked the housekeeper. The woman nodded.

The *arurim* mage frowned at Tris in a well-bred way. "I do not answer to children," he informed her. "Murder was done at the Fifth District Forum. The whole thing looked just as it does here, which means we arrest Kethlun Warder for murder."

"But I just blew the globe, I didn't kill anyone!" protested Keth.

"Quiet," growled an *arurim* as she twisted one of Keth's arms up behind his back. "You'll speak when spoken to."

Tris looked from the *arurimi* to their mage to Keth. She had no understanding of what was going on here — she'd been in Tharios less than a week — but she knew what Niko would say her duty was. Briar and her foster mother Lark both had told stories of what happened to defenseless people who were taken away by those who enforced the law.

"Then I am going with him," she informed the mage haughtily. "He is my student. You will answer to me should any harm come to him."

The mage lost his air of superiority when he goggled at her. "You're joking," he said in a less self-important, more matter-of-fact way.

Tris gave the housekeeper Little Bear's collar, then reached for the ribbon around her neck. She pulled out the medallion and allowed the *arurim* mage to see both sides. When he reached for it, she closed her eyes. The moment he touched the medallion to test if it were a proper mage's token, it threw out a blaze of white light that left everyone but Tris blinking.

"I don't joke," Tris said, her voice flat. "It makes my head hurt. Where are you taking Keth? Who are you, anyway?"

The mage sighed. "My name is Demakos Nomasdina, *arurim dhaskoi* at the Elya Street *arurimat.* That's where we're taking this murder suspect, teacher or no teacher. And who are *you?*"

"*Dhasku* Trisana Chandler," she retorted, giving herself the Tharian title. This superior young man would learn that she could not be pushed around. "And I'm coming with you." She looked at the housekeeper. "Send someone for Jumshida and Niko. They'll want to know about this."

"Yes, *dhasku,*" the woman replied with a bow of the head.

"I hope you are a truthsayer," Tris informed Nomasdina. She knew how to manage this. She had to keep him on the defensive, and not allow him time to think that she was only fourteen, medallion or not. "Because I doubt that *Dhasku* Jumshida Dawnspeaker will be happy to learn a guest of hers was abused." From the looks exchanged by the *arurimi* and the mage, she knew she'd hit a nerve. She'd hoped that Jumshida's name and position — that of First Scholar of Mages' Hall and Second Scholar of Heskalifos — would throw a damper on things. "Or did you not notice whose house this is?"

The mage reassembled his lofty facial expression. "She may vouch for him at Elya Street," he informed Tris. "And there are truth spells I can use. First, though, we are going to see the woman he murdered."

"I didn't —" Keth began, only to receive Tris's elbow in his ribs.

Before he could ask why she'd poked him, Tris told Dema, her voice as lofty as his, "Then I go with him." To Chime, who waited on the dining-room table still, she said, "You stay here."

First they had gone to the Fifth District Forum, where Keth saw the reality of the image inside the glass ball. Numb all over, voiceless with pity over this unknown *yaskedasu,* he was only dimly aware of the quarrel between Nomasdina and the priests of the All-Seeing. He overheard snippets. The priests had wanted to take the dead woman away two hours ago, but they had agreed to wait until the *arurim dhaskoi* confronted Keth with the crime he was thought to have committed. Keth knew he'd disappointed *Dhaskoi* Nomasdina when he didn't collapse and shout out his guilt. All he could do, seeing the tumbler's remains, was address a prayer to Yorgiry, the Namornese goddess of death and mercy, that she grant the dead woman a new, longer life.

When he could bear to look no longer, he turned away and inspected his surroundings. The *arurimi* who'd arrested Keth watched him, as intent as dogs looking at a bone just out of their reach. Keth shuddered. If the *arurim dhaskoi*'s truth spell didn't work, and such spells were tricky if the caster didn't originally have the ability to truth read, Keth knew what came next: torture. Unless they had a truthsayer on duty at the *arurimat.* Somehow he didn't think the district that included the charity hospital, Khapik, and the slums of Hodenekes spent a great deal of money on truthsayers.

A small, nail-bitten hand rested on his arm briefly. "They'll come," Tris said quietly. "Niko and Jumshida. Nobody's going to hurt you if we can help it."

Keth stared at her, numb. How could she possibly say that? Was she so young that she didn't know how things worked for outsiders in any city, in any nation? Jumshida was a Tharian; she wouldn't protest the way things were done.

"That fellow Nomasdina keeps watching me for some sign of guilt," he replied at last, feeling he ought to say something. "I suppose I'm going to have to tell him I knew one of the Ghost's victims."

"The Ghost?" Tris repeated with a frown.

"It's what the *yaskedasi* are calling the murderer. Because he seems invisible. A girl disappears, and the next day she's dead with a yellow veil around her neck."

"You mean to tell me there's been more than one killing?" asked Tris.

Keth looked at the poor dead creature now enclosed in a circle of protective magical fire. "Six, with her."

The *arurim dhaskoi* Nomasdina stamped over to them, a scowl on his dark, lean features. "They can report me to the First *Arurim* all they want," he grumbled, more to himself than to Keth or Tris. "I had to give it a try. Let's go," he ordered his *arurimi*. "Elya Street." To Keth he said, "I have to veil you again."

Unlike the first time Dema shielded them, on their approach to the Forum, neither Keth nor Tris protested. As they had walked there, magically hidden inside a circle of *arurimi*, they had pushed through a crowd of people ripe for murder if they got their hands on the Ghost. Now Tris and Keth huddled inside the guards as the *arurimi* walked them out through the mob. There were cries of "When will you find the *kakosoi*?" and "How long does it take to find a killer?" There were other cries, suggestions of what should be done to the murderer when he was caught, bloody and fiery plans.

"I admire their imagination," Tris murmured to Keth as the crowd jostled the *arurimi* and the *arurimi* jostled her and Keth.

He looked down at her, startled: though they were invisible to everyone else, they could see each other perfectly well. How could she joke at a time like this? "Th-they might think I did it," he reminded her, fright making him stammer. "Hard to admire their i-magination wuh-when they wuh-want to do that to m-me."

"Oh — sorry," replied Tris casually. "But are you the killer? This Ghost?"

Keth started to shout a denial, then remembered he was supposed to be invisible. *"No,"* he whispered fiercely. "Do I *look* like a killer to you?"

"Just for curiosity's sake, how long have you been student and teacher?" Dema asked. The circle of *arurimi* broke free of the crowd and marched toward Elya Street, dodging pleasure seekers on their way to Khapik.

Keth and Tris looked at each other and shrugged. "Two hours?" asked Keth.

"Something like that," Tris replied.

Once inside the Elya Street *arurimat,* they were taken to a room where magic could be worked and kept from spreading to other parts of the building. There Dema positioned Keth inside a holding ring set into the floor and called on its protections so the northerner couldn't escape. Once they were set and Tris was tucked into a chair in the corner, Nomasdina produced vials of powdered sage, coltsfoot, and orris, and blew a pinch of each at Keth's face. The powders hung, sparkling with the magic that made them more powerful. Nomasdina then used a carnelian to sketch the signs for truth and eloquence in the air between them, watching the silvery paths the symbols made as they floated in the air.

"Lie to me," he told Keth. "Tell me something —"

He never finished his suggestion. Keth took a deep breath to speak, and the room flashed with white fire, blinding Nomasdina, the *arurim* who was there to take notes, Tris, and Keth himself. Vision only returned slowly. The first thing Keth saw, when he could see, was that the circle he'd been standing in was a charred mark on the floor. Its barrier was gone, as if lightning had struck the thing and burned it out of the wood. Nomasdina's powders were a small, black clump on the floor. Nomasdina himself was covered in soot. His carnelian, which he still held, was black and cracked.

"Deiina of all mercy, what was that?" whispered the *arurim* clerk.

Tris removed her spectacles to rub her eyes. Keth thought that without the spectacles she actually looked her age, not like some fierce old lady with unwrinkled skin. Nomasdina rounded on her. "What did you do?" he growled. "I ought to put you in irons, and don't think I can't!"

"Excuse me, *dhaskoi*," said the clerk. She was there because she too could see magic. "It didn't come from her. It came from him, and he didn't actually *do* anything. It just surged out of him, like — like lightning. Like he couldn't help it."

"Lightning is part of Keth's magic," Tris informed Dema. "He only found out about it recently. He hasn't learned to control it yet. And if I may, a hint? Don't threaten someone unless you're certain you can carry out the threat."

Nomasdina snorted and turned to Keth. "Well, if your power fights me, then there's only one way to do this," he said. He went to the door and pulled it open.

Keth's knees buckled. He dropped to the floor. Nomasdina was going to call for torturers.

"Just one moment."

Everyone turned to stare at Tris, who had risen from her chair. The door yanked out of Nomasdina's hand and slammed shut, as if a high wind had blasted through the windowless room.

"Keth, get up," Tris ordered, her eyes fierce. Keth obeyed without realizing he was taking instructions from her. Tris walked over to stand between him and the *arurim dhaskoi*. To Nomasdina she said, "Now, I've been nice and cooperative so far." Her eyes blazed up at the Tharian. "We came peaceably; we didn't make trouble. You had your disgusting show back there, exhibiting that poor girl to us without so much as covering her face. But I am at the end of my patience. You are *not* torturing Keth. You're going to get a truthsayer, like a civilized human being."

Nomasdina sighed. "The *arurimat* has no truthsayer funds. It's not like we're in First District here."

"Then you wait until my teacher comes with *Dhasku* Dawnspeaker," retorted Tris. "*She* will tell you that my teacher is the finest truthsayer known, *and* he'll do it for no charge. You should be ashamed, leaping to torture a man on no more evidence than a glass ball!"

Nomasdina looked puzzled as he stared at Tris. Keth knew how the other man felt. "Are you so ignorant of your standing?" asked the *arurim dhaskoi*, genuinely curious. "You're a foreigner, here on sufferance. In Tharios we take the law very seriously. Interference is *not* appreciated."

"We take it seriously in Emelan, too," snapped Tris. "I'm not saying you can't question him, I'm just saying you can't torture him. If you try, I promise you, I will bring this place down around your ears."

Keth saw a spark crawl out of one of her braids, then another, and another. "Please *listen* to her," he begged, suddenly as afraid of her as he was of torture. "You won't like it if she loses her temper!"

"I still want to know why you're in my way," Nomasdina repeated stubbornly, his eyes fixed on Tris's.

"He's my student," Tris said. "Maybe we haven't been together very long, but I learned from the best teachers what a student is owed. I refuse to shame them by letting you do whatever you like to Keth, when anyone but a desperate idiot could have seen back there that Keth didn't kill that woman."

Though she stood only as high as the *arurim dhaskoi's* collar bone, there was no question in Keth's mind who dominated the conversation: Tris. Something in the way he felt about her changed, frightened though he was by the sparks in her hair. He wasn't sure what had changed just yet, only that something was different.

Nomasdina frowned. "You know, I'm beginning to believe you *are* a mage," he remarked slowly. He turned to Keth. "So tell me something. *Did* you kill her?"

"Gods, no," Keth replied, trembling. "I hate the Ghost.

I'd kill him myself, given the chance. Iralima was a friend of mine."

"Iralima? The last victim?" Nomasdina asked.

Keth nodded, then winced. He'd just spoken the fact he'd thought he was too clever to reveal.

"You realize that makes you look even more suspicious," the *dhaskoi* pointed out.

Keth nodded again. Suddenly a breeze whipped around him, and Tris raised a hand. A cocoon of silver mage fire enclosed Keth from top to toe. He touched it: the fire stung.

"I told you, Nomasdina, you're not going to torture him," Tris said flatly.

Nomasdina looked at Keth in his cocoon. Then he looked at Tris. "Do you know how long it would take me to raise protections like that? You're starting to scare me."

"Join the guild," Keth muttered.

Nomasdina glanced at him and smiled crookedly. Then he pulled a stool over to the barrier that sheathed Keth, sat on it. "Right now I'm just asking questions," he informed Tris wearily. He looked at Keth and inquired, "How did you know Iralima?"

"She lived at my lodging house. You were there yesterday," replied Keth. He sat cross-legged on the floor, inside the protections Tris had set around him.

"Did you know any of the other victims?" inquired Nomasdina.

"I knew Zudana by sight," Keth replied. "I used to listen to her sing all the time. She had a beautiful voice."

"She did," Nomasdina agreed. "Before they put me on the murders, I used to sneak out on my shift to hear her. How long have you been in Tharios?"

He questioned Keth for an hour as the clerk took notes. Tris resumed her seat in the corner without lowering her protective barrier. Keth gave Nomasdina the details of his movements for the last two weeks, the tale of his arrival in Tharios and his employment at Touchstone Glass, and all that he'd heard said about the Ghost and his murders. At last Nomasdina went to the table, where he picked up the glass ball with the gruesome scene at its heart.

"I'm sticking my neck out," he admitted, "but I believe you are innocent. That won't be enough for my superiors. I'm new at this. While mages know we must listen to and rely on what our instincts tell us, the regular *arurimi* are quick to tell me I'm a newborn babe in this business of the law."

The clerk ducked her head to hide a smile.

"We'll wait for a truthsayer. If yours doesn't come, I'll pay for one out of my own pocket. Will that satisfy you?" Nomasdina asked Tris.

She smiled sweetly. "I'll wait until I actually *see* a truthsayer, thanks all the same," she replied.

"It grieves me to find one so young who is this cynical," Nomasdina said to no one in particular. "But let me ask you both something." He hefted the globe in his hands. "If Kethlun here isn't the Ghost and this globe isn't a confession, then it *is* a way to see the future, maybe. The time the clerk said the lightning faded and he could see the image was close to the time the dead woman was left in the Forum, or the time we were meant to find her. What if you made another of these, and tried to clear it of lightning immediately?"

Keth scratched his head. "Why would I want to go through that again?" he asked, not unreasonably, he thought. "Perhaps *you're* accustomed to death and murder, *Dhaskoi* Nomasdina. I'm not. I got into glassmaking because I love beautiful things."

Nomasdina drew himself up, his face taking on that lofty, distant, proud cast that it had worn when he came to Jumshida's house to arrest Keth. "Are you a citizen of Tharios?" he demanded.

"No," Keth replied.

Nomasdina's face quivered. A smile made him human again. "Very true. Look, *Koris* Warder, I can understand you don't want to face this pollution, even with glass between you and it. But consider: you might save another *yaskedasu* from death. Better, you might give us a look at our murderer. You can be cleansed after."

Keth sighed. "I don't know how I did it."

Nomasdina looked at Tris. "You might consider making such globes as teaching him his craft."

Tris was not attending to the conversation. She sat up straight, her eyes on the door. It swung open.

"I do not appreciate learning that guests have been taken from my house without my leave." Keth recognized that haughty voice: Jumshida Dawnspeaker. In she swept, dressed for the most elegant circles in a bronze silk *kyten* with beaded hems, heavy gold earrings set with pearls, and a matching bronze stole. Niklaren Goldeye came behind her, dapper in a white silk overrobe, white shirt, and white trousers.

The silver barrier around Keth vanished. He saw threads of it stream back into Tris's hands.

Jumshida looked at the soot-streaked *arurim dhaskoi*, who grimaced and bowed to her, then at Nomasdina's captain, who had followed her and Niko. "As well for *you* he hasn't been tortured," she said sharply. "Kethlun Warder, did you murder the woman who was found tonight?" Niko shaped signs in the air with his fingers.

"No," Keth said wearily. "She just appeared in that glass bubble I made."

Soft white light radiated around him, the sign that he told the truth under a properly applied truth spell.

"Did you kill any of the Ghost's victims?" asked Jumshida.

"No," Keth answered.

Once more the soft light shone.

"Satisfied, captain?" Jumshida asked. She didn't even wait for the answer, but looked at Nomasdina. "If we may have the documents for his release? And next time, I recommend more caution should you attempt to set a truth spell on someone whose magic is rooted in an unpredictable source, such as lightning."

"I'll require *Dhaskoi* Goldeye's signature," Nomasdina said. His brown cheeks were flushed under the soot that marked him when his truth spell went wrong.

"This way," the captain said, bowing. "You understand we must interrogate all suspects in so sensitive a matter. . . ." Jumshida, Niko, Nomasdina, and the clerk followed the man out of the room. The door closed gently.

Keth sighed in relief, and dropped onto the stool Nomasdina had vacated. He looked over at Tris. The girl slouched in her chair, her spectacles near the end of her long nose, running her fingers along one of her thin braids. Silver glinted over every hair of the braid. Sparks followed her hand.

"Please don't do that," Keth said nervously.

Her gray eyes flicked over to meet his. She thrust her spectacles higher on her nose. "Do what?"

Keth pointed, then dropped his hand before she saw that it shook. "With the braid. The lightning thing. You're sparking."

Tris frowned, then looked at the braid she held. "This?" she asked, scraping the lightning from her hair. "It's nothing." She closed her hand, then opened it to reveal a tiny ball of lightning.

The hair on Keth's arms and at the back of his neck rose, prickling against his shirt. "Please put that away."

She pursed her lips and ran the ball of lightning over the braid it had come from. It vanished. "Kethlun, you won't get very far like this. You have to overcome your fear of lightning."

"Well, I won't," he retorted. "You'd understand if it made a cripple out of you and then turned your world on its ear."

"I don't suppose it's occurred to you that you may be immune now," she offered.

"No," Keth said flatly. "Will you *drop* the subject?"

She did, but only because Jumshida had returned. "*That's* settled," the woman told Keth and Tris with satisfaction. "Now, Kethlun where do you stay? Touchstone Glass?"

"I live at Ferouze's, on Chamberpot Alley, in Khapik," he replied.

"Khapik?" Jumshida asked, startled. "You live in Khapik?"

"Lodging is cheap in Khapik," explained Kethlun. "And it's safer than in Hodenekes."

"*Safer?*" Jumshida raised her eyebrows. "But surely they steal from you. *Yaskedasi* are born thieves."

Keth shook his head. "Not the ones I live with, *dhasku,*" he replied. "Besides, everyone knows that if Khapik is the best you can afford, you don't have anything worth stealing."

"Well, I won't hear of your going back to lodgings in Khapik," Jumshida told Keth. "We brought chairs to ride in — you must be exhausted. You need a proper meal and rest, and you and Tris have things to settle tomorrow. Come along."

Keth didn't argue. The truth was that Jumshida's house was pleasant and cool; Ferouze's place was hot and stuffy, and he would have been forced to buy his supper. He'd gotten better at accepting free meals since he'd left his wealthy family's house in Dancruan.

Nomasdina stopped him as he was about to walk out of the *arurimat*. "Think about what I suggested, that's all I ask," the *arurim dhaskoi* said to both Keth and Tris. "One of those balls might turn the tables on this monster."

Long habit brought Tris and Niko downstairs the next morning shortly after dawn, despite their late bedtime. They ate breakfast in silence, the quiet broken only by noise made by the cook as she brought dishes and took them away. When her last plate had been removed, Tris sat with her head propped on her hand, while Niko had a second cup of tea.

All kinds of thoughts had been rolling through Tris's mind. Many of them she preferred to keep to herself. It was the most recent one that bothered her. "Niko?"

"You're the only one who can teach him," he said instantly.

"It's not that," she said. "I know *that*."

"What then?"

"Kethlun's not going to like me telling him to do things, is he?" she asked. "Sooner or later he'll forget the lightning and remember I'm just fourteen."

"Gods," Niko said wearily. "No, I'm not grumbling. You're right. But Tris, teaching mages is different from teaching normal students in any event." He rubbed his temple with his free hand. "It's a matter of persuasion, not orders. Even if a student accepts your command, his magic might not. You have to work around it. Every teacher fumbles a bit until he finds the right approach to each new student. Your task is just twice as hard because Keth is a grown man. Try to understand his feelings."

Tris nodded thoughtfully. It had occurred to her that she also had to find a way around his fear of her lightning before he could learn much. Niko had just confirmed her thinking. If Keth was to catch the Ghost, a cure for that fear should come sooner rather than later.

With breakfast done, Tris took Little Bear into the courtyard and tethered him there with a meaty bone the cook had set aside. Then, with only Chime in a sling on her back as a companion, she set out for the heart of Heskalifos, following the maze of flagstone paths that covered the grounds. Except for the odd *prathmun* clearing away trash, the grounds were deserted. Even the clerks and teachers who worked here would not start their day until the third hour of the morning. That was fine with Tris. She didn't want any witnesses to what she was about to do.

Phakomathen, the Torch of Learning, was the pride of Heskalifos and of Tharios. Its tower rose from the east side of the Heskalifos Museum, soaring three hundred feet into the air. At its peak a figure of Asaia Birdwinged, the Living Circle goddess of learning, faced east, massive wings outstretched. In both hands she grasped a torch. Its flame was made of crystals that flashed in sun and moonlight, spelled against damage from wind and lightning. Twenty feet below the goddess a platform and guardrail were set. From the platform, visitors who had survived the twelve-hundred-step climb could see all of Tharios. On their second day here, Jumshida had brought Niko and Tris up to view the city that had thrown off the ancient Kurchal Empire and pursued its own glorious destiny.

Now Tris opened the doors at the base of the tower and walked inside. It was a point of pride for the university that Phakomathen was never locked, so that stargazers, young lovers, students, and tourists could see the city in each of its moods, if they had the desire and the stamina for the climb. Tris remembered the climb. She had managed it, of course. Though she was plump, the legs beneath her sensible skirts and petticoats were hard with muscle. She just saw no reason why, after a long, dramatic night, she could not cheat.

Besides, she wanted to realize an ambition she'd had since she'd laid eyes on the hollow heart of that tall stone cylinder.

She thrust the doors shut with a breeze, and looped it to

and fro around the latches. It would serve as a rope lock until Tris removed it. The doors secured, Tris sent a few more breezes out to explore the upper reaches. They returned to her carrying nonhuman sounds — settling building, outside winds, birds who nested in the owl figures set over each of the staircase windows. There were no humans in Phakomathen, no one to spy upon Tris.

She summoned all the winds and breezes within reach, calling them in through the windows of Phakomathen. Waiting for their arrival, she walked a large protective circle around the floor. She then called her magic not to form a cylinder or cocoon of protection, but a flat shield within the circle she had made, to protect the elegant, tiled floor.

She took down two of her wind braids and freed half of what they held, spinning around to show them how she needed them to flow. They had been with her a long time: they settled into the spin as neatly as her sister Sandry's favorite spindle. With her palms Tris thrust her winds low and flat, until they shaped a whirling disk of air. When she judged it to be solid, she halted the disk and stepped onto it.

Now came the Tharian winds, pouring through the windows and down the inside of the tower like honey. When they touched the floor, they slid under her disk. Tris gripped the first of them and twirled her finger. Like her own winds, these understood what she wanted. They began to spin, rapidly, under the disk of air where Tris stood.

Slowly, little by little, the column of twirling wind grew in height. Other breezes joined in, giving it strength, bulk, and speed. Steady on her disk of flattened air, Tris let the moving winds thrust her up through the hollow core of Phakomathen, passing the stairway by as she rode her tightly controlled cyclone. Higher and higher she went, until she reached the door to the outside platform, twelve hundred steps high. She tugged on her cyclone. It swayed, letting her step from her disk onto the landing.

With a snap of her fingers her air disk came apart. Tris caught the ends of those winds and twined them back into her braids. The Tharian winds she set free, thanking them silently as they poured back into the city through the tower windows.

"Now, how was that?" she asked Chime.

The dragon, who had experienced the whole thing from her place on Tris's back, climbed onto her shoulder. She rubbed herself, catlike, under the girl's chin, making the musical glass sound that Tris was convinced was a purr.

"I liked it, too," admitted Tris. "Much more sensible than all those steps." She suddenly remembered that people might wonder why the tower were locked. Putting two fingers in her mouth in a way Briar had taught her, she blew a piercing whistle. Chime made her glass-scratch complaining noise as the breeze that had secured the doors below returned to Tris. The girl listened to it for a moment, but the only sounds it carried were those of the tower and of the winds she had summoned, not of people trying the doors in frustration.

"I don't mind walking *down*," she told Chime. "It's the up part that's a pain."

The dragon took flight, swooping and circling through the open air inside the tower. Tris watched briefly, thinking again how beautiful the creature was, then walked outside.

She had not come for a view of the city, though she did admire it. She had not even come for the winds, which pushed her, teasing her for making them work. "Oh, you do it every time you power a windmill," Tris scolded affectionately. "Don't complain."

She looked over the balcony rail. Outside the walls, which had been added to and rebuilt for nearly two thousand years, lay the broad brown ribbon of the Kurchal River, once called "the lifeblood of empire." On it flowed, down through the distant harbor town of Piraki and into Kurchal Bay. Beyond that lay the gray-green sparkle of the Ithocot Sea, more green than gray under the yellowish heat haze that lay over Tharios and everything beyond.

Behind the city in the north lay the grasslands of Ubea, with the farms and villages that kept Tharios alive. To the west lay forests, then mountains; to the east, the rocky stretches that supported goats, olive trees, and little else until they touched the sea. Somewhere in all this, Tris reasoned, a storm was brewing. She just needed to find it, and see if it could be moved. Keth had to overcome his fear, and not just of the little bolts she had conjured in front of him. He would never master his power until he mastered that. She would need big proof, final proof, that his magic now shielded him from the dangers of normal, non-magical, lightning.

There was a storm out there, one that would teach him a lesson he desperately needed to learn. Ignoring the snippets of conversation the city's winds brought to her — bits of gossip, legal proceedings, speeches in the Assembly and the temples of the All-Seeing — Tris made herself comfortable on the platform and spread her spirit on the winds.

She was forced to go farther afield than she'd expected. It made her cross as well as exhausted as she plodded down those many steps, past the first sightseers of the day. It shouldn't have happened, she thought as she rested on a bench near the door. Quietly she gathered the magic that had kept her cyclone from ripping up the floor tiles. It was monsoon season in Tharios and the lands far south of the Pebbled Sea. Storms should have rolled steadily across that open stretch of water between here and Aliput, to die over the waves or to build their strength for an assault on this coast. If she remembered the maps correctly, she'd just gone two thousand miles to find those storms, locked in place around Aliput, piled up like so many logs behind one storm that would not move.

It was even more maddening to realize she would never know who had done it. She wanted to give a piece of her mind and a few other tokens of her esteem to the mage who had pulled this costly stunt. Tris knew this was mage-made. No one else could halt a storm in its track. But it was a stupid mage who had cursed all of Aliput with floods while here in the west the fields withered for lack of rain. She'd given herself an earache, straining to hear a name or any information on the tired winds that reached her. If his name was known, no one had spoken it. If he had spoken, it had gotten lost on the way east.

Well, at least the storms were moving once more. Just to ensure he couldn't do this again for a while, Tris had traveled along the line of weather, tying each storm to the one ahead with a mage-knot she had learned from Sandry. He'd never break the string. She hoped he drained himself trying.

She barely made it back to Phakomathen. She must have looked terrible: when she opened her eyes, Chime sat on her chest, giving voice to small tinkling sounds that seemed to mean dismay. She'd had to reassure the dragon while forcing her weary arms to undo one of her tidal braids. It had taken a third of the strength from that braid before Tris could get to her feet, and another third from the opposite tidal braid to get her and Chime down the steps. In the end she drew off all the power of both braids to feel like her old self. Normally she wouldn't have used so much, not when she would pay the price later, but she and Keth had work to do before he could try another lightning globe. The sooner they got to it, the fewer *yaskedasi* would meet their end at the Ghost's hands.

All the way back to Jumshida's, Tris cursed in Tradertalk and in street slang from two countries. If she could scry the winds, see all they had touched, she might have found the idiot. She might not have used so much of her strength to hunt for storms if she could have seen from the beginning where they were.

She might be able to see the Ghost.

This was mad. As Niko and Jumshida kept saying, their conference was the single greatest collection of vision mages brought together in their time. Surely *one* of them should know about wind scrying!

But she had a duty first, to Keth. She remembered how it felt, to believe she was cursed because so many strange things happened when she was present. She remembered how it felt, to get those things under control. Keth had the first claim on her time. She had to guide him before she tried to chase a kind of magic so rare that even Niko did not know who could do it.

As she walked into the courtyard of Jumshida's house, she heard loud, belligerent voices around the side, by the servants' entrance. Curious, she went to look. The cook stood in the kitchen door, arms folded over her comfortable bosom, the very picture of an outraged Tharian woman.

The person who had drawn the cook's ire was a slender brunette in her twenties, gaudily dressed and even more gaudily made up. She wore pomade with bits of mica in it so her curls glittered, even under her yellow head-veil. A wisp of breeze carried lavender scent to Tris's sensitive nose.

"You obviously have the wrong house, *koria yaskedasu,*" the cook was saying coldly. "This is a decent residence. I assure you that no one *you* might be seeking would set foot in here."

A *prathmun,* collecting night soil from the alley that ran beside the servants' entrance, snorted as he emptied a barrel into his cart. Chime climbed out of the sling on Tris's back to look at the man, who gaped when he saw her glittering in the morning sun. The moment he realized that Tris was smiling at him, pleased he had an eye for Chime's beauty, he turned away and busied himself at his work. The cook and the *yaskedasu* didn't so much as glance at him.

"I was told he was here," the *yaskedasu* told the cook, her hands on her hips. "I'm sorry if it offends you, *Koria* Respectability, but I want to know how he is!"

The cook gasped. "All-Seeing guard us, you hussies get bolder every day!" she cried. She looked beyond the young woman's shoulder and saw Tris. "*Koria* Tris, I apologize that we disturbed you. This — person — was just leaving."

"Not until I know he's all right," the brunette insisted. She turned to look at Tris with large, suspicious brown eyes set over a short nose and full mouth. Tris noted the cheap wool of her *kyten* and the clumsy embroideries in gaudy thread. The *yaskedasu* wore brass bells on her wrists and cheap gilt jewelry at her throat and ears. Under the heavy white face paint and bright red lip and cheek color worn by the entertainers at Khapik, she looked as weary as Tris had felt atop Phakomathen. "We heard the Elya Street *arurim dhaskoi,* Nomasdina, took Keth to the *arurimat* last night, and the desk man at the *arurimat* says he came here with *Dhasku* Dawnspeaker."

"And I told her we'd no more have one of those nimble-fingered Khapik sorts in here than we'd have a camel in the best bedchamber," snapped the cook.

"Deiina!" whispered the brunette, pointing to Tris's shoulder. "What is *that?*" Chime slid her head under Tris's chin to peer at the *yaskedasu.* "It's glass, and it's moving. I've been up much too long."

Tris absently stroked Chime. "You said Keth. Kethlun Warder?"

The brunette nodded. "He has lodgings in our house. He's our friend."

The cook snorted. "Partner in theft, I don't doubt. I've never heard of him."

"Actually, he's here," Tris said. "I'm sorry, Cook. We brought him back with us late last night, after you'd gone home. He's in the guest room above mine." To the brunette she said, "Come in. I'll see if he's awake." As she walked by the cook she explained, "Keth's my new student."

"Keep an eye on her," the cook said fiercely as the *yaskedasu* passed her. "And how does a student have a student of her own?"

"It's a long story," Tris replied. "Have you got honeycakes? I'm famished. And tea would be lovely, if it's not too much trouble."

"She doesn't go past the dining room!" the cook said.

Tris whirled. She'd been quite patient until now, considerate of the cook's lacerated feelings over being wrong and having a *yaskedasu* in the house, but enough was enough. She was tired still and might need some lightning to pick up her step; she was hungry and in no mood for an argument. Just as she opened her mouth to let the cook know her true feelings, the *yaskedasu* stopped her with a hand on her arm.

"It's all right," the young woman told her. "That's the way of things in Tharios."

Tris scowled as Chime stretched out, trying to grab one of the *yaskedasu*'s curls. "The way of things in Tharios is starting to give me a rash," she snapped, leading the way into the dining room. "Please, sit," she said. "What's your name?"

"Yali," the woman replied. She put her head in her hands. "Keth is really all right?" she asked, her voice muffled. "Don't lie to me. Everyone knows the Fifth District *arurim* have no budget for truthsayers, and the truth spells the *dhaskoi* have aren't much good."

"He's safe and well and undented," Tris said as the cook

came in with a tray of cakes, a teapot, cups, and honey. "Thank you," Tris said, lifting it out of the older woman's hands. "I appreciate it, with you being so busy and all."

The cook looked at Yali, sniffed, and returned to her kitchen.

"Let me give you a hint, since you're a *shenos*," Yali said as she sat up straight. "*Yaskedasi* are not in the least respectable. She won't appreciate it that you made her let me in."

"Why aren't they respectable?" asked Tris, pouring two cups of tea. "You just perform, right? It's not like you're prostitutes."

"We flaunt our bodies and our skills before anyone who will look," replied Yali, running her fingers along one of Chime's wings. "We have no chaperons, we keep late hours, we don't work at dull, boring tasks all day, we hold noisy parties, we sing loud songs. We must be half streetwalker and half thief. My goodness, this is a beautiful thing."

"She's not a thing. She's a glass dragon that Keth made two days ago," Tris said, blowing on her tea before she sipped it. "Her name is Chime."

Yali looked at her, kohl-lined eyes huge with astonishment. "But Keth's no mage!"

"He wasn't," Tris said. "He is now. Let me see if he's awake." Leaving Chime and the tea tray, she went upstairs to see if Keth was out of bed.

He was awake, dressed, and shaving when Tris rapped on his door. When he bid her enter, she poked her head inside. "There's a *yaskedasu* named Yali in the dining room," she said as he carefully scraped a razor over his whiskers. "I don't think she'll leave till she's counted all your legs and arms."

"Yali?" Keth hurried to finish his shave and wiped his face. "She should be at home, in bed! Why did she come here?"

"Ask her yourself," Tris said. "I'll be down shortly."

She stood at the top of the stairs, watching as Keth stumbled down the steps. His face had lit up. There was concern in his voice when he'd asked about Yali. If he still had an arranged marriage back in Namorn, he had a problem, but that at least was not her affair. She walked to her own room, closed the door, and sat on the bed. Carefully she took down two of her heavier lightning braids and began to draw a little of their power into her veins, to liven the tidal strength. As she worked, she wondered what would happen to her when this dose of borrowed power was used up, then shook her head. She'd worry about that when it happened.

The cook surprised Keth by making breakfast for him after Yali left. First he said she didn't need to; when she insisted, he apologized for putting her to the extra work. "A good-looking young fellow needs all the strength he can get, to chase off the hordes of girls who must be chasing you," she said with a wink. Keth laughed for what felt like the first time in ages. He stayed in the kitchen while she cooked, talking to her about the news of the city and her children. She shooed him into the dining room when she finished, saying she had the marketing to do, then sat him at the table and ordered him to eat.

Keth was happy to do so: he was *hungry*. She had given him fresh flatbread, cheese, and a dish of eggs cooked with cinnamon, cumin, cardamom, and fermented barley brine. On his arrival in Tharios, he'd tried eggs prepared this way and thought that, with so peculiar a combination of flavors, they weren't fit for hogs to eat. Now it was one of his favorite Tharian foods.

He hadn't been eating long when Tris came downstairs. She was accompanied by a just-fed Chime — Keth could see the coloring agents for purple and blue glass in the dragon's belly. The girl looked odd, strangely awake for someone who had gone to bed well after midnight and risen not long after dawn according to the cook. Tris poured herself a cup of tea and sat across from him.

"Is your friend Yali all right?" Tris asked as Chime curled around the teapot. "She was upset over you being taken up by the *arurimi.*"

"She knows they don't pay truthsayers in Fifth District," Keth replied, carefully producing each word. His tongue seemed to get thicker when she was near. He couldn't make himself forget what she could produce from those thin braids on either side of her face. "She just wanted to know I was in one piece." He scooped up some eggs with a wedge of flatbread. "She didn't really believe they got a truthsayer because you told them to," he added. After he chewed and swallowed, he continued, "I was there. I'm not sure *I* believe it."

"But I was so polite," Tris replied with a razor-thin smile. "*Dhaskoi* Nomasdina was such a gentleman, giving way to a lady's wishes."

Keth blinked, startled. "Did you just make a joke?" he asked. He'd never thought she had a sense of humor. If she did, it was *very* dry.

"I hardly ever joke," Tris informed him, straightfaced as she sat at the table. "It steams up my spectacles."

Keth put down his spoon to give his full attention to her. For the first time it sank in that this odd girl two-thirds his age was to be his *teacher*. He had no idea who she was, apart from a heroic bad temper, a hand for lightning, a claim to handle forces too big for any human to wield, and a dislike of being balked. She was gentle with tweezers and medicine. She loved Chime and her impossibly sized dog. The eyes behind those spectacles were uncomfortably sharp. She also took their new relationship more seriously than he did, which shamed him.

"So we're stuck with each other," he said carefully.

She propped her chin on her hand, her smile crooked. "Yes, we are. Do you think your cousin will let us do magic at Touchstone? Otherwise we'll have to find a glass mage who will give us a place to work. If you were younger, I wouldn't even try to have you do craftwork as you learn basic mage discipline, but we can't untangle the two now."

"Antonou won't mind as long as I keep making glass for him. If we use a lot of materials, I'll have to find a way to pay him, though. He isn't rich." Keth sighed. He would have to stay in Tharios long after he'd mastered his power, just to repay his cousin. Well, it can't be helped, he told himself. "Let's go," he said, pushing back his chair. "The sooner we start, the sooner we catch the Ghost."

Tris stayed where she was, drumming her fingers lightly on the table. Chime woke from her nap and looked from Keth to Tris. "It's not that easy," Tris said at last. "You won't be creating any lightning globes today."

"Yes I will!" he replied. Really, he thought, just because it took her awhile to master her power doesn't mean it will be the same for me. I'm an adult. She was — is — a child. Patiently he reminded her, "I can meditate, I know I have magic now. All I need is practice."

"And if it were just a matter of glass magic, you would probably be right," she replied. "You're a journeyman in your guild. I concede your knowledge of glassmaking. But you've forgotten that small matter of lightning. It's tricky. It doesn't do what you expect. Magic itself is like lightning, only worse."

"You manage to work it pretty well," Keth said, frowning at her. For the first time in months he felt that control of his life was within his grasp, and here she was trying to muddle it.

"How do you think I got so fast at throwing up protections?" Tris asked. "And some unusual things happened to help me grip it better than most people ever learn to do. Those things won't happen for you. Don't expect to hand *Dhaskoi* Nomasdina a clear globe this evening."

"Well, the sooner we start, the sooner we know," he snapped, impatient. The gall of her, trying to patronize him! "So let's move, already."

He stalked out of the house, fuming, without looking to see if she kept up or not. She judged everything by herself and her little friends. Children learned by rote because it would be years before they understood the ideas behind the memorization. He'd seen it over and over with apprentices. Tris had to learn that an adult would learn easily, now that he knew what he dealt with.

Tris let Keth go. Without rushing she put on Chime's sling and packed a basket of the dragon's dishes and foods, then beckoned for Chime to hop into the sling. Once the dragon was settled, Tris went into the courtyard and put a leash on Little Bear. After leaving word with the cook about where she would be, she set out along the Street of Glass with her dog, letting him sniff and ornament whatever he wanted to. It was better to let Keth walk his temper off now. He would be in a quieter frame of mind when she reached Touchstone.

She knew what he was thinking. Over and over in these last four years she had seen it: adults always believed they knew more than younger people. Normally this was true, but magecraft always turned the normal world on its head. The rules that governed accounting houses, craft shops, armies, and trade were not the rules of magic, even craft magic. Keth's problem was not his skill. It was the crazed power that was a combination of air, water, heat, and cold.

Lightning never formed or struck the same way twice. Tris understood that, and managed it. It was something Keth would learn, if she could stop him from getting killed in the process.

"I wish Lark were here," she told Little Bear and Chime as they passed through Labrykas Square. "She can gentle anybody into doing anything. He'd even thank her for it." Tris sighed. "I'm not good like Lark. I don't know how to gentle anybody. We don't have the time for me to step nicely around his being an adult stuck with a teacher who's a kid." When most people used that word, it meant "baby goat," but to Briar, the street urchins of Summersea, and Briar's foster sisters, "kid" would always mean someone who was not an adult.

Mila of the Grain, give me patience, Tris prayed as she walked around the side of Touchstone Glass. Yanna Healtouch, give me coolness to keep my temper down. Shurri Firesword, don't strike him with your lightning arrows.

Kethlun had stripped off his shirt, donned a leather apron, and begun to make something. Carefully he worked a lump of liquid glass at the end of his blowpipe. He wasn't blowing this piece. He used the pipe to hold the glass as he manipulated it with tongs, pulling out long tendrils and flipping them inward at the end. Tris could see that he breathed in the slow, steady count of meditation. In her magical vision his skin flickered with lightning, but it was gentle, a shimmer rather than a blaze. Working glass calmed him. Perhaps she could use that in her teaching.

If he had seen her, he didn't show it. His big hands and blue eyes were steady as he pulled the glass, thrust the piece back into the furnace to heat, then worked it again. Tris and Chime stayed by the door to watch, silent. Little Bear retreated in boredom to the courtyard.

At last Keth finished. He'd made a pale green octopus, its tentacles neatly arranged to touch its head, as if it had thrown up its arms in shock. He gave it a final examination, his eyes sharp as he inspected the piece, then set it in an annealing oven on the far side of the furnace. Tris knew about this step from her earlier questions to glassmakers. Without a final tempering in the oven, glass would be even more fragile than it already was.

Keth scowled at Tris. "It took you forever to get here. Why didn't you interrupt me?"

Now that she wouldn't distract him, Tris came in and took the sling off her back, then set Chime's food and water dishes in an out-of-the-way corner. The dragon began to feed. Only after Chime was seen to did Tris look at Keth.

"I didn't *want* to interrupt," she replied with a shrug. "I love to watch people work with glass. And you were using the meditation pattern to breathe. Did you feel anything different?"

Keth busied himself cleaning the tools he had used. He

was pouring sweat from the heat of the furnace and oven, while Tris remained cool inside her cocoon of breezes. With a couple of flicks of her hands she expanded her breezes until they wound through the shop, freshening the air.

"It, the breathing, it made me feel calmer," Keth admitted in his slow, careful speech. "I just did it for practice. I'm all right with pulling and molding glass. It's the blown stuff that gets away from me. Are we going to start? The lessons, for the magic? I want to try to blow a globe before the end of the day."

Tris bit her lip and counted to one hundred by fives to keep from snapping at him. He needs to learn to listen to me, she thought. When she was calm again, she told him, "Find a comfortable way to sit. I'm going to draw the circle for our meditation."

"But you only do a circle when there's a danger of magic getting away," argued Kethlun. "I was meditating while I worked — I didn't need any circle. We aren't doing magic."

"*I* am," retorted Tris, "just by drawing the circle. And if you're to grip your magic, you'll have to let it out to work it. You'll do that inside a circle until I'm convinced you know what you're doing."

"Has anybody told you you're bossy?" demanded Keth.

"All the time," Tris replied.

"You'll never catch a husband that way, you know," he pointed out. "A little sweetening would go a long way."

She had heard this before. She didn't like to hear it from

him, but she would tell him so later. There was magic to be done now. "If I have to 'catch' a man to get a husband, I don't want one," she retorted. "Now, sit." She pointed to a clear space at the center of the floor. To Chime she said, "Stay put."

First she set her breezes free to roam the city, though not without regret. It would be stifling inside without them, but at best they might distract Keth. At worst, they might carry some of his uncontrolled power into the world to wreak a patch of havoc. It was better to sweat.

Outside Tris walked around the shop to make sure that she could enclose the whole thing in a circle. Once she had, she walked the circle again, laying a stripe of pure magic as she passed. When she reached the place where she had begun, she stepped inside the circle, then closed it. Her eyes shut, Tris summoned her barriers to meet above and below the workshop, enclosing it in a perfect bubble.

Inside, Kethlun sat cross-legged on the floor. "Close your eyes and start to meditate," she ordered. "Clear your mind of all thought. Ignore me, just meditate."

"I wish I *could* ignore you," grumbled Keth, but he obeyed. Whoever had taught him to meditate had trained him well, Tris observed. His eyelids did not even flutter. His magic cast an uneven, shimmering glow in her sight, flaring and retreating, more active now than it had been while he had focused on making his octopus.

Quietly she assembled several articles. When she had

lined them up behind Keth, she set Chime next to them, motioning for the dragon to stay where she was. She had learned this approach from Daja, who had described her teacher's way to show her how to get her power to tell her about metals she couldn't see.

Finished, Tris knelt behind the row of things she had set up at Kethlun's back. If she remembered her own lessons properly, the idea was to keep her voice soft and her movements quiet, until the teacher's voice seemed almost like part of the student's thoughts. As he inhaled she whispered, "Keth, feel for the power that moves in you. Find it in you, find where it runs. Gather it strand by strand to you. Slowly, slowly."

She repeated it over and over, watching as the silver tracework of magic in his body drew in. Multitudes of glittering pale threads that ran through his muscles came together, their tracks thickening as they merged. Once she judged that he had gripped as much as he could manage, she said, "Let that power flow out behind you. Let it spread there. Let it cover everything behind you. Let it run toward me, let it flow. . . ."

His breath hitched in his throat as his mind fumbled with this new trick. The heavier strands of magic began to pull apart. Tris went silent, waiting. At last Keth found his breathing rhythm and tried again.

Three tries later, the power he'd gathered flowed out to cover Tris and the things that she had set there. It was cool on her skin, as if she were coated in fluid, cold glass. Tris savored the relief from the heat, then drew her thumb and forefinger down a thin braid to coax a grain of lightning from her hair. The spark glimmered on her fingertip as Tris touched it to the first thing she had set at Keth's back.

"Stay as you are," she began softly. "Tell me what I'm touching back here." She had meant to say that she used lightning to point, then changed her mind. His magic would know the difference between lightning and glass. "Find me with your power and tell me what I'm touching." That should be easy. They had lightning and fire in common, if precious little else.

"Bowl." Kethlun's lips barely moved, he was so deep within himself. "Blown glass, green, stylized birds impressed around the sides by tongs."

"Do you know this because you recognize the piece, or because you feel it with your power?" Tris wanted to know.

"It — it's there," he said, his voice agonizingly slow. "In the glass. In its shape. It knows — it knows what it is."

Tris raised her eyebrows, impressed. Perhaps his glassmaker's training made it easier for him to know so much about the bowl. She lifted her finger away, still with the spark of lightning on it, and touched the next piece. He identified an undecorated blue glass bottle, a clear vase blown onto a mold of a many-petaled rose, and an overheated piece of cloudy glass that Tris had taken from the cullet, or junk-glass barrel.

The last item at Keth's back was Chime. She had curled into a cat-style ball to nap.

Tris restored her spark to its braid. "What do I touch now?" she asked. Keth shouldn't need her to lead him to Chime, not when the dragon was infused with lightning. "There's one more item behind you."

Keth fidgeted. He twitched his shoulders, then yelped and tried to scramble away, not remembering that his legs were crossed and that he'd been sitting in that position for quite a while. He pitched forward onto his face, his ankles tangled behind him. After a moment he said grumpily, his nose mashed flat on the beaten earth of the floor, "Chime. That *stings*."

"There's quite a bit of lightning in her, even though she's so small," admitted Tris, speaking in her normal volume. "You did really well. I hope you know that."

"Good. Are we done?"

Tris scowled. She had done the right thing, praising him. He should appreciate it; she didn't give compliments easily. A more patient part of her whispered that he didn't know that. She took her own deep breath, counting until her temper settled. Only then did she say, "No. Now you'll try blowing glass."

Chime squeaked and scrambled under a bench. Keth rolled over to untangle himself. "About time. He could be killing a *yaskedasu* right now."

"Start the meditation breathing as you start your gather," Tris instructed as he prepared to work.

"You know what a gather is?" he asked, shaking out his shoulders.

"I like to watch glassblowers, and often they let me ask questions," replied Tris.

"Why?" he asked, checking the crucible to make sure the glass in it was still fit to be worked. "It doesn't have anything to do with your magic."

Tris sighed. "Most things don't have anything to do with my magic," she said, trying to be patient. "I just like to know about them. I almost never have anything to show for what I do. To me glassmaking, weaving, medicines, metal-smithing, now *that's* magical. You make something and it lasts. It isn't gone in the blink of an eye. *And* you'll be able to earn a good living with it."

He raised his eyebrows. "You won't?"

"Not like a craft mage can. Not if you don't want to kill people with lightning. Not if you can only bring rain or winds when you're sure you're not stealing them from others who need them. If you don't want to work that way, it's hard to make a living as a weather mage," she explained. She could see he didn't believe her. Time to get to work, she told herself, and said aloud, "Now, Keth — don't try to blow a globe this time. Let's just see what happens."

He rolled his eyes and sighed, a combination that always made her want to box the ears of the person who did it. "I've blown globes since I was an apprentice, Tris," he told her. "The fishermen of the Syth always need them as floats for their nets. It's child's play. Now that I know what the problem is, it'll be easy."

Tris nibbled on her lip. He could be right, though she doubted it. "Do as you like, then."

He stood for a moment, blowpipe in hand, the light from the furnace casting his face into relief. Tris settled on a bench to watch him. She could feel the forces in the shop come together. Lightning flared from his skin more power-fully than it had before. Quickly Tris sent extra power into the protections that enclosed the shop. She did not want any stray magics to come in now, as they had two days ago. His next accident might not be as wonderful as Chime.

Tris breathed with him and waited as he returned to meditation. At last Keth slid his blowpipe into the furnace. The heat didn't seem to bother him, though Tris had seen journeymen and even guildmasters flinch from it. She re-moved her spectacles and closed her eyes, sketching the sign for fire on her lids with a finger. When she opened them, Keth and his surroundings were a blur, but the quiv-ering heat of the furnace was as clear as his magic. The heat twined around Keth like an affectionate cat, sinking into his skin and bones.

Tris wiped a thumb over her eyelids and restored her spectacles to their proper resting place. Whether it was due to lightning or his own expanded seed of glass magic, Keth could take higher temperatures than most people. He might even be able to hold fire in his bare hands, Tris thought. She would ask Daja, the smith mage, when she got —

"Home" was the next word of her thought. Tris's eyes burned with sudden tears. After all this time, she still tricked herself, thinking Discipline cottage was nearby and that Daja, Sandry, and Briar would be there when she returned for the night. But they weren't. Discipline and Sandry were in Emelan, months of travel to the north. Daja was in Kethlun's home country of Namorn, even farther north; Briar was on the road to Yanjing in the distant northeast. They were truly scattered and Daja wasn't here to judge Keth's magic.

Tris sniffed and locked her attention on her student. Keth brought his gather of molten glass out of the furnace, twirling his blowpipe as he did. His grip on his breathing was shaky.

"Gently," she murmured, watching the reddish orange glass change color as it began to cool. "Remember the feel of your magic."

He kept the pipe spinning and carefully blew down its length. Tris saw the lightning blaze of his power show through the pipe. He blew steadily, far longer than she could have managed. When his lungs were empty, Keth reheated the glass as he took in fresh air. The power in his breath was brighter still in the pipe this time. Tris, about to say something, held her tongue. He reheated again, but she knew he'd lost the count of his meditation. This time, when he blew into the pipe, glass-coated lightning darted from the end and dropped to the earth without shattering. Chime dashed under a corner worktable and stayed there.

"Relax," Tris said as Keth turned beet red with frustration. "Calm down, drink some water, try again."

"Y-you —!" he began to yell, turning on her. Tris met his eyes with her own, wanting him to see that this was normal, it was to be expected. She knew it was maddening to think a thing through perfectly, only to have it go awry the minute she actually tried to do it.

Whatever he'd meant to say, Keth chose not to say it. Instead he walked around the shop, touching vases, bowls, jars, and suncatchers until he was calm. After that he set another crucible to heat and drank some water.

They were so caught up in their work they didn't even notice Antonou's wife had come with Keth's midday. She couldn't pass through the magical barrier or catch their attention. At last she fed some chunks of grilled lamb to Little Bear, then went back to her own work.

By late afternoon both student and teacher were sweat-soaked and exhausted. In addition to the glass lightning, Keth had produced a few other mistakes. When the breath caught in Keth's throat on his second try, droplets of molten glass exploded over the workshop. They glinted in the light of the furnace like dark gems. Next came an egg-shaped blob of black glass, then a lump that sparkled with tiny lightnings. The last failure was a glass coil that burned the toe off one of Keth's boots. Chime had yet to leave her hiding place.

Tris looked at the glass coil, then at Keth. Knowing she was about to trigger an explosion, she said as gently as she knew how, "This isn't working. You're exhausted and probably starving. It's time to stop for the day."

"No," he told her stubbornly. "You don't know the *yaskedasi*. I do. I've been living with them for eight months. The Ghost is killing their sense of, of excitement. Of fun, joy . . ." He fumbled to express his thought. "Khapik was the first place I've been where I c-could forget what h-happened to me. The, the Ghost is killing Khapik." He collected a fresh gather at the end of the blowpipe.

Tris wanted to scream. She was hungry, she was soaked in sweat, she wanted to be out and about. She was pouring magic into the barrier to keep the wild bursts of Keth's power inside. What was so wonderful about Khapik? she wanted to yell. It had theaters, inns, musical performances, women and men who flaunted themselves in form-fitting clothes, gambling dens, and wine shops. Every city had such places.

She said none of these things as Keth drew a shuddering breath and started to blow into the pipe. As a teacher her duty was to encourage Keth, not discourage him. From her own experience, Tris knew he would give himself enough discouragement without help from her.

"Nothing yet, then?" someone asked from outside the barrier. It was *Dhaskoi* Nomasdina, crisply dressed in a clean red tunic and blue stole, his short black hair still wet from the bath.

Keth, startled, made an apprentice's mistake and puffed hard into the blowpipe. The molten glass at the end bulged, coated in tiny lightnings, and grew to the size of his hand. Tris and Nomasdina froze, watching. Tris could see that Keth's hands trembled, but he continued to work, carefully twirling the pipe to see what shape his most recent accident would take. The bulb expanded to a perfect globe, then broke away. Keth reached out and caught it in one hand before it could fall.

That answers that question, thought Tris. He can hold hot glass.

The globe was a twin to the one he'd made at Heskalifos. Miniature lightnings played inside and outside of the glass, growing thicker and longer until they coated it entirely.

"You did it!" cried Nomasdina. "What do you see?"

"Lightning," Keth said gloomily, and sat on a bench with a thump. Tris gently took the blowpipe from him and set it aside.

"May I look?" Nomasdina asked. "Maybe I can spot something. *Dhasku* Chandler —"

"Tris," the girl interrupted. "Just Tris. Don't touch it unless you've got some kind of fire magic, *Dhaskoi* Nomasdina. It's hot, still." She held out her hands. Glumly Keth handed the globe to her. It was warm to her touch, but only warm. She could handle molten rock for brief periods.

"But I could look at it," argued the *arurim dhaskoi*, "maybe see between the lightnings."

Tris turned the globe over in her hands. The lightnings were still excited. They whipped around the globe so fast that she saw no gaps between them. Reaching for them with her own power, thinking to draw them off, she failed. To her magical senses it felt as if the bolts were locked inside sheaths of glass that turned her power away.

Well! she thought, amused by the lightning's defiance, I'm not to tinker with you, is that it? "I doubt you could see through them, *Dhaskoi* Nomasdina," Tris replied. "But you're welcome to look."

"*Dhasku* Chandler," the man said.

"Why is 'Tris' so hard to say?" she demanded, still looking at the ball in her hands, running her own power around it, trying to find a path inside the glass. She could no more do that than she could shift the lightnings outside it.

"But it's the *dhasku* I need," Nomasdina explained. "The *dhasku* who's so strong that all the charms I know to break a circle of protection aren't working. And the ones taught to the *arurim dhaski* are usually effective."

That made Tris look up. Nomasdina stood outside the barrier she had raised, his hands against it. Starbursts of silver light spread around them as he tried to push through her protections. "I'm sorry, *Dhaskoi* Nomasdina," she said, contrite. "You must be pretty good if you can stand to touch it, though." She went to the door and erased part of her circle with her foot, gathering her power back into herself as the barrier gave way. Little Bear came bouncing in to see if anyone was interested in petting him.

"Please — under the circumstances, you should call me Dema," the Tharian told her. As he walked past her, he lifted the ball from her hand. "Ow," he cried, juggling the ball from one hand to the other. "It *stings*."

Tris took the globe back from him. "Lightning has that effect. Among others," she added, looking at Kethlun. "Do you remember how this happened?" she asked her student.

"No," he said with a sigh. He idly scratched the dog's ears. "I wasn't thinking."

"Maybe that's it," Dema remarked as he sat on a bench. Chime trotted out of her hiding place and began to sniff his hands. "Not thinking."

"It's harder than I thought," Keth admitted. "What brings you here, anyway?"

"The honest answer? Hope. I'm on my way to Elya Street for the start of my watch," replied Dema, wriggling his fingers for Chime. "I thought I'd stop by, on the chance you were here. And I was right. Now we have something to work with."

"If it clears in time," Tris reminded him. Eyeing her student, she added, "Keth, you're in no shape to try and draw out your lightning." She passed the globe to him as he slumped on a bench. He'd drained off all of his power for the time being; she saw not a flicker of it inside his skin. At least the lightning on the globe bothered him no more than it did her.

"No," Keth replied, stubborn. "I'll clear it and I'll see what the Ghost looks like. I have to. He'll kill someone else." He began to breathe for meditation, staring at the flashing globe in his hands. Tris and Dema waited patiently.

Finally Keth glared at Tris. "Where is it?" he demanded accusingly. "This magic of mine? I don't feel it. It's a crackly buzz in my head, but I don't hear it. You took it, didn't you?"

Tris folded her hands in front of her, stifling her irritation at the question. She knew all too well how it felt to be as exhausted as he was. "I can't take magic from people," she replied in even tones. "Even if I could, you have none to take. Keth, look, it's the study and the work of magic that builds up your reserves. You just started to learn today. You don't *have* reserves. The only thing that will bring your power back is food and rest. You'll have power to use tomorrow."

"Someone will die," whispered Keth.

"Maybe not," Dema said briskly. "I'll take the globe to the *arurimat*. If it clears before the murder, we'll go where it leads us. And if we don't, well, you'll have other chances to make this work."

Keth slumped forward, resting his forehead on his globe. Tris felt sorry for him, but knew he wouldn't thank her for showing pity. "On your feet, Keth," she said briskly. "Is your octopus done?"

As Keth checked the annealing oven and began to clean up, Tris looked at Dema. "He's been at it since this morning, trying as hard as he could," she said.

"I know," Dema said with understanding. "When you've drained yourself, that's it. You have to eat and rest until your strength comes back."

"It's not just her coddling me?" Keth asked, his voice sluggish. His back was to them.

"I don't coddle," Tris said sharply.

"No, she isn't," Dema added. "Every mage learns, when you're finished for the day, you're finished. You'll only make yourself ill if you try to do more magic. Look here, I know a good eating-house near the *arurimat*. I'll pay — it's the least I can do in trade for this." He pointed to the globe Tris still held. She put it in the basket she'd used to carry Chime's food and dishes, and handed it to him.

Dema accepted the basket with a bow of thanks. "I hope you'll come, too, Tris."

She smiled. "Thank you, but I'm tired. I think I'll go back to Heskalifos. Keth, you are taking Dema up on his offer, yes?"

Dema grinned at her, then looked at Keth. A trace of concern crossed his sharp brown features. "Come on, old man," he urged Kethlun. "They've got a sauce for lamb cooked on skewers that will make you think you dine with the emperor of Aliput."

"Then he goes home to sleep," Tris added. She sighed. "And we wait for the globe to clear."

Dema made the circle of the All-Seeing on his forehead. "Maybe it will clear beforetime," he said.

Keth looked at him and smiled crookedly. "An optimistic lawkeeper. Now *there* is something unusual."

"Have a proper meal and you'll be an optimist, too," Dema said, ushering Keth out of the workshop.

Tris watched the two men walk away, smiling when Dema draped an arm over Keth's shoulder. She'd gotten a very favorable impression of the *arurim dhaskoi* the previous night, once they'd gotten over their original misunderstanding about the use of torture. As he'd questioned Keth, she'd watched his face and listened to his voice. He wanted to catch the Ghost, and she didn't think it was all about glory for Dema. It didn't seem to be much about the *yaskedasi,* either, but Tris would settle for what she thought he did want, the end of the killer's lawlessness.

Once the men were gone, she went into the glass shop to ask Keth's cousin Antonou a favor. Would he mind if she left Little Bear and Chime in the courtyard for a few hours? She would get them later, without disturbing the family. Not only did Antonou agree, but his quiet, shy wife found a meal of table scraps for Little Bear. Tris thanked them, and ordered the dog and dragon to wait for her return. She brushed the soot and dirt from her pale green dress —

woven and sewn by Sandry, it refused all stains and hardly wrinkled — and headed down the street.

This Ghost mess revolved around Khapik, and Tris had yet to see the place. She had heard of it, long before they had reached Tharios. Other travelers, learning where they were bound, sang the praises of Khapik; its gardens, its entertainers, its food, its wine. The best performers worked there at some point in their careers; the guests who saw them spread their names from the Cape of Grief in the south to Blaze-Ice Bay in the north. Some men had spoken more fondly of Khapik than they did of their families. To Tris it seemed that many of the young people they'd met were saving their money for one holiday only, at Khapik.

She'd seen Khapik when they rode into Tharios, of course, or at least, its brightly painted walls. Normally she might not have gone there. While she loved music, acting, tumbling, and food, she thought it folly to pay for such things when she had to watch every copper. Now, though, Keth's globes had given her an excuse at least to look around.

She joined a river of visitors all headed in the same direction, on foot, in sedan chairs, on horse, camel, or donkey back. The caravan master who'd brought her and Niko to Tharios had mentioned that no wagons were permitted inside Khapik. She wondered if the *prathmuni* had to carry the garbage, night soil, and dead bodies out of Khapik by hand, without using their carts. She wanted to ask a *prathmun* who drove his cart across the Street of Glass if that was the case, but there were too many Tharians around, all retreating from cart and driver, most drawing the circle of the All-Seeing God on their foreheads.

Some blocks past Touchstone Glass, above the shabby stores that sold overpriced items to newly arrived tourists, Tris saw the bright yellow pillars that marked Khapik's entrance. They towered over the district's walls, which were painted with dancers, musicians, bunches of grapes, illusionists, wine jugs, plates of steaming food, tumblers, and all the other delights that lay inside. The guards at the gate watched the flood of tourists go by them with blank faces, unimpressed by the number and variety of the visitors.

The moment she passed inside the wall, Tris felt cool moisture in the air. Ahead of her lay a shaded expanse of ground divided into small islands by streams and riverlets, some broad enough to allow boats to pass along their length. Inside the boats, people lazed, nibbled on fruit, talked, or trailed their fingers in the water. Squat candles burned inside flower-shaped cups that floated in the water, like fireflies that skimmed its surface: those who poled the boats avoided the candles with the ease of long practice. Trees grew here and there along the banks, cooling the streets under them. On the islands she saw delicate pavilions lit by lanterns and torches where musicians, singers, and dancers performed for small groups.

Scents drifted on the air: roses, jasmine, patchouli, sandalwood, cinnamon. She heard bits of music and the splash of fountains. Her breezes, which had come back when she lowered her protections on the glassmaker's workshop, whirled around her like small children, eager to run away and explore the maze of streets and streams. She let them go, reminding them to come back to her. As she looked around, watching the guests break up into small groups and disappear down the streets, something tightly knotted inside her loosened a bit.

She had to walk a distance to leave the area where the streams flowed. Beyond them she found the streets where businesses thrived: eating houses, wineshops, theaters, tea houses, gambling dens, and shops that sold trinkets, perfumes, scarves, even toys. Here too were houses where entertainers performed for smaller audiences than those found in the theaters, in courtyards, and in brightly lit rooms with gauze curtains.

Tris saw *yaskedasi* at street corners, beside the many fountains, on the stream banks, in courtyards, on the islands, on balconies and porches. Six tumblers stood on one another's shoulders to shape themselves into a human pyramid, then to leap free, tucking, rolling, and landing on their feet. Next to a many-tiered fountain Tris listened to a handsome boy play a melancholy song on a harp. On the far side of the fountain an older woman juggled burning torches. An illusionist produced flowers and birds from his sleeves under a willow tree, while dogs danced together under a trainer's eye. A woman draped in an immense snake and a handful of veils perched in a low window, stroking her pet. When she saw Tris watching, she beckoned, but Tris shook her head and walked on.

In low houses circled by colonnades, women and men lounged on couches, talked, ate, drank, and gambled. When Tris glanced down the inner passages of such houses into the courtyards, she saw scantily clad dancers, female and male, performing to harp, flute, or sometimes only drum music. She heard lone singers and groups of singers, their melodies twining among the songs played on instruments. In one courtyard a poet declaimed verses on the art of love. In another, a group of people played Blind Man's Bluff.

When her belly reminded her that it was nearly dark and she had not eaten for some time, she found an eating-house whose bill of fare promised a decent meal. The prices would have made her gasp if she had not seen those posted beside houses whose charges were even higher. She chose a table outside, on the street, so she could better watch the crowds. She ignored the stares, thinking it was her pale complexion and red hair that drew attention, rather than her youth and the fact that she looked like no pleasure seeker.

The serving maid brought her a supper of lamb grilled on skewers, lentils cooked with onions and bay leaves, plum juice, flatbread, and cheese. Tris thanked her politely, then turned all of her attention on the street as she ate.

Why the *yaskedasi*? she wondered. Six dead women, all

of them *yaskedasi* — why did he choose them? It wasn't for their money, not from what she'd heard. And why only women?

Did he choose them because he knew that the *arurim* wouldn't care about the murder of entertainers whom respectable folk viewed as disreputable, if not out-and-out dishonest? But if that were so, why had he placed the last two so visibly, outside Khapik, where respectable folk would raise a fuss? If he'd wanted to be entirely a Ghost, he should have stayed inside Khapik, or even turned to the slums of Hodenekes, where no one would care about another dead body.

He was clever, to make use of the Tharian beliefs about death. Tris had helped Niko often in the past, when Niko had raised a vision from the site of an event that had taken place there recently. That would be impossible in Tharios. The priests always showed up on the heels of the discovery of a body, and erased all magical influences to rid the area of death's pollution. They made it easier for the killer to get away with his murders.

Staring into the cup that held her plum juice, Tris idly wondered if she could scry for the killer. It was just an idle fancy. Niko had tried to teach all four of them how to scry in water, oil, mirrors, and crystals. Daja had succeeded once, but Tris had been the only one to find an image each time. It was frustrating. She saw only scraps of things, many of which made no sense, and there was no way to control what she saw. Following her progress, Niko said her images seemed to come entirely from the present; she could not see anything in the past or future. Now she let her mind drift, her eyes fixed vaguely on the dark liquid in her cup, its surface glinting in the torchlight. Scraps of things began to rise to the surface: Niko talking animatedly to a dark brown man in a pure white turban, Market Square back home, a wooden building ablaze as people scurried around it like lines of ants, a small mountain village where a shaggy-haired blacksmith labored at his forge.

Tris growled and drank her juice, ignoring the beginnings of a headache. She was no better at this now than she had been at Winding Circle. No wonder so many seers had a reputation for being odd, if all they saw was a flood of meaningless pictures. Feeling useless, she returned to her meal.

As she finished, a procession came down the street, led by tumblers and musicians, surrounded by a cloud of orange blossom scent. At its center, four muscular men carried a woman in a sedan chair. Its curtains were open, framing her like a picture as she reclined on satin pillows. Her black hair was dressed in glossy, ornate loops, not the curls of Tharian fashion, twisted through with the yellow veil of the *yaskedasi*. Her *kyten* was pure white with golden embroideries, her jewelry gold encrusted with pearls.

"That's Baoya the Golden," a female voice remarked near Tris's shoulder. A breeze carried a drift of lavender scent to the girl's sensitive nose. Tris turned. Keth's friend, the *yaskedasu* Yali, lounged against the low fence around the eating-house as she watched the procession. She was dressed much as she had been that morning, though her makeup and *kyten* were fresh, and she looked the better for some sleep. With her was another *yaskedasu*, a blonde, dressed northern-style with a tumbler's shorter skirts and leggings.

"Who's Baoya the Golden?" asked Tris.

"The Queen of Khapik, the most legendary of all the female *yaskedasi*," the blonde said, looking down a short nose at Tris. "*Everyone* knows Baoya. She's a dancer. She's performed for most of the Assembly and all of the Keepers of the Public Good for the last fifteen years."

Yali regarded Tris. "What are you doing here unescorted, *Dhasku* Trisana?"

"It's just Tris. I wanted to see what the talk was about," Tris replied. "What is it that you do, anyway? You never said."

Yali sighed. "I sing. Xantha, here, is a tumbler — she stays at Ferouze's, too. Look, we're due at the Butterfly Court right now. Why don't you go home? Come back with someone who can look after you, like Keth. You're fine here on the main streets, but in the back ways . . . Not everyone in Khapik is as nice as they're paid to be."

"You mean like the Ghost?" inquired Tris.

Yali and Xantha both made the sign of the Living Circle on their chests. "He's one," Yali replied. "Go home, Tris.

Give that glass dragon of yours a polish for me." The two women disappeared into the crowds, dodging people with the skill of long practice.

Curious, Tris sent a ribbon of breeze after them and called it back. It returned with their conversation.

"Keth's *teacher*?" That was the voice of the blonde Xantha. "Of course! Why didn't *I* realize that? Come on, Yali, if you keep pulling my nose like that, it'll be as long as hers!"

"I'm not joking, Xantha," was Yali's reply. "She's a *dhasku* —"

"And I'm Baoya," interrupted Xantha. "Let's take the short cut. We're going to be late."

Tris smiled at the remark about her nose. She was above all a realist, and her nose *was* long. She also had no intention of going home, but it was sweet of Yali to worry.

What if she listened to her breezes for the Ghost? He took his victims from Khapik — she might hear something. Eagerly, Tris summoned them all to her, adding a double handful of breezes from the streets of Khapik, then sent them out to listen. She couldn't see things on them, but she might hear something worthwhile.

Her meal over, she set off once again, looking at the sights as she listened to dollops of conversation that came to her on currents of air. With the ease of practice she listened only for something unusual in the bath of chatter about money, music, politics, affections, excitement, and boredom. She also considered the situation she and Keth had been plunged into.

If the Ghost was grabbing *yaskedasi,* he did not do it among the processions, clusters of performers, idlers by the streams, or gate traffic. Someone would have seen him. He took his choices in deserted places. Accordingly Tris followed the maze of streets, looking for Khapik's hazards. They were endless. There were too many shadowy nooks, unlit passages, alleys, and blind curves for the *arurim* to patrol. The courtyards shrank; the houses rose to three and four stories. Many outdoor stairways led to flat rooftops. A fugitive could go up there and run the length of the district to escape pursuit, if he knew his way.

Tris wandered down an alley, eyeing the houses on either side. Business was done back here, too. Her breezes told her what sort of business it was. Intent on her surroundings, toying with the end of one thin braid, Tris walked on, ignoring those who offered to sell her various items.

A hand darted from the shadows to grip her wrist; a man pulled her close. "Here's a nice little armful. What is it, wench? What's your price?" The man was big, his tunic rumpled and stained with wine. "If you're sweet to me, I'll be sweet to you."

Tris looked up until she met his eyes. Rage fizzed under her skin, but she gripped it tight. "Let me go," she told the man, her gray eyes glittering as they locked on his. Her free hand itched to undo a spark-braid. "I'm not what you think I am."

The man laughed. "Then what are you doing here, by your lonesome?" he wanted to know. "I know what *you're* looking for. Give me a kiss to seal the bargain."

Tris slammed her hard-heeled northern shoe straight down onto his sandaled foot. The drunk yelled and let her go, then reached for her again. "You little *mirizask*," he said, his voice a growl. "You'll learn respect for me!"

Tris grabbed the little finger of his hand and pulled it back in its socket until he howled with pain. She had learned the stomp from Briar and the fingerhold from Daja, both of whom had given her long instruction in all the ways they knew to end an unpleasant conversation. "It's a dreadful thing," she said grimly as he tried to free himself without breaking the finger, "when a respectable tourist can't enjoy the sights without some idiot getting in her way. And I do so *hate* stupid people."

She stepped back as she released his hand, yanking the tie off a spark-braid. Then she waited, holding it as she watched the man. It would be shameful to turn lightning on someone who was clearly drunk, but she didn't want any more nonsense, either.

The man cradled his aching hand as he glared at Tris. Something in her gaze made him think at last. "Stick to the main streets, then, *shenos*," he snapped. "And bring a guard, next time you feel like a stroll."

"Oh, I don't think I need a guard," Tris replied. "Do you?" She walked off, sending two breezes in her wake to warn her if he attacked. It seemed he'd had enough. He stumbled off in the opposite direction.

It was just after midnight when Tris decided she would not be lucky enough to hear the Ghost snarl, "I'm going to kill you!", then have him wait for her to trace that particular bit of wind back to the killer. Instead she spread her awareness through the ground until she found the web of streams, and followed her sense of them back to the islands, the boats, and the main gate.

Ghost or no, she thought that she had not wasted her time. This walk had been instructive. While she'd dealt with the drunkard, not a single nearby window or door had opened; no one had peered over the edges of the roofs. No wonder there were no witnesses when the Ghost seized his victims. There were too many hidden places, and too few people who cared enough to stop a disturbance.

All that Tharian love of order applies only outside the Khapik fence, she thought grimly as she left the district. All that white marble, good manners, and agreement of equals is only meant for the higher classes, not anyone else. They ought to be ashamed.

The most maddening aspect of her walk, of course, was her failure with her breezes. She'd hoped for *something*, though she knew how unlikely it was that she might hear the Ghost at work. What he did was no doubt accomplished in silence. She needed to *see* what the winds saw, not just hear it. Surely if anyone could do it, it would be her. She could scry the present, though she couldn't control what she saw. And she worked in winds and puffs of air all the time, using them to eavesdrop.

Tris hated to feel useless. Keth had the lightning globes as a goal, though she still believed it would take much more work before he could get anything useful from them. Quite possibly the Ghost would be caught by other means before Keth mastered his globes. She wondered if there might be something about Keth that made him attuned to crimes in general, not just crimes against people he knew. Once the Ghost was accounted for, would Keth make other such globes? She probably ought to suggest it to him, so he could prepare himself. He'd made it clear he wanted to make beautiful glass, not deal in ugly crime.

Her mind busy, Tris strode up the Street of Glass. She stopped to quietly gather Little Bear and Chime from the Touchstone Glass courtyard, then resumed her walk up the long hill back to Heskalifos.

Tris was reading in the workroom when Niko found her. He and Jumshida had been out late, attending yet another party for the conference. On his way to bed, he'd seen the light under the workroom door and looked in.

The moment he saw her, his black brows snapped together. "You've been using your braids again," he remarked sourly.

Tris looked up from her book. "And with very good reason. I need to help Keth with his fear of lightning, and the closest storm on the path to Tharios was stuck in Aliput."

Niko crossed his arms. "Trisana . . ."

"It's true!" she protested. "Some mage over there had things locked down, and I had to pry them loose." As he remained silent, she made a face. "All right, I used winds to lift myself to the top of Phakomathen first. But I'm not joking about the storms, Niko, and I *am* careful, using the stronger powers I store."

Niko sighed. "No, it's true, you are. And I suppose we're beyond the point where I can lecture you about such things. I do like to think you're too sensible to use them so often that they become a drug for you."

"As sick as I'll be once I can stop to rest? That's not at *all* addictive. You don't have to worry," she replied. She inspected his face. "What's the matter? You look cross."

"Did you know they magically cleanse the site where a dead person is found?" Niko demanded. "Scour it of all traces of the events there?" Tris nodded. "It's obscene!" cried Niko. "I talked to the *arurim* officials in a position to allow me to raise a vision of the past to help catch this beast, but they tell me the cleansing isn't just religious, it's magical as well. How do they ever catch criminals here?"

Tris shrugged. "Dema — Demakos Nomasdina, the

arurim dhaskoi you met — and Keth think Keth's globes will do it."

"And you don't." The way Niko said it, it was not a question.

"It'll be awhile before Keth can do magic to order instead of by accident," Tris said frankly. "He seems to think that now he knows the problem, he can just get to work. And maybe he's too involved. He knew one of the women; he watched another of them perform. He *wants* it to work too badly. It's getting in his way."

"You'll have to find a way to calm him down," Niko said, yawning. Suddenly he smiled. "Something I would give a great deal to see, actually."

He'd lost Tris in his thinking. "What?" she asked. "What do you want to see?"

Now he grinned outright. "*You,* trying to calm someone down."

Tris smiled, but wryly. "So funny I forgot to laugh," she retorted.

Niko stretched. "I will laugh for us both, then."

Tris ran her fingers over her book. "Niko?"

"Yes?"

"Have you ever been to Khapik?" she asked.

"Many times. Not since we came, but in my youth," he admitted. "It had the unfortunate effect of sucking all the coins from my purse, so I stopped going." His eyes were distant as he thought. "I remember it was very beautiful, particularly the area of streams and islands around the main gate."

"It's still there, and it's still lovely," Tris informed him. "Why would anyone want to ruin it? Maybe the *yaskedasi* aren't as respectable as they could be, but they do such amazing things, and this Ghost is killing them."

Niko sighed, his dark eyes gentle as he looked at her. "I've never known why anyone would destroy something beautiful, but such people exist." For a long moment there was silence between them. Tris regarded the book in her lap, while Niko watched her. At last he said, "Did you know that Lark used to work in Khapik?"

Tris's head jerked up at the sound of her foster mother's name. "No!" she exclaimed. "She did?"

Her teacher nodded. "There was a year when the performing troupe she was with decided to rest for a few seasons and create new material. They stayed and performed in Khapik."

"She wore that dreadful yellow veil?" Tris asked, the hair on her arms prickling. She loved Lark. The thought that a killer like the Ghost might have gone anywhere *near* her was chilling.

"Actually, I believe she wore it as a neck scarf," Niko replied, his eyes somber. "*There's* a frightening thought."

Tris made the sign of the Living Circle on her chest.

Niko sighed. "It's late. I'm off to bed, unless there's something else you need?"

"Someone to teach me to scry the wind," she said wryly. "I could send my breezes searching for the killer in Khapik, if I could see things in them."

Niko rubbed his temples. "Tris, I've told you, it's very like seeing the future," he pointed out. "You drown in different images and events — how do you sort one from another? That's why future seers are as rare as lightning mages. Most go mad from sheer confusion. Does it really mean so much to you?"

"I feel useless," Tris admitted. "Like a bride's attendant to Keth — I get to hold the basket of herbs, but he's the one who says the vows."

"Do you think I'm useless?" asked Niko. "Or Lark, or Frostpine, or Rosethorn, or Crane?" He'd named the main people who had taught her and her friends at Winding Circle.

"No!" cried Tris, startled. "You're wonderful, all of you!"

"You will produce wonders in Keth, I'm sure of it," Niko said. "Think again about scrying for something that will drown you in visions. The price you pay is every bit as high as what you'll pay when the strength of lightning and tides runs out of you." With a tired wave, he went off to bed.

Tris thought about what he'd said for a long time.

Dema

He'd gotten a proper meal into Keth. It seemed like the least he could do, when Keth had worked himself into numb silence trying to produce a vision of the next murder before it came to be. Dema knew that state of unblinking exhaustion all too well. Every student mage reached that point. He wished he had a *bik* for every time he had poured out all of his power over the course of a day, until he simply had nothing left.

He made sure an *arurim* saw Keth home, giving the *arurim* coins to buy Keth a honeycomb and good tea in one of the Khapik *skodi* along the way. Keth would need both in the morning. If he was like Dema, he would wake feeling as if someone had run a hot wire through his veins.

What would it have done to him, Dema wondered, to wake at twenty with strange magic on his back? He wasn't sure. Like every other child of Clan Nomasdina, at the age of five he had been interviewed by mage testers. Once they proclaimed him a fledgling mage, Dema began the years of lessons, experiments, tests, and study under various teachers. After he'd earned his credential from Heskalifos at twenty-two, he'd chosen a career, knowing that his position as a mage would make his advancement easier.

He had *not* known that the average *arurim*'s view of a new mage was one of cheerful contempt. One of them had advised him to "cast your little spell and don't bump into the furniture." They were laughing at him tonight as Dema went everywhere with a basket on his arm. No matter that the nearness of the lightning globe made the hair on his arm prickle, or that every time he accidentally touched it he got a small, nasty sting. He wanted the thing where he could see it when the lightnings cleared.

In the meantime, he investigated the newest victim. Her name was Rhidassa; she had been a tumbler and a dancer. She left behind a husband and children, all shattered by her death. She had not told them if she had noticed anyone strange loitering about in her last days of work. Her family's blank faces and hard eyes told Dema that they might not tell him if they did know of such a person. Fortunately his truth spell worked; they weren't lying. That was reassuring: his self-confidence had suffered when Kethlun's magic had scorched it from existence. That was the problem with spells cast by those without innate ability as truthsayers: they were easily destroyed by strong magic.

Dema was drinking tea at his favorite shop on Peacock Street when he wondered if Keth *realized* just how strong his power was. Probably not, since he'd taken his failure to clear the globe he'd just made personally. Dema hoped Tris would tell Keth that he had done better today than most student mages did after years of study.

Two hours before sunrise Dema realized he'd brushed the globe without being stung. Looking at it, he saw that the surface lightning was reduced to specks that flashed and vanished. The bolts inside looked as if they were thinning out. At that point he gave up any pretense of investigating further. He ordered a horse saddled and a squad of *arurimi* prepared to ride with him, then sat at his desk to wait for the globe to clear. It did, an hour before dawn, to show a dark-skinned *yaskedasu* in a flowing, silvery *kyten*. She lay on an altar Dema did not recognize, the yellow veil knotted around her throat.

He ran outside to the *arurimi* he'd kept waiting. "Do any of you know where this is?" he demanded, holding out the globe.

They gathered around, bleary-eyed and no doubt thinking of the end of their shifts in two hours. Most shook their heads, but a twenty-year veteran frowned. She traced the line of the altar and the image of a cow-headed goddess behind it with her finger.

"Do you know it, sergeant?" asked Dema. "Quickly, if you do."

"It's a *shenos* temple, one of them inland religions," she replied, squinting. "Oh, aye, the Temple of Ngohi. But *Dhaskoi*, it's near the crossing of Apricot Street and Honor Street in Fourth District. Out of our boundaries."

"I don't care if it's in Piraki," retorted Dema. "Come on." He put the globe in his saddlebag, mounted his horse, and galloped out of the courtyard without waiting to see if the *arurimi* followed or not. He urged his horse onward through the nearly empty streets, the animal's hooves striking sparks from the cobblestones. Late guests of Khapik, staggering home, scattered out of his way.

The temple's doors were unlocked. Dema seized his mage's kit and rushed in, searching for the altar. There was the statue, three times the height of a normal human being. The altar, and the latest victim, were in front of it.

He approached as he fumbled in his kit for heartbeat powder. He didn't know how long it would take for the priests to arrive, but he had to learn as much from the dead woman as he could. He sprinkled the powder over her, watching as its color shifted to the faintest shade of pink. She had died recently, maybe as little as two hours ago.

Next came the vision powder, sprinkled over each bulging eye. Inside Dema felt shame for treating her this way, for using her as a source of information rather than mourning her. Even a *yaskedasu* deserved better.

The powder revealed only smudges over her eyes. She had not seen her killer. In all likelihood he had come up behind her.

Next he got the bottle of stepsfind, took a mouthful, and sprayed it over the body with a fresh, silent apology. Looking down, he saw the killer's footprints, shadows that led through a side door into an alley.

Three white-clad priests were there, building a circle of protection around the temple. "How did you know?" cried Dema, furious past all common sense. "How did you know about this?"

One of the priests, the one who held their supplies, turned to look at Dema. Behind him his partners, a man and a woman, closed the protective circle and brought it to blazing life, cutting Dema off from the killer's traces. "You walk perilously close to the defilement of all you touch, Demakos Nomasdina," the priest who'd looked at him said, grim-faced. "You would have carried the pollution from the corpse you just saw out into this district, letting the rot spread to innocents. We knew you were capable of it. A watch was placed on you."

"You had me *followed*?" shouted Dema. "By what right? I am a citizen of Tharios, a member of the First Class. I am doing my duty toward the city!"

"Your vision of your duty blinds you to the risk you take, involving yourself with the rotting shell that once housed a spirit," retorted the priest. "Continue as you meant to just now, and you will carry spiritual rot to the houses of the First Class and to the temples and offices that serve them."

The female priest looked at Dema. "If pollution spreads over the First Class, the city is doomed," she said flatly. "It is our purity that saved us while an empire was falling to pieces. It is our cleansing and our vow to stay clean despite temptation that makes us a great power now. And you would destroy that, in your arrogance, in your belief that only Demakos Nomasdina of the *arurim dhaskoi* may speak for one of the Fifth Class. She is before the All-Seeing. He will judge her as well as her killer."

"But her killer spreads his pollution, too," Dema said daringly. "He goes out into the city with death all over him. You say *I* risk polluting the city — what of the killer?"

"The city's priests cleanse Tharios in prayer, fasting, and

meditation," said the priest who had first spoken to Dema. "The killer will only pollute those who encounter him. They are plainly of the Fifth and Fourth classes, with the crimes of their last lives to pay for in this one. He is their penance. It is *you* who are the greater danger. You take this vile taint among those who must keep the city from plunging into chaos."

"You have lost sight of what is vital, imagining that matters of this world are as valuable as those of the spiritual realm," the female priest announced. "You will spend this day and tonight among us, to fast, repent, and be cleansed."

"But there is a killing!" protested Dema. "He could kill again!"

"He is in the All-Seeing's hands," said the third priest, who had been silent until now. "As you are in ours."

Dema clenched his fists, his heart racing with fury. "I have an investigation to run!"

"Others will work on it," the female priest said flatly. "Your superiors and your family are being notified. Tomorrow you may take up your work again."

"*If* you have a more fitting vision of what matters, and what does not," added the third priest. "If you accept your true duty."

Dema turned, to discover more priests behind him. He was trapped. He looked beyond them, to his *arurimi*. "One of you go to Touchstone Glass when you are released from here," he ordered. "Tell Kethlun Warder and Trisana Chandler about this." His sergeant nodded. Dema faced the priests. "If he kills again tonight, it will be on your heads," he snapped.

"If he kills again tonight, he will answer to the All-Seeing," retorted the female priest, "as *we* will answer if we allow you to continue in the path of error."

8

Worn out by his day and the taxing of his power, Keth slept the night through. His dreams were filled with lightning.

When he woke, it was to open shutters, early morning light, and three familiar faces. No, four: Yali balanced the silent Glaki on one hip. The child sucked her thumb, her brown eyes large and steady as she looked at Keth. The women were still dressed and made up from the night before. He winced, started to get out of bed, and remembered just in time he had nothing on. He clutched the sheet to his chest.

"The Ghost got another one," Xantha said, yawning as she leaned against the wall. "She was dead in some Fourth District temple. The gossip is that you magicked something that helped the *arurim* find her."

"I wanted to make something that would help them find the *killer*," growled Keth. "Did they?"

The three *yaskedasi* shook their heads.

"You never said you were a mage." Poppy's tone was accusing, as if she thought Keth had made it a secret on purpose.

"I didn't know," Keth retorted.

"How could you not know you're a mage?" demanded Poppy. "Or are you just a bad one?"

"How could *you* not know Arania pays Lysis twice what she pays you to play Laurel Leaf in *The Creation of the Garden*?" Yali inquired. "Maybe you're just a bad actress."

Poppy glared at her. "She does not. It's Lysis who can't act."

Yali shrugged. "Arania thinks otherwise."

"Bring down your pots!" a man yelled outside. "Bring down your pots!"

Keth looked out the window next to his cot. The *prathmun* who collected night soil was in the courtyard below, waiting for Ferouze's lodgers to dump their chamberpots into the small barrel in his cart.

"He's early," said Xantha, running for the door.

"He's late," argued Poppy. No one in Khapik wanted a full chamberpot in their rooms during the day, when the heat made the smell overpowering.

Yali set Glaki by the door and stooped to fish Keth's chamberpot out from under his bed.

"Yali, I can do it," Keth protested, looking around for his breeches.

"But I'm up and awake." Yali stopped on his threshold,

her brown eyes curious as she gazed at him. "Are you all right? Ferouze says you barely made it upstairs last night."

"I was just tired," Keth replied. "This magic wears me out. We went at it hard yesterday, trying to just make a globe, not even to make whatever was inside visible. And I did one, I don't know how, but then I couldn't make it clear so we could see who this killer is." He rubbed his face, then smiled at Yali. "Did you do well last night?"

"Well enough," Yali answered. "I —"

"Last call for pots!" cried the *prathmun* below.

"I'd better go," said Yali, "before he leaves."

"I'll see you this afternoon," Keth promised.

"If that slave-driver teacher doesn't work you as weak as an overcooked noodle," Yali said drily. With Glaki in tow, she ran to fetch her own chamberpot.

Keth got dressed. "I don't think she can work what isn't there," he muttered. He could feel the power inside him, but the best way he could describe it was "floppy," very like the noodle Yali had mentioned. In his skull he could hear the slight buzz he'd come to associate with his magic, but it was not what it had been the day before.

As he shaved, ate a roll for breakfast, and walked out to Touchstone, he tried to recapture the feeling that had shot through him in that moment when Dema had distracted him — the moment when the globe had produced itself. He'd felt like the strain of forcing it down the length of the blowpipe into the glass had broken free to the thing he'd been wrestling with. Was it a matter of not thinking about his magic? or of not thinking about his craft? He wasn't sure, and he wanted surety. He didn't want any more dead *yaskedasi*.

When he reached Touchstone Glass, the glass shop itself was still closed. Antonou wouldn't open for another hour. Keth decided not to bother the family. He went straight to the workshop. As he rounded the corner into the inner courtyard, he saw an *arurim* sergeant leaning against the well. She had been in command of the squad that had arrested him.

Keth stopped cold. "Whatever it is, I didn't do it," he snapped, wondering if he should yell for Antonou. The *yaskedasi* told plenty of tales of those who'd vanished into *arurimati*, to return so bruised their mothers didn't know them.

Don't be ridiculous, he told himself as the sergeant straightened. If you're being arrested, why is there just one of them?

"Your glass ball cleared around dawn," the sergeant said. "You did do *that*, am I correct?"

Keth swore silently as he felt a blush creep over his face. His blushes always made him feel like an idiot. "Yes," he muttered. He met the sergeant's eyes. "The killer . . . ?" he asked, but she was shaking her head.

"A *yaskedasu*, in the temple of Ngohi. Not long dead, from what *Dhaskoi* Nomasdina could tell. He asked me to tell you that you won't see him today," the sergeant continued. An odd expression crossed her face. She rubbed her nose and explained, "He's, ah, he's been granted the chance to cleanse himself and to rededicate himself to the purity of the city."

Keth blinked at her. "What does that mean, exactly?"

"The priesthood of the All-Seeing took him in charge, to pray and fast for a day and a night," the sergeant explained. "He got a little careless about taking death pollution out into the city proper. He's been warned before."

"You know, you'd catch criminals a lot faster if you just accepted death as part of life," Keth pointed out.

"And what of our souls?" inquired the sergeant. "I for one don't want to come back to another life as one of the Fifth Class, or worse, a *prathmun*. Belonging to the Fourth Class is hard enough." She nodded to Keth. "Good day to you, *Koris* Warder." She walked out of the courtyard.

When Tris arrived an hour later, Keth was catching up on work he'd promised Antonou. Seeing he wasn't ready to do magic, the girl produced a large-toothed comb from her sash and began to groom Little Bear. As she struggled with a particularly stubborn knot, Keth told her about the dead *yaskedasu,* and about Dema.

Tris gaped at him. "These people," she said at last. "I won't understand them if I live for a century. He should be trying to find the one who killed that poor girl, not holed up in some temple."

"The Tharians see it differently," Keth answered, and sighed. "To them it's the pollution that matters. I have to wonder if they'd be so concerned about Dema's wallowing in death if the victims belonged to their precious Assembly." He was putting a crucible of sand and chemicals into the furnace to melt when he realized he'd forgotten to use gloves or tongs. He felt nothing except a gentle warmth against his skin. The crucible placed, he held up his hands and looked at them. The only change was a bit of ash on his knuckles. He blew it off, and noticed that Tris was looking at him. "I didn't know," he commented, then grimaced at the stupid remark.

"There are good things about what's happened to you," she pointed out. "You can admit it, if you like. I promise not to say 'I told you so.'"

"Oh, no," retorted Keth. "You'd just *think* it really loudly." He looked at Chime, who'd perched on top of the furnace. "Aren't you afraid you'll melt?" he asked the dragon.

For answer, Chime curled up, tucked her muzzle under one paw, and appeared to go to sleep.

"I don't know how much work on globes you'll do today," Tris remarked after Keth had worked in silence for a time. Once Little Bear was combed, she had taken out a book and begun to read. "I've been watching. While your power's come back, it's not what you started with yesterday."

"It doesn't seem a rush, since he kills every other day or so, but I still want to try," Keth said, twirling his blowpipe in one hand as he pressed a bowl mold to the molten glass to shape it.

"We'll meditate in a while, then," said Tris, "and try for a globe after midday." She went to the doorway and sniffed the air. "There will be rain tonight."

"We need it," Keth said absently as he set his bowl in the annealing oven.

Other chores caught him up. Tris stayed out of his way, though once she startled him when she sang the words to a song he didn't even know he was humming. "So that one made it all the way to the Pebbled Sea," he remarked.

"Here I thought it made it all the way to Namorn," she retorted.

They didn't get to meditate until after midday. Tris enclosed the workshop within her magical protection — Keth's mage relatives would have ground their teeth to see how easy it was for this girl-child to wrap an entire building with her power — and explained that day's exercise to Keth. He thought it was ludicrous. Whoever heard of stuffing all of one's own magic into a small object?

But she insisted, and he agreed to try. First he selected a crucible for the job. Next he imagined himself pouring all of the light of his power into it, as if magic were sand he meant to heat.

What vexed him was that the exercise turned out to be hard. His power fought his grip, sending out darts and flares like those thrown off by his lightning globes. For each spike that Keth grabbed and stuffed back into the crucible, two more seemed to sprout. By the time Tris called a halt, he was hot, sweaty, irritated, and out of patience. The weather didn't help. The air was stuffy, unmoving and sticky. When he begged Tris to lower her barrier, convinced it made the workshop's air stale, she refused.

Keth sighed and prepared a gather of molten glass, though he doubted he could get a globe from it now. His neck was stiff, his hands sore, and no matter how much water he drank, he was soon thirsty again. Around midafternoon he threw off his shirt and leather apron. The apron only protected his clothes from embers. His body ignored small burns now. He rolled his breeches up above his knees. Tris, as aggravating as ever, had arrived wrapped around with breezes that ruffled through her pale gray cotton gown and white petticoats, leaving her with just a slight dew at her temples and the base of her neck.

"One thing I miss about home," Keth remarked, wiping his dripping forehead on his arm as he prepared to take his gather from the furnace, "it cooled off at night. Of course, the winters are a curse from the gods. I suppose no place is perfect."

"Emelan's much like this," Tris remarked, inspecting one of Keth's glass bowls. "So's Capchen. But we get the sea breezes at night, even in summer. My friends and I go down to the beach during the midday rest period, now and then, and swim. Sometimes we don't mean to get wet, but then Little Bear shakes off on us and we're wet anyway."

Keth grinned. "Our dogs at home do that. My mother and sisters won't go down to the Syth when the dogs are along, because they know they'll get splashed." He set the blowpipe to spinning and concentrated on the feel of his magic, letting it flow down the length of the pipe. A breeze wrapped around his body, cooling his skin. When he looked at Tris, she looked back at him, all innocence.

His efforts to make a new globe came to nothing. His magic simply hadn't come back enough. His third attempt gave off a few sparks of lightning, but they soon faded.

"Enough," Tris said when he would have tried again. "Go home, rest. You can't work with nothing."

Keth scowled at her. "I don't want to hear the 'sometimes you have to know when to halt' speech again," he informed her.

"Then don't make me give it," she retorted. "Have you got a globe's worth of magic in you?"

Keth hung his head. Complain about it though he had, the morning's crucible exercise had shown him how to measure the extent of his power.

"Go home," Tris ordered. "Relax. Visit a bathhouse. Something. I know it's maddening, if that helps."

"Do you?" he asked suddenly, wanting to know. "It doesn't seem like you're ever at a standstill."

She stared at him for a moment, then glared, propping her fists on her hips. "The hardest lesson any of us must learn is there's only so much we can do," she informed him, her voice lemon-tart. "We run into it headfirst all the time, knowing what we can do, what we can't, how much we can do. We think of magic as this promise that we will fix anything that comes our way, Keth. We can't. Power's just a tool some of us can use." Her mouth curled wryly. "Now look. You went and made me give a speech. Go home and rest. There's always later." She gathered up her belongings, the dragon, and the dog, and left the workshop.

Keth stood there, frowning. Even if he couldn't produce another globe, he'd have thought she would try another exercise, rather than go. Perhaps she had a project of her own waiting back at Jumshida's.

But now that she had mentioned it, a bathhouse sounded like a wonderful idea. Once he cleaned up the shop and took the finished work to Antonou, Keth headed for the bathhouse he used in Khapik. The steam in the hot bath was unbearable after the heat and damp outside. Keth stayed only long enough to scrub and rinse before he waddled down to the cold bath pools. There he soaked and dozed, comfortable at last.

After she left Kethlun, Tris idled the rest of her afternoon away, exploring Khapik by daylight. There were no lights on the streams, no entertainers at most of the corners. The gates to the courtyard houses were closed. Some shops were open, as were some of the lesser eating-houses. Tris took a light supper at one of these, seated on a stream bank. The help was in no hurry to shoo her away, so she read a book of glass magic as she waited for time to pass.

Now and then she sniffed the air. Her storm was coming on fast, turning the sky greenish gray as it advanced. The little hairs on Tris's arms and at the back of her neck stirred. Her big lightning braids quivered against her hairpins. It was far too long since the last rain, the city's earth complained to her. The very stones knew a downpour was coming. They welcomed it; the water in the streams of Khapik shivered with its approach.

At last Tris left her table and walked into the maze of the district, asking shopkeepers for directions to Chamberpot Alley. It was one of the twisty back streets close to the shadow of the Khapik wall, in an area where the locals dwelled and shady business was done. When she asked the *yaskedasi* for directions to Ferouze's, they gave her and Little Bear strange looks, then reluctantly showed her the way. Tris, they made it clear, was not at all the sort of person they were used to seeing. Chime at least was spared the looks. She was tucked away in her sling on Tris's back.

Ferouze's lodging-house was stucco over crushed stone, three stories high. The street windows were small and barred; the wooden gate that led to the courtyard was open. Tris hesitated by the door inside the courtyard passage, wondering if she ought to knock and ask for Keth, but then she heard voices. Following them seemed more appealing than knocking on an unknown, very dirty, door. She walked out into the open air.

At the heart of the courtyard was a well, one that had been in use so long that the broad stones that formed its rim — and provided a place to sit — dipped at the center from generations of use. Three *yaskedasi* sat there, watching a dark-haired child as she played with a pair of dolls. Tris recognized two of them, Keth's friend Yali and the tumbler Xantha. The third, a curvaceous brunette with a lush mouth and green hazel eyes, was someone Tris hadn't seen.

The child saw Tris first. She gasped, stretched out her arms and cried, "Doggie!"

Little Bear looked at Tris. "Go," she said, "be careful." One of the hardest things to teach Little Bear was that "be careful" meant he was to approach, then hold still. He trotted over to the child, wagging his tail and panting cheerfully. With no qualms at all the girl stood and wrapped her arms around the dog's neck.

The curvy brunette looked at Tris and grimaced. "Who let *Koria* Respectability in?" she asked, getting to her feet. "Isn't anyplace safe from that sort?"

"Leave her alone, Poppy," Yali said with a sigh. "She's a friend of Keth's."

"Well, he's not here," said Poppy. "He's off studying magic somewhere."

"Actually, he isn't," Tris said mildly. "He finished a couple of hours ago. I hoped he'd be home by now."

"You can wait, if you like," Yali said. "He usually comes home before we leave for work."

Tris looked up at the sky. High clouds scudded overhead, the leading edge of her storm. "*Will* you work? There's rain coming," she told them.

Poppy scowled. "How do *you* know?"

Tris shrugged. "It's what I do."

Poppy and Xantha traded glances. "Grab what trade we can, then," Xantha said. She and Poppy raced upstairs.

Tris looked at Yali. "I don't understand," she said hesitantly. "What's the rush?"

"We're street *yaskedasi,* not house ones," Yali replied, watching the little girl pet the dog. "We lose money on rainy nights. Even if it only rains for a short time, guests are afraid it will start again, so they find other things to do."

"I'm sorry," Tris apologized. "But the city really needs the water. The wells are down everywhere, and the gardens are drying up." She nodded toward a small patch of green: Ferouze's herbs and vegetables hung limp.

Yali blinked at her. "Why are *you* sorry?"

Tris opened her mouth to reply, and thought better of it. Confessing that she would cause the *yaskedasi* to lose a night's income seemed like a bad idea.

"Never mind. May I sit?" she asked Yali.

The woman nodded. "Glaki, don't pull the dog's ears," she warned. "He won't like it."

"Sorry, doggie," the child said. She looked at Tris. "What's his name?"

"Little Bear," Tris replied, easing Chime's sling into her lap.

This made Glaki chuckle. "He's not a bear!"

"He's big enough to be one," Yali remarked drily.

"Is she yours?" Tris asked Yali as she let Chime climb out of her sling. When the glass dragon unfurled her wings, the child gasped in awe.

"What?" asked Yali as Chime flew over to land on Little Bear's back. "Glaki, mine? No. She was Iralima's." She lowered her voice so Glaki wouldn't hear. "Our friend who was murdered."

Tris watched Glaki run a careful hand over the edge of Chime's left wing. Chime sang a low, soft note, stretching out her long neck to look directly into the little girl's face.

"What will happen to her?" Tris wanted to know. "Her father —?"

Yali shook her head. "As far as we know, Iralima was alone in the world. No family — if she had a man, she never mentioned it."

Tris frowned. For ten years her relatives had hammered into her mind how their generosity saved her from the fate that waited for a little girl cast onto the street. They had included details about just what that fate might be. "She has no one?"

Yali shrugged. "She's got us. We're keeping her — I am, mostly. Poppy and Xantha mean well, but they tend to get caught up in things. They forget that children must eat and go to bed at regular hours. But they chip in, and the men do, so there's coin enough to provide."

"And when you work?" Tris asked.

"Ferouze or Keth watches her," Yali smiled. "Keth's cheaper — I have to pay Ferouze to do it. But at least she hasn't kicked Glaki out, or me for keeping her." Yali propped her chin on her hands. "I can't believe that Keth made that dragon without knowing about his magic."

"It was a mad occurrence," replied Tris. "The kind that doesn't happen often. He accidentally called a lot of stray magics while he tried to make the glass do what he wanted. With those and his own power mixing, he got Chime."

"And then he tried to break her, he told me," Yali commented, and shook her head. "Men. They're so excitable. Usually over things they can't help."

"I can't exactly blame him for being upset," Tris said. "From what he's said, Chime was the first real clue to what had changed in him since he got hit by lightning. My experience is that adults don't like surprises."

"Oh, it is?" Yali asked, chuckling. "And you with *vast* experience, I take it?"

Tris smiled. She liked this woman. It also couldn't hurt Keth if Yali understood a bit more about his new life. "Vast enough. Our kind of magic — Keth's, mine, what my brother and sisters have — it's tricky until you get to know it. And it's different for everyone, because we're all different inside. It helps if you're younger when you start. You're more used to being surprised as a kid."

"But Keth's going to be all right now?" asked Yali, worried. "He was so haunted when he first came here."

"With a bit of work, he'll be all right," Tris assured the woman. "Right now he's still getting used to the idea that he's a mage."

Chime took off, gliding here and there as Glaki and Little Bear chased her around the courtyard. Glaki was laughing so hard she nearly tripped. Both Tris and Yali started to their feet, then sat again as Chime turned to land on the little girl's shoulder. Glaki carried the dragon over to them.

"Yes, she's very pretty," Yali told the child as she held Chime up for her to inspect. She glanced at Tris. "So yours is with the weather?"

Tris grinned. "The rain prediction gave me away, I take it."

"Well, Keth said. And that's how you became his teacher, because he's got lightning." Yali sighed. "Let's hope he doesn't try to work with it here, or Ferouze will pitch a fit. She doesn't even like it if we hang curtains at the windows." She stared into the distance for a moment, then asked shyly. "Is there anything magic *you* could do? Just a little thing? I love magic."

Tris hesitated, then pointed to a dusty patch of courtyard and twirled a finger. The dust began to rise and spin, until she had a miniature cyclone no bigger than her hand. Moving her index finger, she guided the cyclone through the dust, until she had written Yali's name in the packed earth at their feet.

The *yaskedasu* laughed and clapped her hands, then looked at the gateway to the street. "And here's Keth, before I impose on you anymore. Thank you so much!"

"You're welcome," Tris said, ushering the cyclone over toward Glaki. Little Bear backed away, growling — he didn't care for Tris's displays. Chime showed no interest whatsoever. Glaki waited until the cyclone was within reach, then set her palm on it and pressed the cyclone flat against the ground. When she raised her hand, it was gone.

Keth walked over to them with a smile for Yali and a frown for Tris. "What are you doing here? Shouldn't you be home?"

"I have to change," Yali said, getting to her feet.

"But the rain," Tris protested.

"There are covered walkways where I can sing," Yali told her. "And Glaki needs shoes for winter. Ferouze says she'll watch her," she added, looking at Keth. "Make sure she feeds her more than dates and stale cheese. I paid her five *biks.*"

"I'll keep an eye on Ferouze," Keth promised. When Yali passed him, he stopped her with a hand on her arm. "Be watchful," he told her, blue eyes serious. "Stay off of Falsedice Way, even if you do get customers that pay well there. It's too far back from the traveled streets."

"I've been taking care of myself for years," replied Yali. She kissed him on the cheek. "But you're sweet to worry."

Tris pretended not to watch this exchange. Instead she showed Glaki the spot behind the dog's ears where he most liked to be scratched. Only when Yali had vanished into her upstairs room and Keth had turned to Tris did she say, "Perhaps I should have mentioned your lessons aren't done for today."

Xantha and Poppy ran down the steps, both in their gaudiest clothes, Poppy carrying a cape painted with peacock feathers. They waved good-bye to Keth and blew kisses to Glaki, who blew them back. For Tris, Poppy had a scowl. Xantha only fluttered her fingers in a wave and called, "So long, *Koria* Respectability."

Tris watched them run out to the street. "She says that like it's an insult," she commented.

"From her, it is. What lessons haven't we done?" demanded Keth.

Tris looked up at the sky. "I thought we might talk about lightning a bit."

Keth, too, looked up. The clouds were lower, fatter, and the dark gray of thunderheads.

"Oh, no," said Keth, turning pale. "Oh, no. No, no, no, no."

"No?" asked Glaki.

"Suppertime," Keth told her. He gently removed Chime from the girl's fingers, setting the dragon on the lip of the well. Then he swung Glaki up onto his shoulders as the child whooped with glee. To Tris he said again, "No." To Glaki he said, "Let's see Aunt Ferouze and find out what's for supper." He trotted Glaki to the door in the passageway to the street. Opening it, he called, "Ferouze, I've got Glaki." He looked at Tris, repeated, *"No,"* and disappeared inside.

B{y} the time Keth left Ferouze, the sky was covered with heavy masses of fast-moving gray clouds. He had delayed going to his room as long as he could, first by helping the old woman to feed Glaki, then by telling the girl a story until she fell asleep. Only after that did he gather his courage and go out into the courtyard. There was no sign of Tris, Little Bear, or Chime. Keth knew he should be relieved that she was gone; instead he was puzzled. He was starting to get some idea of what she was like. She wasn't the sort to just go away.

He was also dissatisfied with himself. Why hadn't she made him face the storm? He thrust that idea clean out of his mind. It was just another of the bits of folly that had entered his thoughts after he'd been struck by lightning. Instead he told himself that Tris had finally seen it was futile to argue with him.

With another wary look at the sky, Keth climbed the stair. It would pour at any time. Probably Tris had returned to Jumshida's to dance in it, or something. He hoped that the *yaskedasi* had found indoor work. This storm felt like a big one.

He slid his key into the lock on his door, and turned it. The door locked. Frowning, Keth turned the key in the opposite direction. The door opened. He didn't like that. Had he left the room unlocked all day? Yali would never steal from him, but he didn't trust Poppy or the male *yaskedasi* who lived at Ferouze's. How could he be so stupid as to forget to lock up?

When he entered the room he found that he'd also left the shutters open. He swore: if it had rained in the day, his sketches for designs would have gotten soaked. Then he registered movement beside his door. It was the dog. Tris sat on his stool. A flash at the corner of his other eye drew his gaze to Chime who sat atop the pile of his sketches.

"You found it open and you just walked in?" he demanded. Somehow he was not as surprised to find her there as he should have been.

"No," said Tris, smoothing her skirts. "My breezes found the one with your magic in it, and I picked the lock." She held up a pair of hairpins.

Whatever he had expected her to say, that was not it. "*You* picked a lock."

Tris tucked the pins back into her braids. "Briar taught me. He said I had a gift for locks. It's high praise, coming from him. Not that your lock was much of a challenge."

Little Bear came over, wagging his tail. Keth scratched his ears. "Hello, Bear. Good boy." To Tris, in a less affectionate tone, he said, "You let yourself in, let yourself out."

"No," she replied as a gust rammed through the open window. "Come on. We're going up to the roof." Chime gave off a high, singing note that rose and fell as sparks popped in her eyes.

Keth shivered. He could smell rain on the wind. "I told you, no. Just because there's a storm coming doesn't mean I'm going to play in it."

Tris removed her spectacles and rubbed her nose. "Keth, I'm not asking you to play." Her voice was surprisingly gentle and reasonable. "But I need to show you something."

"I don't need to be shown anything." Keth folded his arms over his chest. He hoped she couldn't see that he was shaking. "Not in a storm, anyway."

"But you do." This time her voice was even gentler; that same kindness was in her level gray eyes. Now she scared him. She wasn't kind. "Keth, as long as you fear lightning, you'll fear your power. It doesn't have to be that way. You're not the same fellow who got struck beside the Syth. I can prove it to you."

He shook his head stubbornly, though he couldn't have said what he was denying or refusing. Outside, the tiniest growl of thunder rolled through the greenish air. His skin rippled with gooseflesh.

Tris took a deep breath and tried again. "So, you'll learn

magic, but only to the point where it starts to scare you. Is that it? How far will that get you? Magic doesn't respond to orders like 'this far and no further.' The more you do, the better you get, so the more power you have. If you don't keep ahead of it — if you don't learn how to release it safely — it will find its own ways to come out. You *really* don't want that to happen."

Keth shook his head again, his heart thudding in his chest. What she said had the unpleasant feel of truth. For all her fiery temperament, she wasn't the dramatic sort who liked to exaggerate. She was irritating, but she was also forthright. And when she spoke of magic, somehow the things she said carried more weight than the pronouncements of his mage uncles. She was fourteen and difficult, but when it came to magic, she seemed as much a master of her craft as Niko or Jumshida, and even more than Dema.

Tris went to the window, turning her face up to the blast of the rising wind. The two thin braids she wore loose on either side of her head fluttered wildly.

Chime flew over to hover in front of Keth as she made a chinking sound. Once she got his attention, she flew to the door and back, as if in invitation. She wanted Keth to go outside.

Tris faced him, the wind turning her braids as they reached toward Keth like yearning hands. Quietly she said, "I don't believe lightning has the power to hurt you anymore. I think it would recognize you as a kindred spirit. But in case I'm wrong, and I suppose I could be, *I can protect you from it*. I can keep it off of you. But Keth, for that to happen, you have to trust me."

For a long moment he said nothing, his mind in an uproar. It did come to trust, didn't it? She was his teacher. Until now she'd been a good one. "You threw lightning at me," he reminded her. "That hurt."

"Because you'd put all of yours into Chime." Quick as a flash her hand whipped forward. A thin stream of lightning — where had she gotten it with her braids all done up? — shot between them to strike Keth's crossed arms. His muscles twitched, then stilled. Nothing else happened.

"You did it again!" he yelled, outraged.

"That's right." Her eyes were cold and steady. "Just a bit I yanked from the air, with the storm almost on us. Did it hurt?"

"That's *beside* the point!" he cried. "You threw —"

"Did it hurt?" she interrupted, steely-voiced.

Keth struggled, trying to think of something cutting to say. Finally he snapped, "You tell me trust you, then you throw lightning at me."

It was her turn to cross her arms over her chest. "Show some sense, Keth. How else am I going to get you to listen to me, if you won't take my word for it?"

Suddenly the wind went out of his sails. She was right.

She was right, and he, a grown man, was wrong. "You won't let it hurt me?" His voice emerged far smaller, and far more trembly, than he liked. "You said you'd protect me."

"I will."

Keth sighed and wiped his sweaty face with a hand that shook. "Let's go, then."

They climbed to the third floor gallery, then up to the roof. Ferouze had already taken the wash down from the lines strung up here, leaving a few buckets and a rough bench to endure the storm.

Keth looked up. Rough black clouds billowed overhead. The wind rose, whistling through the streets and over the rooftops. In a lodging-house across the way someone had not closed his shutters completely: they slammed in the wind until one ripped free of its hinges. The air had taken on the green hue of olive oil. Thunder rolled in the distance. Keth shivered, and huddled in a corner of the rooftop wall, Little Bear on his left, Chime tucked securely in his lap. He had thought he would be safe in this low part of Tharios that would not draw lightning. That no longer mattered with Tris here. With Tris for company, no place was safe.

I'll protect you, she had said. Now he had to learn, did he need protection?

Tris stood at the center of the roof, idly removing hairpins, releasing some braids. They hung below her shoulders, flapping and popping in the wind.

Lightning flashed. Keth waited, counting silently to himself. At thirty he heard the roll of thunder. The storm was ten miles away — plenty of time to scramble downstairs, except that now he couldn't bring himself to move.

Lightning again. Keth resumed his count, ending when thunder boomed at twenty. Six miles. The storm moved fast. Another flash and another. Thunder made the stones under him shiver. He hoped Glaki wasn't frightened. He couldn't remember if Ira had ever said if her child was afraid of storms. Keth had never been afraid, one of the reasons he was stupid enough to be caught in the open when the Syth blew up a surprise.

Lightning jabbed down near the Piraki Gate. Thunder blasted through the narrow canyons made by the buildings.

Here came another bolt, three-pronged, thunder on its heels. It struck Tris squarely, all three prongs twining around her. She held up her arms; she *laughed* as the bolt clung to her without vanishing, a white hot ladder to the clouds. Several of her braids exploded from their ties, the hair in them wrapping around the lightning that secured her to the sky. Oddly enough, the rest of her hair stayed where it was, unbudging, locked in place with pins. Keth's rescuers told him that his hair had been standing straight up when he was found. Why did some of Tris's hair move, but not the rest?

It was her mage's kit. Suddenly he *believed* that she held other forces ready for use in her many braids. She had not been joking when she had described the range of her power. Niko had said nothing that day, not because he liked the joke Tris had played on Keth, but because she told the literal truth.

I'm dead, he thought helplessly. And all thanks to a cross-grained fourteen-year-old.

Chime's claws bit into Keth's breeches, forcing him to yelp and straighten his legs. Free of the bowl of his lap and arms, the glass dragon took flight, swooping and soaring around the trapped branch of lightning that still clung to Tris.

Keth stared. Inside Chime he saw a skeleton of silver. Around it twined veins that flickered and rippled like lightning.

Little Bear had seen enough. The big dog scrambled to the door and into the house, tail between his legs.

The bolt that held Tris shrank. It wasn't dying, Keth realized. It was soaking into the hair that his young teacher had freed of its pins. It grew thinner and thinner, until it was gone. The braids that had absorbed it shimmered.

An immense fist pounded Keth on the head. He fell to his knees, staring at his hands. They blazed — *he* blazed — with lightning. He groped his scalp, and found something stronger and far hotter than the power in the globe he'd made for Dema. A bolt of lightning had struck his head, in the same place the last bolt had struck. His brain fizzed, his eyes filled with a glory of white fire that trickled down his throat, into his belly, through his arms and legs. In that splendid moment Keth saw that all things had some lightning in them. Physical matter did not reject lightning; it was simply overwhelmed by it, as a teardrop was overwhelmed by the ocean. Lightning struck objects because it was drawn to the ghost of itself within them.

Except there was no ghost of lightning inside Keth: he had the true thing. He drank the power in like a thirsty man drinks water and, like Tris, raised his arms to call even more to him.

Later, as they staggered down into the house, he found the voice to croak, "You promised you'd protect me."

"I did," she replied, her voice as rough as his. "I saw that your power was calling to the lightning, and I made sure that you weren't hit by so much you'd panic."

"You made me think you'd —" he began.

She interrupted him. "What? Wrap you in a cocoon of magic? In a nice safe blanket? I would have done so, had there been the need. There wasn't. It's my job to know these things, remember? I wasn't about to lose my very first student because he didn't have the sense to come in out of the rain."

They had reached Keth's door before he'd summoned the energy to say, "You are a wicked girl."

Tris shrugged. "So I've been told. I've learned to live with the shame of it." She looked at Little Bear, who huddled by Keth's door. "Come on, Bear. Lightning's done." She turned her sharp gaze on Keth. "Answer me truly — have I done you a disservice?"

It was his turn to shrug. He hung his head for good measure. "You know you didn't."

"*I* knew. I wanted to make certain that *you* did, too." Before Keth could jerk away, Tris stood on tiptoe to kiss his cheek. A spark jumped between them. They both grinned. "If you have any leaks, put a big pot under them," she warned. "It'll rain all tonight and all tomorrow. Not my doing — this storm built up a lot of power while it was stuck in the east, and coming this way has made it stronger. I hope you've got a hat to wear to the shop tomorrow."

Though he wasn't sure if he would like the answer, Keth heard himself ask, "How do you know so much about it?"

Tris grinned, waved, and left him without a reply. Chime, riding on her shoulder, flapped her glass wings in farewell.

The rain continued to fall as it had fallen all night, steadily, without letup. Tris was glad for it. She felt like parched ground in the first showers of spring, greedily drinking up the moisture in the air.

Rain washed Tharios. Gutters ran clean on both sides of the Street of Glass, their burdens of trash swept away the night before. The white stucco of the houses and storefronts blazed; the orange-colored roof tiles shone. It was all scrubbed clean, right down to the soaked and sullen *prathmuni*. They were almost the only people in sight as they went about their endless chores. Those Tharians of the other classes who walked abroad did so in oiled straw hats and capes, or with oiled silk umbrellas over their heads. Tris simply ushered the rain away from herself, Little Bear, and Chime. She'd had her fill of rain the night before, and the heat of Keth's workshop would make a wet dress unbearable. Let the passersby stare at her and her dog, shedding drops as if a glass bowl lay over them. It was time they learned that they did not control all the wonder in the universe.

Keth was hard at work by the time she reached the shop. "Did you sleep at all?" Tris asked, seeing the lightning's power blaze through his skin.

"A little," he said, "but I had an idea, and I wanted to test it." He grinned. "Close your eyes," he ordered. "I've got something for you."

"It had better not be slimy," Tris warned as she obeyed.

"Spoken like a girl with a brother," Keth said, moving behind her. "Even in Khapik I'd have to look hard for anything slimy." Something light fell around Tris's neck as Chime crooned.

Tris opened her eyes and looked down. On a black silk cord around her neck dangled a bright red flamelike piece of glass, its tail twisted to provide a loop for the cord. On either side of it hung two smaller, blue glass flames. "Keth, this is beautiful," she whispered. "How did you make it?"

"Actually, Chime did most of the work," replied Keth, standing back so he could see the full effect of the necklace. "I found these on my sketches when I woke up this morning. She leaves them everywhere she goes, practically. I guess because she eats the ingredients that make and color glass."

Tris nodded.

"Well," continued Keth, "I got to thinking that we could sell them as novelties, to pay Antonou for supplies and to buy more food for Chime. The hardest part was actually heating the tails to bend them for the loop. Whatever's in those, it resists fire." He poured a handful of glass flames, all with looped tails, into her hands. "I kept some for the girls at Ferouze's," he confessed. "I didn't think you'd mind."

Tris frowned. "You aren't thinking of taking Chime back, are you?"

Keth shook his head. "I gave up my responsibility to her. Besides, I think she belongs with you."

Chime underscored Keth's words by twining around Tris's neck.

"I love you, too, Chime," mumbled Tris, her cheeks crimson. "Thank you, Keth. It's a wonderful idea." She patted her necklace, then looked at him. "Ready to meditate?"

Meditation that day was easier than it had ever been, particularly the exercise in which Keth placed his magic into a crucible. It was as if the night's lightning had cleared his mind of fear and increased his strength. Tris watched as he treated the lightning in him just as he did glass, with a friendly but firm hand. Today he gripped the power just hard enough to control it, but not so hard that it erupted through the weak places in his concentration. On his fourth try he managed to pack it all into the image he held in his mind of a crucible: Tris could see its shape as it folded in on itself, reduced to a blazing, fist-sized sun. He was so giddy with his success that he repeated the exercise two more times, just because he could.

"We'll stop for midday," Tris said, gathering in the magic she had used for her circle of protection. "Then let's try for another globe."

"That's what I hoped to do," Keth replied. "I might be more successful, now that I have some idea of how my power works —"

"Tris. Keth." Dema stood in the doorway, wearing a rain hat and cape. He looked harried, and he would not meet their eyes. "The Ghost struck last night — another girl from Keth's lodgings. I need you to identify her," he explained, tight-lipped. "I've got horses. Can the dog keep up?"

Keth turned white and rushed from the shop. Tris followed, throwing her rain shield over all of them. In silence they mounted the horses Dema had brought, Chime riding on Tris's shoulders.

Dema led the way to Elya Street, past the *arurimat*, and onto Noskemiou Way.

Tris kneed her horse even with Dema's. "Where?" she asked. "Where was she? Back in Khapik?"

"No," Dema said tersely. "She was at the foot of the last emperor's statue in Achaya Square. They didn't tell me until she was taken to Noskemiou Thanas, so I wouldn't risk pollution by getting too near the body." His mouth tightened into a grim line. "They won't try *that* little trick again."

They rode on to Noskemiou Way, where the great hospital lay directly across the Piraki Gate from Khapik. Tris gasped when she saw the sprawl of buildings, larger than any of Winding Circle's infirmaries or Summersea's hospitals. Four stories high, white stucco over brick, Noskemiou was laid out like a series of ladders. Between the wings that were the ladders' rungs lay courtyard gardens where the healers grew herbs for their medicines.

Dema led them past the wings, each with a sign that named it as a House in Tharian, Kurchali, and Tradertalk, the main languages spoken here. They rode by Children's House, Mothers' House, Elders' House, Poverty House. Beyond them the blazing white stucco was painted black. This part of the hospital had no windows, only a few doors, and no signs at all. An *arurim* stood in front of one of its small doors.

Dema rode up to him and dismounted. "The *arurim* will mind the horses," he said curtly. "It would be better if the dog remained, too."

"Little Bear, stay," ordered Tris as she slid out of the saddle. "What is this place, anyway?" she asked.

"Noskemiou Thanas," Keth said, his voice more crackly than usual. "The House of the Dead."

They followed Dema into the building. Magical signs of preservation, cold, and permanence shone in Tris's vision from the walls and floors. The people who walked here were civilians — who quarreled, wept, or bore their losses silently — or they were those who worked here, silent *prathmuni* dressed in black tunics or *kytens*.

Dema led them to a door that bore a brass number five and opened it, motioning for Tris and Keth to go in. Two black-robed *prathmuni*, at work there, turned toward them. "Number eighteen," ordered Dema. They led him, Tris, and Keth to a covered form on a wooden table.

Tris clenched her hands until her ragged nails bit her palms. She hated the sight of dead people: they looked sad, alone, abandoned. Though she had seen a great many dead since her career as a mage began, they still made her flesh creep.

The *prathmuni* drew the cover away from the dead woman's face.

Tris bit her lip. The woman had been strangled. Under the mud splatters of last night's storm the weapon showed yellow at her throat: the head veil of a *yaskedasu*. While she and Kethlun had reveled in lightning, rain, and cool air, the Ghost had struck. His way of killing had changed the woman's face enough that her own family might not recognize her, but Tris knew the lavender scent, the soggy brown curls, and the embroidery on the dead woman's *kyten.*

Keth was not as slow as Tris to recognize the victim. He dropped to his knees, burying his face in his hands.

"Oh, Yali," Tris murmured, her lips trembling. She closed the dead woman's staring eyes with one hand. From her sash she brought out a pair of coppers and used them to weight Yali's eyelids, so that the soul could not return to its old home, which had begun to decay. Chime crept onto Yali's body, making the screeching of metal on glass sound that was her distress cry.

Now the *prathmuni,* who had seen people behave as Tris and Keth did a thousand times, showed emotion. Chime caused them to step away nervously as they sketched the circle of the All-Seeing on their foreheads.

Tris put a hand on Keth's shoulder, then offered him her handkerchief. He ignored it, though tears dripped to the floor through his fingers. Tris looked around: where had Dema gone?

She found him in the hall, talking to an *arurim.* "I don't care what it takes in bribes to the secretaries, I'm good for it," he said fiercely, his dark eyes ablaze. "I want to talk to the Keepers of the Public Good *today.*"

"But, *dhaskoi,* what can they do?" inquired the *arurim.* "They aren't equipped to investigate criminals!"

"They can shut down Khapik!" snapped Dema. "Close it down until we find the rotted polluting Ghost! So get moving. Lay those bribes on as thick as you can. Stop by Nomasdina Hall and get chits from my mother for it, but I need the Keepers' attention *now*."

There was sufficient iron in Dema's voice; the *arurim* left at a trot. Before he could open the door to the outside, a man and a woman in the white robes of priests emerged from a room next to the door. The *arurim* halted and raised his arms as the man surrounded him with incense smoke from a censer, and the woman rattled off the prayers for cleansing. Tris gritted her teeth. They all would have to undergo this nonsense when they tried to leave.

Dema turned to her. "What?" he demanded.

Tris shook her thoughts about cleansing. "That was badly done, in there," she said, pointing to the room where Yali lay. "Springing it on us like that. You could have warned us."

"I didn't know," Dema retorted. "Wouldn't it be just as cruel for me to say I think it's a woman I've only seen for thirty minutes in my life, and have it turn out not to be so? There are two other *yaskedasi* at Ferouze's, remember. And I have other things on my mind."

Tris folded her arms over her chest. "Such as?"

"We have to shut down Khapik, forbid the *yaskedasi* to work. We need to put extra *arurimi* on this, as many as can be spared. I don't want any more dead women. They *have* to listen to me this time," Dema insisted, trembling with urgency. "He's moving closer to Assembly Square. He's taunting us — it can't be allowed to go on, and it won't!"

"Well, while you're enraged over being taunted, Keth just lost somebody he cared for," Tris said coldly. "I wish you had thought better, Dema."

He took a step back, startled to be addressed in that tone. "I'm trying to save lives, in case you hadn't noticed."

"So in your rush to save lives you don't care if you shatter one or two? And they tell me *I'm* not kind," Tris said flatly. "Her name is Yali. She was a friend of Iralima, and she was taking care of Iralima's daughter."

"You don't understand," Dema said wearily, rubbing his forehead.

"I don't want to," Tris replied.

The door to the room where Yali lay opened. Keth emerged. His eyes were red and puffy with weeping. Chime stood on his shoulder, steadying herself by gripping his hair in her forepaws. She looked at Dema and hissed, spraying him with tiny glass pellets.

"I agree," Tris said, glaring at Dema.

Keth ignored her. To Dema he said harshly, "You have to close Khapik. Before he kills anyone else. How does he come and go unseen, even in Achaya Square? I know the *arurimi* patrol up there."

"I'm going to see the Keepers of the Public Good today, to petition them to shut down Khapik," replied Dema, leaning against the wall. He looked exhausted. "As for how . . ." He grimaced. "There are service and sewage tunnels throughout the city."

"Wonderful," Keth said sarcastically. "Let me guess. Nobody wants to see the *prathmuni* and servants at work."

Dema nodded. "This city is a giant sieve. It *can't* be guarded well, though I'll bet the Assembly authorizes the money for more guards. They'll have to pay a lot to get them into the sewers, and they'll have to have priests to cleanse them, or no one will do it. Even the *arurim prathmuni* refuse sewer duty." His voice, cracking with exhaustion, softened. "Keth, I'm sorry. My mind was going in six different directions. . . . You were close."

Keth nodded. "I have to go home," he said. "I want them hearing it from me."

"Did she work last night?" asked Dema.

"Yes," Tris replied softly.

"You know how it is for the street *yaskedasi*," explained Keth. "If they don't work, they don't eat, they risk losing their lodgings. . . . And Yali was clever. She wouldn't take risks." He looked at Tris. "I can't go back to Touchstone —"

She shook her head. "I'll go to Ferouze's with you," she said, thinking, Maybe I can do him some good.

After a moment's hesitation, Keth nodded.

"Let's get cleansed, then," said Dema, leading them to the priests. "Keth, take our horses. Just have someone return them to Elya Street."

Tris endured it as the priests worked their cleansing with incense and prayers, her mind racing furiously. As they mounted their horses, she asked Dema, "Do you think your Keepers will listen?"

"They must." Dema gathered the reins and urged his horse to a trot down Noskemiou Way.

Dema

As Dema trotted through Achaya Square, he saw that the priests of the All-Seeing had already erected cloth barriers around the defiled statue until it and its surroundings could be purified. They turned to watch him pass. Seeing their eyes on him, Dema remembered his own, slow process of cleansing at their hands — a day and a night stolen from his hunt for the Ghost! — and the priests' complete lack of interest in the methods needed to trace a murderer. What if the Keepers of the Public Good ignored his arguments? When all was said and done he was still an *arurim dhaskoi* of less than a year's standing, without enough service to Tharios to give weight to his words. He must not waste a trip to Balance Hill or worse yet, waste the clan's bribe money. In theory the Keepers were duty bound to hear any Tharian, but there was a great deal of difference between the ear of the Keepers when they were awake, and that of vexed, half-asleep Keepers. There was also a difference between the Keepers and their obligations, and the interests of those who served the Keepers.

It was the sight of Phakomathen, stabbing into the gray mists of rain, that gave Dema an idea. The Keepers would *have* to listen to him if he came with support from Heskalifos, particularly those mages who attended the conference on visionary magics. He turned his mount aside, and rode to the university.

He arrived at the conference hall shortly before the midday break. He waited outside until the doors opened and mages of all races and nationalities spilled out, then strode through them into the hall. The morning's speakers were still on the dais, talking to one another and collecting their notes. One of them was Jumshida Dawnspeaker; another was Tris's teacher, Niklaren Goldeye.

Jumshida smiled when she noticed him. "*Dhaskoi* Nomasdina, is it not?" she asked, her rich voice friendly. "Have you come to join us?"

"Actually, no," he said, nervous. "I've come to beg you for help. The Ghost killed another *yaskedasu* last night — another woman who lives in the same house as Kethlun Warder." Jumshida drew the circle of the All-Seeing on her forehead. Dema continued, "I'm on my way to Balance Hill to speak to the Keepers. It was my hope that you would lend me your support."

Was it his imagination, or did she stiffen?

"I fail to see what use I might be to the *arurim*," Jumshida said.

"You underestimate the honor you have in the city," Dema replied. "You are First Scholar of Mages' Hall, Second Scholar of Heskalifos. You are responsible for bringing together the greatest vision mages of our time, to produce a work that will define vision magic for centuries." Children of the First Class also learned the art of flattery. One of their maxims was that bees went to sweet-smelling flowers, not earth-smelling mushrooms. "How would the Keepers not value anything you have to say?"

Everyone but Goldeye left discreetly, watching Jumshida from the corners of their eyes. "What, exactly, do you wish them to value from me?" asked Jumshida, smoothing the folds of her mage's stole.

"That Khapik must close until this monster is caught," replied Dema. He took a breath. "And that cleansing the site of a murder must wait until the *arurim* can trace every influence present."

"Very sensible," Goldeye said tartly. "I can't believe this hasn't been raised before."

"Why should the Keepers listen to any thoughts I might have on Khapik?" asked Jumshida. "Have you considered the serious hardship a closing would place on the shopkeepers and the *yaskedasi*? They exist day by day on their earnings. As for the other . . ." She looked at Goldeye. "You don't understand, Niko. Killing destroyed the Kurchali emperors, with their mass executions and their gladiators fighting to the death on sacred days. Why else would the blood plague have begun here, where people bled to death through the very pores of their skins? It was a thousand years ago for you of the north, but it took *us* three centuries to recover from the disorder of those times." She turned a stern face to Dema. "You are a Tharian, Demakos Nomasdina. You already know these things. It was the cleansing, and the banishment of pollution through death, which saved us from the chaos that followed the emperors."

"But it hurts us now," argued Dema, wanting her to *understand*. "In the case of these murders —"

She covered her ears with her hands. "You speak blasphemy," she retorted when he stopped talking. "So the rumors are true. You risk your soul and the safety of Tharios in your pursuit of the Ghost. I will not sully my hands by association, *Dhaskoi* Nomasdina. And *you* must decide which is of more value: a few lives, which are fleeting at best, or your family's standing and your own immortal spirit." Her body stiff with disapproval, she picked up her notes and walked away.

"I'll go with you," Goldeye said, his voice clipped. "I may be only a *shenos*, but perhaps the Keepers will listen to me."

Dema hesitated. Would support from a *shenos*, even one as famed as Niklaren Goldeye, hurt or help him?

As if he read Dema's mind, Niko said, "I've been wanting to talk to them in any case. I want permission to scry the past on the sites where the victims have been found. It's possible your priests missed something as they cleansed."

At that Dema bristled: surely the priests knew their craft! Still, he told himself, it couldn't hurt to have a reputable mage at his side.

Most importantly, he was desperate. He'd seen the look on Keth's face, when the glassblower recognized the dead woman. He remembered the accusations the people had thrown at him in the Forum and elsewhere, that he didn't care about their lives. Recently, to enter the *arurimat,* he'd had to pass through a crowd that grew larger with each murder. They watched him in silence, their eyes accusing: how many more would he allow to die?

"Do you have a horse?" he asked Goldeye.

One of the Nomasdina clan servants awaited Dema at the First Class entrance at Serenity House. The woman greeted him with a bow, took charge of his horse and Niko's, and handed Dema a heavy, jingling purse.

"Your mother says that coin always gets a quicker response than chits to be redeemed," explained the servant. "She also instructs me to tell you to take care. She hears what is being said of you, and worries that you risk forgetting your obligations to the clan in your eagerness to meet your obligations to the *arurim.*" She bowed again and led the horses away.

Dema had visited Serenity House with his family and knew how things worked here. As servitor passed him on to servitor, he distributed the bribes that would ensure he was being sent in the right direction, a silver *bik* each. When he and Niko reached the greeting room set aside for the First

Class, Dema gave five silver *biks* to have his name presented to the Keepers. Then he and Niko were granted a private room in which to wait. Servants came with food and drink; others came with dry tunics for them both.

After a short time a clerk arrived to write down the reason they had come; Dema bribed him appropriately. Several hours later, when their clothes, dried and pressed free of wrinkles, were returned to them, another clerk came to clarify what the previous clerk had written down. She too received the proper bribe.

As the long hours dragged by, Dema and Niko talked of all manner of things: their educations as mages, Niko's travels and how he'd come to teach Tris, Dema's family history. They even napped for a time. It was nearly midnight when Niko asked, "I know the customs of Tharios and the blood doctrine. I confess, I'm curious — why *do* you keep sticking your neck out to trace the killer's steps? You risk a great deal for a procedure that may not lead you to him."

Dema looked at him, startled. "You don't think I could catch him if I could dog his trail?"

Niko smoothed his mustache. "If there had only been one murder, I would say, almost certainly. But with each killing he has shown he is clever — and in our world, clever criminals always have ways to foil magical tracking. In any event, you have put your standing in Tharios in great danger. Why? He's killed no one close to you. Is it the defilement of public places?"

Dema raised his eyebrows, shocked. "Defilement? That's for priests to worry about. The busier you keep priests, the less chance they have to pry into our private lives. But the Ghost . . ." He thought for a moment, then sighed. "The All-Seeing, in his wisdom, arranged my birth to an honorable family in the First Class. I have privileges, but I also have a duty to the lower classes, to protect and guide them. Not everyone takes that duty seriously, but we Nomasdinas do. Even if it's to *yaskedasi* and the rest of the Fifth Class. They trust us to watch out for them. That's what I mean to do."

"And if the Keepers don't listen?" Niko asked gently.

Dema wanted to tell the older man that this was ridiculous, but he couldn't. Refusal was always a possibility. "I'll have to think of something," he said, feeling defensive.

"Perhaps you ought to start thinking now," suggested Niko. "Just in case."

Tris watched as Keth roused everyone and gathered them in Ferouze's sitting room to break the news of Yali's murder. The result was chaos. Xantha collapsed in hysterics. Ferouze punched the wall before she started to cry; Poppy sat and rocked as tears streamed down her face; the male lodgers hammered Keth with questions. Glaki clutched her doll and screamed for her dead mother and her Aunt Yali.

"Get her out of here!" shrieked Ferouze. Poppy lurched to her feet and scooped up the child, taking her outside.

Tris went to the wailing Xantha and considered slapping her out of her hysterics. A seed of pity stopped her. Instead she took the scent bottle she carried for such occasions from the purse on her sash. She removed the top and waved it under Xantha's nose. Immediately the blonde inhaled and coughed. The men standing near her flinched from the smell.

"What *is* that stuff?" demanded the flute player, a pretty

young fellow with bronze skin and gray-green eyes. "It's hideous!"

"The friend who made it calls it 'Infallible,'" replied Tris, corking the vial. She chose not to mention that her foster mother Rosethorn had no respect for hysterics. The herbs in her version of smelling salts were chosen with that attitude. "We need some water."

As Xantha drank the water, Tris looked around. The drummer held Ferouze, his muscled arms tight as he kept her from lashing out again. Tris remembered hearing something shatter as she brought Xantha around: the pieces of a basin lay on the floor at Ferouze's feet. Glaki could step in that mess, she thought, and fetched the broom to sweep up the shards. Finished, she looked for Glaki. The child and Poppy were still missing.

One of the male *yaskedasi* was also gone. He soon returned, having spread the news throughout the neighborhood. Others came with him, men and women, old and young, to weep and to curse the killer and the city that didn't care if *yaskedasi* died. It wasn't long before Tris's head ached fiercely. Little Bear and Chime had escaped the room when the first guest arrived.

When Tris gave a final look through the crowded chambers, she saw Poppy had returned. The brunette sat with Ferouze as they shared the contents of a jug with their neighbors. Poppy wept still, without making any sound.

Tris asked one of the men for directions to Yali's room,

where she assumed that Poppy had left Glaki. She figured that the little girl would cry herself to sleep, but Tris didn't like the idea that Glaki would wake alone.

Tris walked out to the courtyard, glad to be in cooler, less stuffy air. She let rain fall on her head for a moment, enjoying its comforting feel on her braids. It was over the rain's soft patter that she heard hiccups. Glaki was huddled on the stair to the upper galleries, weeping into Little Bear's fur. Chime sat on her shoulder, crooning as she groomed the child's tangled hair with her claws.

For a moment Tris could only stare, appalled. Did Poppy just bring the child out here and leave her to cry alone?

How often had Tris herself done this, crept into a corner to weep, knowing the only ones who cared about her were the animals of the house? She had not lost a mother or an aunt as Glaki had, but time after time she had been passed on to yet another relative. It was overhearing the talk that decided that she and her many strangenesses would be sent to some other family member that had always sent Tris to cry in secret. When Cousin Uraelle, who had kept her the longest, died, Tris had wept not for the mean, stingy old woman, but for the loss of the most permanent home she could remember.

She touched the girl on the shoulder. Glaki flinched against Little Bear, throwing up an arm to protect her face. Gently Tris pressed her arm down. A handprint showed clearly on the girl's cheek. Poppy had slapped Glaki to silence her.

"It's just me, Glaki. You saw me yesterday, remember?" Tris kept her voice gentle as she sat on the flagstones of the ground floor gallery. She leaned back against a wooden pillar.

"Mama," the child mumbled at last. "Aunt Yali. When do they come home?"

Tris drew her knees up to her chest and wrapped her arms around them. She knew she wasn't good with children, though her heart went out to this one. What could she say? What *did* people say?

She could only know what *she* would say. She hated people who tried to evade the truth. "They died, Glaki. Mama and Aunt Yali died. They won't be coming home."

Fresh tears welled in the girl's eyes. They spilled over her stained cheeks. "No," Glaki replied, shaking her head. "No."

"I'm sorry," Tris said gently. "Yes."

Glaki began to sob again, then to wail. Tris bit her lip, trying to decide what was right. In the end it was her knowledge of Sandry, her good-hearted sister, that guided her. Tris sat beside Little Bear and pulled Glaki onto her lap. The little girl fought, straining to get back to the dog. "Doggie!" she screamed, her face turning beet red.

"It's Little Bear. That's his name," Tris explained, panting as she hauled on the struggling child. "He's not going anywhere. If you sit with me, he'll be here, and so will

Chime. We must talk, Glaki. You have to learn some hard new lessons. I wish I had someone nice to teach them to you, but you're stuck with just me." She finally got the little girl onto her lap. Glaki howled, battered Tris's chest with her fists, and drummed her heels on the ground. Tris held on grimly, still talking softly. "It isn't right, what's happened to your mother and Yali. I hope you grow to be someone incredible, to repay you for all this misery. Why is it, do you suppose, the gods are said to be favoring you when they dump awful things into your lap? Is it because the other explanation, that sorrow comes from accidents and there are no gods doing it to help you be a strong person, is just too horrible to think of? Let's stick with the gods. Let's stick with someone being in charge."

As she continued to speak, rattling along about any topic that came to mind, whether Glaki could understand or not, she held the girl close. Tris was so used to the child's struggles that she didn't notice at first when Glaki's screams began to grow softer, her small body relaxing into Tris's hold. It was only when Glaki was quietly sucking her thumb, whimpering against Tris's chest, that the older girl realized she could loosen her grip. Her hands and arms stung from being locked in the same position for so long. She smoothed damp, tumbled curls away from the child's face. "That's very good." She hesitated, then awkwardly kissed Glaki on the forehead. "We can't let you make yourself sick on top of everything else."

It was some time before Glaki would let Tris get up without hysterics. Each time the child's voice rose, Tris would settle back into place. Finally Glaki herself climbed off Tris's lap. "Pot," she whispered, not meeting Tris's eyes.

"Chamberpot?" Tris asked. Glaki nodded. With a groan Tris struggled to her numb feet. "You don't have a real privy here?" Glaki shook her head. "Wonderful," Tris said, easing the kinks in her spine. She held out a hand. "Show me where," she said.

Glaki took her hand and led her up the stairs. Little Bear, with Chime on his back, followed them.

"Let's go to where you sleep," Tris suggested.

From the neatness of the room and the absence of dust, Tris guessed that this was Yali's room, not Iralima's. As Glaki used the chamberpot, Tris opened the shutters to let some air in. She leaned outside for a moment, calling her favorite breeze to her. It had come all the way from Winding Circle and was Tris's most faithful attendant in the hot south. When she held out her hand, the breeze wound around it. "Find Niko," she instructed it. "Tell him I'm all right and that I don't know when I'll be home." It sped off on its way.

It had been frustrating to send her winds out before in search of a woman being killed, but what else could she do to help right now? Keth was torn up in spirit, too much so to attempt to make another globe. No one had mentioned it, but it was plain to Tris that they couldn't rely on the killer waiting a day in between strikes, not when he'd taken Yali just a day after the previous victim.

She had to do something. Her breezes were all she had.

Tris looked around. Glaki and Little Bear had curled up together on the bed, the child watching the dog as he slept. Chime sat on the windowsill beside Tris, cocking her head, her eyes curious.

"Will you stay there a little while and be quiet?" Tris asked Glaki. "There's something I need to do. It's going to be windy in here, but don't worry. It's just me. I'm a mage. There are things I do with winds and breezes." She wasn't sure that the child understood, but she thought it did no harm to talk to her as if she could. Tris had never understood the need for adults to address children in baby talk.

She walked over to the door and flung it wide, summoning her breezes from the courtyard. She also called any of the Khapik air currents that would respond, drawing them to her through door and window. In they sped, making blankets, curtains, skirts, hair, and fur dance, spinning around Glaki, Little Bear, and Chime in curious exploration before they circled Tris.

She let her power spill out around her, doing her best to magically convey the sounds she wanted to hear, frustrated because it would be so much easier if she could just *see* what they passed over. Only when she was sure that she could explain no more did she let them go. "All of Khapik, mind," she told them. "Every street, every alley, every courtyard."

The breezes sped away to do as she asked. With a sigh, Tris lit the cheap tallow lamp, then sat on the bed, resting her back against the wall. Glaki inched over and tucked herself under Tris's left arm. Little Bear belly-crawled until he was sandwiched between Glaki and the wall, then resumed his slumbers.

"You know, I lost my mother when I was small, and some of my aunts," Tris confided. She chose not to mention that her mother and aunts had not been lost to her through death. "It was scary, going from house to house. Everyone has different ways of doing things, and they yell at you if you don't do them properly, have you noticed that?"

Glaki nodded, her thumb firmly in her mouth.

"But animals are always friendly, if you don't hurt them," Tris said. "And you can tell yourself stories, just like your mother and your aunts tell you stories. You could tell yourself stories about the family you will have one day. I have a wonderful family now. And you know, Glaki, that your mother and your aunt still love you, wherever they are."

Glaki took her thumb from her mouth. "Did you cry?" she asked.

"I cried like you did, where nobody would hear and yell at me, or slap me," replied Tris softly.

"Tell me about your family?" asked the girl.

Tris was telling Glaki about the day Briar stole a miniature tree when she realized that Keth stood in the doorway.

She glanced at the little girl, who was fast asleep. "How is everyone?" Tris asked Keth in a whisper.

"Frantic," Keth replied abruptly. "Angry. They're talking about a march to Balance Hill in the morning, to tell the Keepers that they'll stop working if something isn't done. Khapik brings a lot of money into the city; it's the place foreigners usually visit first. Maybe the Keepers will listen."

Tris frowned. If that was true, that the district brought income to the city, what chance did Dema have of making the Keepers shut Khapik down?

Keth rubbed the white spot in his hair. "Look, I'll get a chair to take you home. You —"

Tris cut him off. "You're out of your mind," she said flatly. "This child just lost the two most important people in her life. I'm not taking her from the only home she knows, and I'm not leaving her with *this* lot. That Poppy slapped her, for Mila's sake! I've sent word to Niko. In the meantime, I'm staying here."

"But she's not your problem," Keth protested. "You don't have to do this."

"I know how she feels," replied Tris. "I've been in her shoes, or a pair that looked a lot like them. If Little Bear and Chime give her some comfort, I'm not taking it away. Have you heard word from Dema?"

"Tris, this isn't necessary," argued Keth stubbornly.

Tris glared at him, refusing to share any more of her private miseries to explain why it *was* necessary. "I asked, have you word from Dema?"

He may not know about her childhood, but he did understand the look on her face. "Nothing." He wandered to the window and leaned out, letting the rain fall on his head. "At least not that many *yaskedasi* are out working in this." Struck by an idea, he turned to Tris. "Could you keep it raining a few days? The fewer people on the street, the fewer targets."

Tris shook her head. "The storm's already moving on."

"Then stop it," replied Keth.

"You don't stop storms," she explained. "You usher them on, guide them down a path they might have taken anyway, but you can't stop them. That's why you had a drought before this — someone was holding the rains in place across the sea. Besides, Keth, the rain won't stop him from killing. If he can't find someone on the street, he'll go elsewhere."

Keth jammed his hands into his pockets. "You mean he'll go to the nice, sheltered women of the city. Women with families who care what happens to them. Women who aren't as shady as *yaskedasi*."

She had only meant that the killer would try the back alleys, the courtyard *yaskedasi,* or even go after Khapik's women in their homes. There was nothing in this room to stop anyone from coming in who wanted to; Yali's lock was even worse than Kethlun's. It hadn't occurred to Tris that the killer might leave Khapik, to find victims in the rest of the city.

Once he'd said it, though, the truth became clear. "They'll refuse him, won't they? The Keepers, and Dema. Between the money this place brings, and the risk the killer will go elsewhere, they won't let Dema shut Khapik down."

Keth slumped into the room's sole, rickety chair. "No. I don't think they will." He looked down at his clasped hands. "I don't know what Dema can do if the Keepers won't help."

Tris leaned her head back, staring at the ceiling. "Me neither," she admitted.

For a long moment Keth was silent. Finally he said, "I need to get back to work on the lightning globes. I'll make them clear sooner. I'll make one that will show us his face."

"Then sleep," Tris advised. "Try, anyway. We've a long day tomorrow."

Her breezes reported back to her all through the night. They brought Tris nothing.

In the morning Tris made sure that Glaki, Chime, and Little Bear were comfortable in the workshop at Touch-stone Glass with Keth. He had agreed to watch them while Tris ran some necessary errands. Once she had purchased breakfast for the group, Tris headed back up the Street of Glass, dodging two brawling *prathmuni* whose wagons had collided. Other pedestrians and riders swerved around the brawlers as if they didn't even see them.

The skies were clear; the brooklets that had run in the gutters were shrinking. The city sparkled, rinsed clean for the moment. Atop the two hills ahead, the white marble structures of Heskalifos and the Assembly gleamed like hope and dignity given shape. For the hundredth time Tris wondered how Dema had fared with the Keepers of the Public Good. She was almost positive that she and Keth had been right, that the Keepers would not shut Khapik down, but she wanted very badly to be mistaken.

At Jumshida's, Tris found her hostess seated at the breakfast table, reading a book. "Niko's still abed," she told Tris. "He made a late night of it, at Serenity House."

Tris frowned. "What was he doing there?"

"The *arurim dhaskoi*, Nomasdina? He came to us for reinforcements for when he talked to the Keepers yesterday. I felt badly for him," Jumshida said, peeling an orange, "but he's so obsessed with catching the Ghost that he forgets what truly matters here in Tharios. I tried to remind him of the duty he owes his clan, but he would have none of it. He persuaded Niko to go to the Keepers with him. The Keepers didn't see them until after midnight. I think it was the third hour after that when Niko returned to us."

"Do you know if the Keepers listened?" asked Tris.

Jumshida shrugged. "Niko said nothing to me, but I

would be much surprised if they changed the way we have done things for a thousand years, just to meet a temporary emergency." She met Tris's eyes with her own gray-green ones. "We are great believers in time, here in Tharios," she explained. "Time, and the eternal balance of things."

The cook walked into the room with a tea tray. "He rang for this," the woman explained.

"I'll take it up," Tris offered. The cook was more than happy to relinquish the heavy tray to her, and Tris was more than happy to get away from Jumshida, before the woman patronized her any more. Sheer survival over centuries isn't a guarantee of virtue, Tris fumed as she climbed the stairs. It's just a guarantee that nothing will change for the better!

Niko was busily cleaning his teeth when Tris came in and set the tray on a table. "Jumshida said you went with Dema," she said as Niko spat, rinsed, and spat again. "Will the Keepers do anything?"

"Nothing," he informed her waspishly, throwing down his facecloth. "They will not close Khapik. They said it would alarm the populace and cause financial hardship to those who work there. They will not intercede with the priesthood of the All-Seeing to let the *arurim dhaskoi* or even me work seeing-spells over the dead. They will not risk the purity of the city and of the conference. Even though I am a foreigner, they will protect me for my own good. Arrogant, hidebound, unimaginative —"

He might have gone on, but Tris interrupted. "Niko, Yali, the woman who came here to see if Keth was all right? She was the most recent victim."

Niko sighed. "So Dema told me." He took the cup of tea Tris handed to him.

"Well, she left a foster daughter, the child of one of the other dead women. I mean to stay with the little girl — her name's Glaki — until some provision is made for her. I don't think she ought be left to the other women in the lodging-house, and Keth wants to concentrate on the globes."

"Is he Glaki's father?" Niko asked, sipping his tea.

Tris hadn't thought of that. She considered it, then shook her head. "Glaki's Tharian clean through. Anyway, I'm back for some clothes, and I wanted to ask about scrying again." Tris smoothed a wrinkle in her dress. "I sent my breezes through Khapik last night, to let me know if they heard a woman being strangled, but it doesn't work very well. Has anyone arrived yet who can see things on the winds?"

"You are still determined to learn?" asked Niko. "Even after all I've told you?"

"*You* survive being pelted with images," Tris pointed out. "It hasn't driven you mad — though you can be quite odd, when you put your mind to it."

Niko sat on his bed and looked at her. "So much of it means nothing," he pointed out. "So much of it you don't even really see because it's gone in a flash. The headaches are ferocious. Every account I've read of wind scrying compares it to seeing the future, and the grief involved in *that* I know all too well."

Tris sat next to him. "Has *anyone* come who knows it?" she asked again. "Niko, these women deserve better than to have a monster pick them off one by one while those who should protect them say it's all right if they die, as long as they don't spread the pollution of their deaths around. I could go as mad from not being able to help as I could from being drowned in visions."

Niko sighed. "Start looking at and through a particular breeze, clearing your vision as you clear your mind. According to what I've read, you should first begin to see colors, then movement. . . . Tris, you *do* realize that only one mage in thousands can do this? One in a generation?"

"I have to try," replied Tris, her voice low but passionate. She wouldn't meet his eyes, but stared at her hands, fisted in her skirt. "It's not right, what's happening here."

Niko stood and went to the trunk of books he carried everywhere he traveled, opened it, and pushed back the lid. These were the texts of his craft of seeing, volumes on ambient and academic magic, and other books that helped him in the exercise of his own power. He brought out a small, leather-bound volume closed with a strap and a catch, lifted it in his hand as if weighing it, then held it out to Tris. "Take it. There are exercises that may help. The writer could scry the wind."

Tris looked at the tiny volume and gasped. "Niko! You have a copy of Quicksilver's *Winds' Path*, and you never told me?"

He smiled. "My fears for your sanity are real, you know. My best friend at Lightsbridge, when I was a student there. She went mad from the study of wind scrying. She was — more easily distracted than you are, though. I always meant to let you see the book in time. I suppose that time is now."

Tris stroked the embossed lettering on the cover with reverent fingers. It was said to be the ultimate book on wind magics. It was also very old. "You can't lend this to me. What if something happens to it?"

Niko smoothed his mustache. "That's why I'm giving it to you, so you needn't worry if anything happens to it. I've learned all I can from it, and you need the half that's about scrying the wind. Just remember, it takes *time* to master it, if you can. You may not learn enough to stop this madman."

That Niko would trust her with such a prize told her more about how he saw her than anything else that had passed between them in recent months. It said that he believed she was a full-fledged mage, an adult and craftswoman. She met his eyes, her own filling with tears. What would happen to her now? Was he saying he wanted her to leave him?

"Not that you get rid of me," he added, as if he'd read her mind. Neither of them was good at being sentimental with the other. "We've places to go yet, libraries to search. Now, scat, so I can dress."

"I need to go back to Touchstone Glass," she said. "You'll find me there or at Ferouze's, Chamberpot Alley, in Khapik, if you need me."

"I will be here or at Phakomathen, scrying the future," Niko said. "The conference can manage without me, until this monster is caught."

Tris sighed in relief. "Thank you. You'll probably see him long before we will!"

Tris packed, then visited the university baths. Dressed in clean clothes, her pack slung over one shoulder, she visited the Achaya Square *skodi*, or market. There she bargained with a jewelry seller for a price on the glass pendants Keth had made with Chime's flames, selling a quarter of them. At Jumshida's she had collected all of Chime's flames she could find, as well as the spiral glass circles that were the dragon's vomit and the lumpy glass rounds that were Chime's dung. If she and Keth were to create more lightning globes and look after Glaki properly, they would need cash for glassmaker's supplies, clothing, and food. Tris had money set away, but saw no reason to dip into that if Keth were right about the attraction of the pendants.

Once the bits of glass were sold, Tris set off for Touchstone. The day was heating up. By the time she arrived, she was red-faced and puffing under the weight of her things. Inside the workshop, Glaki napped on Little Bear's flank as Chime tried to wrestle the cork out of a jar of coloring salts. Keth was pacing as Tris set down her pack.

"Where have you been?" he demanded. "Most of the morning has gone! I made three vases already!"

"I had things to do," said Tris. "Whenever you propose to upend your life, arrangements have to be made."

"Nobody asked you to come live with us," protested Keth with a glance at the sleeping child. "We managed before you."

"You'll manage better *with* me." Tris went to the well and gulped down a ladle of water, then looked at Keth. "Are you ready?"

Once her circle of protection was drawn and the magical barriers raised, Keth meditated, popping all of his power into and out of his imaginary crucible in the blink of an eye. "Well?" he asked Tris. "I think I remember how to create a globe. I'm going to try to make it big, so we see as much of the surroundings as we can."

"All right," Tris said. "Try."

He got excited as he picked up the blowpipe. His fingers trembled, though his hands were steady enough as he collected a gather of molten glass from the crucible. Tris breathed with him as Keth inhaled, counted, held, and counted, forcing himself to calm down. Raising the pipe to his lips, he exhaled into it steadily as he twirled it. He continued to twirl the pipe as he stopped, inhaled, and held to the count. His second exhale expanded the bulging gather from the size of an orange to the size of Little Bear's head. He reheated the glass and blew a little more. "It cools faster when I work it this way," he grumbled, reheating the glass again. "I *hate* going slow."

"Keth, watch —" Tris began, but it was too late. He'd let himself get worked up. When he blew into the pipe, a fat streamer of his power went with the air, straight into the glass. It lengthened and burst, spraying droplets onto the wall.

Tris surveyed the damage. Luckily the walls, though wood, had been treated to resist fire. "You know, a few more of these, what with the drops you put on the wall the other day, and you could make a design," she remarked, falsely cheerful. "It looks pretty, in an overenthusiastic way."

Under his breath Keth told Tris what he thought of her comments. She caught the small puff of air from his mouth and twisted it in her hand until they both heard "— clay-brained flap-mouthed impertinent —"

"Now, was that nice?" Tris asked, releasing the puff of air. "I was only trying to help."

Very gently Keth beat his head against the wall, rousing Glaki from her sleep. "Ow," the four-year-old observed, watching Keth.

"Men are like that, little one," Tris replied. "Keth, feel

sorry for yourself later. Start again." She dug inside one of her packs until she found the dates and dried figs she'd bought at the *skodi*. These she gave to Glaki, who ate silently.

Keth cleaned his blowpipe, then thrust it once more into the crucible. Chime glided over to sit on a shelf beside the furnace and observe. Keth drew out the gather and began to count, breathe, twirl, and blow. Gently he coaxed the bubble along, reheating and twirling, enlarging it each time, growing more confident as everything went smoothly.

"One more," he murmured as he drew out the gather. "One more go."

Tris saw his magic spike, leaping to flood down the barrel of the blowpipe and out over the skin of the ball. Burdened with its strange weight, the glass ball dropped from the pipe and onto the floor, where it sprayed outward.

"I used to be able to do this!" yelled Kethlun, furious. "I used to be able to do this in my sleep! How can it be so hard? Why does the magic fight me? Why do *I* fight me? This will *never* work!" He flung the pipe into the corner and got to work cleaning up the mess.

Tris leaned her chin on her pulled-up knees, watching him through slitted eyes as she thought. One day she, Briar, Daja, and Sandry had been on the roof of their home, basking in the sun and talking. They had spoken of their first real experience with their crafts, the one they didn't actually associate with magic. Talking it over, Sandry and Daja could see how their teachers had used magic to teach them something about spinning with a hand spindle, in Sandry's case, and drawing thin wire from thick, in Daja's. Maybe what Keth needed was help with his craft.

She waited until Keth was ready again. Glaki moved into a corner with her doll as Tris got to her feet. "Here," she said, walking over to Keth. "Let's try something. You're going to meditate like before, and blow like before, but you're going to close your eyes and let me help you."

"I don't need help!" Keth snapped, red-faced and out of patience with himself and the world. "I know perfectly well how to do this!"

"You know perfectly well how to blow glass," she said. "That's what you're going to do. You're not going to interrupt yourself by sticking it into the furnace to reheat, that's all. I'll keep the glass warm."

"How can you do that?" demanded Keth. "Your lightning will fry it."

"I won't use lightning." She walked her fingers through her braids until she found the loops on either side of her head that she used to store warmth. She removed their pins, then undid an inch of each braid. Pulling her fingers through the freed hair, she collected two palmsful of that heat, drawn from the molten rock of the earth's core. She pressed her hands together to mix their contents, then drew them apart. Now she had a square foot surface to use on the glass. She checked it against the furnace, making sure they were equally as hot, before she looked at Keth again. "Stand at right angles to the furnace, once you have your gather," she told him. He looked green, as he always did when she fidgeted with her braids. "Now, start breathing."

Once he had his gather on the end of the blowpipe, he backed away from the furnace. Tris moved until she stood in front of the gather. "I don't think that's a good idea," Keth said. "Or weren't you watching when the last two splattered?"

"Just breathe, and close your eyes, and blow, Keth."

He hesitated. "I can't shape it that way," he warned.

"It shaped itself the first time. Stop talking and get to work."

Counting, Keth twirled the pipe as Tris held her outstretched hands on either side of his gather. Closing his eyes, he exhaled into the blowpipe for the count, drew his mouth away without stopping the motion of the pipe, then blew again.

Tris kept the heat she had summoned just beyond the glass, watching sharply as the globe got bigger. Tiny lightnings, magic that Keth mixed with the air he breathed, darted along the glass surface like minnows in a pond. When the globe had reached the proper size, she grabbed a pair of cutting tongs and put them around the glass still attached to the pipe. "Keth," she said quietly. He opened his eyes as she pinched with the tongs and twisted, freeing the globe.

Keth yanked the pipe back and caught the globe in one hand. It didn't burn him. He stared at it, awestruck. As the lightnings in the glass played, they grew to fill the inside of the globe and to run amok across its surface. By the time Keth had gotten the composure to set his blowpipe aside and cup the globe in both hands, it was a ball of miniature lightnings.

"It's pretty!" cried Glaki. She clapped her hands and reached up. Before Tris or Keth realized what was happening, the globe left his hands and flew toward her.

"It'll burn," Tris said quickly. "The glass is hot, Glaki. Only Keth can hold it."

Glaki pouted and sent the ball soaring back to its creator. The child had just confirmed a suspicion that Tris had held since the child stopped the cyclone Tris had used to write Yali's name in the courtyard dust.

Keth stared at Glaki. "I can't deal with this now," he said hurriedly. "Tris, don't expect me to. I just can't."

"You won't have to," Tris replied with resignation. "The responsibility is mine. Find somewhere to put the globe."

"Why?" asked Keth. "We have to make it clear up, don't we?"

"First we stop. You need a walk, and a breather, and food," Tris informed him.

"No! Let's work on it now, get the lightning out. I can do it!"

Tris sighed. He was dead white and covered in sweat, shaking so hard he could barely hold onto the globe. "When did you last eat?" she asked.

Keth had to think. "Breakfast."

"And drink? And visit the privy? And sit down?" she demanded.

Keth glared at her, his blue eyes reflecting the lightning on his globe. "I don't need any of that," he said, and swayed.

Tris propped her hands on her hips and glared back. "You've been working all morning and part of the afternoon in this hotbox. If you don't eat, you'll collapse, and if you collapse with this thing, you might break it, so stop arguing with me!"

Chime swooped over to land on Tris's shoulder. She chinked worriedly at Keth, who wiped his forehead on his sleeve.

"Just for a moment, perhaps," he admitted. He swayed again. Quickly he placed the ball on his workbench.

Tris began to say something rude but decided to hold her tongue. Keth needed to rest before he fainted, now that his excitement and the strength he had built up by repeated use of his newly gripped power had drained away. Rather than speak hastily, she took down her magical barrier on the shop.

"Sit," she ordered. "I'm going to the *skodi* across the street for some food. Glaki, why don't you tell Uncle Keth what your doll did this morning?"

As the child walked Keth to the bench by the well, Tris left Touchstone Glass. Only when she was three doors down did she stop to sag against a shop's wall in relief. She hadn't been sure that her help would work.

II

They were almost done with their belated midday when Keth looked up to see Dema in the workshop door. "Sit," he offered through a mouthful of flatbread and chickpea spread. "Eat something."

Glaki towed Dema over to the bench, where he sat abruptly and took the food Tris offered. A handful of olives and a wedge of cheese revived him a bit, as did the ladle of cold water Glaki fetched for him. "Hello," he said to her, "what's your name?"

Glaki, suddenly shy, stuck her thumb in her mouth and hid behind Tris.

"She's Glaki," Tris explained quietly. "Iralima was her mother, Yali her foster mother."

"Gods," Dema said, dejected. "That's more ill luck than anyone should have in one lifetime." He looked at the globe that sparkled on a counter. "Another one. Splendid. If the last two are any indication, he'll strike tonight. Any luck in getting the lightning to clear?"

"We're going to work on that after we eat," Keth replied with a sidelong glance at Tris. "They turned you down, didn't they? The Keepers."

"Niko said they did," Tris murmured.

Dema looked at the hard-boiled eggs and helped himself to two. "They said the city can't afford the loss of income from Khapik," he said, shoulders drooping as he peeled an egg. "That the people would lose confidence in the Keepers, even the Assembly. That it would look as if they were admitting defeat at the hands of a lone madman. That all order is lost. In the audience chamber, while Niko asked about the cleansing, I heard someone whisper that if Khapik closed, the Ghost might come for respectable women." Chime clambered into Dema's lap, purring musically. He smiled absently at her, ate half an egg, then continued. "The Keepers asked why they shouldn't replace me now and let my family deal with the loss of status. Thank the All-Seeing I had a fallback plan to give them. If I don't find the Ghost in ten days, Nomasdina Clan loses one of our Assembly seats as punishment for sending an idiot like me to work for Tharios. I asked how could I save our honor with Khapik open and my hands tied, but they were done with me. *How can they not care?*" he burst out, looking from Keth to Tris. "Women are *dying!* Why won't they do whatever is necessary to save them?" He stuffed the other half of his peeled egg into his mouth.

Tris laid a hand on Dema's arm. "Why are you up? You need sleep. Tired folk make mistakes."

Dema swallowed, drank some water, and sighed. "I'm on my way to Elya Street now. There's a room in the back I can use."

"What about your fallback plan?" Keth wanted to know, curious. "What's that?"

Dema peeled his second egg. "My sergeants will find as many *arurimi* as they can, particularly females, to bring into Khapik disguised as locals. I can do that if I pay for it myself, or rather Nomasdina Hall pays. With an Assembly seat at risk, Mother will let me spend the money." He looked at the globe. "Come for me when that clears?"

Keth nodded and squeezed Dema's shoulder. "Get some rest," he said. Dema nodded and left, eating his second egg.

"So they won't close Khapik," Tris mused, "but if he can find people to act the victim for him, and if he pays for their time, he can do that. This city doesn't make sense."

"It does in a strange way," replied Keth as he gathered their leavings. "If you belong to a great family, your power is shown by what *you* give to the city that grants you greatness. The city gives to you, you give to the city. It's worked for Tharios until now." He dumped their trash in the barrel by the rear gate. "And honestly, Tris, have you ever heard of anything like these murders? Women in the same line of work, killed the same way by one person, left out in public for everyone to see?"

He watched as she tugged her lower lip. "Sandry — my foster sister — wrote me that some assassins worked like that in Summersea a few months ago," she replied slowly. "But they were killing the members of another family as part of a trade war, in a way that would frighten anyone who might think to cross them."

"I don't think the Ghost does it for that," Keth said. "*Yaskedasi* aren't exactly anyone's rivals for anything. I think he likes it. And maybe he looks to shame Tharios, by showing that no one can stop him."

"And if you can't afford fountains or extra *arurimi,* like the *yaskedasi* and the Fifth Class, the city does nothing to help," Tris remarked tartly. She got to her feet and stretched to loosen her back. "Back to work, Keth. I've got an idea. Why don't you try to blend the lightning on the outside of the globe, so you can clear the surface. Maybe then you can look into it and see what's inside."

Keth tried to do as Tris suggested. First he tried to combine the outer lightnings into one large bolt he could peel away, but things distracted him from the task. Chime produced a shower of glass flames that rained on the laughing Glaki. The dog wriggled on the workshop floor to scratch his back. Street noise seemed louder than ever.

Only Tris didn't disturb Keth, though he wanted her to. He wanted her to thrust him aside and growl, "Oh, here, *I'll* do it!" Instead she read from a small, leather-bound volume. She seemed lost in it, though every time Keth glanced at her, she looked up, raising colorless brows over the brass rims of her spectacles.

Frustrated after what seemed like a dozen interruptions, Keth grabbed a hank of lightnings with thumb and forefinger, literally trying to jerk them off of his globe. For a moment he saw its frosty white surface. An image grew there: long brown hair, large brown eyes, a full mouth with a wicked twist to the side. It was Yali.

Keth trembled; his eyes stung. After he rubbed them to make sure no unmanly tears fell, her image was gone. The lightnings he'd yanked away escaped his hold to coat the globe again.

Keth set the globe down and covered his face with his hands, trembling with grief. He and Yali had only kissed once. For the most part they had just talked, something Keth had never done with his betrothed in Namorn. They'd discussed food, music, plays, even the customs of their countries. Something in Yali spoke to his heart. She'd had a restful quality unlike that of any girl he'd ever known.

The Ghost had taken that from Keth, just as he'd taken a loving mother and a foster mother from Glaki. What else would he take?

Settling the globe on his knees, Keth tried again.

Late in the afternoon Tris roused herself from her reading and proclaimed that Keth had worked enough today. Plagued with a savage headache, Keth didn't argue. Instead they cleaned up the shop, bid Antonou and his family good-bye, and left for Khapik. Headache or not, Keth took Tris's pack, though it seemed to get heavier as he walked.

By the time they saw the yellow pillars of the Khapik Gate, he felt as if someone had worked on him with hammers. Every bone in his body hurt.

As they passed through the gate, strong hands removed the pack from his grip. "You need a bath," said Tris, her eyes sharp and knowing. She hung the pack on her own shoulders. "You're exhausted. It happens when you aren't used to working magic for hours, I should have remembered. Make sure the bath attendants know to wake you up and send you home. Do you cook in your rooms?"

Keth wiped his forehead, trying to think. "No," he said at last. "We buy food cooked at the Lotus Street *skodi*. It's cheap, and not bad. Instead of turning into Chamberpot Alley, you turn right and follow Peacock Street to the wall. The Lotus Street *skodi* is right there." He fumbled in his pocket.

"Never mind," Tris said testily. "I sold some of those pendants you made for me. We've money enough. Go wash."

Keth stood there, staring down at the plump girl who looked up at him. If he hadn't been drunk with exhaustion, he never would have said what he did: "You're actually a nice person, aren't you?"

She went beet red. "No," she retorted. Steering Glaki ahead of her, she walked away, disappearing into the crowd of early visitors to Khapik.

*   *   *

They were eating the supper Tris had bought when Xantha stuck her head into Yali's old room. "There's a Farewell for Yali at the Thanion," she said. "If you want to go, Keth. And you," she added with a glance at Tris.

Tris looked at Glaki. The little girl had been fine for most of the day, until they returned to this room. Now she was silent, eating little, burying her face from time to time in her battered rag doll.

"Thank you," she told Xantha, "but I'll stay with Glaki. It's been a long day."

Keth lurched to his feet, tired as he was. "I'll drop the globe at Elya Street with Dema," he told Tris. "I think it's starting to clear."

She nodded. Keth had placed it on the table, where it sparked and flashed. She had watched when he tried to clear it once he returned from his bath, but as before, he'd used up his magical resources. Now the surface lightnings were growing thin, showing the bolts that still shone thick inside the globe. If it cleared as the last one had, it would be another hour before they could see anything. Since Keth was exhausted, it was better that Dema get the thing before the lightning was gone.

Xantha's blue eyes widened. "Keth, did *you* do that? You did magic!"

"Not any that'll be of use," Keth said bitterly. He picked up the globe and ushered her outside.

As the door closed behind them Tris heard Xantha say,

"Can you do anything with complexions? Mine chaps so easily these days."

Tris shook her head. Then she looked at Glaki, who sat on the floor with her back to Tris. Here was another problem, one she needed to sort out. "Can you make a picture in fire?" She picked up the table lamp and walked around in front of the child, then sat on the floor and placed the lamp between them. "Would you show me a picture in the flame?" she asked gently. "It's not much of a fire, but I bet you can do it. What do you see there?"

Glaki frowned at the lamp, her fine black brows knit, her deep brown eyes intent. Slowly the lamp's flame rose, then spread until it formed an oval the size of Glaki's hand. A face appeared in it, that of a woman with Glaki's large, heavily lashed brown eyes, glossy black curls, and olive complexion. "Mama," whispered the child. The image dissolved: the lamp was out of oil. Glaki began to weep.

This time she didn't fight when Tris dragged her into her lap. Softly she cried into the front of Tris's sensible pale blue dress. Tris patted her back and crooned softly, letting her weep. Now she was certain. Glaki had shown two of the three signs of academic magic: moving things and producing images in fire.

As if my life weren't complicated enough already, Tris thought, grouchy, though she was already making plans. Glaki would not be pushed from household to household as Tris had been. She would have a proper home and all the things a child needed to hold her head up in the world. Tris would take her to Lark, Rosethorn, and Discipline Cottage when she and Niko returned to Emelan. Glaki would become part of the household that was rooted there.

Chime's flames would help. They had to pay Keth's cousin Antonou for the sands, scrap glass, and coloring agents that Keth used to study his magic, but part of the money to be made from Chime's flames would go to Glaki, to give her the things that little girl-mages needed. Tris nodded, her mind made up. She would not leave Glaki to scrabble for a living in Tharios.

Outside Tris saw that the sky was growing dark. In the street under the window she could hear the chime of dancers' bells, chatter, and laughter, test notes played on musical instruments. Khapik was coming to life, which meant the Ghost would be stirring, too.

Glaki dozed on Tris's lap. Carefully the older girl got to her feet. Glaki protested sleepily, just as she grumbled as Tris got her into her night clothes; but once tucked into bed, with Chime on one side and Little Bear on the other, she slept. Tris suspected that, like Keth, Glaki was probably exhausted from her first deliberate use of magic.

She went to the window and leaned out, summoning breezes. As she had the night before, she sent them out to bring her word of violence done with silk and a woman's stolen breath. Then she refilled the lamp, lit it, and sat down with *Winds' Path*. She had little hope for what her breezes might learn tonight, but she wanted them to get used to searching. They might find something and take her to its source, and they would be practiced at exploration when Tris learned enough to scry what they had touched. She didn't care about seeing the future, as Niko did. She just wanted to catch the Ghost before any more little girls were left motherless.

Keth returned from the Farewell for Yali to bid Tris good night. The city's clocks chimed midnight. Some time after that, Tris closed her book. She was unable to grasp another word; what she *had* read was a jumble of complex ideas that would take time to sort out. With the tides and lightning still moving in her veins, she wasn't sleepy. She needed a walk.

First, she discovered that Chime did not want to be left behind, which meant Tris had to don the sling and settle the glass dragon. Then she went downstairs. As she'd hoped, Ferouze was awake. The old woman kept the same hours as the *yaskedasi*. "I'd like to go for a walk," Tris explained. "Would you watch Glaki until I come back? She's asleep in Yali's room."

"She pays no rent for it," Ferouze grumbled through her handful of remaining teeth. "And I'm no children's maid."

Tris got two copper five-*bik* pieces out of her purse. "One of these to watch Glaki. One to pay a week's rent, and don't tell me Yali paid more than that. Will you do it?"

"I'll do it." Ferouze reached greedily for the money.

Tris held up a finger in warning, then stroked a thin braid with her free hand. Sparks of lightning jumped onto the copper coins. She loved copper: it held lightning for hours. "When I come back, I'll take the sparks off these," she said, placing them on Ferouze's table. "I wouldn't do that," she added as the woman grabbed for the coins.

"Ouch!" Ferouze sucked on her stinging fingers. "That *hurt.*"

"I know," Tris replied. "Better hope that I remember to take the spell off when I get back. Of course, I'll find you up where Glaki is, won't I?"

"You *dhaski* are hard folk," grumbled Ferouze as she followed Tris into the passage. "Your mother would be ashamed."

"I'll tell her you said so," Tris promised, turning onto Chamberpot Alley.

Khapik was as fascinating as ever to both Tris and to Chime. Together they went down alleys and through streets designed to tempt the coldest heart, up to rooftop gardens and down to sunken open theaters where dancers, jugglers, and fire-eaters entertained the public. She passed rough taverns overflowing with drunkards and select wineshops where people sipped and talked about vintage and palate. Her breezes sought her out wherever she went, carrying snippets of conversations, including some that made her blush.

"They say you'll get an education down here," she confided to Chime. "They just don't say if you'll like what you learn."

Only once did she encounter a problem, on a street off Willow Lane. A man drew a knife when he saw her, showing bad teeth in a nasty grin. "Just the purse, girl. I'm doing you a favor here, teaching you about walking dark streets alone." He came so close to her that Tris could smell his breath. She moved back a step before he grabbed her by the arm.

Tris tried to yank away. "What if I don't want the favor?" she asked coldly, trying to decide how she would punish him. She felt Chime clamber onto her shoulder.

"That's life, Dimples," the robber said, fumbling for Tris's purse. He was on the girl's far side, in the light. Tris's right shoulder, and the dragon, were in shadow.

Chime pulled herself onto Tris's braids, leaned forward, and spat a handful of needles into the man's cheek. The robber yelped, released Tris, and backed away, pulling the sharp bits of glass from his face. His fingers bled as the needles cut them.

"Maybe I'd better call for an *arurim,*" Tris remarked, though it seemed to her that Chime had punished the man enough. "Men like you are probably terrible for business."

"Mage!" croaked the robber. He turned and fled into the darkness, still trying to pull glass from his skin.

"I don't have dimples!" Tris called after him. She sighed and walked down a broader street. "That was well done," she praised Chime. "I'm impressed by your aim."

The glass dragon butted her head against Tris's ear. A breeze circled them, carrying the voice of someone who yawned and said, "I'm done for the evening, Nerit."

Tris caught herself yawning. "Sounds like a good idea," she murmured, and returned to Chamberpot Alley.

When they arrived at Touchstone Glass in the morning, Dema was there, waiting for them. Keth halted in the courtyard, fists clenched. Get it over with, he told himself, and asked Dema, "Who, and where?"

Dema's face was covered with sweat. He wiped it on his stole. "Stenatia, a courtyard *yaskedasu* from Swansdown House. He left her on the steps of the Hall of Records on the Keeper's Road."

"A courtyard . . . ?" Tris asked, not sure what that meant.

"From one of the entertainment houses. *Yaskedasi* there are a cut above those who perform on the street," explained Keth. "Their customers pay just to get in, plus whatever they give the performer. And the houses have watchmen to make sure the guests don't get rowdy."

"Which means he took her from under the nose of someone who was supposed to stop that sort of thing," Dema added. "You have good instincts for this, Keth, to remember about the watchmen."

"I don't think that's a compliment," Keth said bitterly. "When was she taken, do you know?"

As they talked, Tris set out the breakfast they had purchased on the way to the shop. Glaki took a honeycake to Dema, who smiled wearily at the child. He was ashen-faced with exhaustion. "Around midnight, between performances. Last anyone recalls seeing her, she was on her way to the privy in back of the house."

Heat — temper, magic? he didn't know — welled up in Keth until he thought he might burst. The courtyard houses were *safe*, particularly for *yaskedasi*. There were hazards to performing on the streets, enough that those who could afford to do so and those who had gained some measure of fame thought it worthwhile to pay the monthly fees to those who operated the houses. "Does he walk through walls?" he cried, furious. "Is he invisible?!"

Inside the shop two tall vases shattered. Everyone turned to stare at the pieces on the floor until Tris remarked, as sensibly as ever, "The problem with bringing your magic under control is that it gets more powerful. If your control isn't perfect . . ." She went into the shop and found the broom. "We'll work on that today."

"And the globes," Keth said grimly. She sounded unmoved and levelheaded, but Keth knew her a little better now. He could see the quiver at the corners of her mouth. She was as upset as he was. It startled him to realize that even though he knew she was upset her braids remained where they were, without movement, without sparks. For the very first time he wondered at the amount of emotional control it took, for her hair *not* to give her feelings away.

"And the globes," agreed Tris as she swept up glass. "You said you have a fallback plan. When does it go into action?" she asked Dema.

"Tomorrow night at the earliest," he replied, inspecting his honeycake as if he'd forgotten what it was for. "The *arurimati* have to rearrange schedules. The women, some of them, have families to be looked after. At least Mother isn't screaming over the expense. She knows how close I — we — are to disgrace." He took a bite of the cake and chewed as though it were made of wood. "I wish I could explain how maddening this is!" he cried when he had swallowed his bite. "Nine times out of ten — no, better than that — ninety-four times in a hundred, the victim knows her killer, his killer, whoever. We question the family, the neighbors, fellow workers, and usually it's one of them. But how do we handle a thing like this? We question those who knew the dead, who saw them before they were taken, but all of the possibilities have turned to lead. We've found no one who knew all of the victims, no one at all. And no one who saw anyone suspicious around even two of the *yaskedasi*."

Carrying broken glass to the cullet barrel inside the door, Tris saw a *prathmun* pick up the trash from Antonou's house and carry it to his wagon in the alley. "Have you questioned the *prathmuni*?" she asked, turning to Dema. "Maybe they saw something."

"Of course we've picked up and questioned a number of them already," Dema replied, suddenly uncomfortable as well as unhappy.

"Did they have anything to do with Khapik, or the victims?" Keth wanted to know.

Dema shrugged. "They're Khapik *prathmuni*. And they haven't admitted anything so far."

"You're torturing them," Tris accused.

"That's how we handle *prathmuni*," replied Dema. "Everyone knows a *prathmun* lies as easily as he breathes. Since the *arurim prathmuni* bring them in anyway, it's easiest to go right to it. If you were Tharian, you wouldn't even ask about this."

"So you get the torture out of the way, whether there is reason to suspect the *prathmuni* you arrest or not," Tris said angrily.

"That's how things are done here," replied Dema. "Our ways aren't yours. Could we change the subject? It's not exactly a decent one, particularly in front of a child." He got to his feet, half of his honeycake still in one hand. "If you create another globe today?"

"We'll let you know," Keth said.

Tris, Keth, and Glaki watched Dema trudge out of the courtyard. Only when he was well out of sight did Keth hear Tris mutter, "Barbarians." She looked at Glaki and scowled. "It's fine to talk about torture in front of a child, but gods forbid we talk about the people who get tortured." When Glaki's eyes went wide with fright, Tris smiled crookedly. "I'm not angry with you," she assured the little girl. "Not even a bit." Glaki relaxed slightly, and returned to playing with her ragged doll.

"Tharian customs," murmured Keth, though he understood Tris's feelings. "We're only guests here."

"Slavery is more honest," she retorted. "At least the only thing anyone ever blames slavery on is bad luck, not impurity."

Keth nodded. "We'd better start. I want to get some ordinary pieces done for Antonou today besides the other things. He's been very good about me using up his supplies."

Tris settled Glaki with her toy and placed her magical protections around the workshop. Once more she and Kethlun settled into meditation. That morning, at her direction, Keth worked on letting his magic fill just his skin without going outside his body. Tris barely said a word, apart from letting him know that his efforts were successful.

Once they finished pure meditation, Keth blew glass. Working slowly, taking pains, he produced three balls. None of them held lightning; all had lightning that flickered over their surfaces, but only in bursts that did nothing to hide the glass underneath.

Glaki was placing the third globe where the others sat —

the lightning on these globes didn't sting — when someone outside the barrier cleared his throat. It was Antonou. "Keth? Cousin? Might I have a word?"

Tris lowered her magical barrier. "Keep an eye on Glaki," she told Keth, walking past Antonou into the center of the courtyard. "I'll be right here, but don't disturb me."

Standing beside the well, Tris took off her spectacles and tucked them in her sash, then closed her eyes and began to meditate. The men's voices and the sound of Glaki as she played with her doll, Little Bear, and Chime, faded from her attention, along with the street noise. Once Tris was ready, she opened her eyes.

The day's breezes slid before her sight: they were clear in her vision, though nothing else was. She saw the air's eddies and pools, the change in currents where heat from the kitchen flowed through cooler air. Chime soared past her nose. Tris's eyes picked out the curling and parting of the air as the dragon cut through it, as water parted around a boat.

Whispering a magical formula, Tris drew signs first on her left temple, then on her right: the crescent for magical vision, the seven-pointed star for the strength to manage what she would see, and the four small waves of the winds. Then she clasped her hands before her, and waited for her sight to improve.

A wisp of color shone on a current of air, like the glint in the depths of an opal. Another wisp. Another. The air streamed with flares in many hues, threads of fast-moving color. The wisps grew infrequent, then rare. At last they stopped appearing to Tris's eyes at all.

She sighed. Her first try was over. Using a counterclockwise motion, she wiped the signs from her temples, and lurched. A strong arm caught her. She looked up into Keth's face. "Why are you mauling me?" she demanded, struggling weakly. She felt as wrung out as a sheet on laundry day.

Something on Keth's face looked suspiciously like a smile. Tris gave up her fight and groped in her sash for her spectacles.

"I had to stop you from falling into Antonou's well," he explained, his voice quivering. "They'd never get the taste of mage out of the water."

Tris shoved her glasses onto her nose and glared at him. He *was* smiling. "What's so funny?" she growled.

"You. Did you know it's almost midday?" Keth set Tris on her feet.

She swayed as she looked around. There was the lip of the well, just a foot away. Little Bear, Chime, and Glaki sat on the ground nearby, staring at her in fascination.

"Come on, great teacher," Keth said, wrapping an arm around Tris's waist to steady her as she tottered over to a bench. "Rest your weary bones."

"It *can't* be nearly midday," Tris argued, though her magical senses told her it was. "What happened to the morning?"

"It passed while you gazed into the air," Keth replied, easing her onto the bench. "You didn't even twitch when the Bear chased a cat in the garden. We owe Antonou basil plants, by the way."

"I don't know why that dog bothers," muttered Tris. "Every time he corners a cat, it beats the fur off him. I should get our midday." Her head swam. Odd sparks flared in her sight as she moved her head.

"Antonou is bringing it," Keth assured her.

Tris looked at him sharply. "Why? He's under no obligation to feed me or Glaki."

Keth grinned and sat beside her. "There's been a change in our arrangements," he explained. "Antonou likes having a glass mage in the shop — that's why he's left us alone. And he *really* likes those globes." He pointed to his morning's creations, which continued to glitter and spark, pale copies of his lightning globes. "If he sells anything I create that I don't need to keep, I'll get half the price. It solves a lot of problems, Tris. He says what he can make just from the globes will pay for my time and materials, and we'll have plenty left over. I thought you'd approve, since you sold those pendants I made of Chime's flames."

"Ah, she is back with us." Antonou approached from the kitchen wing of the house, a tray of dishes in his broad, scarred hands. "So, *Dhasku* Tris, does Keth need these globes? As mementoes, or for study? I can get a *very* good price for these. People love magical novelties that don't carry unpleasant consequences." He set the tray down on a table near the kitchen garden and took another tray from his wife, who had followed him.

"But I won't always be making magical devices, will I?" asked Keth, placing benches around the table. "I'll be able to do plain glass again?"

"You can do whatever you like, when your magic is completely under control," replied Tris. "And those globes are your work. They're yours to dispose of. Just let me test them this afternoon, to be sure they don't hold any surprises." She looked for Glaki, and saw that the girl was now hiding behind Little Bear. Both she and the dog stared at the good-smelling dishes with yearning.

"Here, you are too skinny," Antonou's wife said, putting things on a plate for the child.

While Keth tried to blow another lightning globe that afternoon, secure inside Tris's protective circle and working on his magical control, Tris inspected the new globes, exploring them with her power. They held not a flicker of true lightning, or of anything else. When she put the last one down, she noticed that Keth watched her. "They're empty," she said. "If Antonou wants them, and you want him to sell them, go ahead."

He nodded. "So Khapik is safe for tonight," he said, inspecting the globe he had just finished. It glittered like a round piece of ice in his hands. "As far as we know."

"As far as we know," Tris repeated with a sigh. "We should tell Dema." She was tired.

Keth finished his work, cleaned the shop, and told Antonou the globes were there for him to sell. At last he, Tris, Glaki, Little Bear, and Chime set off toward Khapik. "How's business?" he asked the guard who stood at the district gate.

"Not good," the man replied, disgusted. "The *yaskedasi* are scared. Some are leaving. And the guests are falling off, too. I suppose they think there's a chance this madman will mistake him for one of us."

"How bad is business off?" inquired Keth.

"A quarter," the guard replied.

Keth winced as they passed through the gate. "This will hurt everyone," he told Tris. "We've *got* to catch him."

Tris looked up at him and saw lightning flash in his eyes. "Keth, calm down," she ordered. "Breathe and count. You're sparking."

"I'm what?" he asked. "Where?" Tris pointed to his eyes. "Oh," Keth said sheepishly. The lightning in his eyes faded. "That never happened before," he pointed out, breathing slowly and carefully.

"But the lightning found a path through you it likes, so

it will keep following it. You'll have to learn to control your temper," Tris said firmly.

He grinned unexpectedly down at her. "And *you're* going to teach me?" Though he knew she kept a tight hold on her deepest feelings, he'd also gotten enough of the tart edge of her tongue to find the idea funny.

Tris drew herself up. "I can lose my temper because *my* power is under control," she said in her primmest voice. In a return to her normal, dry speech she added, "And quite a fight it is."

At Ferouze's, Xantha, Poppy, Ferouze, and the four musicians were in the courtyard, talking. Keth went to his room. Tris and Chime settled on a step, watching Glaki and Little Bear stretch their legs in a game of chase.

Xantha, relaxing as Poppy combed her long gold hair, began to hum, then to sing, her voice a sweet soprano. Poppy joined in to sing the counterpart in her lower voice. From overhead they heard the sound of a Namornese *balaka*, a plaintive, sharper version of a lute: Keth descended the stairs playing it. Ferouze and one of the men fetched common lutes to play. One musician brought a recorder, another a set of graduated wooden pipes, while the fourth backed his deep bass voice with a harp. One song passed into another, as naturally as the late afternoon breeze flowed through the galleries around the courtyard.

It was the kind of time Tris had never expected to find in

Khapik, like the evenings when her foster mothers, sisters, and brother all sat in the main room of their cottage, working on projects and singing, talking, or telling stories as the sounds of Winding Circle came through the windows.

As Tris watched the players, sparks appeared in the air's currents. She thought they might be part of a picture, but when she strained to see them, they disappeared. At last she gave up, relaxed, and drifted.

The gathering broke up as the shadows lengthened. Everyone but Ferouze, Keth, and Glaki had to work. Keth, seeing that Tris was not inclined to move, took Glaki and Little Bear to the Lotus Street *skodi* to fetch their supper.

That night the three of them ate in Yali's room, washed their dishes, and settled in for an evening's study. Keth pored over a book of glass magic Tris had borrowed from Heskalifos. Tris continued to read *Winds' Path*. When she caught Kethlun yawning, she ordered him off to bed. Glaki was already asleep — she barely twitched when Tris changed her dress for a nightgown and tucked her in. Little Bear curled up beside the child. Tris napped, exhausted by her day, but she woke some time after the clocks had struck midnight, the mix of lightning and tidal strength in her veins fading but strong. Her magic told her that dawn was still hours away, but she was no longer sleepy.

She went to Ferouze and made the same bargain as the night before, that the woman would stay with Glaki. She barely trusted Ferouze, but Keth needed his rest. With Ferouze to watch over Glaki and her lightning-sparked payment, Tris went out into Khapik. Once more Chime rode on her back, as fascinated by the changing worlds inside the district as Tris.

Tonight there was a festival in which *yaskedasi* dressed as butterflies, their wings huge creations of gauze and bamboo painted in a variety of designs. They paraded around the streams and islands in a soaring of flutes and the silvery tones of bells and hand cymbals. Guests and other *yaskedasi* showered them with confetti, dancing around the butterflies.

When Tris tired of the noise and crowd, she turned down one of the quieter streets, venturing into Khapik's darker areas. She came upon two women taking a purse from a drunken man. Tris considered putting a stop to it. She finally decided that if the man were fool enough to get so drunk that he could be separated from his friends and robbed, perhaps the missing purse would teach him a lesson he'd remember. The women looked at Tris, eyes glittering, as if they considered doing something about *her,* but when she walked by silently, they left her alone.

The encounter made her wonder again about what manner of person the Ghost was. He must look normal enough, to come and go everywhere with no one the wiser. He was clever, to turn the city's dislike for the dirtier side of life to his advantage. That he loathed the female *yaskedasi* was obvious. Did he want to be caught? Given that he left his victims in public places, it would seem that he did — or was that due more to his contempt for the city as a whole? Perhaps he didn't hate just the pretty, shady entertainers. Perhaps he hated all Tharios.

Tris shook off her musings. Thinking about what drove the Ghost, while fascinating, was Dema's job. If she were to help, if she were to do more than shepherd Keth as he followed his strange connection to these deaths, it would be through wind scrying. The air was everywhere. If she could see what the moving air touched, she could trace the killer, and avenge Glaki's loss of the women who loved her.

Her breezes, sent out that night from Ferouze's, found her now and then with their burden of sound. She listened to the conversations and noise they carried, finding nothing she could use. She also strained to view something, anything, in them. Once she thought she saw the curve of a gauze butterfly wing. She froze, trembling, needing to see more, but if she had actually glimpsed anything, the air that carried it had moved on, one of a hundred currents that flowed down the street.

"Probably just my imagination," she muttered to Chime, and sighed.

Deep within Khapik, she walked down a service alley for the first time, having avoided them for their trash and smell until now. Two *prathmuni* sat there with a wagonload of garbage, eating supper. Tris was about to pass them by, but curiosity made her stop. "Have the *arurimi* talked to you?" she asked. "About the murders? Whether you've seen anyone or anything suspicious?"

The *prathmuni* — a woman with muscles like a bull's and a teenage boy — regarded Tris with equally flat eyes. Finally the woman spit on the flagstones at her side. "*Shenos,* get some local idiot to explain what happens if you're caught talking to one of us. We'd as soon not catch the whipping. And go away."

"No one will hear about this talk from me," Tris replied. "So will you answer my question?"

"Why?" demanded the boy. "What have you done for us?"

"Shut up," growled the woman.

"It's what I *can* do for you, if you pass the word around," Tris replied. "If I tell the *dhaskoi* who's charged with finding the Ghost that you're helping, he can stop the *arurim prathmuni* from taking your people in for questioning."

"He must be a god, then," said the woman. "How 'bout it's more likely the *arurimi* will just keep torturing till one of us confesses and gets executed for it?"

"What if it *is* one of you?" Tris asked, curious.

The *prathmuni* looked at each other and drew the circle of the All-Seeing God on their foreheads. "They beat that out of us long ago," said the woman, but she looked uneasy.

"One of us — gods," breathed the boy. "They'd slaughter us all."

"*Is* it one of you?" Tris asked again.

"No," they said at once.

"Never," added the boy.

"But surely you've angry folk among you," Tris pointed

out, watching as sparkles, a fistful of them, flowed past her eyes.

"Plenty," replied the woman. "But they know better than to risk everyone's lives. They know how the upper classes feel about us."

"That's right," the boy agreed weakly.

There was no image in the passing clump of light. Tris sagged with disappointment. To the woman she said, "Madmen aren't guided by what their people need."

The woman spat to one side again before she said, "You're strange even for a *shenos*. Are there more at home like you?"

Tris smiled ruefully. "No, mostly they're traveling, too."

"I hope not here," the woman said. "Now please go away."

Tris woke to a hammering at the door. Glaki opened it to reveal Kethlun standing in the morning light. He was trembling. Lightning flickered in his eyes. "I think I have one," he said nervously. "Another globe. It's an itch, only in my skull where I can't scratch it."

Tris sat up. Her bones ached with weariness and too little sleep; the tides and lightning she had used to keep going were starting to run out. She would have to pay with days in bed once their strength was gone. "Go to Touchstone and get things ready," she croaked. "Don't start till I get there. I've an idea."

Keth, about to leave, stopped himself. "*Will* you get there?"

he wanted to know. "You look like death walking. Maybe you — never mind."

Tris, taking the pins from two fresh tide braids, looked at him sharply. He was stepping away from the door. "Never mind what?" she asked. "What's the matter?"

"It's just that when you start to fiddle with your hair I want to leave. No offense," Keth added hastily. "It's lovely hair, I'm sure." He fled.

Tris looked at Glaki. "Can you put your *kyten* on without my help?" she asked.

"Yes, Tris," replied the girl. "And my belly band, except you have to tie it." Tharians wore an undergarment like a diaper that tied at the waist with a drawstring.

"Put it on and come here, then," Tris ordered. When the girl's belly band was secure and she was wrestling with her worn, faded tunic of pale blue wool, Tris returned to her tide braids, undoing two inches of each. She drew their strength in, letting it slide through vein and bone, foam through her lungs, and race to her head. When she had taken it all in, she redid the braids and pinned them back into their patterns. She hoped they caught the Ghost soon, before the price she had to pay to keep awake and alert through all this got high enough to be painful, not just exhausting.

Her strength restored, she dressed, put a leash on Little Bear, tucked Chime into the sling on her back, tied Glaki's sandals, and bustled everyone out the door.

*   *   *

At Touchstone Keth assembled everything he would need, put ingredients into the crucible to melt, checked his work from the previous day, tried to read the book of glass magic Tris had lent him, gave up, and paced, unable to stand still. He blinked when she arrived with Glaki, the dog, and Chime. At Ferouze's she'd been the color of ash, her smattering of freckles darker in contrast. Now she was so full of vigor she nearly threw off sparks. If he needed a reminder that those cursed braids truly were her mage's kit, packed with magic both powerful and invisible, this was it.

She was the strangest girl, he thought as she settled Glaki in the corner. Kind when she was teaching, testy when people argued with her, briskly caring with the child. He would love to know her life's story.

"We did business with a family named Chandler out of Ninver in Capchen," he said abruptly. "Natron, mostly."

About to walk her protective circle around the workshop, she looked over her shoulder at him. "My family handles natron imports," she replied, a little stiff. "My Great-uncle Murris. Not exclusively, of course. My family deals in all kinds of goods." She smiled crookedly. "Except defective ones. Those they don't handle very well." She set to work, leaving Kethlun puzzled. They had thought *her* defective? he wondered. Then he remembered the way she handled lightning. He could see where that might unnerve even his own family.

Once they were enclosed in her magical shield, Tris turned to Keth, hands on hips. "Meditation first," she ordered.

"Do we have to?" he asked, trying not to whine as if he were still a restless boy in the schoolroom. "I don't think I can concentrate."

"But you *will* try, won't you?" she asked, in the sweet way she used when she was about to close the steel fist in her steel glove. "Because you won't control anything without first working on your control."

He took a breath to argue, but memory made him breathe out without speaking. She sounded just like the guildsman who'd taught the apprentices how to master their breathing and how to use as much of their lungs as possible, vital skills for a glassblower. "I'll try," he mumbled, thinking, What kind of a world is it, when a chit of fourteen sounds like a guildmaster?

To his surprise, it was easier to reach the state she demanded in meditation than he thought. Keth felt sheepish when he realized that. He considered an apology, and decided against it. She would only be smug, and he hated it when she was smug with reason.

Maybe if I didn't keep putting my foot in my mouth with her, he thought as they got to their feet and stretched. A scary thought occurred to him. "You say there are three more of you in Emelan?" Keth asked, goosebumps covering his arms at the thought. "Just like you?"

"Oh, no," Tris replied, mischief in her gray eyes. "They're *much* worse than I am."

Thinking of the kind of people who could be counted

on to survive long acquaintance with her, Keth said, "I believe you."

"It could be worse," Tris assured him. "We could all be here. Now," she added, going from playful to brisk, "Let's think about this next globe. Am I wrong, or when you blow into the gather, do you deliberately allow your power to flow on your breath?"

"Sometimes," Keth admitted, thinking it over. "Sometimes not."

"Let's make a choice, then," she suggested. "This time, try to let only a trickle of your power run through the blowpipe. Just a thread. Can you do that?"

Keth picked up first one blowpipe, then another, not liking the feel of either, though both were favorites. "I believe so, but it'll be hard," he admitted. "It feels like a flood behind a dam, Tris. It wants *out*. It wants to say what it has to say."

Up went her near-invisible gold brows. Tris pursed her mouth. "It's your magic, isn't it?" she reminded him. "It's time you taught it who's in charge."

"It is," mumbled Keth, choosing a blowpipe he'd never handled before. It felt right in his hands.

"Go on thinking that your power is in charge, and it will stay so," she explained. "Your single most important tool as a mage has to be your will, Keth. What you want, what you don't want. Your magic feeds on those things. You have to make it feed only on what you grant it, or it will rule you and ruin your life."

He nodded.

"Imagine the crucible in your mind, can you do that?"

Keth nodded.

"Now put all of your power in it, but for a single thread that you'll blow into the globe," she directed.

He did as she suggested and imagined his power flowing into the crucible. Imagining it, he could also feel his magic disappear endlessly, like an illusionist's trick, into some part of himself that held it neatly. In his mind's eye he saw the lone thread hanging from the opening like the loose end on one of his mother's balls of yarn. After a pause to make sure his grip was solid, he opened his eyes. "Done," he told Tris.

She nodded. "While you blow the globe, let that thread and only that thread travel with your breath into the glass. Maybe the problem has been that all of your magic is pouring into the globe until it explodes. Give it a try."

Keth's hands trembled. This was exciting. This might actually help. He glanced down at the blowpipe in his hands, the one he'd never used before. Set into its sides was a line of Kurchali, like advice from a seer who knew that one day a mage would hold the pipe: "Grant me steady hands, and steady breath."

Normally he didn't use an unfamiliar blowpipe on important projects, but this one, with the advice cut into it, seemed like an omen. Keth slid the pipe into the furnace, until its end was firmly set in molten glass. He began to twirl as he withdrew the rod. Up came the gather, a nice, red-orange blob. Frowning in concentration, Kethlun sent breath and power sliding through the pipe. The gather began to spread.

By the third reheating his magic began to fight its way free of the crucible in his mind. Keth clamped down. In that moment of distraction the glass developed an irregular bulge on one side: he'd slowed at twirling the pipe. He controlled its movement and blew, reshaping a perfect globe. A moment later he saw that the merest thread of his magic had thickened.

Then the force that had urged him to blow a globe expanded up and through Keth, filling the glass. The piece was finished.

Keth sighed and cut the globe free of the pipe. A veil of lightnings shimmered softly over the surface, a tamer version compared with the others Keth had made. Inside it was the same, a multitude of lightnings that moved, flashed, and split so much it was impossible to see anything.

Tris was reading from her leather-bound volume again. She looked at the globe he passed to her. "Some got away from my control," he admitted.

"Not as much as before," she murmured as she turned the globe over in her hands. "You know what you have to do now, right?"

Keth sighed. "Wait for that thing to clear."

"And waste the time while you wait?" she asked.

Keth glared at her. "Slave driver."

"A bad name is just a fart with consonants," she informed him loftily. "Well?"

Once more Keth sighed. "I need to work on my control."

"For a while. Then you can just blow glass if you like," his taskmistress said. "From the looks of you, most of your power today went into that globe. I'm going outside to do my own work. I'll make sure the barriers are sealed."

She was being an alarmist, Keth thought. He felt just as good now as he had on getting up that morning. Shaking his head over her lack of faith in how much magic he could work at one time, Keth sat cross-legged on the workshop floor. Tris opened her protective barrier and walked outside, Little Bear following. As she resealed the barrier around the workshop, Keth looked at Glaki. "You must get bored, sitting around here all day."

The little girl shook her head: she and Chime had discovered a game in which she would point to one of the dragon's food dishes, and Chime would eat, then produce colored glass flames for her. Keth noticed the little girl's brown curls were glossy and thoroughly combed, her face, arms and legs clean. Yali and Iralima had both belonged to the "do as well as can be expected" school of grooming a child. Most of their time had to be used on their own appearance, in preparation for a night's performance. Keth decided that of course Tris would do an exacting job on Glaki's hair: only look at what she put her own through.

He glanced outside, where Tris, veiled by the silver glow of the magical protections on the workshop, stood in the courtyard. Her spectacles were tucked away somewhere. She stared into space, eyes wide and unseeing. What was she doing? That was another thing he'd ask her, when he found the courage.

This wasn't helping him to control his power. Taking a deep breath, Keth began to meditate.

Glaki roused Keth from meditation when Dema arrived. It took both Dema and Little Bear to bring Tris back to the real world. Keth frowned as the older man helped his teacher to stand so she could remove her magical barrier on the workshop. As Tris's student it was *his* job to look after her, not Dema's.

Both Keth and Dema rushed to catch her when she staggered through the workshop door. When Keth touched her, a fizzing power like his own, only a hundred times stronger, flooded his body. He gasped and flinched back, then steeled himself to steady her on the left as Dema steadied her on the right.

"Oh, stop that," she said when they placed her on a bench inside. "Give me a moment to catch my breath." She looked at Dema. "Why are you crying?"

"I'm not crying!" he retorted. "My eyes are watering. Girl, what were you *doing*?"

Her eyes darted to and fro, as if she tracked the movement of a dozen insects inside the workshop. "Meditating,"
she said shortly. "Is there water?"

Glaki brought it, steadying it as Tris drank. Keth was
silently grateful to the girl as he sat unnoticed on one of the
benches. His knees were a bit unsteady.

When she finished her water, Tris looked at Dema and
Keth. "Did you show him, Keth?" she asked.

Keth blinked, puzzled, then remembered his globe. He
reached over to the nearby workbench and picked it up,
turning it over in his hands. "Do you send your people into
Khapik tonight?" he asked Dema.

"All four women, plus the guards we're putting on them,
arurimi in civilian clothes," the older man replied. "The female *arurimi* will wear the yellow veil with the ends knotted, so they can be identified."

"Will they perform?" asked Keth. He was trying to ma-
nipulate the lightning inside his creation, without result.
He only felt as if he simply pretended to have magic.

"Gods," Dema said, sinking onto the bench next to Tris.
"Don't ask. I've seen them try. They won't get any customers with music or dancing."

"What about weapons exhibitions?" asked Tris. "That's
entertainment for kings and emperors up north."

Dema rubbed his lips with a knuckle. "That might work
for some of the more hopeless ones. I'll suggest it."

Keth handed the globe to Dema. "Surface lightning's not so bad, but the inside's as clouded as ever."

"I'll take this back to the watch commander at the *arurimat.*" Dema said. "He'll watch it while I look our *yaskedasi* over. Thank you, Keth." He got to his feet, looking old. To both Keth and Tris he said, "Try not to kill yourselves, whatever you're doing. It makes the city look bad." He left them, the lightning globe cradled in his hands.

Instead of following the Street of Glass straight to Khapik when they finished for the day, Keth asked to stop by the Elya Street *arurimat,* to see how his globe fared, though his head ached thunderously. When they walked in, the *arurimi* present gave them a wide berth. Only one, a hard-faced woman in charge of the main desk, didn't inch away from their small group, Keth saw, but perhaps she felt safe behind her wooden barrier.

"I'll tell *Dhaskoi* Nomasdina you're here, *Dhaskoi* Warder," she said.

Keth started. It was the first time he'd been given the title of mage. He started to say, "I'm only a student," but caught himself in time. After facing the prospect of torture in this building, it was very pleasant to be treated with respect and a little fear.

"If you'd like a seat, *dhaski*?" the woman asked, indicating the benches against the walls.

Keth and Tris sat gratefully. Once settled, Keth leaned over to Tris and murmured, "Different from my last visit."

She smiled back, her eyes busy following some movement Keth was unable to see. "Mine, too. Chime, how many times have I told you to stay out of the ashes?" she asked as the dragon hiccuped and expelled a cloud of dust. "I don't care if you like it, you don't seem able to digest it." She looked at Glaki. "If you catch her at it, don't let her eat ashes." Glaki nodded. She pressed close to Tris's side and took the older girl's hand. Keth was surprised at her apparent affection for the redhead. The Glaki he'd known in the company of Iralima and Yali had been shy.

"Keth! Tris! Hello, little one," Dema said to Glaki as he walked into the waiting room. He held the lightning globe in his hands. The surface bolts were gone; shapes and colors were dimly visible inside. "I'm about to ride uptown so we can be close when it clears, since uptown seems to be where our *kakosoi* is headed. Do you want to come?"

Keth was eager to go. He wanted to catch this beast, not just tell others where to find him. He glanced at Tris, who frowned. "Not me," she replied. "I'm not going to leave Glaki by herself." She pursed her mouth, then looked directly into Keth's face for the first time since she had meditated that morning. "Are you sure that you feel up to this?" she asked sharply. "Because you have maybe a pinch of magic left in you, no more than that. My experience is that when you're that drained of magic, your body's on the edge of exhaustion, too. You may collapse before too much longer, no matter how good you feel right now."

"I'm *fine,*" Keth said testily, through the pounding in his head.

Tris shrugged. "Please yourself. Glaki and I are going to Ferouze's." She looked at Dema, her face serious. "I hope you catch him," she said quietly. "Good luck." She levered herself up from her bench, gathered up dog, dragon, and girl, and left the *arurimat.*

Dema turned bright, eager brown eyes on Keth. "We're going to ride. Come on, let's get you a horse."

Progress up the Street of Glass toward Assembly Square and Heskalifos was annoyingly slow. Time after time Keth wanted to shout for people to get out of the way, but with the globe's contents still shrouded in lightning, it made no sense to hurry. The press of humanity on the streets was loud and colorful, a constant irritation to Keth's nerves. He also didn't like it that Dema kept sneaking looks at him.

At the Apricot Street *skodi,* Dema halted at a street vendor's stall that sold small eggplants stuffed with lamb and rice, a Sotaten dish that was popular in Tharios. He bought enough for everyone, and ordered Keth to eat. Keth bolted the food: he hadn't realized how very hungry he was. Dema paid another vendor for skewers of grilled kid marinated in olive oil, cinnamon, and onion, and a third for plum juice. They moved their horses to the side of the street to devour it all, licking their fingers when they were done.

The thickest crowds were bound for Khapik, but even headed uphill there was plenty of traffic as the city's shop-keepers, clerks, and merchants turned their faces toward home. The First and Second classes would not venture out for their evening's entertainment until dark, Dema told Keth. Their servants ran last-minute errands at the *skodis,* doing business at a trot that made their hobnailed sandals strike sparks from the stones of the roadway.

Dark drew down slowly. Torches were lit at eating-houses, other shops that stayed open late, and inns. Foot traffic began to thin out, replaced by horses, chairs, and lit-ters. Keth's headache eased after he'd eaten, but now he was dizzy. He bit his lip, determined to say nothing to Dema.

They halted at Achaya Square, where the Ghost had left Yali's body. At an open-air eating-house they bought dishes of olives, dates, liver patties, dried apricots, and flatbread, along with a pitcher of grape juice, and settled down to wait. The globe held the place of honor at the center of the table, drawing attention from diners and from passersby. Keth and his companions watched as it cleared inside, the lightnings fading.

Keth couldn't eat a thing once they were seated. He tore a piece of flatbread into the tiniest of crumbs, to the approval of the pigeons who came to forage by torchlight. It was unfair, to wait for his own device to reveal something in *its* time, not Keth's. Magic, he thought ruefully, is more the master than the pet dog. In his mind he heard Tris say scornfully, "Whoever told you it was anything else?"

He tried again to draw the lightnings out, but it was as if his magic no longer existed. It was maddening to sit here and wait, and risk the chance that they would be too late to save the next victim.

Dema put a hand on Keth's arm. "It's clear what you're thinking," he said quietly. "But Keth — she's probably dead by now, whoever she is."

Keth sat bolt upright, his mouth dry. "That's a *horrible* thing to say! We might see her in that, still alive!" He pointed to the globe. "Don't pronounce her dead until you've found the body — as well invite the gods to kill her, not the Ghost!"

Dema leaned closer, inspecting Keth's face by torchlight. Suddenly he placed the inside of his wrist on Keth's forehead. When Keth jerked away, Dema calmly produced a black leather case from his sash and opened it to reveal a lens. He held it up to one eye, then put it away, shaking his head. "She was right, and I was too eager to get moving to realize it," he muttered. "Your skin's clammy, you're hot, and you're sweating a river. You've overdone it. If you try more tonight, you'll make yourself ill. You need rest."

"I'm *fine*," Keth retorted. "What is it, getting a mage's credential turns you all into old women, forever fussing and worrying over someone? I made that cursed globe and I'll see it through. You and Tris can go nursemaid each other!" He struggled to his feet and stood, wavering, as sweat trickled down his cheeks. "*I'll* settle the Ghost —"

His ears buzzed. His legs turned to overcooked noodles. Shadows filled the edges of his vision, shadows that grew and expanded as the buzz turned to a roar.

In the room that Tris shared with Glaki, they sat together on the bed, the little girl freshly bathed. Glaki petted Little Bear as Tris explained how Sandry, Briar, and Daja had decided that Tris would miss the dog most of all of them during her travels. She had reached the point at which Little Bear had to be coaxed onto the ship when she heard Ferouze's hoarse bellow in the courtyard below.

She stalked out to the gallery over the courtyard, ready to berate Ferouze for raising such a noise when it was nearly Glaki's bedtime. Looking down, she saw the old woman at the entrance to the street passage. Three men stood with her, two in *arurim* red. The third, sagging between them, was Keth.

Tris tucked Glaki in, ordered her to sleep, then went down to her student.

"Just keeled right over," the older *arurim* said as Tris guided them to Keth's room. "*Dhaskoi* Nomasdina was saying he overdid it, and Keth here was giving him what-for when his eyes rolled up and down he went." The *arurimi* laid Keth on his bed and set about removing his boots. "Will he be all right, *dhasku?*" the man asked. "*Dhaskoi* Nomasdina said he would, but then, *Dhaskoi* Nomasdina didn't see this lad was reeling in the saddle."

"He won't even know he was ill in the morning," Tris assured them. "This is normal enough, when a student's too big for the teacher to order him to bed." She waved them out and returned to open Keth's shirt and bathe his sweaty face. "You want to cure all the ills of the world in one day, because you think magic can do that," she murmured as she drew a sheet over the unconscious Keth. "You'll learn."

Dema

Less than an hour passed after Dema had sent Keth home when the globe began to clear. The men he'd sent with Keth were riding into Dema's view when one of his *arurimi* leaned in to stare at the globe. "I know that balcony! It's at Lagisthion, the debate arena at Heskalifos!"

They scrambled for their horses, Dema tossing coins from his purse onto the table to pay for the dishes they broke. They rode to Heskalifos like fiends, scattering people left and right as they galloped up the Street of Glass. Bolting through Achaya Gate, they ignored the yells of the university peacekeepers as they sped over paths not meant for riders. Where the paths failed to provide the most direct route, Dema led them across carefully tended gardens between buildings.

They reined in before a small, round hall built of white marble with pillars all the way around. Dema slid from the saddle, the globe clutched to his chest. He raced up the bank of steps that served as pedestal to the hall.

"Brosdes, open that thing," he ordered, pointing to the door.

One of the *arurimi,* a short black man with knots of muscle in his arms and legs, approached with a heavy pack over one shoulder. He inspected the double doors with an expert eye. "Right," he said, kneeling to extract a chisel and mallet from the pack. "Majnuna, give me a leg up," he ordered.

The *arurim* Majnuna, a huge, olive-skinned woman who stood a full head taller than any of the others, knelt beside the door. Brosdes jammed hammer and chisel into his sash, then climbed onto Majnuna's shoulders. The big woman stood and braced herself.

Brosdes cut the head off the pin that secured the hinge with two hammer blows, then knocked the pin out. When Majnuna lowered him, Brosdes did the same for the lower hinge. Everyone moved aside as half of the door trembled, groaned, then fell to the marble floor.

Inside the globe, Dema saw a limp woman on the stage of the debating hall. He led his *arurimi* inside, motioning for them to spread out in every direction and cover the doors out of the place. They obeyed, lighting torches from those that blazed outside the front entrance. The outer lobby was empty. Two *arurimi* vanished up the curving stairs on either side to search the balcony.

Dema and three *arurimi,* each with a lead-weighted baton in hand, passed into the immense theater where the university's famed debates were held. Opposite them was the stage.

It was empty.

"Is the globe wrong?" asked one of the men.

Dema looked at the globe, where the image was rapidly fading. Keth had done it, Dema realized. He'd made the inside visible *before* the Ghost could display his victim. His success wasn't complete — what Dema wanted was a look at the murderer himself — but Keth had come a long way toward their ultimate goal.

Hope burned in Dema's chest like a red-hot coal. The killer might be nearby. "Quietly," he whispered. "Fan out and search. Inside and out."

He and Majnuna were in the wings of the stage when one of the *arurimi* came for them. The *arurimi* outside Lagisthion had found a service entrance to the hall's underbelly. It was hidden by a clump of brush a hundred feet away.

Dema cursed. He had forgotten the service entrances. "They didn't want to ruin the beauty of the building with anything as sordid as taking out the trash," he panted as he and his *arurimi* raced outside. "They never do anything simple if they can think of a complicated way around it."

Quickly they found the path into the greenery and followed it to a circle of open ground. An open door yawned at its center. On top of the steps leading down lay the body of a *yaskedasu*.

Dema clenched his fists. They were too late, again.

He looked around. They had been quiet since coming outside. There was a chance that the killer was still nearby.

An application of heartbeat powder over the dead woman told him she'd been dead less than an hour. He didn't waste time with the vision spell, but immediately gulped a mouthful of stepsfind and sprayed it over the *yaskedasu*. In the gloom of the night it drifted to one side of her, and shimmered in the form of footsteps on the ground.

None of the *arurimi* said anything. They followed. They tracked the Ghost through the back ways of Heskalifos, through alleys and service entrances hidden with brush and trees, until the trail of the killer turned downhill. They followed him right up to the white marble columns and stones of a building so thoroughly protected by cleansing magics that all trace of him was lost. Dema's curses brought the priests out to discover who was making so unholy a racket.

Seeing them, Dema literally ground his teeth. The killer had vanished into the bowels of the Heskalifos temple of the All-Seeing. He had carried his pollution into the temple's foundations, where the guardian spells erased all trace of him. Once more he'd managed to be a ghost in fact, vanishing from a trail so plainly marked Dema could have followed it blindfolded.

"You take too much upon yourself," a priestess informed Dema. She had found him on the temple steps, waiting as his people searched outside the grounds in case the Ghost had not vanished into the service tunnels. "You think that magic is not a force of nature but something dead, a tool to be used," she continued, standing beside him. She was robed and draped as a high-ranking priestess. She had the age for it, with laugh lines and the lines drawn by long watches framing her eyes. Her nose was a straight edge with delicate nostrils, her thin-lipped mouth painted the same red that decorated her robes.

"Magic's not dead," protested Dema, watching for his *arurimi*. "But it is a tool, a device we can use to set the balance of justice right."

The priestess shook her head. "Magic is a living force that obeys its own time and its own laws. We must accept that and learn to live with it, for our own serenity's sake. Magic leaves us no choice."

Dema shook his head stubbornly. He *hated* not having a choice.

The priestess rested a hand on his shoulder. Dema looked at her, wary. So far his contacts with this particular priesthood were less than encouraging.

"Your heart is in Tharios, Demakos Nomasdina," she told him.

Dema flinched. He hadn't mentioned his name, not wanting to be punished for tracking the polluted steps of a killer.

"You are a true and noble servant to our city," the priestess continued. "When you have laid hands upon this Ghost, return here. I shall see to it that you are made clean by rite and magic, so that you may do your work unhindered. I trust that your clan takes pride in so devoted a citizen." She drew the circle of the All-Seeing on Dema's forehead, bowed, and retreated into the temple. Dema stared after her, mouth agape.

"*Dhaskoi.*" There was reverence in Majnuna's deep, thick voice. The *arurim* had come up while Dema was speaking with the priestess. "You've been blessed by Aethra Papufos!"

Gooseflesh crawled up Dema's spine. The high priestess of the All-Seeing almost never appeared in public. Her prayers guarded Tharios; she was considered to be the voice of the All-Seeing on earth.

She had set her hand on him in full view of a handful of priests and *arurimi*. She had called him a "devoted citizen." And she had virtually told him that he would be able to find killers unhindered by considerations of pollution — once he caught the Ghost.

The worst part, Tris thought as she groped her way down Imperial Alley, was how confusing it all was. She felt as if she walked through an opal when she tried the magics of *Winds' Path,* an opal alive with glittering bits of color that threatened to overwhelm her sight. None of them served to make any kind of a picture for her, not even so much as last night's glimpse of a gauze butterfly wing. Worse, they made her half-blind in Khapik, not precisely a good thing to be. Tonight she had Chime and Little Bear with her, and her breezes to warn her, but her head was spinning. Floods of dizziness came and went.

"Enough," Tris told her companions. "I'll just have to try again tomorrow."

Chime rubbed her head against Tris's cheek. The girl sighed and closed her eyes, willing the magic away. At last she put her spectacles back on and returned to Ferouze's. She doubted that she could sleep, thanks to the tides in her blood and bones, but at least she could read further. Maybe there was a way to sort all these firefly bits until they showed her something real.

About to climb from the second story of Ferouze's to the third, she saw that Chime scratched at Keth's open door. Tris looked into his room. Her student lay awake on his bed, watching the ceiling shadows by the light of one candle. He pulled the sheet up to his bare chest when she came in and smiled ruefully. "Yes, they had to send me back because I was exhausted. Please don't say 'I told you so,'" he begged.

Tris sat on a chair, Chime at her feet, Little Bear dropping with a groan in the doorway. "It's the farthest thing from my mind," she assured him, watching threads of color in the breeze that flowed between the window and the door. The threads all came to hover around Keth, lighting on his eyes, his jaws, his chest, making him sparkle in Tris's sight.

"I suppose you never did anything of the kind," Keth accused.

"Never," replied Tris, straightfaced. "And if Niko tells you that one time I decided to halt the tides, and the rocky cove where I tried it is now called 'Gravel Beach,' well, he exaggerates."

"You. Tried to halt the — the tides." There was awe in Keth's voice.

"The important word there is 'tried.' I was very foolish, and lucky enough to survive the experiment," Tris informed him. "Are you hungry at all?"

Keth shook his head. "Sleepy, a little. Trying to think of

ways to pull the lightning out of the globes. Where were you? I went upstairs, but Ferouze is with Glaki."

"I'm trying something of my own," Tris said. "I need to be in open air for it to work. It's not going as well as I had hoped," she confessed, and sighed.

"You have trouble? But you wear the medallion," Keth protested, sitting up on his elbows. "I thought, once you have that —"

Tris shook her head with a rueful smile, wishing that were so. "Different spells make different kinds of trouble," she explained. "Nobody can do every kind of magic, and the more complex a spell, the harder it is to work." She sighed, remembering. "Three years ago there was an epidemic in Summersea," she told him. "Nearly thirty of us, including my brother Briar and two great mages, worked day after day, trying to make a cure using magic. Every time something went wrong, we knew more people were dying. And there wasn't a thing we could do except keep working, one hard step at a time."

She looked at him. She could see that he listened to her with every particle of his being. Finally now, to Keth she was not fourteen and unworthy; she was a mage, with a mage's wisdom. They had come a long way since their first meeting. "Every mage knows what it means to fail at something," she continued, "or to bungle it, or to do so much you just collapse. One of our great mages got the essence of the disease on her by sheer accident. She got sick and nearly died."

"I thought magic made things simpler," Keth protested. "Just a wave of a hand, and poof! You have answers. This slowness, this plodding, it's —"

"Too much like the everyday world?" suggested Tris. Keth nodded.

Tris leaned over to pat his arm. "In some ways, magic *is* the real world, complete with fumbles, sweat, tears. . . . All the happy things. Go to sleep, Keth. Tomorrow your magic will be fresh. We'll try again."

"My heart flutters with joy," he grumbled. With a groan he turned on his side. "I'd like to tuck this killer into the furnace, let *him* anneal for a while. It might burn off the impurities."

"I like that," Tris said, imagining it. "Try not to dream about it, though." She got up and blew out his candle, then went outside with Chime and Little Bear. Quietly they climbed back up to their room.

Tris halted outside the door, staring into the dark, or at least into a dark punctuated by the occasional spark of color. Her head ached; her eyes burned. She *would* learn how to do this. She wouldn't allow herself to be driven mad by a flood of sparks. The trick would be to learn it in time to capture Yali's murderer. She was beginning to doubt that she would.

She woke the dozing Ferouze and sent her back to her rooms, her payment of five *biks* stripped of sparks. Glaki, sound asleep, lay half out of bed, her head nearly touching the floor, as limp as her ragged doll. Tris gently lifted her back onto the bed, and arranged Glaki's old doll on her left side. On her right Tris placed a new doll she had bought earlier, a pretty thing with brown hair, a yellow veil, and a costume much like Xantha's. Beside the doll she also set a brightly colored ball so Glaki could play with Little Bear. They were just tokens, not that expensive, but Tris had owned few toys. She knew it could be lonely, sometimes, to have only one doll.

Tris washed her face and hands and settled in the chair to read. The flicker of the candle was too hard on her weary eyes. She blew it out. Making herself comfortable, she combed one of her thin braids until enough lightning had collected on the end to make it glow. With steady light to read by, Tris opened *Winds' Path.*

At Touchstone the next morning, Tris and Keth were preparing to meditate when Tris looked at Glaki. The girl sat in her usual corner, out of the range of any molten glass accidents. She had arranged her dolls, Chime, and Little Bear around her, but she was looking at Keth and Tris, loneliness in her eyes.

"You'd find it boring, most likely," Tris warned.

Glaki shrugged.

Tris looked at Keth, who also shrugged. "As long as she doesn't make noise."

Before Tris could invite her, Glaki raced across the shop to plop herself onto the dirt floor between Tris and Keth. "I do things and count to seven," she told Tris.

"Right," the older girl said. "Breathe in and count, hold it and count."

Keth vanished into his meditation, his magic back to its former strength and tucked into his imagined crucible, where it shone brightly in Tris's magical vision. Once she saw Glaki knew how to breathe, Tris began, deliberately using her power to reach for water without using her eyes as a change from her normal exercises. She found it. Water ran in the gutter outside as shopkeepers washed their doorsteps; it splashed in fountains on the Street of Glass, rushed in streams throughout the city, churned in the bed of the Kurchal River as it raced to the sea. Further off, in the marrow of her bones, Tris felt the pull of the sea and the draw of the tides. When they would have taken her far from shore, Tris shook herself free and returned. Glaki was asleep, her thumb in her mouth. Keth looked much improved.

They spent the morning quietly. Tris went to try wind scrying again. Keth molded glass bowls and pressed signs for health into their bases. When Glaki awoke, she played with her dolls, Chime, and Little Bear.

The city's clocks had just struck midday when Keth shouted, "Tris?"

The redhead's still figure in the courtyard didn't move.

Keth frowned. "Chime, bring Tris out of it?" he asked.

Chime soared into the open air, the sun gliding from her wings as she flew. She lit on Tris's shoulder and looked back at Keth. He nodded.

Chime sank glass fangs into Tris's earlobe. Tris let out a yelp, swatted the dragon, and fumbled for her spectacles and handkerchief. "What did you do *that* for?" she demanded. Her vision was filled with colors. She groped around her as a blind person might, trying to see past everything that filled the air. Chime stayed just out of her reach as Tris snatched at her.

"Tris, I've got that feeling again," Keth called, his voice shaking. "Another globe."

"Start," she ordered. With her handkerchief pressed to her earlobe, she carefully made her way over the stones of the courtyard, seeing them dimly behind washes and currents of moving color. "Keth, did you tell Chime to bite me?" The dragon, chinking in distress, lit on Tris's shoulder beside the unwounded ear.

"Of course not!" Keth said, picking up a blowpipe. "But I'm glad it worked."

"I'm sure you are," she said sarcastically. "Next time I'll send her to get you out of bed in the morning, see how *you* like it. Get started, Keth, don't wait for me. Try what you did yesterday. Make the lightning thinner, if you can." Without even looking she called her protective barrier out of the ground outside the shop. That was one of the benefits of laying protective circles in the ground: the earth remembered them if they were made on the same lines several times.

Tris sat on a bench to watch as Keth collected his gather and brought the pipe up. His hands were more deft than they had been when she'd first seen him. He barely looked inside the furnace, sensing when he had enough glass for his needs. Best of all, Tris could *feel* the change in him. He must have been this way before the lightning struck him, in casual command of fire and glass, born to work in a place like this. She wished she could tell him so, but doubted he would listen. To him a lightning globe that caught the Ghost was his way to buy his life back. He wouldn't realize he'd already gotten his life, with some changes, until afterward.

Once he finished, the globe was as full of lightning as it had been the day before, though only a handful of miniature bolts shimmered along its surface. "Tris, I want to try something," Keth said. He took the finished globe off the blowpipe and held it in one hand. "I want to see if I can take back some of the lightning I put in."

"Now that the globe's closed?" she asked with a frown. She supposed it could work. To her the glass shielded the lightning inside, but it might well be a barrier that would not affect Keth at all.

"I think I can do it," replied Keth.

"Have you ever taken in lightning you just got rid of?" Tris asked, still trying to think it all through.

"No. There doesn't seem to be any reason why it *won't* work." Keth grimaced, then admitted, "I'm scared, a bit."

Tris chewed on her lower lip, calculating. "It could be tricky. One moment." She went to the cullet barrel with its mix of broken and discarded glass. She saw plenty of sparks from Keth's magic in there, from the pieces they'd thrown in. Perhaps her next move ought to be a container for mag-icked glass, to keep the power from spreading, or perhaps Keth could learn to remove the power and make it harmless. She put those thoughts in the back of her mind to brew, and threw the protective barrier she used to guard Keth around the barrel. With it in place, she raised her hands and lowered them, opening the protections on the top of the barrel, until it was sheathed from rim to ground in white fire.

"Now try," she advised Keth, shooing Glaki and Little Bear into a far corner of the shop. "If you can't bear it, throw it into the cullet." She stood beside the barrel, her hands loose at her sides.

"But I should be able to call it back, like you do when you take the circles down," he protested. "I can feel you re-claim the magic that was in them."

"That's magic. *This*" — she pointed to the globe — "is lightning, even if it's sheathed in magic to keep it from burn-ing everything in sight. Once you free lightning, I'm not sure you *can* reclaim it."

"It's my lightning. I can reclaim it," he replied stub-bornly.

"Lightning doesn't belong to anyone," she said, but he ignored her. Tris sighed. He might be right; if he wasn't, he'd soon realize his mistake.

Keth cradled the globe in both hands. Tris watched as his power flowed out around the globe to envelop it. First he peeled away the surface lightnings, pulling them back into himself. Then he reached deeper, through the glass. Slowly he drew some of the inner lightning out, pulling it back into his chest.

She could see it hurt him. His face went red; sweat popped out all over his upper body. He grimaced and continued to draw on the lightning, until he was gasping. "Tris —" he began to say. She pointed at the cullet barrel. He turned toward it and opened his mouth.

Lightning roared from his throat and slammed into the junk glass. The moment the last of it came out of Keth, Tris enclosed the barrel in a globe of protective magic.

She backed away, feeling his power batter her globe. For a moment nothing happened. Suddenly the barrel quivered, shook, and exploded with a roar, hurling charcoal and glass into the magical barrier. Smoke filled it as if her power were glass, whirling and twisting inside.

"*Beautiful,*" whispered Glaki.

"Stupid," said Keth with chagrin.

"You needed to find out," Tris told him, hands on hips as she watched the smoke and ash settle. "Now you know."

"I have to pay Antonou for the cullet, and replace it," Keth remarked, glum. "We need it to make other glass. But it *should* have worked, curse it!"

Tris shrugged. "It's lightning. It's no more amenable to 'should haves' than you are."

"Ouch," Keth said, wincing. He looked at the globe in his hands. The surface was clear, but he'd drawn hardly any lightning from inside it. He sighed and sank onto a bench. "So we wait," he said, resigned. "I —" He stood, swaying.

"I'll get our midday," said Tris, seeing the magic under his skin gutter. It was funny how academic mages were never exhausted by their first workings, she thought, but ambient mages were. "Why don't you see if Antonou has a crate and shovel, so we can clear out the mess when it settles."

Keth flapped his hand at her in gloomy resignation and walked out of the shop, smack into the barrier around the outside. "Just what I needed," he moaned as she retrieved its magic. "A knock on the head."

"Well, it's not like it hurt anything important, is it?" Tris asked tartly.

Keth turned, expecting to see that disgusted expression on her face. Instead she grinned at him. "Why aren't you one of those teachers who believes in coddling students?" he demanded.

"I couldn't," she said, straightfaced. "It would be bad for your character."

He fled, before she could think of another joke to make at his expense.

The globe began to clear as their afternoon's work, getting rid of the mess of molten glass and charcoal, came to an end. They were packing to leave Touchstone for the day when Dema arrived. Under the shade of the courtyard trees he told them of the fruitless search the night before, then took charge of the globe.

Keth had recovered after his midday, enough to help clean up and to blow the small globes that Antonou liked to sell. Tris wasn't sure that he ought to go with Dema after the previous night's collapse, but Keth didn't give her the chance to debate it. He simply followed Dema out into the street.

With Keth gone, Tris turned to Glaki. "Have you ever been up on the wall?" she asked. "The wall around the city?"

"No," replied the girl. She had begged a scrap of cloth from Antonou's wife and fashioned it into a sling like the one Tris used to carry Chime. Into it she had tucked her dolls. Little Bear carried his ball. All afternoon he and Glaki had played with it, until it was covered with dirt and dog drool.

"Would you like to climb the wall, Glaki?" Tris wanted to know. "I want to try something. I'm always better at new things when I'm up somewhere high."

"Let's go," the four-year-old said eagerly, grabbing Tris's hand. She towed the older girl down to the city's gate.

As Tris had expected, Tharios's wall was a favorite with visitors: the guards waved them straight to the stair. When they reached the top, they found a broad walkway, thirty feet above the ground. From there they could see the roads that led around the city, the river bridges, and the road that led southeast to the seaport of Piraki. To their left, a tumble of huts and hovels clung to the rocky hillside between Tharios and the Kurchal River. A number of huge pipes dotted the same rocky ground, pipes that emitted streams of brown, clotted water that flowed into the river: the city's sewer outlets. Swarming over the hillside, hanging out wash, minding goats and chickens, talking, grinding grain, playing, and cooking, were *prathmuni,* recognizable even from this height by their clothes and haircuts. Tris felt cold, seeing their dwelling place. She knew the mages at Heskalifos had to be aware of the connection between sewage and disease, yet they allowed people to live where the night soil of Tharios was dumped. How many *prathmuni* children lived even to Glaki's age, let alone her own? Tris wondered. How many old *prathmuni* were there?

"Tris, please don't," whispered Glaki, tugging Tris by the sleeve. "Please don't."

She glanced at the little girl. "Don't what?" she asked, her voice clipped.

Glaki actually backed up a step. She still found the courage to say, "Please don't thunder inside. It's scary."

Remorse flooded Tris at the fear in Glaki's eyes. She knelt and held her arms out. "It's not about you, Glaki," she said, deliberately gentling her voice. "You could never make me angry."

Glaki clung to her, even with a doll in each hand. Tris soothed her until she was sure the little girl was calm. This too was something she knew all too well. The anger of adults almost always had meant packing her bags and moving on to a new home. An adult in a temper meant new relatives with new rules and new places where she was not welcome.

When Glaki was calm, Tris sat her on a bench with Little Bear and Chime, and gave the child her spectacles. Closing her eyes, she entered the trance she needed to scry the winds. When she opened her eyes, colors and half-images assaulted her, flashing by so quickly she couldn't track them. Time after time she tried to seize an image and hold it, but by the time she'd picked one, it was gone. Grimly she persisted until her eyes began to water and ache.

Once more, she thought, biting her lower lip. One, just one . . . She imagined hooks magically tethered to her eyes, and sank them into a flash of crimson. Then she fought to keep her eyes in one position. They wanted to flick aside to capture another of the images that raced by like a river in flood. She widened her eyelids and refused to let them jitter, staring instead at what she had caught. Slowly the image cleared as the fight to keep her eyes steady got harder.

Suddenly she realized what she saw. Excitement surged through her, cutting the vision free of her grip, but Tris didn't care. Her eyes began to dance again as eyestrain tears streamed down her cheeks.

She had seen something real.

"A ship, Glaki!" she said, reclaiming her spectacles. "I saw a ship on the wind! A ship with a crimson sail and a sun emblem on it!"

"Course you did," the little girl replied, for all the world as if she were Tris herself. "There's all kinds of ships down in Piraki harbor."

It took some time for Tris's vision to clear. When she could actually see, she asked Glaki, "Show me the ships?"

The girl pointed. Far below, through a gap in the rocky hills between Tharios and Piraki, Tris saw the antlike shapes of vessels anchored in the harbor. Above one was a dot of red: the red-sailed ship Tris had seen life-size on the wind.

"Supper now?" Glaki pleaded, tugging her skirt.

Tris hugged the child to her side. "Definitely supper." She looked around for Chime and saw the glass dragon on the wall several feet away, inspecting the guards and tourists as they inspected her. "Chime, come," Tris called. The dragon took flight and returned to her, while the tourists clapped. "Show-off," Tris murmured as Chime wrapped herself around Tris's neck.

"But she's *beautiful*," protested Glaki. "She *should* show off."

Tris smiled. "Spoken like a *yaskedasu*'s daughter," she said. "Come on. Maybe Keth caught the Ghost." Her pride would suffer if he did, but her pride wasn't important. Sending that murderer to a place where he could kill no more was.

Two hours after he left the *arurimat*, Keth returned to Ferouze's. To his considerable surprise, Dema was there with Tris and Glaki. The older man stared gloomily into a cup of water. "You can hear it from me," he told Keth. "We found her in a trash bin, in Perfume Court. We tracked him to the temple of the All-Seeing, where it looks like he vanished into thin air. Of course, the place is hip-deep in cleansing spells, enough so that they stick to you when you come out of it. He's gone, and we lost him." He got to his feet. "Sorry, Keth. You did all that work, and we failed you." He walked out without even saying good-bye.

Keth sat down hard. "All I did was stop for supper on the way," he complained. "And a bath. And this Ghost killed and escaped. Maybe he *is* a ghost. Maybe we need an exorcist, not mages."

Tris shook her head. "He's just a man who knows Tharios from top to bottom," she told Keth. "Look at it this way — tonight your globe brought the *arurimi* down on him before he could even smuggle his prey out of Khapik. You get closer every day."

Keth smiled crookedly at her. "I won't be happy until he's in chains, and neither will you." He looked at Glaki. "So what did you have for supper?"

They had just finished the dish washing when Tris straightened, staring at the door. "What is *he* doing here?" she asked. Before Keth could inquire into "his" identity, Tris had run out of the room. Little Bear galloped at her side, barking furiously as his tail wagged hard enough to create a breeze.

By the time Keth could reach the door, Niklaren Goldeye had stepped onto the third floor gallery. "No, Bear, you know better," he informed the dog as Little Bear danced around him. "Just one pawprint on my clothes and I will make myself a Little Bear rug."

Keth's eyes bulged as he took in Niko's appearance. Even for Khapik the mage dressed well: tonight he wore a crimson sleeveless overrobe with a gold thread subtly worked into the weave, loose black trousers, and a cream-colored shirt. His long hair was combed back and secured with a red-gold tie.

Tris looked entirely unimpressed by her teacher's splendor. She crossed her arms over her chest and scowled. "Those aren't Khapik clothes," she informed Niko tartly. "Those are Balance Hill clothes."

"Actually, they're Phakomathen clothes," Niko told her, allowing Chime to light on his outstretched arm. "*You* are more beautiful than ever," he told the dragon. To Tris he said, "You look dreadful."

"I don't *feel* dreadful," she retorted. "I know what I'm doing, Niko. I don't need a nursemaid."

He raised his black brows at her. "And did it ever occur to you that I might need reassurance that you are well and sane?"

To Keth's astonishment, Tris turned beet red. Looking at the boards under her feet, she mumbled something that sounded like an apology. Keth stared at Niko in awe. In one sentence he had transformed Tris from a short, plump, sharp-nosed terror into a fourteen-year-old girl. It occurred to Keth for the first time that perhaps magic wasn't simply a matter of fires, lightning, and power in the air, if spoken words could also create such a transformation.

Niko turned his dark eyes, with their heavy frame of lashes, on Keth next. Keth managed to meet them for a moment, before he too gave way to the urge to inspect the floor. Suddenly he remembered that Niko's magic revolved around sight, and that if he saw magic, he would know the state of Keth's power. "She keeps telling me not to overdo," he said hurriedly, thinking Niko might feel Tris was careless in her teaching. "And we try, really, we try so I don't go too far, but I need to stop the Ghost."

"Any kind of weather magic is hard to regulate," Niko said mildly. "Academic mages have trouble building their strength up, because it all comes from within them. Ambient magics suffer the opposite problem, struggling to manage a great deal of power that is drawn to them without their knowledge. Lightning, of course, only increases the levels of power that run through you."

"Of course," whispered Keth sheepishly. He felt like an apprentice who hadn't seen the obvious.

When Niko remained quiet, Keth looked at him, and saw that the older man stood still, his hand out. Keth looked to see who Niko was trying to lure to him, and saw that Glaki was peering around the door. Slowly she inched forward as Niko's hand remained where it was, steady in the air. At last Glaki put her fingers in his. "Good evening, young one," Niko said quietly. "What is your name?"

"Glaki," whispered the girl. "Glakisa Irakory."

"She's an orphan," Tris murmured. "And she's staying with me, Niko." She met Niko's glance with steady eyes this time.

"We will discuss the details later," Niko replied. He smiled at the child. "It is very nice to meet you, Glaki Irakory."

He sees her magic, Keth realized. What *doesn't* he see?

Niko left soon after, once Keth and Tris described the things they had done since Tris left Jumshida's house for Khapik. When he stood to go, he looked as weary as Keth felt. "I've started to scry for this Ghost," he said, rubbing one temple. "It's more useful than listening to my fellow mages blather, which doesn't mean a great deal."

"Have you seen him?" asked Keth. It would smart if someone else caught the Ghost after so much work, but not as much as it would hurt if he killed another *yaskedasu*. "What does he look like?"

Tris went over to help Niko adjust his overrobe to a perfect drape while Niko smiled wryly. "I'm sure I have seen him somewhere, in the thousands of futures that have appeared to me since I began to look," he said. "I am sure I have seen him imprisoned, killed, making a successful escape, murdering others. . . . I only need to sift through all of the futures I've seen, in addition to all the futures that result from the next thing you do, or Dema does, or the Ghost does. I told you it was only a *little* more useful than listening to my peers argue about the foreword to our text."

Tris followed him out as Keth collapsed onto the bed.

"What was he talking about?" Glaki asked.

"About the idea that mages are powerful being a great big joke," Keth replied. "Is that a new doll? Let me see it."

14

Tris went out after Glaki was asleep, leaving the child under Keth's drowsy eye. She found a very different Khapik. *Arurimi* were everywhere. There were new faces among the *yaskedasi*, strong, stern women who tumbled or did exhibitions of hand-to-hand combat with no-nonsense faces and without any trace of the alluring smiles one usually found in Khapik.

"I suppose they think nobody can tell the difference," Tris heard a *yaskedasoi* tell one of the musicians who lived at Ferouze's.

He replied, "I'm surprised they remembered to take the red tunic off."

Tris shook her head. She would have to tell Dema his volunteers had to work harder at pretending to be true *yaskedasi*. If these people knew the difference, chances were that the Ghost would know, too.

Other things were different with the newcomers' arrival. Laughter and music sounded forced. *Yaskedasi* and shopkeepers gathered on corners, talking softly, their eyes darting everywhere.

Of course, Tris thought. With all these disguised *arurimi* under their noses, they can't ignore the fact that the Ghost exists. Now they have to face it. They can't tell themselves pretty lies.

Seated for awhile by the Cascade Fountains, Tris eavesdropped on a group of girl singers. Tris could see they were frightened, watching their surroundings and jumping at unexpected noises.

"I don't understand," one of them told the others, her mouth trembling. "Why does the Ghost do this? What have *yaskedasi* done to him?"

"Nobody cares when we disappear," an older girl replied. "If the dead weren't showing up outside Khapik, do you think they'd have the *arurimi* out now?"

"That *can't* be all of it," retorted the girl who'd first spoken. "Look how many he's killed. If it was people nobody cares about, he'd pick *prathmuni,* or those who live in Hodenekes."

A *prathmun* who swept the sidewalk glared at the *yaskedasu.* Tris wanted to tell him that the singer hadn't meant it the way it came out, but she knew the girl had indeed spoken the truth as she believed it to be.

Tris walked on, still thinking about the conversation. They would have to catch the Ghost to learn what truly drove him. After so many deaths, she had come to think it wasn't the simple matter of a grudge against the *yaskedasi.*

He went to considerable trouble and risk to rub Tharian noses in death's reality. He must know that when he despoiled public spots the city would be forced to hold long, expensive rituals before its people could use those places again. He even turned those same Tharian beliefs about death to his benefit, to cover his tracks from the *arurim*.

The Ghost staged his show of hate not for just one group, or two, but all of Tharios: for its people, its lifestyle, its religion, its customs, its history. Tris couldn't imagine a hate so thorough as that of the Ghost for Tharios. Once she reached the headache point of a case of hate, she simply walked away. She had a feeling the Ghost *enjoyed* hate headaches.

Something else occurred to her as she trekked the back alleys of Khapik. Thwarted of his display at Heskalifos, the Ghost had killed the very next day — and he hadn't been able to display *that* victim, either. "He'll kill again tomorrow," Tris told Chime. "He's shown he can't stop himself."

And who was to stop him? He knew the city so well he'd turned its laws and customs against it, coming and going as if he were invisible. How could anyone arrest a ghost?

Though she hadn't slept after her return to Ferouze's, the power of the tides kept Tris awake and alert the next day. When her strength ran out in a few days, she would have to accept the consequences and not try to revive it again. There was only so much of the ocean's might a human body could stand before the blood turned to salt water and the muscles to braids of kelp.

At Touchstone that morning, Glaki joined Tris and Keth at meditation. As before, she ended up napping. Keth, his power at full strength again, crafted bowls, small globes, and vases for Antonou, to make up for the materials he used for his magical work.

As Keth blew glass, Tris returned to her scrying. She let the flood of colors, textures, and half-recognized shapes wash over her, her mind snagging on images of a temple cornice, a finch in a tree, a ball rolling across an empty courtyard, and angry people in motion against the white marble splendor of Assembly Square.

It's about time they protested, she thought when she came out of her trance. Then she realized that a public outcry might drive the Keepers to remove Dema from the investigation, disgracing him and his clan. He would be made to pay because, as he'd said at the beginning, he was green and expendable.

"No, they won't get rid of him yet," Antonou said over lunch. Keth's relative knew much of the city's gossip. "Nomasdina clan pays for the *arurimi* to patrol Khapik for the Ghost." He made Glaki's *yaskedasu* doll jump, surprising giggles from the girl. "The Assembly may be sniveling cowards when it comes to popular opinion," Antonou went on, "but they're also cheap. Getting rid of young Nomasdina means they must come up with a plan and pay for it from the Treasury. If this goes on another week, I'm not certain, but for now your friend is safe."

"How reassuring," drawled Keth.

"That's Tharios," Antonou replied. "Reassuring in its miserliness. Now, I happen to know a bunch of grapes I believe a certain girl would like very much. Who will carry them back from my house for Keth and Tris to have a share?"

"Me, me!" Glaki cried, jumping to her feet.

Tris watched the girl and the old man walk back to his residence. "Your cousin's a good man," she remarked thoughtfully, seeing a swarm of rainbow sparks part around him as the air flowed around his body.

Keth looked at her, surprised. "He gave *me* a berth, didn't he? *And* he was a curst good sport about me destroying the cullet. Plenty of masters would have thrown me out on my ear."

"And you're repaying him with those globes," Tris said. "It all works out."

"I'd like to work the Ghost out," Keth muttered. "Before he orphans another child."

While Glaki napped and Tris read in the shade to escape the hottest part of the day, Keth went to visit other glassmakers. He found enough journeymen at work while their masters rested to buy three crates of cullet glass to replace what he had destroyed. As he filled the new barrel that Antonou had provided, he felt the first twinges of a globe coming on. The feeling was distant, not the roaring pressure it would be soon. When he finished with the barrel, he doused himself with a bucket of well water to cool off and hunkered down by Tris.

"Taking the lightning back yesterday helped some, but I didn't pay for more cullet just to explode it again," he announced when the girl put down her book. "What can I do, o wise mistress of all knowledge?"

She made a face at him. "If I were such a mistress, I'd have this killer in a lightning cage," she informed Keth. She looked up. Gray clouds rolled over the sky above, a promise of more rain now that Tris had put an end to the blockage overseas. The normal summer storms flowed over Tharios as they should. "I think I can, um, redistribute your lightning," she said, gray eyes as distant as the clouds overhead.

Keth looked up. *"There?"* he asked, startled.

"Why not?" she wanted to know. "It's already brewing some of its own. A little more won't hurt."

"Most girls your age worry about husbands, not the redistribution of lightning," he pointed out, getting to his feet.

She grinned up at him, showing teeth. "Most girls aren't me," she reminded him.

And thank Vrohain for that, he thought, paying tribute to the Namornese god of justice. I hope I never meet those sisters of hers, or that brother, he told himself as he checked

TAMORA PIERCE

the crucible in the furnace. I'd probably have nightmares for weeks.

That afternoon he blew globe after globe to hurry along the one he wanted, but he may as well have blown smoke. Antonou was pleased to have more trinkets to sell, but Keth thought he would put his own head through the wall in frustration. Tris helped as she did that first time, shaping the glass with heat drawn from the heart of the earth, but even that produced no visions of death.

Taking a break, Keth worked on an idea he'd had. He blew a handful of tiny glass bubbles as fragile as a butterfly's wing, almost lighter than air. That alone was enough to make him glow with pride: since he'd begun to master his power, his old skill and control were slowly returning.

He didn't stop there. With Tris to advise him, he infused each bubble with a dab of his lightning-laced magic. They sprang to life like a swarm of fireflies, darting around the workshop, then the courtyard, as Glaki and Little Bear chased them.

"Signal flares," Keth told Tris as he tucked them very gently into his belt purse. "Or tracking aids, I'm not sure which."

She smiled at him proudly. "Very good. You're learning the most important thing an ambient mage can learn. Your power shapes itself to your need, if you put some thought into it."

Keth's need to create a globe with a new image of a

murder blossomed at last, shortly before they would have
stopped for the day. Keth worked the glass with care. When
it was done, he and Tris went outside. There he drew the
lightning out of the globe, imagining his hand as a pair of
tongs and the lightning itself as glass that he pulled into a
new shape. Once he worked part of the lightning free of the
globe, he sent it streaming to Tris. She guided it up into the
sky, where it slithered into thunderheads that had already
begun to voice the odd rumble or two.

A white mist remained inside the globe, hiding whatever image was there. Keth gritted his teeth in frustration,
so hard that he heard them creak, and closed down the
workshop for the day. He, Glaki, Tris, Chime, and the dog
were on their way to Elya Street when Glaki pointed to the
globe in his hands. It was clearing.

The sky opened up. Instantly Tris did something. The
rain that drenched their surroundings slid around them.
Under that invisible umbrella they walked up to the steps of
the Elya Street *arurimat*, where a soaked Dema waited for
them. Tris instantly spread her rain protection to include
the *arurim dhaskoi*. When she was close enough that she
could speak quietly and be heard, she told him what she'd
heard the *yaskedasi* say the night before about the disguised
arurimi.

"Ouch," Dema said, glancing at Keth's globe. "I never
realized . . ."

"Tell your people not to be so grim," advised Tris. "Real

yaskedasi smile and laugh all the time, even if they don't want to. They know they have to be pleasing and pleasant for the customers, and never show what they really think."

Keth raised his eyebrows. *"You've* learned a lot," he pointed out as he passed the globe to Dema.

Tris shrugged. "Are you going to try to hunt the Ghost again tonight?"

Keth hung his head. "I know I'll probably go all weak in the knees and have to come home before we even get a whiff of him, but I have to try," he confessed. "I hate sitting about doing nothing while he's out there."

From the way Tris looked at him, he suspected that Tris felt much the same way. "Well, I can't keep Glaki out until all hours," she replied, confirming his suspicion. "We'll see you later."

Dema ushered Keth and his globe into the *arurimat.* The outer chamber was crammed with *arurimi,* both those in standard uniform and the ones disguised as *yaskedasi.* They gathered around eagerly as Keth and Dema inspected the globe. It showed a Khapik stream bank. A lone *yaskedasu* took shelter from the rain under a huge willow there. Keth turned the globe, but no matter how they shifted it, no one could see behind the tree or into the shadows behind a shrine in the background. All they could tell was that it was one of many dedicated to the gods of entertainment.

"We stick to the streams, then," Dema ordered. "You women, keep your eyes open and your whistles handy. If you even *suspect* something, don't play the hero, whistle for your team. I don't want to lose any people to this human *malipi*, you understand? My command post will be at the Sign of the Winking Eye on Fortunate Street." He looked at each of them. "Any questions?"

"Oh," Keth said, remembering his day's work. He carefully extracted one of the bubble globes from his purse and called to the fire and lightning in it. The bubble threw off a burst of darting colors. "If you see one of these, it means we know something," he told them. "Put your hand up to stop it, then follow it back to us."

Dema took the bubble. Its lights gleamed through his long brown fingers. "I'll be switched," he murmured. "Oh, I *like* these." He handed it back to Keth. "Could you make more?"

Keth shrugged. "Given materials and shop time, yes."

"That'd be a nice thing for patrols and such," said a sergeant. "Be nicer if they weren't so showy. If it were empty, like, it could fetch your partner back to you, without everybody hearing the whistle."

"Let's discuss this later," Dema told Keth. "Even if they throw *me* out on my ear, I know the *arurim* will commission a batch of these. The army, too, might like them. Excuse me." He looked around the group once more. "*Yaskedasi*, both sexes. A moment, if I may." He gave the bubble and the stream-bank globe to Keth and went apart with the disguised *yaskedasi*.

Keth slid the bubble into his shirt pocket, then held up the globe. "Does anyone recognize this place?" he asked.

His *arurimi* companions shook their heads. "Problem is, there's willows and shrines all along the streams," explained a woman in uniform. She could well have been somebody's sweet-faced old grandmother, but for her muscular arms and the baton, knife, and thong restraints that hung from her broad leather belt. "Willows are the symbol of the *yaskedasi*. You know, they bend but they don't break. When Khapik was rebuilt about five hundred years back, they dug the streams with all these nips and tucks so folk could have privacy for their entertainment."

"And since it's raining, it's dark out anyways, so we can't tell if this is day or night," added one of the young *arurimi*. "Though the light's greenish, so maybe it's late day?"

"Near sunset," another woman said. "We've an hour, maybe two, to get in place."

The false *yaskedasi* streamed out of the room, on their way to their posts. When Dema came back to Keth's group, they told him what they'd worked out from the scene in the globe.

"There's one more thing," Dema told them. He pointed to the globe. "Look at her. She's *alive*. We've a chance to find her and set a trap around her before he even gets there."

"All-Seeing, make it so," murmured the grandmotherly *arurim*. The believers around her drew circles on their foreheads.

Keth stayed close to Dema as they entered Khapik, keeping a watchful eye on his surroundings. At first he saw very few human beings. The storm was at its height, its thunders bouncing through the streets. Lightning jumped overhead, lacing the sky. Keth wondered if Tris was on Ferouze's roof right now, and wished he were there with her, gripped by lightning. Then movement and a flash of yellow caught his eye: he looked and saw one of the *arurimi* dressed as a *yaskedasu*, sheltering in a doorway. She smiled wickedly and beckoned; Keth grinned and shook his head. As far as he was concerned, she behaved like real *yaskedasi*.

Dema settled to wait at their command post, upstairs in the Winking Eye. Keth decided to go walking on his own. He was known here; he belonged. If the Ghost knew Khapik, the sight of Keth, who had lived there eight months, would raise no alarms in his mind.

Up and down the streams Keth rambled, hands in pockets. The rain thinned, and stopped. He heard the sound of a flute on the air, then a tambourine. Now business would pick up, though many customers would stay home rather than risk a second shower. *Yaskedasi* moved out into the open. Normally they were discouraged from using the neatly clipped stream banks for performances, but Khapik guards could be persuaded to look the other way for a coin or two, if the *yaskedasi* weren't too noisy or didn't get enough of an audience to trample the grass.

Here came the customers, pleasure seekers from all over

the known world. Some visitors left after seeing one red tunic too many. Keth grimaced. The fewer genuine tourists there were on the streets, the more likely it was that Dema's people would stand out.

A light rain began to fall. Now Keth really searched the stream banks. He found what he sought on Little Rushing Brook, which ran beside Olive Lane. The *yaskedasu* was far downstream in the shadow of the city wall. She huddled under a willow on the opposite side of the brook from Keth, peering out at the rain.

Keth dared not leave: the Ghost might be here already, in the shadows. Slowly Keth reached into his shirt pocket and drew out one of his bubbles. He closed his eyes briefly, willing it to seek out anyone in a red tunic, then sent it flying on its way. The *arurimi* would be here in a hurry, and the *yaskedasu* would be safe.

Keth sighed in relief, then froze as the yellow veil slipped off the girl's head. In a flash it looped out of the dark to drop around her neck. The Ghost had used the shadows and rain to creep up behind her. She staggered back into the darkness behind the willow, flailing as she clawed at the strangler's noose.

If Keth waited, she would die before the *arurimi* came. Yelling, he plunged into the stream and slogged up the far bank, toiling in slippery mud to get to her and capture her assailant. He stumbled over a root on the outskirts of the willow. As he struggled to stay on his feet, the girl flew at him out of the dark, yellow veil wrapped twice around her throat and knotted tight. Her face was plum-colored, her fingers increasingly feeble as she dug at the silk. Keth wavered between helping her and chasing the Ghost, then unsheathed his belt knife. The veil was expensive silk, his knife not at all good. Finally he cut the knot and unwrapped the cloth from the *yaskedasu's* swollen neck just as his glass bubble and the *arurimi* found them.

"Which way?" demanded their sergeant. Keth pointed wordlessly with his free hand, his other wrapped around the coughing girl to keep her from falling into the stream. The *arurimi* pelted away, their feet striking great splashes from the wet grass.

Keth pulled the girl farther under the willow's shelter and waited with her. Her racking coughs slowed, then stopped. She clung to Keth as if he were her last hope in the world.

"He's gone," Keth told her over and over. "He won't come back. Let me fetch you some water from the stream. . . ."

She shook her head furiously. Her fingers dug deeper into his arm.

"Or not," said Keth. "Let's go sit, at least." He swung her up in his arms — she was just a scrap of a thing — and carried her over to the shrine. The topmost step was dry, protected by the domed roof from the rain that pelted down with a roar. Keth reached out with cupped hands and ferried mouthful after mouthful of rain to the girl. She drank greedily, wincing as the liquid passed through her bruised throat.

The rain had slowed to a drizzle again when the *arurimi* returned. Dema and a number of other *arurimi* came with them, summoned from the command post. Judging by the mud that splattered all of them royally, Keth guessed they had searched all through the downpour at its worst.

Dema stood in the rain, hands on hips, water pouring from his sopping mage blue stole and *arurim* red tunic. "What were you thinking?" he asked amiably enough. "What, if anything, was passing through your mind?"

Keth glared up at him as the *yaskedasu* shrank into the shelter of his arm. "He was killing her. I didn't know when your people would arrive."

"You *let him go*," Dema said, bright-eyed. "He was right there, almost within our grasp, and you let him escape."

"She would have been dead if I hadn't cut the scarf from her throat," Keth insisted. To the girl he said gently, "Show them, please."

She raised her chin to show them the plum-and-blue mass around her neck.

Dema refused to meet her eyes. "The fact remains, he was right here, and you scared him off."

"What did he do?" Keth asked knowingly. "Run through another of those ridiculous cleansing temples you have?"

"A mage's storeroom," grumbled one of the *arurimi*, smearing mud as he dragged his forearm over his face. "There's no telling where he went from there."

"He's probably got escape routes all over the city," Keth said.

"I *know* that." Dema's voice was thick with awful patience. "That's why we needed to catch him *in the act*."

"She would have died," Keth insisted stubbornly. "Where's the honor in catching him if you let him kill someone else?" He held Dema's eyes with his own, trying to get the other man to see his point.

The *yaskedasu* at his side muttered something, and coughed.

"What?" asked Keth.

The *yaskedasu* looked at him, then glared at the *arurimi*. "*Okozou*," she said in a voice like a dry file drawn over broken glass.

"Your murder isn't an *okozou* matter to me," Keth said fiercely. "And it shouldn't be *okozou* to you," he added, with a glare of his own for Dema.

Dema sighed. "All right," he told the *arurimi*. "You know the drill. Search the area once more, then resume your patrol pattern. Move out." To Keth and the *yaskedasu* he said, "Come on. We'll get you dried off and looked after. And then we'll try and find out what you saw."

"Din't see nothin'," the girl rasped.

"I know," replied Dema with heavy patience. "But we'll try to dredge something from you anyway."

Keth got up and helped the girl to her feet. They followed Dema as the rain slowed, then stopped.

Glaki was restless that night. Tris finally settled her late, by telling stories of her time at Winding Circle. Outside she felt the rain slack off, build, pour, then stop. There would be no more rain for two days; this storm had moved on. With Glaki asleep at last, she wished the storm well and gave Little Bear a much-needed combing. Chime was a useful dog's maid, her thin claws easily working their way through the matted coat.

When the clocks chimed midnight and Glaki did not so much as twitch, Tris collected Chime. Little Bear, worn out by the process of beautification, snored on the bed next to the sleeping child. Once Tris set the usual terms with Ferouze and watched the old woman climb up the stairs to Glaki's room, she settled Chime in the sling at her back and walked out into Chamberpot Alley.

The air was cool and fresh, the winds that explored Khapik lively and curious. Tris slipped off her spectacles and tucked them in her sash, dropping into the trance she would need to scry the winds. As color, movement, and shapes soared by, she set off into Khapik. She kept to the back alleys, not wanting the sight of *arurimi* in disguise to distract her.

The winds were interesting that night. They came from the northeast instead of the usual southeast. She caught a glimpse of towering, snow-capped mountains, red stone fortresses, and a small, crazed jungle that was once a garden in a dry land. She gasped with wonder at that last. Not only was it infused with magic from root to leaf, but the magic was familiar: Briar's. She would have loved to know how a garden that was such a mess had anything to do with him, but the wind had carried the image away while she groped for more of it. She leaned against a building with a sigh, waited to regain the calm she needed to do this, and set forth once again.

It was easier to see wind-borne colors and images in the less frequented areas that night. Torchlight leeched the color from her surroundings. Feeling more confident in her ability to navigate, Tris wandered down Woeful Lane, through the mazes of back-of-the-house paths and service alleys to Painted Place, then out along Drunkard's Grief Street. She saw very few people, which was how she wanted it. These were the paths taken by servants, *prathmuni,* and those whose business in Khapik was suspect. As she made her way the air showed her things: silk gliding along a woman mage's arm, the flare of magic at hennaed finger-tips, and a metal bird coming to life. She wanted to see that bird.

Not tonight, she told herself. You're looking for other things tonight. Standing at the intersection of three streets, she turned, eyes wide, searching for any hint of the Ghost. There: the air blowing down Kettle Court showed her a dirty hand fumbling at a ragged tunic. It yanked out a yellow head-veil, a *yaskedasi* veil.

The Ghost. It was him. He was running headlong into the breeze that took his image to Tris.

She ran, her eyes fixed on that current, following it along Kettle Court. Her feet pounded along the cobblestones. Rounding a corner, she stepped in garbage and slipped, the movement jarring the image from her eyes. A thick hand gripped her arm. A yellow scarf wrapped around her neck.

Dema paced as the *arurim* healer examined the rescued *yaskedasu*. If the healer pronounced the girl fit to bear it, Dema would try a spell to enhance her memory of the attack, to see if she could describe the man who had so nearly killed her. In the meantime, he alternated between chewing his nails and berating Keth. For his own part, Keth understood Dema's frustration, but he was preoccupied. The globe, which had earlier cleared to show the *yaskedasu* under her willow, had clouded again. Keth sat with it gripped in his hands, Dema's words falling on inattentive ears. Sparks of lightning flowed from Keth's fingertips, lancing through the mist inside. There was an image in the globe. He could see the outlines of it, dark buildings, a back street, wooden fences.

A girl raced down a street, sling around her torso, twin braids flapping against her cheeks. She wore no spectacles, but Keth had no trouble recognizing Tris. If these globes were connected to the Ghost, then Tris was in danger.

"Where is this?" he demanded, trying to recognize her surroundings. "Dema —"

"I tell you we don't have *time* to deal with whoever's in charge!" a crisp voice shouted. The speaker was downstairs in the Winking Eye, where Dema had his command post. "A woman is in danger right *now*, you boneheaded behemoth!"

Dema looked at Keth. "Niko?" they chorused. Both ran for the stairs.

Below stood the *arurimi* Brosdes and Majnuna. Each of them held one of Niko's arms, impervious to the mage's fury. "He says he knows where our boy is and who's the next victim," explained Brosdes. "Wants us to turn out the whole force to track 'em."

"Let him go," ordered Dema. "What is it, *Dhaskoi* Niko?"

"*Dhaskoi?*" muttered the taller of the *arurimi*. "He never said nothin' about bein' *dhaskoi.*"

Keth thrust the globe at Niko. "Is this it?" he demanded. "Is this why you're here?"

"Where did that come from?" Dema wanted to know. "Where — Tris?"

"I made it clear again," Keth explained.

"This is why I'm here," snapped Niko. "I was scrying for the future, and this time the images came together." Hands trembling, he laid them over the globe, his fingers touching Keth's. Both of them concentrated, Keth letting what power he had left pass into the glass. The image of Tris shrank as the vision grew wider and wider. "Where is that?" demanded Niko. "Where is she?"

"Cricket Strut?" asked the thick-voiced Majnuna, squinting at the image. "Brosdes?"

"Cricket Strut," confirmed Brosdes. "Near Silkfingers Lane."

"I've frozen it where she is right now. She won't be there when we arrive," Niko said hurriedly. "We need Little Bear. He can track her. We need him and we need to move. This takes place in fifteen minutes, twenty if we are fortunate. Her life is about to intersect with the Ghost's — I don't know how, but if you want him to be alive when you question him, we must go!"

"The Bear's at Ferouze's," Keth told Dema. "I'll get him and meet you at the corner of Chamberpot and Peacock." As he raced out of the inn, Keth heard Brosdes mutter, "If we want *him* to be alive?"

Tris, dazed by her wind scrying, hadn't even heard the man. As she dragged at the cloth he fought to twist around her neck, Chime lunged up from her sling over Tris's shoulder and spat needles into the man's face. He screamed, clutching a punctured eye, and staggered back, releasing the girl. Dragging the cloth from her throat, Tris kicked out, hard, catching the man between his legs. Down he went into the gutter muck.

She blinked hurriedly, clearing her vision of magic, and yanked her spectacles from her sash, putting them on. At last she could see what she and Chime had brought down: a *prathmun*, wearing the dirty, ragged tunic and chopped haircut decreed for all of his class. Tris pulled a length of yellow silk off her neck and clenched her fingers around it.

"Do I *look* like a *yaskedasu?*" she wanted to know.

He scrabbled back, away from her, his right eye a ruin. Tris closed on him. "You're here, ain't you?" growled the *prathmun*. "Night after night I seen you, out walkin' where none of the outsiders go. You consort with them, you're as good as them, ugly little filth-wench to be left all dirty on their nice, white marble." He tried to pull the needles out of his face.

"What did the *yaskedasi* do to you?" demanded Tris. "They aren't that much better off than you, or much more respected."

"One whelped me!" the Ghost snarled. "Her and her Assembly lover, they got me, but they wouldn't keep me. They throwed me into the sewer to live or die, till the other sewer-pigs found —"

She wasn't expecting it; later she would scold herself. He slammed her in the chest with both bare feet. Tris's head cracked on the cobblestones as she fell, adding the white flare of pain to the colored fires that remained from her scrying.

Chime leaped free as Tris went down. Now the dragon swooped on the killer *prathmun*, spitting needles into his scalp, as he crawled toward Tris to snatch the yellow veil from the girl's hand. He jumped to his feet with a snarl, arms flailing as he tried to knock the glass dragon away. With no torches to illuminate her, Chime was nearly invisible. She swooped again, raking the Ghost's head with sharp claws.

Tris kicked out, catching him behind the knees. He stumbled, lurched, gathered his feet under him and ran.

"Chime, go!" Tris ordered. "Slow him down!"

The dragon followed the Ghost, her glass body silent

and hidden in the night. Tris got to her own feet, passing her power over her eyes again and again to clear her vision. All of her braids sprang from their pins, hanging free. The ties popped off her two lesser lightning braids.

Tris reached to the top of each thin braid and ran her hands down, sparks leaping under her fingers. She molded them into a ball to see by and let it hang in the air as she drew a good, stiff breeze from two wind braids. She sent it after Chime as a living rope, so she wouldn't lose the glass dragon, then followed. As she trotted along she thanked the gods of earth and fire for Chime. If not for the dragon, her corpse might be on its way to defile one of Tharios's proudest places right now.

The child of a *yaskedasu* and someone from the First Class, tossed in among the *prathmuni*. It made a kind of warped sense, if the Ghost told the truth. Maybe he *thought* it was the truth. Maybe it was simply the excuse he needed first to murder women who showed him temptation they would never give to a *prathmun,* then to rub the noses of those who used *prathmuni* in the worst thing they could imagine — public, unclean death.

She heard the claws-on-glass screech that was Chime's alarm. Tris ran, sending more breezes ahead to keep the Ghost from opening any doors. As she rounded the corner into the next street she found him, tugging frantically at the handle of a door set in a cellarway. The building above it looked abandoned.

Tris slowed, panting. Chime flew at the Ghost's face, slapping him with her broad wings. He ducked his head and continued to tug, refusing to let go of the handle.

"There's no escape tonight," Tris called. "Not here. You've used your last yellow veil."

That got the *prathmun's* attention. He struck Chime, throwing her against the building, and scrambled up the stairs into the street. He fled down its length until he reached a brick wall. Digging his toes into its cracks, he began to climb.

Tris lifted her hands to the single heavy braid that went from her forehead to the nape of her neck. The tie dropped from it; strands pulled free of the braid. The power they released flowed, ripe and heavy, into Tris's palms.

She took a deep breath. The *prathmun* raised a hand to hit Chime, who had recovered quickly, and fell from the wall to the ground. With the persistence of a terrier he began to climb the wall again.

Tris held out her hands. The power in them trickled into the soggy ground of the alley. She set down protective barriers on either side, sinking them deep in the earth and up the walls of all the buildings. Only when her control was locked in place did she release what she had taken from that one braid. It followed the channel made by her protections straight down the street. The ground quivered. The quivers spread and rolled forward, taking the shape of waves in the soil, rolling on like a small earthquake. The floor of the alley turned to earthen soup as Tris harnessed the tremors, directing them to flow as she wanted. Her teeth hurt, they were clenched so hard. Her eyes were locked on the Ghost.

He was three quarters of the way up the wall when the tremors struck. The brick under his feet quivered. Old plaster and mortar dropped away as the waves hit directly under the wall, held there by Tris. With a cry the *prathmun* fell to the street, into now-liquid ground. It swallowed him up to his hips before Tris shoved all of the force she had released deep into the soil. She jammed it down through stone cracks and veins, letting it disperse into the earth that had lent it to her for awhile.

In the ringing silence that followed, the brick wall grated and dropped. Tris's winds thrust it back from the Ghost, into the yard it had shielded.

Tris walked down the alley, the dirt reasonably firm under her sensibly shod feet. She reclaimed her protections from ground and buildings, satisfied that she had done them no damage. No one here would die because she'd allowed a place to be shaken past the point where it could stand.

At last she stopped a yard away from the trapped *prathmun*. He stared at her, sweat crawling down his face.

"You orphaned a little girl twice," she said quietly, as cold as if she were trapped inside a glacier. "You took two of her mothers. A little girl who never did you harm." Lightning dropped in fat sparks from her hair to her feet. It lazily climbed back up her plump body in fiery waves. "You left her among strangers who might have thrown her into the street. Never once did you think of her."

"Never once did anyone think of me!" he snapped back, his eyes black and empty. "Fit to haul dung but not fit to be seen — this place is rotten. If she don't like the smell of rot, she shouldn't live here, and neither should you."

Her lightning blazed as it flowed down her arms, gloving her from fingertip to elbow. "No," Tris said quietly. "*You* shouldn't live." She put her hands together, then pulled them apart, creating a heavy white-hot thunderbolt.

"No, Dema, let her do it!" The familiar voice was Kethlun's. "Don't stop her!"

"For her own sake, she *must* be stopped," Niko replied. Tris should have known that Niko would see this piece of the future. There were times when having a seer as a teacher was a pain.

"Tris, give him up," Dema pleaded. "If you kill him, I'll have to arrest you and have you executed."

"No!" argued Keth. "She's doing Tharios a service. He killed Ira. He killed Yali. Let him cook!"

"Is this what it comes to, Trisana?" Niko called, his normally crisp voice gentle. "When you sank the ships at Winding Circle, you defended your home. If you do this, it's murder. You will be a murderer by choice."

"He deserves to die," she shouted.

"But do you deserve to kill him?" Dema asked quietly. He was much closer to her. "Leave him to the State, Tris.

That's what it's for. His first debt is to Tharios. Let him pay it."

She should have just killed the Ghost the moment they arrived, she thought ruefully. Now she was afraid they made sense. She let the lightning trickle into the earth, following the route of her tremors. The molten lava far below the surface wouldn't mind the extra power.

When the last bit faded, a long, wet nose thrust itself under her palm. Little Bear whined and wagged his tail, nudging her for a scratch behind the ears. "Traitor," Tris murmured. She knew very well that the dog had helped to track her.

Chime landed gently across her shoulders. There she voiced the ringing chime that was her purr. Tris rubbed the dragon's head with her fingertips, looking down at the Ghost. "Take him then, Dema," she said clearly, "but I won't dig him out for you."

"Send for the *arurim prathmuni*," Dema ordered one of his people. "I won't befoul myself by handling the likes of him."

And that's where your world goes wrong, thought Tris as she walked by him.

As she passed Niko he took her arm. Gently she pulled free. "There's something I have to do right now," she told him. "It's *really* important, Niko. Life and death, literally."

He released her. "Go," he said, his voice soft. "But we

need to talk later, you and I." He frowned at Keth. "*And* I'll need a word with you, Kethlun Warder. You too had better learn that mages don't kill unless it's unavoidable."

Tris hurried on. She sent her breezes out, searching for someone in particular. Soon enough a current of air returned, carrying an unmistakable smell. She followed it back to its source, the *prathmuni* woman and boy she met several days ago.

They backed away from their cart as she approached at a trot. Then the woman stopped, and squinted through the back alley gloom. Tris drew a handful of sparks from a braid to illuminate her face.

"*You,*" said the boy. "What do you want with us now?"

Tris waited until she was very close to speak. "They've caught that killer, the one they call 'The Ghost,'" she informed them. "He's one of you."

They both drew the sign of the All-Seeing on their foreheads, though the woman snapped, "Impossible."

Tris nodded to her partner. "*He* knows the truth of it."

When the woman scowled at him, the boy said, "Not even Eseben would be that foolish." He didn't sound as if he believed himself.

"How do you know?" the woman demanded fiercely.

"I caught him," Tris replied. "He's confessed. The *arurimi* have him now. It won't be long before the news gets out."

"Massacre," breathed the woman.

"Have you ways to leave the city unnoticed?" asked Tris. The youth nodded. "Then alert everyone you can," Tris continued. "Let Tharios manage without her *prathmuni.*"

The pair traded a look, then turned their backs on Tris and raced down the alley without a word. Tris hadn't expected thanks. "Shurri Firesword guard you all," she murmured. They would need the goddess's protection. Tharios was a big city, and there were many *prathmuni.* Not all of them would escape by dawn. Perhaps some wouldn't even try to flee, though she hoped they would have better sense.

She walked back to Ferouze's, warning every *prathmun* she glimpsed.

In Yali's chamber, Ferouze was nodding off as the little girl slept on the bed. "Thank you," Tris said, pressing a five-*bik* piece into the old woman's hand. "You were good to stay with her."

"Like Keth would have given me a choice," Ferouze grumbled, stuffing the coin into her sash. "So what's going on? He came racing in here like the Hounds of War were at his heels. He took that dog of yours away with him."

If I tell her, all of Khapik will know by dawn, Tris realized. Ferouze was a notorious gossip. She shrugged. "I don't know. I found Little Bear waiting for me outside."

"*Dhaski,*" muttered Ferouze as she let herself out. "All mysteries and no explanations."

Tris sat on the bed and bent to unlace her shoes. The room started to spin. Her fingers were suddenly too weak to hold onto the laces. In controlling her earthquake, she had burned up the last of her borrowed strength. It was time — past time — to pay for it.

She lay back, before she collapsed in a heap. I hope they think to look here for me, she thought before a tide of unconsciousness swamped her.

When she awoke, five days later, she was in Jumshida's house. Niko sat by her bed, reading. He didn't even wait for Tris to clean up. Instead he proceeded to relieve his feelings about girls who tapped the power of the earth, looking after children who weren't their own, and searching for dangerous madmen, as they avoided wise elders who would see the folly they committed and bring them to their senses. When he showed no signs of calming down, Tris went behind a screen to change clothes. Someone, she hoped Jumshida, had dressed her in a nightgown. Tris replaced it with a shift, a single petticoat, and a pale gray muslin gown that fit more loosely than it had before she'd gone to Khapik.

"Are you even *listening?*" demanded Niko.

"Not really," she replied wearily. "Either I'm adult enough to have a medallion and a student and make my own stupid choices, or I'm not. It's not like I did it for party entertainment, Niko."

He sighed. "No, I know you didn't. I suppose I feel guilty

because I should have helped you more, instead of letting conference politics sap my strength."

Tris looked around the edge of the screen at him as she did up her sash. "Help me with what? I didn't help find him, I walked bang into the man, Niko! Is he dead yet?"

Niko's large, dark eyes filled with distress as he watched her. "Do you care so little, Tris? He paid in blood, yesterday."

"I feel sorrier for the *prathmuni*," she retorted. "There *was* a slaughter, wasn't there?" She had dreamed it, seeing knots of *prathmuni* disappear under the stones and clubs of outraged citizens.

"Sadly, yes," Niko admitted. "Twenty-nine *prathmuni* dead, four of them children. The Keepers finally decreed martial law and ordered the *arurim* to get the city under control."

Tris paused, her sash half-tied. She emerged from behind the screen, frowning. "Twenty-nine?" she repeated. She had expected far more.

"I was shocked, too," admitted Niko. "But that's all that were found. Tharios's *prathmuni* have vanished. The Assembly is fighting about who will do their work."

Tris grinned. They had listened to her, then. They had escaped.

Niko tugged at his mustache. "I find it interesting that they left at almost the same time the Ghost was captured. Do you think they were warned?"

Tris ignored so foolish a question. Niko was too clever not to realize she had alerted the *prathmuni*. "Where's Glaki?" she asked. She wished everyone had escaped, but if *prathmuni* were like most people, some must have insisted that no one would blame their entire class for the acts of one man. At least the number of dead was far smaller than it could have been. "How's Keth?"

"He's in the workroom, meditating," replied Niko. "Glaki is helping in the kitchen. They're staying here for the time being — Khapik was closed during the riots. What do you plan to do with the girl, Tris?"

"Keep her with me," Tris replied. "She needs something constant in her life, and she has no family." She held up a hand to silence her teacher when he opened his mouth. "I know I need to provide for her properly. I'm too young for motherhood. And she's an academic mage, though too young to work with it much. I want to learn to be an academic mage myself; I don't know how to teach one."

"She has used her power somewhat," Niko remarked. "She is far more disciplined than I would expect for a child her age."

"It's the meditation, I suppose," Tris replied. "I suppose that will do for now. I was thinking of taking her back to Winding Circle when we go home." Searching an open drawer for a scarf for her hair, which was a mess of half-undone braids that had to be washed, arranged, and pinned afresh, she found Chime sound asleep in her belongings. "Hello, beautiful," she murmured, stroking the glass dragon as she eased a blue scarf out from under her.

Chime opened one glass eye and chinked at her, then resumed her slumber.

"Come eat something," Niko said. "You don't have to plan Glaki's life today."

"Good," Tris replied, clutching a chair. "Right now I'd be hard put to decide between honey and syrup for my bread." She took the arm Niko offered, leaning on it more than she would have done had her strength been normal. "How's Dema?" she asked as they went downstairs.

"Vindicated. About to receive a more prestigious appointment," replied Niko. "We thought it was best for all concerned if he got sole credit for the Ghost's arrest. Some grumblers say he should have sent disguised *arurimi* into the district earlier, but they're in the minority. Do you mind?"

"Dema getting credit?" Tris asked as Niko let her sink onto a dining-room chair. "He's welcome to it. I told you, I didn't find the Ghost, I ran into him. Does Keth mind?"

"He says no," replied Niko, ringing the bell for the cook.

"Tris, Tris!" Glaki plunged out of the kitchen, arms upraised, spoon in one hand. Tris managed to hold off the spoon while welcoming the four-year-old's passionate hug. "You're awake!"

"We thought you'd sleep all year," said Kethlun. He'd come downstairs without Tris realizing it. "So tell me, if you were storing other things than lightning in your hair, why didn't we feel them tear up the house while you were snoring?"

"I don't snore," Tris retorted. "And there are protections on my head to keep the power from escaping even when I'm not in control of it. I renew them every time I wash my hair, all right?"

Keth sighed. "Here I was, all hopeful you wouldn't even have the strength to pick on me once you woke up. So much for boyish dreams." He wandered into the kitchen.

"Tris, look," said Glaki impatient, bouncing in the older girl's lap.

"I'm looking," Tris replied. "Don't do that, I might break."

Glaki pointed to a dish on the table. It rose, shakily, three full inches, then settled again.

"Very good," Tris said. She hesitated, then kissed Glaki on the cheek. "Your mother and aunt would have been proud."

Keth had continued to work at Touchstone Glass while Tris slept, with Dema to keep him enclosed with protective magic. A week after Tris got out of bed, she rejoined Keth at the shop, along with Glaki, Little Bear, and Chime. They said hello to Antonou on their arrival, then retired to the workshop.

The slip into their old routine was as easy as Tris's slip into sleep. The three of them meditated. Glaki settled into her corner to play with her dolls as Tris drew her protective circle around the shop. Watching Keth work, she thought that she would dispense with the barrier after today. He kept his power firmly in hand as he created the small, sparking globes that Antonou could sell.

Comfortable with Keth's skills, Tris let herself out through her barrier, to practice scrying the winds. Her bit of success in pursuit of the Ghost had given her confidence. She could master this in time, and who knew? Unlike her other magics, she might be able to make a living with this.

She only had the strength for less than a half hour of work. Sweating, she lowered her barrier on the workshop and left it down. As she sat on a bench, watching Keth, she realized that his eye was on her.

"What are your plans?" she asked. "Niko says they're going to move the conference to an island off the coast. I should go with him." She smiled wickedly. "It seems our fellow mages don't find Tharios, with all the garbage piling up, much fun as a place to write their text on visionary magics."

"I'm going with you," Keth says. "There are glassmakers on the island related to Antonou. They'll take the work they can sell to him, and he'll pay them for my supplies. Later . . ." He gouged at the floor with his foot.

"Later . . . ?" Tris nudged.

Keth looked at her. "I want to study investigators' magics. While you slept, Dema shielded me while I made two more globes with crimes in them. It's not something I want to do constantly, understand, but if I can help, I'd like to."

Tris nodded encouragement. "That sounds like a wonderful idea. I wouldn't want you to give up your glassmaking, but even a little help from time to time would make a difference, it seems to me."

Keth grinned at her. "I figured you'd approve. And Tris, I had another thought." She raised her eyebrows. Keth said, "How would you like to learn how to work glass?"

Tris blinked. "You mean, learn to work it like an ordinary craftsman does."

"Exactly." Keth sat next to her. "You won't get further than journeyman, probably. You don't have the time to spend just on glass, for one thing. But you could learn to mold and pull glass. I've seen how you admire the work."

Tris looked at the ground to hide her blush of pleasure. "I'd love to."

Keth laughed. "Oh, I have you now!" he said, rubbing his hands together. "A little repayment for your hours of torture —" He went into the shop and took down two leather aprons.

"I did *not* torture you," Tris retorted. She accepted one apron and tied it over her gown. "No more than you deserved, anyway. And I'm still your teacher, so mind your step."

"I am going to enjoy this," Keth said. "Come here. We'll start with the basic mix of materials you need to melt down." As Glaki invented stories for her dolls, Keth proceeded to instruct his young teacher on the mysteries of glass.

They were cleaning up for the day, or rather, Keth and Glaki cleaned up while Tris sat on a bench and sweated, when Dema walked into the courtyard. Little Bear greeted him with earsplitting barks as Chime flew around his head. "You look *terrible*," Dema informed Tris. "Are you even ready to be out of bed?"

"Nice to see you, too," she mumbled.

"Slumming, or moving to a more respectable *arurimat*?" asked Keth, grinning at Dema.

"Neither." When Keth and Tris stared at him, Dema coughed into his fist. "I'm, ah, staying at Elya Street," he confessed. "I, well . . ." He looked at them and shrugged. "I like it down here. I asked the Keepers to promote one of my sisters instead." When Keth and Tris continued to stare at him, Dema flushed under his brown skin. "They need me more down here than they do farther up the hill. And after catching the Ghost, the *yaskedasi* are talking to me. I've been able to solve three old crimes since that night." He sighed. "The Keepers rewarded me anyway. At least, they *said* it was a reward. I'm also assigned to the Hodenekes and Noskemiou *arurimati*. I guess they think if I like the lowlife, I ought to get a belly full of it." He looked at Tris. "Which reminds me — who tipped the *prathmuni* off, do you suppose? Let them know to flee the city?"

Tris knew that sooner or later someone would think to ask. Though she was not generally in favor of lying, she saw no reason why anyone should know the truth. She looked Dema in the eye and said, "For all you know, there were *prathmuni* everywhere on that street. They're not stupid, Dema."

"No, they're not," he said grimly. "They're negotiating a contract with Tharios right now from hiding. They won't return until the Assembly grants certain concessions, like pay for their work, and better living conditions."

Keth and Tris exchanged grins. "What a shame," Keth remarked.

"I feel for you," said Tris, innocent and earnest. "I feel for all Tharios."

"Me too," said Glaki, hugging Dema around the knees.

Dema lifted her up and kissed her cheek. "I'm glad someone around here feels sorry for me." To Tris he said, "We can't change overnight. Not Tharios."

"But a little change won't kill you," replied Tris as Chime began to purr in her lap. "It might even help Tharios to stand another thousand years."

ACKNOWLEDGMENTS

First and foremost, I owe heartfelt thanks once again to my friend, Thomas Gansevoort, whose knowledge of crafts and the perils attached to them has saved my grits time after time throughout both The Circle of Magic and The Circle Opens quartets. I owe him a particularly large debt for his guidance with regard to the perils of glassmaking. I owe thanks at a researcher's distance to William S. Ellis's *Glass: From the First Mirror to Fiber Optics, the Story of the Substance that Changed the World* and to Christina Schulman, who showed me the book. The Circle Opens is also the result of years of reading about the acts and psychology of serial criminals in books by writers such as Jack Olsen and Anne Rule and in the groundbreaking study *Sexual Homicide: Patterns and Motives* by Robert K. Ressler, Ann W. Burgess, and John E. Douglas.

Closer to home, I owe tremendous debts of gratitude. First and foremost, I thank my editorial staff at Scholastic — editrix Anne Dunn, who inspired and signed

ACKNOWLEDGMENTS

up the quartet and who helped me to shape *Magic Steps;* editrix Kate Egan, who took over where Anne left off and has been a support, mainstay, and guide through the rest of the quartet; Elizabeth Szabla, who has stepped into the breach with able, gracious assistance and support when Anne and Kate were not there; and Jennifer Rees, line editrix and able hand-holder for wifty authors — and at Scholastic in England, to editrixes Holly Skeet and Kirsty Skidmore, whose intelligent commentary and suggestions did so much to influence the final shape of the quartet. My thanks also to my eagle-eyed agent Craig Tenney, who always has cogent points to make; mapmaker to the scale-challenged, Rick Robinson; to my beloved spouse-creature, Tim, whose creative fingerprints are all over each and every book I write, including this one; and to my friend, Raquel, who also gives me ideas and keeps me steady. Without these people, *Shatterglass* and the entire Circle Opens quartet, would either not exist or have a very different shape and intent.

Last, but never least, I thank teachers, particularly those in grade school, middle school, high school, and college, who taught me what good teaching really is. Our teachers are never paid enough and never thanked enough, yet they create the future when they shape the people they instruct, guide, and encourage. No book I write would exist if it weren't for a steady succession of teachers who gave me hope and the belief that I had something positive to offer.

Other Books by TAMORA PIERCE

The Circle of Magic Quartet
Sandry's Book
Tris's Book
Daja's Book
Briar's Book

The Circle Opens Quartet
Magic Steps
Street Magic
Cold Fire

The Song of the Lioness Quartet
Alanna
In the Hand of the Goddess
The Woman Who Rides Like a Man
Lioness Rampant

The Immortals Quartet
Wild Magic
Wolf-Speaker
Emperor Mage
The Realms of the Gods

The Protector of the Small Quartet
First Test
Page
Squire
Lady Knight

ABOUT THE AUTHOR

TAMORA PIERCE is a New York Times *best-selling writer whose fantasy books include* The Circle of Magic, The Song of the Lioness, The Immortals, *and* The Protector of the Small *quartets as well as* Magic Steps, Street Magic, *and* Cold Fire. *She says of her beginnings as an author that "after discovering fantasy and science fiction in the seventh grade, I was hooked on writing. I tried to write the same kind of stories I read, except with teenaged girl heroes — not too many of those around in the 1960s."*

In her Circle of Magic *quartet, Ms. Pierce introduced the unforgettable mages-in-training who are now four years older in* The Circle Opens — *Sandry, Briar, Daja, and Tris. She began the new quartet at the urging of her many readers, who encouraged her through letters and e-mails to explore the mages' lives further. She chose their next turning point to be when they each acquire their first students in magecraft while still in their early teens.*

Ms. Pierce lives in New York City with her husband,

Tim Liebe, their cats (Scrap, Pee Wee, Gremlin, and Ferret), two parakeets (Timon and the Junior Birdman), and a "floating population of rescued wildlife." Her Web site address is http://www.tamora-pierce.com, *and she is active on the discussion web she co-founded,* http://www.SheroesCentral.com.